GOLD
FEVER

GOLD FEVER

by
DUANE L. PETERSEN

Published 2020 by:

D&D Books
P.O. Box 458
Cascade, Idaho 83611
USA

ISBN 978-0-9763421-2-0

Book Format and Cover Design, Photo by
Don Dopf, Cambridge Litho, Inc.
Cambridge, Idaho 83610

Photo: High Dive, Road to Black Lake
Seven Devils Region Idaho

Printed in the United States of America

CHAPTER 1

The towering peaks of the Tetons rose as a back drop above this long narrow sagebrush covered valley. At the upper end smoke rose this cool morning from a long log building surrounded by other log structures of all sizes. As you got closer you could see smoke curling from a couple of the buildings. These building belonged to the ghost town of Garnet. The smoke was rising from the only business still operating, Crawford Trading Post. When the town of Garnet was first born this business was called Crawford General Store. The owners were Dan and Kate Crawford, Later on as the miners moved on to better diggins leaving Dan and Kate, who decided to stayed on. They combined the store and the saloon next door together and changed the name to Crawford Trading Post. Dan died during the winter of eighty one after trying to save the families from a religious village high up in the canyons above this valley. Now Kate and Benny her half breed handy man were the only full time residents of this forgotten town.

During the winter months the town grows to sometimes twenty to twenty-five people. A few older prospectors who have decided they've chased the gold mining camps far enough have made this area their home. Each summer they head back up into those peaks to search for that pure gold vein that has always alluded them. Most make enough to live well during the winter months in one of the cabins still left in Garnet. Kate stays on to sell these men their supplies and the trading post becomes their second home during the winter.

Kate was going to board up the saloon after the last of the other business in town gave up and moved on. Then, one day the stage which traveled through the valley once a week dropped off a passenger along with the mail. The passenger was April, who had been one of the dance hall girls in this saloon when Garnet was a booming town. She was just a few years younger than Kate, but was now at the age she couldn't find work as an entertainer any longer. She had the choice of heading to the bigger towns and working the brothels south of the tracks, another term you might use would be the slums. April heard Kate was still in Garnet so she headed north to see if she could find work. Kate had always treated the dance hall girls real good, when April was here before.

1

By the next day the two women had made a deal, April could run the saloon on a percentage. The saloon had rooms upstairs from the earlier days. Kate told April she could rent them out rooms or whatever she wanted, as long as no fights or trouble got started. As the miners drifted in from the mountains that fall, they, all welcomed the new business. Before the first snow, two more girls showed up on the stage, like April they were passed their prime for the showgirl business.

One morning they woke to gentle falling flakes as the ground was beginning to turn white out across the valley. Kate's only full time helper was a breed by the name Benny. He had showed up one fall the same year Dan died. Benny limped pretty, bad at times and Dan had told Kate he was missing his toes on that foot. Dan had seen his bare foot once, he, said the toes looked like they had been chopped off. Benny insisted he worked just for his board. Kate tried to pay him a wages. He told her if she did, he would leave. Benny never said what tribe he was from or where he came from. He didn't drink anything but water and coffee, so Kate didn't have to worry about him getting drunk. He could read and write along with other things making Kate think he was maybe raised by whites. He knew of religion but every time it was brought up he would leave.

That morning when Kate walked into the kitchen like always he was busy peeling potatoes for her. The stove was hot and ready for the first customer. Kate fixed their breakfast, as they ate he looked up at her. "Don't worry, Kate. Ben will be showing up before long."

He was talking about Ben Jasper one of the miners that called Garnet his home during the winter. He and Kate were very close. He lived in his cabin back on the knoll behind the trading post during the winter. Benny had already cleaned up the cabin so it would be ready for Ben when he came in.

Kate nodded, "I know he's probably alright Benny, but I still worry about him being gone all summer. Most of the others drop by for supplies at least once a summer, but not Ben. Once he leaves in the spring I never see him again until late fall. I'm always worrying he will try to get up to those mines that cult bunch had in those cliffs and fall off."

Ben Jasper was a tall man with big shoulders. He talked real slow in a very low deep voice. Kate knew he had come west as a young man in the cavalry. After his hitch was up he stayed in the Dakota's for a year working in the mines around Deadwood. When he had enough to buy an outfit he was off from mining camp to camp in Montana. Later he'd been in the Oregon Territory like all miners looking for the mother lode. He's been in the Idaho territory, down into Colorado before coming to these mountains.

He came about the same time those religious miners were about. The first of the group that prospected in this area would trade with Dan and Kate but only outside the building. They wouldn't go into any place that sold whisky or tobacco. Nobody ever saw much of them, then one spring after the roads were good a large wagon train came up through the valley. It was loaded with women and kids and stock. When the snow melted enough to get up closer to those cliffs, the other miners saw for the first time the settlement that was built during the winter. It was located in a small valley just below those sheer cliffs. Somehow during the fall before many more men had showed up to build this settlement. It had been an easy winter as far as deep snow in the area, so they had picked a good winter to build this settlement. For the next two years they only saw a few people from the settlement in Garnet. One man did most of the buying a packing of supplies for the group. They always paid Dan for the supplies in gold, so Dan figured they had hit pay dirt somewhere up in those rugged cliffs.

At the upper end of the valley about ten miles from Garnet they built a cabin and a few barns. This is where they had left their wagons and stock. Twice Dan and the others saw wagons moving south on the other side of the valley. Then a month or so later the same wagons came back, using the same route. The stage driver said he saw them camped and those wagons were filled with blasting powder. It was soon after that at times the dull boom could be heard way off in those peaks. It was this same fall that the miners started moving out, they headed for the Salmon River country. Gossip of a large strike was in the wind, so off went most of the miners of Garnet along with many of the businesses.

That was the winter Dan and Kate first met Ben Jasper. He came in one day riding a big black horse, leading three pack animals. Dan was working out front of the store when he rode up, "You folk's going to move out too," he asked.

Dan shook his head, "No, Kate and I decided were going to stay as long as we can survive. Are you, just passing through?"

"No, not if you're staying. The name is Ben Jasper. I was kinda looking for a place to hold up for the winter. If you're staying then I can get supplies so I'm staying too. Are any of these vacant cabins for sale?"

Dan stepped over as Ben swung down, "Dan Crawford. My wife Kate and I own this place. As far as the cabins, most of them you can

3

have for just moving in. I do have one I would like to sell. I can give you a deed to it. I grub staked the owner and builder to enough supplies to get him to the Salmon River country. You got twenty bucks you can own one of the better cabins in Garnet."

Ben grinned, "You just sold a cabin. Where is it located, so I can unload these mules?"

Dan motioned, "Follow me. I'll take you over there."

With the last of the packs inside Ben looked over at his new friend, "Now where can I stake out these animals until I can find an area to winter them?"

Dan motioned to the gate over in the next draw, "Put them in that pasture for the night. Tomorrow I'll show you a place you can keep them for the winter."

That's how Kate and Ben first came to know each other. Ben had been coming back to Garnet every winter since. It was an un-talked about subject, but the other miner knew Kate had eyes only for Ben. With April and her girls, they had all they needed.

The next morning Kate came walking out from the living quarters in the back to stare out the front windows. The snowing had stopped but the wind had shifted to the north and it was cold outside. Kate turned to the kitchen, Benny was grinning at her, "How come you're so happy this morning?" she asked him, as she poured a cup of coffee.

"There's smoke coming from the chimney of the cabin on the knoll, this morning," he answered.

About then the front door opened, in stepped the tall missing man, "I thought you two would never get up this morning so I could get some breakfast."

Kate grabbed him as she rushed up, "Dam you Ben Jasper, why are you always one of the last to come in?" She buried her head in his chest. She stepped back, "When did you get in, last night?"

Ben took off his coat as Benny offered him a cup of hot coffee. He turned back to face Kate, "Oh it was late. I was figuring on camping last night up on Chipmunk Creek, then come on in this morning. When that north wind started blowing, I decided I'd rather sleep inside instead of out in the wind so I came on in." He looked back at Benny in the kitchen listening to them, "How come I had a warm cabin? How did you know I'd be in?"

Benny kept his same face, showing nothing, "You know, how us Indians are? We just know these things."

Ben looked at Kate, she just shrugged. "I didn't know anything about a fire up there." She looked over at Benny, "How did you know

4

he was up there when you told me of seeing the smoke if you lit the fire yesterday? Don't tell me it's an Indian thing!"

Benny shrugged, "I saw him walking down the hill just before you walked in from the back."

Kate looked back at the tall miner, "Did you have a good summer?"

Ben nodded, "You know, I did pretty, good. I think. I got a bunch of work to do to clean up the concentrates I brought in. After I get that done I'll know more. I got enough to last me the winter unless you've raised your prices." Then he grinned.

Benny walked over to join them as they finished breakfast. Ben looked up from his plate, "How long ago was it when that religious character with the young boy came though looking for that mine in those cliffs?"

Both Kate and Benny looked up real quick to stare at Ben. "Why are you asking, Ben?" Kate asked as she stared at the tall miner sitting across from her. "You haven't been up there snooping around have you?"

Ben smiled, "Now Kate, don't get all huffy. I was just asking how long ago that was when they rode though. I just got to thinking about that yesterday when I looked up at those sheer cliffs when I rode by. I also was thinking that Benny here and me should take your team and go up and bring down some of them wagons before the snow gets deep. I stopped at the old cabin and looked around. Four of them big wagons are in pretty good shape yet. We could maybe do a little work on them on the warmer days this winter, then come spring maybe sell them."

Kate kept looking at Ben, then she looked over at Benny, "Okay Indian, how long ago was it when that creep came through here with the boy?"

Benny never changed expressions as he looked over at Kate, "Moons or years?" Ben started laughing. "This is the fourth winter since they rode through," Benny answered.

Clayton Moore one of the other miners had walked in and had been listening to the conversation. He nodded, "I believe Benny's right. I was the one who brought their horses in when I came by that pasture that fall. They never would have survived the winter in that ate down pasture. Coby's still got them down on the river." He looked over at Ben, "What you figure happened to them two? That boy was pretty young."

5

Kate smiled, "You know that boy could read. While that creep was buying a few supplies the boy was reading the prices to him. He also wanted one of the books that I brought down from the old school. I told him they were free so he took it."

Ben shrugged, "Well I figure they must have either starved or got killed trying to climb around on those ruins. You know that slide didn't leave much of that mill they had hanging on those rocks. You can see walkways just hanging up there in space. Each year more of it falls down."

Kate glared at him, "I thought you said you hadn't been up there."

"Kate when you ride that trail over to Fall Creek you ride right under where they worked," Ben fired back.

Clayton nodded, "He's right Kate. I've seen all that too. You know I often wonder how many died that winter. I know those four men camped up there almost all summer burying bodies as the snow melted to show them. I was going to ride over and check out that knoll to see if they left any sign of those graves."

Benny who was clearing the table stopped, "Many of the small children were buried with the grownups. I watched from the ridge one day as they put four people in one grave, two women and two small kids. I know that wasn't the only time they done that."

Kate slowly shook her head, "I guess I'm not thinking to straight this morning. Dan and the men from here went up the next day after we heard the rumbling coming from those peaks. Everyone got so wet trying to save the few who survived when that slide wiped out the mine and the settlement below. Dan never got over that chill, he died that spring. That's the year those few men showed up from somewhere to bury the dead. Then it was the next summer when that man and boy came by looking for the mine. He kept mumbling something about inheriting the mine from his father and his followers or something like that."

A couple of the other miners had walked in and sat listening as Kate and the other talked of that winter. Henry Corn spoke up, "That was my first year to winter here, was the year after the big slide. I know I about spooked and left the country the first time I heard him wailing from those cliffs. I camped at Chipmunk Creek one night, it was the full moon. About midnight the horses started raising hell, I jumped to my feet and grabbed my rifle. When it woke me I thought it was a mountain lion screaming. Then I heard the wailing again and figured out it was a human making all that racked. Hell nobody had told me anything about that character living up somewhere in those cliffs. I packed up and

6

headed down the trail in the dark. It was Kate here that told me about that religious nut when I told her what I'd heard during the night."

Kate nodded, "You know Henry I believe you were one of the last or even the last one to ever hear him.

Clayton laughed, "You know that guy had one hell of a set of lungs. Hell he could hold that wail a lot longer than any coyote or wolf I ever heard."

Kate looked over at Ben, "That whole thing was a mess. When those first people showed up looking for a place to mine is when it all started. Then when they built that settlement up in that canyon was the last straw. Dan and everyone else kept telling those people who would talk to strangers that on a bad winter that slides from above covered that narrow valley. This all seemed to be lost on deaf ears." She stopped and looked at all the men looking at her, "Some of you weren't here then. The next day after we heard the thunder like noise, Dan and the others headed up there. They heard the screaming and wailing long before they got to what was left of the settlement. Broken bodies were every-where along with small kids still in their sleeping clothes. They moved the ones still alive down to the cabin where they had left their wagons. Dan sent two men back here for a couple of tents and all the medical supplies we had. He also sent word that I wasn't to come up there."

Clayton went on as Kate wiped away the tears, "Benny here headed for Springfield to get more help and let the law know about the slide. By the next morning wagons and men were pouring through here on their way up to help. Two doctors from Springfield were with the men. As we packed the living down to the cabin, many of them didn't want our help. A couple of the women we had to tie to the littler, to keep them from going back up the mountain. We combed through the rubble sticking out of the snow searching for survivors. I found one baby still wrapped in blankets sound asleep under the body of a young woman, I figured she might have been the mother. That about got the best of me."

Everyone was quiet, the Kate spoke up. "Dan always figured that the blasting in that mine is what caused that slide to cover so much area. You know that afternoon a crew of men who had been working that night came down from those cliffs. They had to rig ropes to get down because the slides had taken all their walkways down. They just stood and stared at all the bodies and the rubble which had been their homes. The Marshal from Springfield finally got one of them to talk. When all the wagons loaded with the survivors head out the next morning, those eight men refused to go. They turned down Dan and the men from here offer to help bury the dead."

"When Dan got here he was chilled to the bone, along with a couple of the others. I wrapped him in warm blankets and set him near the stove, to try to break the chill. I thought he was getting better, then, he got that terrible cough. The other two men were upstairs in the saloon being cared for by April when she was one of the saloons main attractions before the saloon closed down. One of the miners like Dan got that deep cough, Kate sent Benny riding to Springfield for a doctor. The doctor said they both had pneumonia real bad and there was little he could do. They built a tent like cover over both beds and filled it with a warm steam mixed with different medicines trying to loosen the congestion. The miner Miller died the second day after the doctor got here. Dan lived another two weeks. The third man survived, but he left the next spring to go to a lower dryer climate to see if maybe he could breathed better in that dryer air. Kate got word a year later that he also had died. Three of Garnets main citizens had died trying to save the group who shunned all help from outsiders."

Clayton nodded, "You know about ten more men showed up that next spring from somewhere. As the snow melted they slowly finished burying the last remaining dead as the bodies were exposed. By summer they loaded up and headed off leaving everything up by the cabin. They didn't take any of those wagons Ben here wants to bring down to work on. I found the remains of one of them later that year high up under the cliffs. I built a mound of rocks over him up right where he laid. I think he was probably working up at the mine when that snow broke loose. I know of a couple more piles of bones others have found since then."

April had walked in from next door while the group had been talking. "Those were weird people. I was here working for Patterson in the saloon when they first came here to buy from Dan and Kate. I was standing up on the balcony one morning when they were loading supplies. I just had a wrap on as I enjoyed the cool breeze that morning. That one spotted me and he never took his eyes off me until they went out of sight. I had bad dreams about those eyes for a week. It was like he was looking plumb through me." She shivered.

"Hell April, he was sizing you up to add you to his household of wives. You probably missed out on a lot of praying and a gold mine," Clayton kidded her.

April looked over at Kate, "His drinks just went up," Kate nodded.

8

Kate and her partner in the saloon were two different people. Kate was always in Bib overall and a man's shirt with bandana around her head. April was always in a dress, with her hair in curled in ringlets.

CHAPTER 2

The weather warmed up after that first storm when Ben came in. So, Benny and Ben with Kate's team on lead ropes headed up the valley one morning. Up at the cabin where the wagons were parked Ben started looking over which one he wanted to take first. As they were hooking up Clayton and Henry showed up, "Hell, you left without us."

Ben laughed, "I figured you two would still be sleeping in this morning. Anyway I was just looking over to see how many of them I want to take. Maybe tomorrow we can make two trips if I find two more worth taking."

Clayton and walked with Ben as he crawled around looking over each wagon. Henry walked up to the two barn buildings. He was out of sight for a while then stepped out where they could see him. "Hey Ben, did you know all the harness and other gear is hanging in this back barn? The mice and porcupines have eaten some of it, but nothing that can't be fixed. I think we should take this gear too."

Ben, Clayton along with Benny walked up to where Henry was. Inside the building they found the harnesses and other gear belonging to the wagons. Ben was the last to walk out and he went out a back opening. He stopped and looked at a track in the dirt where the snow here close to the building had melted away. He dropped down to study the light imprint. This was fairly new track. It was something like a moccasin track except for the sole. The sole had been made of something hard, like maybe harness leather. Ben looked all around. The snow was melted in the sun out away from the buildings. He followed the faint track until the soil stated getting rocky, then he could find them any longer. Ben heard his name called and headed back around the barn to where the others were getting ready to move out. Clayton and Henry had loaded two sets of harnesses and a few other items to the wagon they were taking back with them. Benny drove the team pulling the big wagon while the others rode the horses back. Henry rode up alongside of Ben, "I wonder what they did with the canvas covers for these wagons?"

10

Clayton had rode over closer to the others and heard Henry's question. "I was wondering about that, too. They surely wouldn't have packed them up to the settlement. Tomorrow I'll climb up into the top of that one barn and look around."

When they got back to Garnet, Kate walked out to see the big wagon. While Benny was unhooking she walked around the new addition to town. "This seems to be in pretty good shape for sitting out in the weather for a few years. How many more are you going to bring down?"

Ben had walked up, "Well, there's six just like this and a few more that need work to move them. The cart that fella with the boy had, is there, but I don't think I'll bring it down. It looks to be the back axle off one of these bigger wagons. I think maybe that fella put it together from pieces after the maybe the big wagon broke down. Maybe that why, he was late getting here, his wagon broke down and he couldn't keep up." Kate looked up at him with a question look in her eye. Ben shrugged then grinned, "Just a thought."

Back in his cabin that evening Ben sat staring at the darkness through the window. His thoughts were back on that track he had found. 'Could one of those people still be alive up there? I need to go back up there alone sometime and look around more.'

The next day broke clear with a cool breeze blowing down off the peaks. This was going to be mail day and Kate had supplies coming in on the stage. During the summer a freight wagon moved through the valley every two weeks, but in the winter they didn't run. Kate had contacted the stagecoach company about hauling supplies to her during the winter. They had jumped at the chance to add a little extra income to the route. It freight was mainly food supplies, nothing big and bulky in size. Kate wanted Benny to help her stock the shelves so he wouldn't be helping Ben move down another wagon. Henry had spent the night at the saloon and was in no shape to help, so Clayton and Ben headed back for another wagon.

On the way up Clayton came up with an idea, "Ben, why don't we make two trips today? This weathers going to break one of these days and we'll have a hard time moving them."

They loaded a few more of the gear from the barn and Clayton headed back for Garnet with his horse tied behind the big wagon. Ben looked for way to get up above the manger in the big barn. Then he spotted a ladder pushed back alongside the, feed manger, mostly out of sight. They had taken down the ladder from the wall for some reason. He pushed it back up and climbed up. As he looked in the shadows he stopped, there was smudge prints in the dust of the floor. Again he found that same print as he saw outside.

Ben walked around the big area following the tracks. They stopped at a large trunk. When Ben opened the lid, he found many wood working tools, then, he found an oily canvas all rolled up. When he unrolled it he stopped to stare, before him on the canvas was two 45-70 trap door Springfield carbines. These were army issue, it was, well oiled, and in good shape. He rolled them back up and dug deeper into the trunk. In the bottom corner was a wooden army issue ammo box. Inside a few rounds were missing, but the rest were untouched. Ben put everything back and closed the lid. Scattered about, the area different type of furniture, most in good condition. As Ben climb down and put the ladder back where he'd found it.

Outside he looked around for more tracks but saw nothing. Over in the other barn where the harness hung he looked about. As he walked toward the far side of the barn it was dark, so he walked over along the wall where he could see light showing around what looked to be a square opening. When he moved a small block on the wall, a door swung open revealing an opening looking out over the parked wagons. Now with light shining in he walked back to other side of the building. That's when he saw another doorway, leading into another room. Inside Ben smiled when he saw the big rolls of canvas. The room had been built to store the big covers for the wagons, now Henry could solve his puzzle.

Ben moved back outside and sat in the sun chewing on a stick of jerky as he waited for Clayton to get back. He wished now he'd brought along a coffee pot this morning. It was a little afternoon when he saw Clayton coming. As he watched he noticed the second rider, then, as they got closer he saw it was Kate.

"Well Clayton how come you brought along more help?"

Kate reached behind her saddle to take a towel all wrapped up from one saddle bags. "Now don't get smart or you won't get this fresh sandwich," she said as she handed it to him.

They hooked up, then, Clayton moved out for Garnet while Ben sat down to enjoy his sandwich. Kate looked about, "How come nobody ever looked this place over before? Henry and Clayton have been talking about everything still here."

Ben shrugged, "I just never felt right to stop and snoop around before. You know those were strange people and wanted to be left alone. I guess the others are like me when it came to nosing around. This fall when I rode by I had a change of heart. I just couldn't see these big old wagons going to waste. Somebody paid big dollars to buy this type of wagons. I never even thought about nosing around until Henry found those harnesses. I did look in that cabin a while ago. That is one fine built cabin. Somebody in that bunch was a good craftsman."

Kate kept looking up to those high peaks in the back ground. She looked back at Ben, "I know you've been up there. Why did they look for gold in such a rough place, they should have known the snow got deep up there? Are there any natural caves of tunnels up there?"

Ben looked over at her, "Kate, I was up there before those people showed up. I did find some good looking samples, but I'm not half Billy goat. I really don't like working on those narrow trails. I'm real curious on what kind of ore they found to bring their families all the way up here. If I'd been involved I think I would have built the settlement down here for the families. They could have built quarters up those cliffs for the crew to stay during the week. They came back down here to see their families on their off days." He stopped to eat another bite, then, he looked back at her, "You know it was too bad we didn't have a heavy snow year when they spent the winter building that settlement. Some of them might have got buried, but at least they wouldn't have taken their families up there when they got here. I'm like the others back in town, I think all their blasting in that mountain might have caused that whole mountain to slide at one time instead of a bunch of small slides." He shrugged as he stood up.

The next day Henry joined them again, along with Benny. Ben showed Henry the room with all the canvas bundles, while Benny helped Clayton hook up the wagon. Ben looked over at Henry, "I guess until we need them to cover a wagon we should just leave them where they are."

Henry nodded as he turned to look over the building. "Have you been up above those mangers in the other barn?"

Ben nodded he had, but he figured for now the trunk was something to just keep to himself. "Yeah, there's some old furniture on the west side. On the east side there's some farming implements, but nothing worth getting down. They must have figured on farming somewhere around here."

Henry glanced over at Ben, "Hell they picked a poor place to try to farm at this elevation. I guess maybe you could raise a few spuds, along with short termed vegetables if this soil is any good. This wild grass seems to survive up here."

Ben grinned as he looked over at Henry, "You sound like you know a little about farming?"

13

"I know enough to know this is no country to farm in. I watched my mother grow old quick trying to raise enough greens to keep us kids alive. The old man homesteaded a rock farm. All he cared about was hunting and fishing along with fathering a passel of snot nosed kids for mother to try to feed. When she died he hurried off to find another young one to breed. She had a temper, one night after he beat the hell out of her she stuck a knife in him after he went to sleep. She took the younger kids and told us older ones we were on our own. I was thirteen at the time. Yeah Ben, I know a little bit about farming."

Ben nodded, "I didn't mean to pry into your past."

Henry chuckled, "Hell Ben you're the first one I ever told that. My sister a year older than me left together. We wondered into Kansas living on what I could shoot and what we could find. We came upon a camp out in the middle of the prairie of people probably a lot like these folks were. They feed us and the woman soon had Sis converted to their way of thinking. The old leader of the bunch said we had to be baptized to rid our bodies of all evils. Ruth let them dunk her out in the river, but I high tailed it out of there before they could dunk me. I never saw any of my family since then. Hell for all I know Ruth could have been part of this bunch." Ben just looked over at him, but didn't say anything.

As they all headed back for Garnet Benny was driving the team with Henry riding with him. Ben and Clayton rode on each side of the wagon so they could talk as the team slowly moved along. Henry motioned up at the sky, "Looks like maybe our weather going to change. We may be made our last trip for a while."

Ben laughed, "Well we got plenty of work to keep us busy for a few days. I've been wondering if we can get one of these wagons at a time, into that old blacksmith shop. We could build as fire in that old forge to warm out hands and heat a pot of coffee while we work on them."

Clayton nodded, "You know I think we can if we work on that back door so it'll swing open. Benny, didn't Kate have you nail that shut after the wind blew it back and broke one hinge?"

Benny nodded, "One new board will fix the door and then change the hinges and they will swing."

They woke the next morning to a warm rain. As Ben walked down to the store he looked to the peaks, but they were hidden by the low clouds. He laid awake that night thinking about those tracks. He hadn't even mentioned it to Kate, but he was curious of who made those tracks and when.

14

The rain stopped by afternoon, but warm breeze was blowing in from the south. Benny and Ben went over to the blacksmith shop to look over repairing the door. Soon half the men in camp were helping with the door. Benny hooked up the team to a wagon and moved around to come in the back door. With Ben standing in the wagon bed watching they slowly moved it into the barn. The bows only cleared the top of the door by a few inches. Once inside they closed the doors and found they had plenty of room to work around the wagon. With that done they headed for the saloon to toast their big venture.

Ben stopped by the store after he left the saloon. Kate smiled as he walked in, "Party get too rough for you?"

Ben smiled, "No, I just didn't feel like drinking all night. I guess I'm getting old or something, that hangover come morning just don't appeal to me anymore. The reason I stopped by was to ask you if you needed any fresh meat. If the weather is clear tomorrow I thought I'd go see if I could find a deer."

Kate nodded, "Sure, I can stand some fresh meat. Do you want me to send Benny with you?"

Ben shook his head, no, "No, I'd just as soon go alone." He grinned when she frowned at him, "You see that way I can talk without having to answer any questions."

Kate grinned, "Do you make a habit of talking to yourself?"

Ben turned toward the door, "Sure I do. That's why I stay gone all summer. I don't have to answer questions like that. I very seldom ask myself a question when I'm out there alone."

"Ben Jasper, at times I think you do spend too much time alone in those mountains," she turned and walked back into her living quarters.

On his way back to his cabin he detoured over toward the old school house. Kate had Benny board it all up so the building would last in case the town ever needed a school again. Ben walked it leaving the door open so he could see, better. A few books still lined the shelves so Ben started looking through them. Many of the men who wintered here that could read often took books to read, then, brought them back. Ben took four books and headed back to his cabin.

After cooking his supper, he started packing a pack sack with items from his kitchen. He had restocked when he moved in for the winter, so his pantry was full. He packed a water tight container of salt, in another water tight can with flour, one of rice, with another of beans. To this he added some sour dough, along with a box of matches. Then he took a box of candles from a shelf in pantry and added them to the now full pack. To another pack he put in the books, along with a spool

15

of waxed thread and an awl with extra needles. He sat back in a chair and looked about the cabin. 'I can't think of anything else.' he mumbled.

The sky broke clear the next morning as Ben saddled his horse and loaded the pack horse. The sun was just topping the peaks as he rode out of town. He rode toward the river in case anyone was watching him leave. Later once out of sight of the building he headed back toward the peaks. He tied the horses behind the biggest barn and unloaded the pack. Inside he put the ladder back up to the loft, then climbed up to the top. As he looked at the floor a smile came to his face. Fresh smudges were in the dust of his tracks when he'd been up there. He pulled another trunk that he'd saw earlier over next to the one with the rifles and other gear. He took the tools from the second trunk, then, replaced them with the items he'd brought from his cabin. He closed up the lid and climbed back down. After the ladder was back in place he walked back out to the horses. He stood for a moment looking to the peaks high above. As he stared up at them he could still see of few of the broken walkways and timber still hanging from the sheer cliffs. He shrugged then mounted his horse, leading the pack horse he rode away.

He took the same way back so he wouldn't be riding in from the direction of the barns. He spotted a small herd of deer in a draw, they moved over the small knoll when they saw him. He tied his horses, pulled his rifle then moved off in the direction the deer had gone. He studied the deer below him, then settled on a young buck standing away from the other deer. He figured that bigger buck with the doe's had chased him away. Later with the deer loaded on the pack horse Ben headed back for Garnet. As he unsaddle and was hanging the deer in the woodshed he heard footsteps behind him. He turned to find Kate walking toward him. "Well I see the hunter was successful in getting his meat."

Ben turned, "Now be nice, I did bring you the liver."

She took his arm, "Well good. How about if I don't ask too many questions, you come down and eat with me tonight?"

Ben laughed, "Sure don't take much to ruffle your feathers, does it? I suppose you're going to make me eat what I said last night?"

Kate smiled as she took an extra knife lying on the work bench and started helping him skin the deer. Ben hung the hide over a rafter, "I'll tell Benny he can have this hide for a pair of gloves."

Kate nodded as she put her coat back on, then picked up the cloth wrapped around the liver "You coming down with me now?"

16

"No, I'll take the horse back up to the pasture, then, I'll be down. You want any of this meat now?"

She shook her head, "No, let it hang a few days, then I'll have you bring it down to my cooler. See you at six or before, we'll have a quick drink before supper."

Ben cleaned up and headed down the slope to the store. Later Benny, April and Clayton all sat down to the liver supper with Ben and Kate. As they ate Clayton looked over at Ben, "Why didn't you say anything about going hunting, I'd joined you?"

Kate started laughing and before Ben could answer, "Oh he wanted to alone so he could talk to himself."

Everyone looked over at Ben who was just looking at Kate, slowly shaking his head. This look just made Kate laughed all the harder. "I'm sorry, Ben, I just couldn't let that go by."

It snowed in the night time and rained during the day for the next week. Ben and the others had stayed busy working on the wagon in the blacksmith shop. One piece was broken on the front axle. Henry thought he remembered enough about a forge to make a new one. As Ben stopped by the store for coffee one morning the sun was trying to break through the clouds. As Kate sat a steaming cup on the counter, Ben looked over at her, "You want to go for a ride this morning if this sun keeps shining? I've been thinking about going up to see if one of those wagons we left up there still has this part we need."

Kate nodded as she looked over at Benny who just walked in from the back, "Benny, how about watching the store while I go for a ride with Ben?"

Benny who never showed any expression nodded, "I need to straighten out the store room. Tomorrow is stage day. You send in a good sized order in last week, so we'll need the space."

Ben rode up out front leading Kate's horse along with a pack horse. Clayton and the Henry had the front door of the shop open to let the sunshine in. Ben stopped out front as Clayton walked out toward them, "I'm going to ride up to see if that wagon with the broken wheel has that part we need. If it does I'll bring it back."

Clayton looked up toward the peaks, "Looks like you'll have a good day for a ride. Boy those old peaks look like all this rain has been snow up there. You can see those huge overhangs from here this morning. You might get to see or at least hear some rumbling today. This is good weather for avalanches."

Up at the wagons Ben crawled under the wagon. Later with the part loaded on the pack horse, it wasn't heavy, just bulky. He had left

17

the metal part attached to the wooden frame work. With it all tied down and the horse tied to the corral fence, he motioned for Kate to walk with him. Inside the big barn he left the door open so they could see better in the darkness. He took the ladder from its hiding place and stood it against the manger wall. He climbed up and stopped on the top rung, looking for tracks in dust. He looked back down at Kate, "I'll be back down in a minute. I found something up here you might like." He walked to the back where the old homemade furniture was and picked up a rocking chair. As he walked back by the trunk he stopped and lifted the lid, it was empty. In the bottom was a small pouch. Ben picked it up and dropped it into his inside pocket of his coat. Then he closed the lid, picked up chair and climbed down.

Kate looked the chair over while Ben dusted himself off, "This is well built. It needs a few things fixed, but it's good chair. What else is up there?"

"It's so dark back in the back I really can't see too well. There's more furniture, but most of it I've looked at isn't in very good condition compared to this. Come spring well bring a light and look around more."

As they were tying the chair on top of the pack, Ben stopped and looked over at her. "Kate how about you let me tell the boys about where we found this for you. I really don't want anyone climbing up there right now." Kate just looked at him, "I've got an idea, about something up there. When I figure it out, then I'll tell you about it" Okay?"

Kate nodded, "Okay, but why so secretive? Is it bad?"

Ben chuckled, then, Kate stepped over to, punched him on the shoulder, "Oh I know, too many questions. Ben sometimes you make me so mad." She smiled, "Okay, I'll let you tell the boys whatever you want. I know you could have just left the chair up there and not got it down for me."

The clouds were getting lower and a brisk breeze hit the two riders before they got home. Ben cut across and rode down the back street to the back of the store. He untied the chair and put it on the back porch of the store. Benny stepped out as Ben sat the chair down, "I'll put the horses away while you warm up."

Ben nodded, "Okay, I need to unload this part down at the blacksmith shop. Then you can have the pack horse too."

Benny led the packhorse around to the blacksmith shop back door. Clayton opened it when he heard Ben knocking, "How come you're sneaking up on us? I've been watching out the front window for you to ride by."

"I took Kate home first, that wind been cold the last few miles. I thought when we left this morning we were in for a good day for a ride."

Clayton helped Ben unload the wagon part and carry it up to the forge. Henry walked over to look at it. He looked over the metal part, then, shook his head, "Good thing you went up and got this. There's more to it than what you see when it's on the wagon. I went out and looked at this on those other wagons, but when it's in place you don't see this part of it," as he pointed to the piece. He walked over to the forge and brought back the broken part. "When it broke that part I just showed you must have, fell off. Well now if we find any more of them broke I can make a new one from this pattern. Hell this, calls for a drink over at April's. Ben, go over to the store to see if Kate wants to join us?"

When Ben walked in the store Kate was all snuggled up to the stove with a hot cup of coffee. When told her what Henry suggested, she smiled, "Thank Henry for the invite. Tell him I'm just now getting warm and I'm going to stay that way." Ben smiled and walked back out.

Later that night back in his cabin Ben took the small pouch from his coat pocket. He poured the contents onto a cloth on the table. Two small gold ingots dropped onto the cloth. These had been poured into a mold to cast them. Ben walked over to a shelf on the back wall and took down his gold scales. Each ingot weighted the same, each one was three ounces. As, Ben looked them over this looked to be pure gold. Someone knew how to refine the ore they had into this pure form was a very smart man. Ben leaned back in his chair staring at the wall behind the stove as his mind wondered. 'So someone had survived that slide or maybe that nut with the small boy did find the mine. The cabin started getting cold before Ben came out of his trance and stoked the fire up. Even after curling up in bed his mind was still on who was still alive in those peaks. Light was showing in the windows when Ben woke up. This was late for him to be rolling out of bed. He stoked up the fire and started to slide the coffee pot over the firebox, then, he pushed it back to the side. 'Hell, I'll let Kate cook my breakfast, besides she makes better coffee.'

It was quiet outside so he knew the wind had died down. He walked over to look out the window. It was a sea of white. Big flakes were floating straight down. He banked the fire and put on his coat for the walk down to Kate's place. He was surprised when he stepped out from under the porch roof. The snow was up half way up to his knees. It was fluffy and easy to walk in. Inside, he brushed off the snow by the door and took off his coat. At the big table in the back was full of men looking back at him. Clayton spoke up, "Hell, Ben it's not like you to sleep in, that ride yesterday must have been tough on you."

Henry butted in, "It didn't seem to bother Kate," everyone laughed.

Later it was decided they would go watch Henry build a copy of the part Ben had brought back yesterday. Benny went out to fill the wood boxes in the trading post and the saloon leaving just Kate and Ben at the table. As they talked the back door opened, Benny came shuffling in with an arm load of wood for the inside wood box. When he turned to leave he stopped and looked over at Ben, "Where was that rocking chair you and Kate brought back? I thought I'd been though all those buildings, I sure never saw that."

"It was in that back bedroom of the cabin, behind the door. I missed seeing it the first time I was ever in that cabin too," Ben was hoping the Indian would believe his tale.

Benny nodded, "I guess I never really looked at anything except the main room in that cabin. I told Kate I'd fix those loose parts, then, she can start using it." Benny went shuffling out.

When Ben looked over at Kate she was just staring at him, he smiled, "Kate I just don't want anyone nosing around above the stalls until I get something all figured out in my mind. I know it driving you nuts because I won't tell you more, but right now there's nothing to tell.

CHAPTER 3

It kept snowing for the next week and when the blue sky reappeared, it was nearly a two feet of snow in town. Ben walked up and checked his horses, with the fluffy snow they were still able to paw to find feed. He, decide he'd better move them down to Coby Kline's place on the river until spring. It was only four miles down there but the snow very seldom piled up along the river. Kate had Benny put up hay down on a meadow just south of town each summer. After it cured out he hauled it up to the fill the small hay loft in her barn. That way she could keep one horse for her to use close to town. Dan had done this when he was alive, so Kate kept up the practice.

Ben passed the word around about taking his horses to the river, before long he had ten head to take. Kate, decide to have him take her team too. That night before he was to head out, Benny stopped by the cabin. "How about I take those horses down for you, tomorrow? I got a trade I need to make with Coby for some hides he's got. I can take Kate's horse so I won't have to walk back."

Ben smiled, "Sure go ahead." Ben walked into his bedroom, he walked back and handed Benny a twenty dollar gold piece. "Give this to Coby tell him I'll settle up when I come down after the horses come spring."

Without having the team around to move the wagons around, they used men from camp to help Kate saddle horse with the chore. Clayton had helped Benny using the team move all the wagons into the corral behind the barn earlier, this really helped now.

By the time the spring rains started melting the snow at the end of March, the wagons were all finished. Kate had made up an advertisement and sent it out with the mail stage to neighboring towns. The men told Kate they would bring down a few of the canvas covers before they all headed back to the mountains for the summer.

By the first of April green grass was beginning to cover the south slopes. Benny brought Ben's saddle horse and Kate's team up on a trip down to the river to see Coby. He also surprised everyone with a deer he got along the river. The deer that wintered down there were in good shape compared to the ones closer to town. Kate had a big liver feed along with a fresh meat meal for anyone wanting to come. The saloon was full that night.

Ben woke one night to rumble that was shaking his cabin windows. After a pause it happened again. Ben felt a hand squeezing his arm, Kate scooted up even closer. "Is that what I think it is? Ben, that's as loud as it was that year it killed those people." He lay back down next to her, pulling her close to him.

The peaks had been loaded with huge overhangs, visible even from here in Garnet. Ben was sure the rumble was avalanches causing the windows to rattle.

She kissed him, then, sat up. "I guess I better head back to my own place before someone starts pounding on my door wanting to know if I felt the shaking. We need to move your cabin closer, so I don't have to get dressed to go home."

"You know I could be the one walking in the wee hours between beds?" Ben said a she pulled on her bibs.

Kate laughed, "Like I told you before, I don't want someone finding you in my bed down there. I just feel better if I come up here."

Ben waited until daylight before he walked down to Kate's. Three or four of the regulars were already sitting around the big table. "Did you feel the old mountain shaking us this morning, Ben?" Henry asked as Ben sat down.

"I sure heard the windows rattling. Come sunup we'll probably be able to see what part broke loose. This may have ripped lose the last of that frame work left hanging on those cliffs. Pretty soon there won't be any trace of any mining ever been done up there. I still wonder what they found in those sheer cliffs. I've looked through those rock slides down below. I never have seen anything that looks like mineral in any of it."

Jess Garret was one of the oldest miners still staying in Garnet during the winter. This morning he had joined the group. He looked up at Ben and nodded. "I agree Ben. I spent a lot of time up there one summer long before the religious group showed up. I found one rock that showed a little color, but nothing to get excited about. That upper frame work I think must have been a portal to a tunnel. You can see high up under where it was, that they dumped tailings, but that a real steep climb for someone my age. Maybe this slide moved some on those loose rocks down closer to the trail, so we can look at what they were digging into up there."

Clayton looked over at Jess, "I thought about try to climb up there last year, but looking at that loose frame work just hanging up there discouraged me. I figured it, be just my luck I'd get up there and one of those pieces would break loose and clobber me."

Two days later Ben and Benny rode up to the cabin, the snow was now gone in the flats. As they sat staring up at the peaks, they could see where those huge overhangs had scoured the cliffs down to the bare rock as they came roaring down. Ben looked all along where the timbers had been and found nothing now, the cliffs were wiped clean. Later Benny and Ben walked up over the snow to where they could look up into the basin where the settlement had been. Both men, just stared, the whole basin was just a huge wall of snow.

Ben shook his head, "It doesn't look like any of us going north to our diggin's will be going this way. We'll have to take the lower route. Hell it'll be August before this upper trail melts out with that much snow in that basin."

As they walked back toward the cabin, Benny motioned toward the barns. "I think I'll go check on those canvass to make sure that room didn't leak with all the rain we got last winter."

Ben nodded, "While you're doing that I'll check that other barn for damage."

Ben pulled out the ladder and climbed up and hurried over to the trunk. Inside were the empty tins he had left when he left the flour, bean and rice and other stuff. Ben closed the lid and hurried back down the ladder. When he walked out Benny was just closing the doors to the other barn.

"Canvas, are still dry, looks good inside the whole barn," Benny said as he walked up.

Ben motioned to the two wheeled cart that the crazy guy and the boy had when they passed through Garnet. "You know we could use that when we come after a few of those covers. It'd be easier than using one of the big wagons." Benny nodded as they swung up for the ride back to town.

The miners started getting ready to head for the mountains. They had brought all the horses up from the river and were busy trimming hooves and shoeing them. Kate was busy getting all the orders ready for each miner. With the freight wagons again on the main road, she had stocked up on supplies.

Bens last night in camp Kate lay beside him in bed. Most of the other miner had already left. "I wish you could find a mine closer in so you could come in once or twice during the summer. I hate it when I don't know how you are from spring until snow fall. Dam it, Ben we need to do something different with our lives."

Ben pulled her close, "I agree Kate. How about, I see if I can find someone who will buy me out this summer. You know I do miss you too, but hell its long trip back here from the mine. Old Bowers who owns the claim next to my mine has been bugging me to sell to him. I'll have him make me an offer on my claim when I get up there."

She kissed him then she smiled, "You're serious aren't you? Oh Ben, that'll be great if you move closer."

"Kate I can't get much closer than, I'm right now," she buried her head in his chest.

"We could do this every night, if we were married."

"Yeah, we could I suppose. Who knows what will happen."

In one of Ben's packs was a separate load of supplies. With the late start from town Ben camped that night at the cabin. After supper he took the extra supplies from his main packs and headed for barn. No one had been there since his trip with Benny. He filled the tins and packed everything else into the trunk. Closing the lid he climbed down.

It was still an hour before dark so Ben took some papers from his saddle bag and six tins he had brought from his cabin. He walked off to a corner of the corral and fastened one can to the post. Then he paced off so many feet and built a mound of rocks and placed another can under one of the top rocks. Again pacing off until he was past the corner of the far barn he mounded up another marker. Later he hung the fourth can on a post between the two barns.

Then he paced off past the second barn to a fence post, there he hung another can. Back at the cabin he fastened the last can to the corner of it. Inside each can was a claim notice. He grinned, 'Well Kate, we're now partners in what later may become our home.'

The next morning Ben packed up and head south to hit the lower trail back to the mountains where his claim was. The day was sunny and Ben was glad to be on the move again.

Back at the trading post Benny walked in and handed Kate an envelope with her name printed on the front. "When I went up to close up Ben's cabin this was on the table."

Kate sat down and read the letter. She opened the envelope that was inside the first one. A few tears appeared. Benny looked at her, "What's the matter Kate?"

She handed him the letter. Benny smiled as he finished reading it, "Why the tears Kate? You've, been, wanting, him to settle down here and quit climbing all over these mountains. This sounds like that's just

24

what he's going to do. I suppose that other envelope is the claim notices he wants filed for you and him on that cabin and barns up above."

Two weeks later Ben was unpacking his supplies into his cabin at the claim. The trail had been hell, even using the lower route. The heavy snows high up during the winter plugged a lot of the trail that were usually open by this time of the year. Ben had to back track a few places in order to keep traveling. He normally made this trip in about a week if he could use the upper trail. He needed to add a couple of days by using this lower route. This year it was tough all the way. Snow was still on the mountain just above Ben's claim and the water was cold to work in.

By evening the cabin was beginning to heat up after sitting empty all winter. This cabin wouldn't be a good place to stay during the winter. Ben had built it just for his summer use. Like always Ben last fall before he left had set the water into the sluices so they would pick up the spring runoff. This year it looked like the run off had been higher than usual. With the banks sloughing off into the creek during the high water brought fresh material through the sluices. Ben normally each spring had a good clean up before he ever shoveled any dirt himself. The first three days Ben was busy cleaning up. One afternoon he sat in the sun by the cabin picking all the bigger nuggets from his clean up. This was a good haul. He smiled as he filled a pouch with the shiny pieces that he could pick with his fingers. 'Kate, this is why I love my work,' he said aloud.

The next morning Ben saddled up his horse and headed over the ridge to see if old Nate Bowers had shown up yet. He smelled the smoke before he could see Nate's cabin. As he rode into the clearing he saw Nate hard at work splitting wood by the cabin door. Nate's dog was barking and Nate turned to see Ben as he rode up. He waved, "Well high neighbor, looks like you wintered good."

"You do too, Nate. How, was your travels, getting up here? Mine was real slow. I had to use the lower route and still needed to make a few detours just to get here," Ben said as he swung down.

"Yeah I did too. That snow was deep this year in the high country. Well at least we won't be running out of water very soon," then he laughed. "Come on in, I got fresh pot of coffee on."

Once they sat down Nate look over at Ben, "Well I'm not going to be alone this year. My youngest son showed up from back in Missouri along with his young wife. He's going to join me and be a partner in this claim. He was only five years old when the old lady kicked my ass out of the house. Every year since I've had this claim I send back a good sum to her and the kids. She never writes, but when I got back to town last fall I had this letter from Rodney. He asked if I cared if he came west to join me. I wrote back and told him, he was plumb welcome." Nate chuckled, "When he showed up he had this cute little filly with him. I guess she was the reason that his mother kicked him out too. Old Ester was a daughter of a bible thumper, she pretty straight laced. Anyway she didn't approve of Rodney's new wife. With her being the daughter of a preacher, I always wondered why she married me in the first place.' He grinned, "I guess she thought I'd be a good, stud. We had four kids before she booted me out. You'll like Rodney and that little wife of his, Rose Mary."

Ben laughed, "When they coming up?"

"Oh that cabin of mine in town was too small for three people especially when one was a woman. I left him a list of gear to buy for him and her, then, I bought some extra horses. Old Levi the livery stable owner and me are good friends. He's taking a few days off and going to help Rodney bring up the pack string with all the supplies. They should be showing up by weeks end."

As they walked out into the sunshine Ben stopped and turned to face Nate, "You still interested in buying my claim? I've decided to change my way of life and more or less settle down in one place. I'm really in no hurry to leave. I just want to get it done before I leave this fall."

Nate sat down on a block of wood, then, looked up at Ben, "Yeah Ben with Rodney joining me I will think hard on that. How about I wait and talk it over with Rodney? He laughed, "You know by the time he gets up here he might change his mind about mountain living. He's never been anywhere but that flat Missouri land along the river all his life."

Ben offered his, hand, "Sounds fine to me. I just wanted to ask you first. So take your time on deciding. Now I better get back to work." as he swung up he look back at his neighbor, "Did you get a good clean up this spring?"

Nate chuckled, "Yes I did. I've always been glad you taught me about setting up those sluices each fall before I leave. Hell I've already made enough to pay for all the extra gear and supplies I had to buy this year."

Ben waved as he turned his horse then headed back toward his own claim. Ben was reworking the upper end of his operation to pick up all the material the high water had brought down. One morning he was just dropping the riffles back into the sluice when he saw riders

26

coming through the trees. Nate was in the lead with three other people single file behind him. He waved when he saw Ben. "Howdy neighbor," he said as he swung down at the corral.

Nate waited until everyone was dismounted then looked at Ben, "Ben I'd like you to meet my son Rodney and his wife Rose Mary. The tall drink of water over behind them is my winter partner Levi Davis, folks this is Ben Jasper.

Ben shook everyone's hand including Rose Mary who offered her hand. "Well how do you Missouri people like our home up here in these mountains?"

Rodney just shook his head, "If I would have ever thought Dad lived in a place like this I'd been here long before this. Rose Mary and I both just can't believe where we are. This is like heaven to us."

Levi stepped forward to grasp Ben's hand, "I've heard many good stories about you. It's good to finally meet you."

Ben led them up where he was getting ready to start working virgin ground again. As they passed along his flume that carried material down to the sluice he stopped and reached down to pick up a good sized nugget caught up in a root running across the smooth bottom. Every so often down the smooth bottom Ben added a riffle ever so often to help break up the dirt clods before they got to the main riffles. This root holding the nugget was one of these. He held his hand back to Rose Mary, "Here's your first gold nugget."

When she held out her hand, he dropped the shiny nugget. "This is mine to keep? She almost yelled.

Ben laughed, "Yes, you can keep it."

Nate chuckled, 'I'll bet you one thing. This little gal will get even with you on that gift. She's one hell of a cook."

It was evening by the time Ben was again alone. He finished locking down the riffle in the main sluice, then headed back to the cabin. The next morning he was hard at work when about noon he saw a rider coming toward him. He stopped to see who it was, then, he recognized Rose Mary. She waved as she dismounted beside his cabin. She took down a small pack from behind her saddle then disappeared into the cabin. She came right back out without the bundle and started walking up where Ben worked. "High, I brought you some fresh bread and biscuits I baked this morning. I just love my present you gave me," she pulled a fish line from around her neck and held up the nugget. "Levi drilled a hole in it and made me this, necklaces from some fish line Dad had in the cabin."

Ben laughed, "I'm glad you like it, Rose Mary. He looked closer at it, "Levi, did a good job of making that."

"Dad Bowers told us last night you're going to sell him this claim. How, come you don't want to mine up here anymore?" then she blushed. "I'm sorry for being so nosy. It's none of my business why you want to sell."

Ben sat down on a nearby log. He motioned for her to sit next to him, "I don't think you're being nosy. You just asked the question straight out. That's what I person should always do if you really want to know something. Don't beat around the bush, just asked it straight out. Then if the person doesn't want you to know, then he should just say so. You just continue to be straight forward and no one will think your being nosy in this country. Now that's enough of my preaching for this day," he laughed.

"Now back to why I'm selling the claim, well Rose Mary there's a woman living over in Garnet a semi ghost town running a trading post. I kinda like her. It's about a week's ride from here when all the passes are open, this year it took me almost two weeks to get here. Her name is Kate Crawford, her husband died a few years ago. Besides the trading post she owns the local saloon along with her partner, April. During the summer she gets business from travelers and sells supplies to the local miners still working the area. Then in the winter she gets a couple dozen of us miner who work the summer miles from Garnet then move back to town to winter there. Mainly because, there good winter feed for our pack animals a few miles from town, down along the river. Plus Kate and April provide a good place to winter. When the gold rush moved onto new ground those town folks left some nice cabin there vacant. I've got one of them for myself along with all the others who winter there. We can leave all the stuff we don't need for the summer in our places and come fall nobody has bothered it. Kate and her hired hand Benny make sure nobody bothers our cabins. Kate, been complaining about me being gone from when the snow leaves in the spring until the ground again white in the fall. I've decided I miss her too, so if Nate buys me out I'm going to find me a claim somewhere close to Garnet to work. I already stake a claim on some ground we can build us a place to live together."

Rose Mary had a big grin on her face, "I'm so glad you've found you a good woman. A person shouldn't live alone all their lives. I know that as I look at Dad Bowers. I'm so glad Rodney and I are here. We now can make the family he needs so badly. You know Rodney's

28

mother Ester has remarried, in fact Rodney don't think she ever divorced Nate. Nate wasn't even gone year when she moved another man in. Rodney has never told his dad that she remarried. She's just been keeping that money he's been sending all these years. That's how Rodney found out his Dad was a miner was when the local banker there told him about the money he'd been sending every year. That's when Rodney decided to write to see if we could join his father out here. We'd just about give up, then, Nate's letter showed up telling us to come west. He also sent money for us to come join him."

After Rose Mary left Ben went back to work. Two days later, Nate, came riding up just after Ben finished breakfast. He poured him a cup of coffee. "Well Ben I decided I'd better get over here to see what kind of deal we can make. You know I haven't dug enough gold this spring to pay you the full amount for this claim. I was wondering what you wanted to do."

Ben nodded, "Well, Nate, make me an offer. That will include everything just the way it is right now, except for my personal gear and enough grub to get back to Garnet."

Nate studied the man that had been his neighbor for the last few summers. He thought a moment then looked back over at Ben, "I don't need the supplies, Rodney and Rose Mary brought enough to last us a year, so without the supplies, how about twenty thousand in gold dust? I can give you ten now and the rest by fall. You keep the papers on this mine until I pay you in full."

Ben grinned, "Neighbor, you just bought a mining claim. I'll make a point in coming back over in September to collect the balance, I'll bring you the deed then," he stood up and offered his hand.

Nate shook his hand, "I'm going to miss you Ben. I know we haven't spent much time together other than a pot of coffee now and then. But I still knew you were close by if I ever needed help. I think I'll move up here to this cabin and let Rodney and Rose Mary use mine. It's a little bigger and it'll be easier for two people to live in."

Ben nodded, "How about you move up day after tomorrow, I'll head out the next morning?"

Ben cleaned up the sluice then packed up his gear for his trip back to Kate's place. That evening he and Nate sat there sharing a jug that Ben always carried for such purposed. Rodney and Rose Mary had ridden up with Nate to tell Ben good-bye then they headed back for their place. Rose Mary had given Ben a big hug, "You will treat that Kate real nice, won't you?"

"Ben smiled, "That I will, little lady. Now, don't you spoil these two men you've got in your life now."

As Ben finished his loading the next morning, he turned to Nate, "I'm going to try to go back on the high trail. It's been pretty warm so it should have melted out by now. If not I'll double back and drop down on the other trail." He reached for Nate's hand, "I'll be seeing you come September."

Ben looked back as he topped the highest point after leaving the mine. 'That's one hell of a good claim to just ride away from.' Two days later Ben started getting into the high country. He found a few small slides across the trail. He would tie the horses and walk across each slide to make sure of it before he led the horses across the snow. He stopped on a wide point in the trail when he started hearing the roar of water ahead. He tied the horses and took his rife and headed on up the trail. As he rounded a sharp corner he stopped to stare, the trail was totally gone. Where a fairly dry draw had been was a raging river of water cascading off the cliff. On the next point beyond the water he could see the trail again. Ben turned and walked back to his horses. As he headed back down the trail he started trying to remember the country below him. He had prospected all of this area before he found the mine he just sold. That night be camped at fork of the trail, the ground was flat here with plenty of feed for his stock.

As Ben packed up the next morning he decided he would try this lower trail to get around to and back up on the high trail. By noon the second day he was to a flat where the water from above had somewhere above had gotten back into the right channel. At the ford the water was up to the horses belly but they crossed with no problem. The next morning he was again back up on the high trail. Ahead he could see the beginning of the peaks where the religious clan had been.

Ben looked ahead real fast when the horse stopped all of a sudden. He'd been looking ahead for any sign of the timber still hanging from the cliffs above. The trail was totally plugged with rocks is why his horse had stopped. Ben moved back to the back pack animal and slowly eased it back down the narrow trail until he found a place to turn the horse around. He tied the horse at the first wide place, then, headed back for the next animal. It took about an hour to get all three animals back to a place with a little feed. He off loaded them and tied them where they could get a little feed sprouting among the rocks. Taking his rifle he headed back up to the slide blocking the trail. As he surveyed the slide he noticed nothing was real big, so he decided in time he could clear the trail. By evening he had opened a good section of trail, ahead

30

he could see the open trail. He walked back down to his animals to camp for the night. A small trickle if water was coming down through the rocks. Ben cleaned out a basin for the water to pool so the horses could drink. With a full stomach Ben laid there staring up at the stars as darkness closed in.

The next day about noon Ben was walking on up the trail above the slide when he came to a wide place in a draw. As far as he could see ahead the trail was open except for a few rocks scattered on the narrow shelf of a trail. He walked back and loaded the horses and headed up the trail leading them. As he moved past the area where he'd walked before he began to see timbers scattered below the trail. Now ahead he could see the basin where the settlement had been. Off in the distance he could see the roofs of barns near the cabin. Darkness was beginning to close in as he walked onto a grassy flat where the cliffs began to tapered, off. He knew it was going to be too dark in another couple of hours to try to make the cabin for the night. With good feed and water he pulled the packs and staked out the horses. While he was gathering wood for a fire, his eyes caught the faint trail in the rocks above him. He dropped the wood he had gathered into a pile, then, moved up along the narrow path. He got into a place where you could see places that had been used for hand holds he stopped. It was getting too dark to be hanging out here on an open faced cliff. As he turned to go back down he felt the ground under his feet start to move. Then a roar came from above him as rocks started bouncing by him on the narrow shelf. He hugged the rock wall as the roar got louder. He felt the rock under his feet move, then, he was falling.

As he waken by the terrible pain in his leg. Ben tried to move and he couldn't. It was dark. Ben then moved his right arm to his face. He could feel rocks all around him, but he was smelling dust. He moved a couple of rocks on his left then got his left arm loose. His legs seemed to be penned in. The pain in the right one was almost making him sick because of the pain. Then he got dizzy and then nothing. He opened his eyes, a small ray of light appeared out through an opening in the rocks around his head. Then the world went dark again.

Twice he regained a little knowledge of what was going on around him, then, it would go dark again. His eyes flickered open, above him was a face staring down at him. The face was covered with whiskers and his hair flowed down over his shoulders. All Ben could really see, was, the two very clear blue eyes looking down at him. Ben saw his lips move then everything went blank again.

Sweat was running off him as Ben again opened his eyes. He was covered with blankets, his arm moved trying to move the blankets and they wouldn't move. It was like they were tied down on both sides of him. Sweat was getting into his eyes, then, he felt a cool cloth wiping his forehead. Again that same face stared down at him. He felt a hand under his head, tipping it up and then he felt the lip of a cup on his lips. A cool liquid began to cool his parched throat. Then his head was gently laid back down. "Lay quiet my brother the pain will soon pass," Come a voice that sounded miles away. Darkness again took over Ben's world.

CHAPTER 4

Back in Garnet, Benny walked into the trading post. Kate was busy fixing breakfast at the stove. Benny poured a cup of coffee, "Did you feel that old mountain shaking last night? I felt my bed moving a little."

Kate nodded, "Those peaks sure have been acting up this summer. I don't ever remember this much activity during the summer."

Benny looked over at her, "Maybe mother nature is closing up all those holes those religious nuts put in her mountain."

Kate laughed, "Now quit trying to convince me the spirits are in that mountain doing all of this. You and your Indian voodoo would scare a normal person. Benny, are you sure you wasn't a medicine man or witch doctor when you lived with your tribe? I'm thinking they run you off for your wild tales."

Benny gave her a blank stare, Kate laughed just as April walked in, "What's so funny this morning? Did you feel the shaking last night or was it just me?"

Kate motioned over to Benny, "Our spirit leader over there thinks the mountain is getting even for those miners putting holes in it."

April looked over at him as she filled her cup, "Benny, how do you come up with all this stuff? Maybe Kate is right about you being a witch doctor or something before you came here."

Benny took his plate from Kate and headed for the big table. As they were eating Kate looked over at Benny, "I suppose that upper trail is plugged again. It seems like every time some miner clears the trail, the mountain shakes and plugs it again. Clayton said he would be back in before the fourth of July to get supplies. That's only a couple weeks away, so he may have a hard time getting through that upper trail."

Two weeks later, Henry Corn, came riding in leading his two pack mules. Kate walked out to greet him as he swung down in front of the trading post. "Good to see you Henry. I guess that upper trail must be open if you made it down here. That old mountain been shaking all spring, it seems to plug the trail every time someone opens it."

33

Henry grinned, "Tell me about it. I've been up there a day and a half getting it open enough to get my animals by it. I can see where someone else has been doing the same thing before me." He stopped to look around, "Kate I got a pretty full pack I need to leave with you. I need it shipped off to Springfield bank on the Well Fargo stage."

Kate nodded, "Okay, the towns empty right now so no one will see you unloading it right here in the street. You want me to go get Benny to help you?"

Henry laughed, "It ain't that big Kate. I wish it was, that way I could quit trying to kill myself out there mining from dawn to dark." It's been a good clean up from the wet winter. I got little nervous with this much gold in the cabin, so I came in a couple weeks early for supplies."

April had walked out from the saloon to see Henry, "When you your animals put away I buy the first round."

Kate joined in, "Then I'll buy supper."

"Hell ladies, with a deal like that I may never go back to that mine," as he took the lead ropes and headed for his cabin.

While the four people were eating that evening Henry looked over at Kate, "Where you hiding that Ben? When I saw his animals up in the pasture by the barns I thought he was living in the cabin. I swung down and looked in, it's been all cleaned up but no one was around."

Kate jumped to her feet, "What do you mean his animals are up in that pasture? Ben hasn't been here. Henry, are you sure those were Ben horses?"

Henry shook his head yes, "Yeah, Kate those are Ben's horses alright. They haven't been used in a while. There all three right fat and sassy looking."

"I was up there and stayed a couple nights, about a month or so ago. Benny, you were up there not long ago, you didn't see any horses did you?"

Benny shook his head, "There wasn't any horse's there, when I was there. In fact I fixed the fence a couple of places where the elk torn it down during the winter. The only, tracks around that pasture then was wild game."

Henry looked over at the people across the table staring at him, "You mean Ben hasn't been here at all? Hell when I came down I stopped by to see Clayton at his claim. He said he rode up to see Ben around the first of May and found out he'd sold out to his neighbor. He said old Nate told him Ben had headed for here, then."

34

Henry sat there a moment as if he was in deep though, "You know Clayton told me that upper trail washed out this spring. He said he had ridden up there and the trail is totally gone. One of those bigger creeks for some reason has changed canyons. What was a dry draw is now almost a river. Between that and the lower trail the water went back to the right channel. So Ben couldn't have come out that way, he had to come out the way I just came in."

Kate slammed her fist on the table, "One of those dam slides must have got him! She almost yelled.

Benny reached over to grasp her arm, "Kate, calm down. If a slide had got him his horses would be gone too. Henry says they look in great shape, so that means a slide didn't get him. Henry was his gear in the cabin?"

"I sure didn't see it. When I saw the cabin was empty I just figured he was here so I just rode out without looking around anymore."

"Come on Benny were riding up there, now," Kate said as he grabbed Benny arm.

"Kate it's dark outside. We'll ride up there come morning. If he's camping there somewhere he'll still be there in the morning. Now sit down. April pour her another drink, maybe that will calm her down."

Henry nodded, "Kate, Benny right. Come morning I'll even ride up with you two. Clayton should be riding in a couple of days, maybe he knows more about where Ben is now."

The sun was just being to flood the valley when the three riders swung down at the cabin. Kate had them in the saddle long before dawn. The three horses in the pasture came running to the fence when they rode up. Kate walked over to rub their heads, "Oh I wish you three could talk." The big black Ben always rode looked good, no sign of any injuries. It had been a while since it had a saddle on, no cinch or saddle marks showed anywhere.

Kate stood there staring up at those peaks she was beginning to hate. First they had taken Dan now it seemed maybe they had also taken Ben from her. Benny and Henry came walking back from the two barns, both shaking their heads, "No gear or any fresh sign back there," Henry said as he walked up.

Benny was walking back up the trail toward the peaks, studying the ground as he walked. Soon he was out of sight. Kate looked over at Henry, "Where's he going?"

"Hell Kate you know Benny better than I do, but I'd say he looking for horse tracks. He's more Indian than we realize when it comes to tracking people or game."

35

Kate walked into the cabin and soon had a fire going. She filled the coffee pot hanging on the wall from her canteen, added coffee beans she had brought with her. The water was just beginning to boil when Henry called from outside, "I can see Benny way up there, he's coming back down the trail now."

Benny looked at Kate, slowly shaking his head, "I'm sorry Kate. It's been too long to find any tracks other than the fresh ones coming down the trail. I walked up to where the rock ledges start. I did find where someone had gathered wood, but didn't, used it."

Kate walked back outside and just stood there looking at Ben's horses in the pasture. "Ben, where in the hell are you?' Benny walked up alongside her, she looked over at him, "What shall we do with these horses?"

"Kate the pasture is still in good shape, so let's leave them for a while. I'll keep a watch, if the pasture starts getting ate out I'll move them to town." Kate rode in silence as they rode back to town.

A week later, Clayton rode in late one night with his pack animals for supplies. The next morning he walked in to the trading post as Kate was cooking breakfast for the early riser's already drinking coffee at the big table. Henry looked up as Clayton walked in, "Well look, who, final showed up."

Clayton looked about grinning, "Hell I thought I better get here to celebrate the fourth with you rebels." He looked over at Kate by the stove, "Where that partner of yours? Is that his horses up at the cabin? I was going to spend the night with him when I saw his stock, but the cabin was empty."

Henry spoke up before Kate could answer, "All that showed up was his stock. We've never seen Ben. I saw them as I rode down by the cabin coming in. When I got here, these folks didn't know a thing about them being there."

Clayton looked over at Kate, then back at the crowd at the table, "Has anyone looked for him? I wonder if a slide got him, you know you can see where a bunch of them came down this year. I had to move one slide yesterday to get by. Were the horses bunged up?"

Benny looked up from the table, "They came in just like they are now. No saddles or gear on any of them."

"Dam, old Nate Bowers said he was in high spirits about getting back down here to Kate when he left the mine. He had to ride the same trail I just came in on. Nate said Ben was coming back this fall to get the other half of the gold from the sale. Nate is living in Ben's old cabin since he bought him out. Nate's son and daughter in law are with him this year, their staying down on Nate's old claim." Clayton just sat there staring at the walls, slowly shaking his head. "When I get back to the mine I'll ride over to let Nate know about him being missing."

With a few bad hangovers in town after the 4th celebration Clayton and Henry started loading up the next morning for their trip back to mining their claims. They told Kate as they moved along they would keep an eye out for any sign of Ben. If they found out anything they would come back to let her know. As they rode away Kate and Benny stood watching them until they were out of sight. Benny looked over at Kate, "If I didn't have that hay already cut, I'd ride along with them to look for sign. In fact when I get done with the hay I might take a few days to ride up there and look for myself."

Kate glanced over at him, "I might just go with you."

When Benny finished his haying job he started packing up to head up the trail. Kate had decided one of them needed to stay here to run the trading post. With the road traffic going north Kate had been busy. April and her girls were busy in the saloon, so she didn't have time to tend the store for Kate.

Benny was gone a week, then he rode in one afternoon. Kate saw him ride by toward the barn so she walked out the back door. He swung down just as she got to the corral. He shook his head, "Nothing Kate. I really spent a lot of time looking for any sign that could have been him, I found nothing."

That evening Benny sat with Kate at the big back table, Kate was having a drink, while Benny nursed a cup of cold coffee. "Kate, that one section of trail really bothers me. Its right where those miners worked, it's like I'm being watched. When I rode up through there the hair on the back of my neck stood up. Then when I came back down today I got the same feeling. You laugh when I talk of spirits, but there is something strange going on up in those rocks. I don't believe in ghosts, but this is something different. You just wait and see, one day you'll agree with me."

Kate looked over at her very good friend, "Benny, I may kid you about your goofy beliefs at times, but I also think you are serious about your spirits in those mountains. Those dam mountain peaks have cost me Dan and now we can't find Ben. Like you, I think that mountain has something to do with Ben being gone."

The nights were getting colder, so everyone knew the miners would start drifting in before long. This morning the sun was warming the front porch of the trading post and the saloon. Kate walked out to sit in the sun with a cup of coffee. April came out to join her. As they sat there warming to the sun, April motioned up the trail, "Rider."

An older man stopped his horse, he look down at the two ladies, "Fine morning. Would one of you ladies be Kate Crawford?"

Kate nodded, "I'm Kate Crawford. How can I help you?"

The old man swung down, and walked up to the porch, "The name is Nate Bowers. I'm the miner who bought out Ben Jasper up on the Middle Fork. I came down to try to settle up on my buying Ben's claim. That Clayton fella stopped by this spring to see Ben then later stopped by to say Ben was missing. Is he still missing?"

Kate stood up and offered her hand, "This gal here is my partner April. Come on in Nate, I'll fix you some breakfast then I'll bring you up to date on Ben."

April excused herself and headed back for the saloon. Inside as Nate was eating Kate told him all they knew about Ben. Benny had walked in while they were talking so Kate introduced him to Nate.

Nate pushed back his plate, "Mighty fine meal, Kate. Now back to business, I owe Ben the second half of the gold for the mine. I asked him to keep the papers on the mine until I paid in full. He said he would ride back in September with the papers. Well, I got the gold with me. Do you know of any way I can get something to show I now own the mine?"

Kate looked over at Nate, "We had talked of getting married this year if he sold the mine. Well as you know he didn't come back, his horses did. That cabin and those two big barns you passed coming down here belong to Ben and me. He staked those out for us when he left this spring. His horses showed up there at the end of May with no gear. Someone put them in the pasture, but left no sign. Now as far as the papers on that claim, I'll go up and look in his cabin. I think I know where he kept that stuff. If it's there, I'll bring it down for you. I'll sign it and hope no one questions it."

Nate spent the night before heading back to his claim. As he was saddling up Kate walked out to see him, "Nate if we find Ben I'll let him know what I did. If he shows up at your diggin's he can sign over my signature. I will get this gold dust down to the bank in Springfield on the stage." She held out her hand, "Nate, it was great to meet you. Now you have a good trip home."

Nate held to her hand, "Kate I wish you the best. I deep down believe that Ben will show up one day. You just keep the faith, things will work out." He mounted and waved as he rode away.

Ben eyes popped open, a faint light made shadows on the walls of the room he was in. His eye's moved as he gazed around. His eyes stopped when he saw a figure of a man humped over a small work bench. The man's back was to him, but in the faint light he could see the long shinny hair down the man's back. "You are awake my friend," came a voice so soft it was almost a whisper. The man stood up then turned to face Ben. Slowly he walked over to where Ben laid. He put his hand on Ben's forehead. "Good, your fever finally has gone. Do you feel like eating some broth?" Ben nodded he did. As the man turned away Ben couldn't get over those eyes, they were so bright blue even in the dark. How did he know Ben's eyes were on him as he working at the, bench.

Ben tried to sit up but he had no strength to move, then he was dizzy. Again that voice broke the stillness, "It will take time before you can move about. The leg has healed very well. It too will take a long time before you have back your old strength." He slowly spooned a warm broth into Ben's mouth. It tasted so good, then, all of sudden Ben was again asleep.

When he woke the next time, no one was around but more light came from down the long hallway. As Ben stared around he saw he was in a cave or manmade rock room. Across where the man had been sitting Ben could see what looked to be a shiny figure of some sort. The more he studied it he decided it was like a small statue made of maybe gold or something that almost glowed. Then he started seeing all the things in the room made from gold. Candle holder next to the bed looked to be made of gold too. Ben would have jumped had he the strength when from alongside the low voice said, "Good you are awake, I brought you more broth."

"Where am I?" Ben asked between, spoonful of warm broth.

"You are in my home in the mountain. This mountain is homey combed with tunnels and large rooms all built into this mountain by I think the Spanish with slave labor long before settlers ever found this country. You can travel inside this mountain from top to bottom and never see the outside world except out those windows along the outside tunnel. These were added by the family so they could get the ore out and down chutes to their mill which never got completed before the slides wiped everyone out. I will tell you more as you get better, now you need rest."

He started to turn away then turned back, "You don't remember me, but I remember you. The lady from the trading post gave me books to read. You have also brought me many things to the barn to make my life easier. The salt is what I needed most, but I've used it all. Now maybe I can repay you."

"You were the small boy with the man looking for mine left when the religious group all got killed by the slide. Where is the man that was with you, now?"

"He was my father, he is now dead. He died that first winter. When he found the gold had to be mined from the rock for him to be rich, he just gave up. Father had been asked to leave his people because of his ways. My mother stole off into the night carrying me just to get away from him. He followed and stole me back one night when I was about a year old. With his ways we were chased out of every town he went into. Later when he heard about my grandfather and the brothers here being killed, he came to collect what he thought was his. My father was crazy, but he was also very smart. He could read and write real well but he didn't want anyone to know it. He taught me all the time, later I became his spokesman to everyone met. Now you must sleep, soon we will start getting you up on your feet."

"Why am here? The last I remember was the ground shaking under my feet, then, I was covered up. I remember the terrible pain in my leg whenever I came to."

"In time I will tell you of your trip back from dead, now you must rest." He turned a moved away.

Ben laid there staring up at the rock ceiling above him, 'trip from death?'

He looked at his arms, they were all shrunk up he hardly recognized them then as his own. He felt the long beard on his face. He now wore clothes made from skins, where were his clothes? How long had he been here? He wondered.

By weeks end he was sitting up for sometimes an hour now before losing his strength to hold himself up. He watched for hours as the silent young man worked with his gold figures. Ben had never seen a man with this kind of talent before. His meals now had big pieces of meat that was so tender it just fell apart.

Ben didn't know how much weight he had lost, but this young slender man lifted him like he was a feather. He had built a place for Ben to stand with supports under his arms. The third day he placed a square stone about 4 inches high in front of his feet. "Take turns trying to step up on the rock, then, step back off. This will get your muscles built back up in your legs. You must be patient with the right leg it will take longer to build back."

As the man walked away Ben asked, "How long have I been here?"

A voice drifted back to him, "Four full moons," as he disappeared from sight.

Ben slowly walked out toward the light ahead. He stopped back from the opening to gaze out over the valley below. Far below were the big barns and the cabin. Off in the distance he could see building of Garnet. His legs were getting better, but walking was still a chore to go very far. Jacob kept after him to keep moving every hour he could stand the pain. He had walked back to where the rich ore vein was to watch the silent man work. This man was a craftsman at everything he did.

One evening when a cold wind could be heard whenever they passed a skin cover that blocked on hallway. Jacob looked up from his silent pray or whatever he called it, "We need to get word to the woman who comes to the cabin alone to look for you to bring a wagon for you before the snows come. If you will write a letter to her to come alone without telling anyone, I will deliver it down to the cabin."

Ben nodded, "How will you get me down there? Those cliffs are straight off."

Ben thought that through that long flowing beard maybe a smile had appeared. "You can walk down, it may take you two days, but you can make it. I will be by your side all the way down. Long before our people mined here others have been here. Many tunnels are scattered all through this mountain. It was not my grandfather who first found the gold in this mountain, his faith to lead him to this mountain. The forge that I use now was built many years ago. Come I will show you some of their work, whoever they were."

Ben hobbled along slowly as Jacob led him through room after room filled with wooden furniture of all types. You could tell these were very old, but looked to still be usable. Back in the room with the forge built into the rock wall, Ben looked about. He looked above and you could see the rocks were blackened from the smoke from the forge. As he looked higher, the smoked rocks became lighter as they entered the blackness high up through the cracks.

Jacob had been watching Ben as his eyes searched where the smoke should have been, "I have never found where the smoke passes out of the mountain. The people before us were very skilled." He motioned to the gold bars lying along a shelf built into the rock wall, "These I have poured using the tools they left behind. It is like they just

41

walked away leaving everything except their gold they had mined. I have no idea where they produced the coke used to fire the forge. In a supply room back there is more choke than I can ever use." He took Ben's arm, "Now we must return to your quarters so I can watch for the woman from the trading post."

Ben looked at the young man for a long spell, "Jacob, I will have Kate bring supplies when she brings the wagon. Can you make me a list of what you need?"

Kate sat alone in the cabin one night, a few scattered tears at times rolled down her face. This would be her last trip until next spring, if she even came then. With Ben being gone so long her hope of him showing up grew weaker each day. She jumped as she heard a light thump against the door. She picked up the rifle lying on the bed and eased to the door. It was totally dark outside as she slowly cracked open the door, nothing. Then she saw the pouch hanging on the door handle. She closed the door, turned up the oil lamp she had brought from town. She took the piece of paper from the pouch, when she unfolded it she stifled a scream. "Oh, My God!" As she read the note, tears started rolling down her cheeks. When she finished she walked to the door, all was quiet as she gazed out into the darkness. "Thank you whoever you are, my prayer have been answered."

Kate couldn't get to sleep that night. At first light she was headed back for Garnet. She never said anything to Benny or April about the letter. That evening Benny said he wanted to go down on the river to see Coby for one night. Kate told him to go, ahead. This would make her trip easier without having to lie to Benny about her load of supplies.

After Benny disappeared over the ridge Kate got busy packing supplies on the list. She packed everything out onto the back porch, so she could load it fast when she brought the buggy. With everything ready and loaded on the buggy, she walked around to the saloon. April and both girls were eating when she walked in. "April would you watch the store for me until Benny gets back tomorrow. I decided to take a few supplies up to the cabin in case someone gets stranded up there this winter during a storm. Tell Benny not to worry if I don't get back for a few days."

The girl called Meg looked up from the table, "How about I do that for you Kate? Things are real slow right now. By the time you get back the miner should be starting to show up, then we'll be busy for a few days," then she laughed.

Kate parked the buggy close to cabin while she unloaded her supplies, then, moved it over by the barn. She unloaded all the rest of the

load onto the work bench close to the door as Ben's note had said..
Benny had a mixture of something that smell terrible that they used to
keep mice from the storeroom at the store. She had brought two tins of
that, so she set them on each end of the bench. After parking the buggy
next to the cabin she unhooked the team and took them to the pasture.
Benny had moved Ben's horses back to town early in the summer, so
the team had plenty to eat. Back in the cabin she built a fire to warm up
the cabin. As darkness settled in she started fixing herself something to
eat. She had walked out many times to study those terrible peaks, nothing was moving. She didn't sleep much as she kept waking to every
sound from outside. Finally she saw dawn breaking in the window. She
got up and built up the fire and pulled the coffee pot over the main fire
box. It was coffee she had made last night, but she had only drank, a
half a cup. It was lukewarm but now she wanted hot coffee to help calm
her down. "Ben, where are you?" Her voice echoed in the cabin, then
she shook her head, "Damn it Kate the letter just said he would bring
Ben down, but it didn't say what night. Just calm yourself down.
What's one more day to have Ben back with you?"

Unknown to Kate later that afternoon Ben was getting closer as he
sat resting along the hallway after the long walk down from high above.
Later they stopped in a room full of gear, that Ben recognized they were
his. Saddles, packs everything from his horses. Soon the smell of cooking meat drifted to where Ben lay on his own bedroll. As they ate Jacob
slowly began the story of Ben being here. "I was watching as you rode
by that evening. Then I saw you stop and make camp. I watched as you
walked back up the trail to foot path coming up here. I was surprised
you had spotted it while riding by. Then I felt the mountain starting to
move. As I watched I saw the big slab break off above you and then the
path where you walked disappeared in the dust. I waited until the dust
cleared, there was no sign of you or the path left below. I hurried down
from the high point to see if you survived. I was above where the forge
is, it took me hours to get down here. It was totally dark when I got to
where the path leads from the mountain."

He stopped and filled Ben's bowl again with the thick meat stew.
At dawn I moved out onto the slide, a few rocks were still rolling as I
looked for you. I was about to give up when the wind all of a sudden
stopped, a stillness was almost unreal. I heard a slight moan coming
from below my feet. I got down, too look into every crevice then I saw
you. I reached down, you were alive but I knew your time was short. I
moved a few rocks with help from the one above helping me. Your leg
was almost cut off and you had lost much of your blood. I stopped the

bleeding and carried you into this same room. After I gave you something to make you sleep I moved your gear into a cave below here where it wouldn't be found. I carried you up into my quarters. I knew I must fix your leg and get blood flowing through it or you would lose it. I spent the night putting your leg back together. Twice while I worked I thought you had passed on, only to find you still had the will to live. By morning I had blood again flowing in your leg and the bones set into place. For the next two weeks, only your will to live kept you from the hereafter. It was a month before you first responded by opening your eyes. I fed you with a tube to your stomach."

Ben looked over at the man who he owed his life, "How did you know about how to do these things? It's like you were a doctor."

"Grandfather must have had a man trained in medicine or even a doctor in his group. Next to grandfathers room is another room with many books on medicine. Also there are many tools for operating. The books I've read many times to pass the time day away since I've been here. It is from these I knew how to repair your leg and to feed you. I also have had help from the one who looks after us all."

Ben nodded, as he studied this strange young man. Ben was trying to remember when he'd ever met a man with the knowledge of this man.

"If you keep moving about each day your leg will become as strong as it once was. I do fear as you get older it will give you problems when the weather changes." He got up and walked to the other room and returned with Bens clothes. "I don't think you can wear the boots, but in time maybe you can. In your pack I have places another pair of moccasin's for you. Now when you're ready we can leave for the cabin." As Ben changed clothes Jacob picked up one of Ben's packs which he had tied onto his pack board. "Each trip down for the supplies I will take your gear down to the room of the wagon covers."

It was a cool clear night as they walked toward the barn. Inside Jacob set Ben's pack down and started loading the pack board with the supplies from the bench. He finished then walked over and placed his hand on Ben's shoulder. "I will truly miss your company. If you ever need to see me light the three torches, in the trunk above the manger on the north side of the cabin. Place them in a triangle and let them burn until midnight then put them out. I will come down the following night. Now I have something I need you to do," he took a pouch from his shirt. "I need you to mail this. Then if a person shows up at the trading post asking about me please bring them here. If this happens only use two torches to signal me. Of this I wish you tell no one, my brother."

"It shall be that way, Jacob. If you need anything from me, leave message in the trunk." He grasped the tall young man's hands, "Travel well my friend. You'll always be in my thoughts."

As Ben headed for the cabin he didn't hear a sound of Jacob leaving. He smiled, this man moved about so easy that Ben very seldom ever heard him coming before he spoke. The cabin was dark as Ben walked up onto the porch, he gently knocked. He could hear Kate moving about inside, then the door slowly opened. "Kate, it's me, Ben."

The door opened wide as she stepped out to grab him, she jumped back. It had felt her hand on the long hair and beard before she jerked away. "It's alright, Kate, I need a haircut and shave real bad." A match flicked by the stove then a candle lite up the room enough to see Kate by the table lighting the lantern.

When he glowed bright she walk over to him, "My God Ben, you look like a ghost. If it wasn't for your voice I would have grabbed my rifle. Ben, are you alright?" She moved into his arms.

He stroked her head, "Yes Kate I'm alright. It'll probably be spring before I get my strength back. Kate, I kinda need to rest a little, my walk down here from the barn was longer than I remember it being."

Kate was still staring at him, "Are you alone?"

"Kate I haven't been alone for the last six months. Its story I have all winter to tell you, most of it you won't believe when I do tell you." He laid, down on the bed as Kate snuggled up tight against him. She smiled in the darkness as she heard his deep even, breathing, she closed her eyes then fell into a deep sleep.

Dawn was breaking when Ben woke, as Kate slipped from the bed. He heard her adding wood to the fire. He turned over to watch as she moved about the kitchen. Finally she looked over to see Ben watching her, "So you're awake? You died as soon as your head hit that pillow last night. How do you feel this morning?"

Ben smiled, "I feel great. I'm kinda hungry for some of your biscuits."

"How about after I feed you we do something with all that hair? All I got with me is a pair of scissors, but at least I can get you to look more like a human than some caveman," then she laughed.

Ben nodded as he swung his feet off the bed. "You got a deal. I think if I go out to the barn and find my pack we'll find my straight edge razor. After breakfast we'll walk over there. I need to walk all I can to work this leg back in shape."

Three cups of coffee and half a dozen biscuits along with four strips of bacon Ben pushed back from the table. "Jacob was a good cook, but I still missed your cooking."

Kate looked up from where she was cleaning the plates, "Jacob?"

Ben chuckled, "In time I'll tell you about him."

It was cool as they walked out toward the barn, inside Ben grinned as he looked at the bench which now was empty. Kate looked over at him, "Where's all the supplies I piled up here?"

Ben walked over to open the door leading into the room with wagon covers. There was most of his gear from the cave. Ben shook his head as he mumbled, 'Jacob, you we busy last night.'

Kate looked over at him from the door, "You're mumbling Ben. I couldn't hear what you said."

He picked up the small pack he knew held his personal items from the pile. He carried it over to where Kate stood staring at him, "My razor is in this pack."

He motioned back toward the gear, "We need to hang this gear for the horses up before we leave. I suppose I better take my saddle. Did my horses ever show up in town?"

Kate shook he head and then smiled, "No, Henry saw them here in the pasture when he came in from the mine on the fourth of July. That was the first time anyone had seen them. Benny had fixed the fence a couple of weeks earlier. They weren't around then. When Henry asked where you were when he rode in, is when we found out they were here. Someone had put them in there and closed the gate. You didn't know about that?"

"No, I just figured they had gotten loose after I didn't make it back to the camp. The last time I saw them they were picket out up on that flat up above here. That's where I was going to camp for the night." He pointed up toward the peaks towering above them. Kate just stood watching as he turned and started back for the cabin.

His neck started feeling cool as Kate started working on his hair. She stepped back to look at her work, "I think I'll quit right there. If you decide you want it shorter, I'll do it when we get back to the trading post. I got better hair cutting tools there." She took a hold of his whiskers, "You ready for this next?" He nodded, "Ok, how close do you want it?"

"Leave a good beard. It'll cover my bony face until I gain some weight back. You shave it close I'll look like a skeleton," Kate laughed nodding she agreed.

They had just finished and settled down for a cup of coffee when they heard horses outside. "Kate, are you in there?" came Clayton voice from outside.

Kate hurried to the door, "High Clayton, step down I got fresh coffee already brewed, besides that I got a surprise for you."

Clayton was pulling off his heavy coat as he walked in. He stopped cold when he saw a man sitting at the table, then he recognized Ben. "Well Holy Christ man, what happened to you? You look like hell." He rushed over to grasp Ben's hand.

Ben laughed as he took his hand, "Like I just told Kate, we got all winter for me to tell you the story. The main thing for me is I'm now home for good."

Clayton looked over at Kate, she shrugged. I found a note tacked to this door from him saying to bring a buggy to the cabin. I got here day before yesterday. Then last night after dark I heard this light knock, when I opened the door I jumped back. I never saw so much hair on a bony face in my life. Then I recognized his voice." She motioned over to pile of hair by a chair over by the window, "That all came off him just before you rode up."

"How did your horses get here last spring?" Clayton asked as he looked at Ben.

Ben shrugged, "Like I said before, I'll tell you more later on. Right now I don't even know how my horses got here."

Clayton looked at Kate standing behind Ben, she held up here hands as she shrugged her shoulders, "The main thing he's home. I don't care how or where he's been, he's mine to take care now and that's all that counts."

Clayton help hang up all of Ben's gear he wasn't taking to town. Then they loaded his saddle in the buggy. They closed up the cabin and headed for town with Clayton riding in the buggy with them, his horses tied behind. Kate pulled up behind the kitchen. Clayton helped Ben down from the buggy. Benny came running out to grasp Ben when he saw who it was, "You're the reason Kate took the buggy to the cabin? Man you look like hell. You need a lot of Kate's cooking to put some fat on those bones." He studied Ben's eyes, then, smiled, "I see by your eyes you're not going to say where you've been."

Kate looked over at her helper, "Benny, sometimes I still wonder about you. How can you tell from his eyes he's not talking about where he's been?" Benny grinned as he started unloading the buggy while Kate helped Ben up the steps into the trading post.

47

Ben looked back, "Benny just take my gear up to the cabin and build a fire for me."

Kate swung around and took Ben's arm, "Ben Jasper you're not going up to your cabin. Benny you put his gear in my room. I lost you for the summer, by God from now on you've got a shadow everywhere you go."

Clayton looked over at Benny who was just watching Kate, "Benny unless you want to start cooking for yourself, I think I'd do what the lady just asked!"

Benny grinned as he grabbed an arm load and headed for the door. Clayton took a load with him too. Inside Ben walked over to sit down by the stove. Clayton moved over to face him, "Well old partner, it's great you have you back. I think I'll head up to my place to start unloading my outfit. I'll stop back by tonight if I can talk Kate or the girls next door to cook my supper." The front door opened and in walked April, with Meg and Charlotte close behind. April kissed Ben's cheek, "I thought that was you in the buggy when Kate drove by."

Benny moved over by her, "No sense in asking where he's been, he's not going to tell you." Everyone laughed as April looked over at Kate, who was nodding she agreed with Benny.

Ben sat back in the living quarters of the trading post that evening as he waited for Kate to call that supper was ready. Benny stepped on from the back porch, "Henry just rode in. I just saw him turn up the street toward his place. He must have had a good summer, he leading four pack horses and there all loaded."

Ben got up and walked over to his pack he'd started unpacking just before he sat down. As he pulled his personal gear out, out came a small pouch that he recognized real quickly as something Jacob had made. Inside he found a note, he opened it, 'To the lady who long ago gave me books, and now comes to rescue her man, my friend, Jacob.' Ben took another smaller doe skin pouch from the bigger one, it was heavy. When he opened the draw sting a small all gold statue slid into his hand. It was like the ones Ben had looked at in the gold room in the mountain. This one was much smaller, yet every little detail on it was perfect. At the bottom, in old English scrip, "To Kate," Ben just stared at the beautiful work, the lettering was perfectly drawn. He re wrapped it then slid it into the bigger pouch then put it back in the pack. Kate called from the kitchen, so Ben walked out into the trading post.

Kate looked up from the stove, "I sent Benny up to get Henry."

Just then the door opened, Benny and Henry walked in. A big smile broke out on Henry face as he rushed over to grasp Ben's hand.

48

"Benny said you were kinda on the skinny side. The main thing is you're alright. Benny already told me you're not talking about where you've been." He looked over at Kate, "Kate I'd surely buy a drink for the house, if you got any booze over here."

April and the girls were helping Kate get ready to feed everyone, "April looked over at Kate, "I'll run next door to get one. I got a special bottle a drummer left for me to try, we'll drink that."

Ben glanced up at Kate as she set glasses around before everyone, "Make mine small. My last drink was last spring with Nate up at the mine the day I sold out to him. I may get a little light headed and fall down if I try too much."

Ben chuckled, "I just remembered I was supposed to meet Nate up at the mine in September for my final payment. I'll bet he wondering what in the hell happened to me."

Kate put her hand on his shoulder, "He was here a couple months ago to settle up. Clayton had let him know about you being missing. I'll tell you about it later." Ben nodded.

Clayton and Henry left early, for them it'd had been a long trip in. April stayed to help Kate clean up while the girls headed back to the saloon. Meg had seen one of the miner pass the window that was already in from the mountains walking by for his evening drinks.

Later with everyone gone Ben and Kate moved back into the living quarters for the evening. Ben walked over to his pack and took out the small pouch. "I found this when I was unpacking, it belongs to you."

She looked up at him as he handed it to her, "For me?"

Ben nodded, "Read the note first."

Kate read it then looked up at Ben with a question like look on her face. She slowly, unwrapped, the small statue, "Oh my God, it's beautiful. Is this pure gold?" Ben nodded, "Where did he get this?"

Ben smiled, "He made it just for you, I guess. I just found it, so I didn't know anything about him sending it to you."

Kate just kept looking at the small figure in her hand. She finally looked up at Ben, "The person who saved you is that boy who was with the crazy man?"

Ben slowly nodded, "Kate you're going to have to be patient with me on this. I spent four months up in that mountain with him, but yet I really don't know him. He moves like a ghost, you never hear him coming or leaving. His eyes, look beyond you or maybe even through you and his speech is so soft. Kate, I just need time to think about what happened while I was healing up. I don't know what he used but I never

49

felt pain, until he started making me move around. As far as that present, he is such a Craftsman. He had a room full of this type work. This is the smallest I ever saw up there. He mines the ore, melts it down and pours these from molds he makes."

Kate just looked at him then back to the gold figure she was holding. "Kate for now I ask that you don't mention anything about him or show your new present. I know eventually him living in that mountain will come out, but I need time to figure out how to handle it. The thing I need most is to keep quiet is the fact he's mining gold up there. I doubt if anyone trying to find him and rob him would ever even find their way in there. In fact I'm not too sure I can find my way back in there from the bottom."

"I gather the crazy man no longer is up there?" Ben grinned, shook his head no. Kate slowly wrapped up her new present. "I hate that people can't see this, it's so beautiful."

The next morning Ben walked up to his cabin to get a few items he wanted. He was carrying what looked to be his empty pack. As he got closer to the cabin he saw the smoke rising from the chimney. Inside it was nice and warm. From the empty pack Ben took the packet Jacob had given him to mail. He un-wrapped the outside doe skin cover. Inside he found the packet Jacob wanted mailed. It was addressed to St Louis, Missouri. The lettering on the packet was block type lettering. Then up in the left corner was drawn a statue much like the ones in the gold room. No wording just the figure. Ben wrapped it back up and put it back in his pack. Kate had said this morning that the south bound stage would be through this afternoon. He would ask the driver to mail it for him instead of putting it with the trading post mail.

During lunch Kate looked over at him, "Ben I need to go to Springfield to do some business later this week. Is there anything you need me to do while I'm down there?"

"Are you going, to drive the, buggy? Or ride the stagecoach?" Ben asked.

Kate shrugged, "I just figured on riding the stage. I was figuring on riding down Wednesday and then back on the early stage Friday. That would give me all day Thursday to get my business done. Why?"

Ben looked at her for a minute, "I was thinking about riding down with you. If we take the buggy I could get out once in a while to, stretch this leg a little. The stage would be a lot more comfortable and a lot dryer if it happens to storm."

Kate smiled, "I'd like having you along. You know its four hour ride to Springfield by coach. They stop at Tolivers for a half hour for lunch, you could walk around then."

"Okay, we'll go by coach then." He reached out for her hand, "Kate, I think while we're there we maybe could get married. What do you think?"

Kate smiled as she squeezed his hand, "Ben Jasper, I think Jacob way of thinking is getting to you. I don't think, we've been living in sin the way it is now, but I would love to get married, if that what you really want."

Ben winked as he stood up, "Someone needs to keep you on the straight and narrow, Kate."

Wednesday as they got ready to leave Kate had already trimmed his hair and beard. As he walked down from his cabin after getting his clothes for the trip together, she looked down at his feet. "Are you, going to wear those moccasins?"

Ben nodded, "I don't think I can stand a boot yet. I've got a new pair of Moccasin's in my gear."

Kate just nodded, "They look fine, I was just wondering."

Kate was wearing a dress with all the trimmings. April and the girls were making a fuss over her outfit. Ben grinned as the stage pulled up, "Come my lady. I will help you into the stage. I must say you look stunning today."

As they walked to the stage Kate leaned over, "I really need to talk to Jacob. You're coming up with things I've never heard before. I'm beginning to worry about you," then she squeezed his arm.

Ben walked around the Toliver station yard while everyone else finished their lunch. He was surprised that his leg didn't bother him as much as he thought it would.

In Springfield the stage pulled up in front of the station which was next door to a hotel. When they checked in Ben wrote Ben and Kate Jasper on the ledger. They put their gear into the room then headed out to do some of the things on their lists. As they passed by the building on the corner, Ben stopped, he took Kate's arm. He motioned toward the door, "We might as well get our license now. If you want we can find a preacher or just let the local judge marry us." Kate grinned as they turned into the big building.

With the paper work filled out they headed down the hall to a door with Judge Adams name in big letters. Inside they were greeted by an older lady, who on hearing their request, smiled. "Please be seated, I'll see if the Judge can perform the ceremony now."

A tall older man walked out, "I'm Judge Adams, I hear you two want to get married.

Ben and Kate both stood up, Ben offered the judge his hand, "Ben Jasper, this lady is Kate Crawford. Yes we would like for you to do the honor of marrying us."

The judge looked at Kate, "Would you be the owner of the Crawford Trading Post up in Garnet?" Kate smiled and nodded. "Well, I real glad to know you, Kate. I've heard so many stories about you over the years. You seem to have a winter haven for the miners in that area. I hope you're getting married doesn't mean you will be leaving Garnet."

Kate smiled, "We really haven't talk too much about that, but I assure you the trading post will still be operating. Ben and I have filed on the ground and building the religious group built before they were wiped out in the avalanche. So we will be close by."

Judge nodded, "I've always heard you lost your first husband during the rescue of those people, along with a couple more men from Garnet."

"Yes, I did loose Dan. He died a month or so after he got back."

Later they walked back out on the street, "Mrs. Jasper, how about we look for a place to buy you a ring? This is my first time doing this marry thing, I never even thought about getting you a ring before the ceremony."

Kate looked up at him, "I got you, that's what counts. If you want to buy me a ring, I sure won't say no."

The jeweler sat a tray of rings for them to look at. As Kate looked at each one she stopped and took one out. "Do you like that one?" Ben asked as he looked over her shoulder at her hand with the ring on her finger.

Kate smiled up at Ben, "Sure I like it, but look at that price. We'll pick out something a little cheaper."

Ben looked over at the Jeweler, "Will you take gold dust? I haven't had a chance to sell my gold yet."

The jeweler nodded, "Yes I will be glad to take dust. In fact if it's good quality gold I may just buy whatever you have with you. I make my own jewelry so I need good pure gold, that way it saves me a lot of work."

"Ben, that's too much for you to pay for my ring."

Ben winked at the jeweler, then, looked back at Kate, "We've only been married less than an hour and you're already questioning my decisions?" Then he laughed as she frowned at him. "Kate, this is what I

52

really want to do, so please except this as my gift to you for taking me as your husband."

A small tear appeared as she took his arm, then smiled up at him as she nodded, "Thank you, Ben."

Back in their room Kate sat looking at the new ring on her finger. As Ben sat down she pulled his lips down hers, "Ben, thank you for making me the happiest woman in the world right now." Then she kissed him again.

Ben held her for a long while, "Why don't you do whatever women do before going out to celebrate getting, married. While you're doing that I need to walk across the street to the post office." He opened one of his bags and took out a packet. This is errand I promised Jacob I do. I was going to put it on the stage Monday, then, you said you wanted to come here, so I decided to mail it myself from here." He handed it to her.

Kate studied the small statue up in the left corner and the address-ing, "He writes so beautiful. This statue is perfectly drawn. It's just like my gold piece." She handed it back to him.

The clerk stood looking at the packet, "That is a beautiful job on drawing that figure. Is that some sort of return address? He looked up at Ben, "You draw this?"

Ben chuckled as he shook his head no, "I have a hard time just writing my name without adding all that fancy stuff. He's just a friend who asked me to mail this."

After supper in the hotel dining room, they retired for the evening. That night as they got ready for bed, Kate looked down at Ben's leg. "Can I look at what Jacob did you repair your leg?"

She ran her hand over the scares that almost cover his leg from the knee down. "My God Ben, your whole leg is scares. It's like the whole leg was opened at one time or another." She looked up at him while still holding the leg, "You said you didn't feel any of this while he put your leg back together?" Ben nodded. Her fingers traced each scar, "What did he used to sew this, it's so smooth now. Usually scares are rough when you touch them?"

Later she went to sleep all snugged against him. Ben laid there for a long while looking up at the ceiling. Finally he drifted off to sleep.

The next morning while eating breakfast, Kate was going over a list of things she needed to do. She looked up at Ben, "Do you have any errands to do while I'm busy taking care of trading post business?"

"I was thinking last night about trying to find a store with books for Jacob. You know medical books, mining books, book's, on metal

53

work like sculpturing. He loves to read and study ever thing he reads, then, put it into practical use. Would they have anything like that here in Springfield?"

"Look for a book store, if you can't find that, go to the library," Kate answered.

Ben nodded, "I also need to check at the recorder's office and make sure Nate's claim went through alright. Do I need to check on our claim of the barns and cabin?"

"You can check to make sure but I got the documents back soon after I files them for you," Kate answered. She stood up, "I'll meet you back here at noon."

Ben went to the claims office first, everything was right on both claims he was looking at. When he finished he asked the lady behind the counter about a book store in town. She named two, so he headed out to find them. In the first store the clerk kept showing him books more for someone just beginning. He finally said, "I need something for a man trying to master these types of work, not for someone just starting."

The man looked at him, "I do have a section over here that is too technical for most people to grasp. I hardly ever sell any of these to anyone around here."

Ben thumbed through many of these books. He found four or five he thought maybe Jacob would get some use out of them. The clerk kept watching as Ben stood there, "Are these for you or someone else?"

"They're for a man who is very talented and wants to learn more. I think some of these he would maybe like. How much are they?"

"Mister, you give me three dollars a book and you can take all you want. These books have been here since I opened the store two years ago."

Ben took ten of the books. Do you have a box an old suitcase or something I can carry these in?" Later Ben walked out of the store with his purchase and headed for the hotel. Back in the room he left the box of books, then opened his pack again and took out three pouches. This was gold from his mine, before he'd sold to Nate. He emptied his canvas type suitcase and placed the three pouches in it. Back on the street he headed for the assay office to sell the gold. As the man was weighing out his gold another man walked from the back, "Looks like you did right well. Is your mine close by?"

Ben looked over at the man, "I just sold out over on Third Fork last spring. I've been slow getting back over in this area. You know always looking for that ledge of pure stuff. When the weather starts getting cold I always look for a warm place to winter."

The man nodded, "You miners are always looking for the mother lode, even though you already got a good claim."

Ben laughed, "You know I think it's the hunt to find it. Once you have to start working to make a mine pay, you lose interest. Anyway I think that's my problem."

The clerk was totaling up the amount, then, looked up at Ben, "This is a good chunk of money to be carrying around. Do you want a bank draft or the cash?"

Ben looked over at the clerk. He was remembering Kate said she had an account for the trading post in one of the banks here. "I'll take a draft for the full amount." The clerk nodded as he filled out the draft. Later Ben walked out onto the sidewalk, as he looked around he saw Kate coming out of store up the street. He waved and she saw him, she waited while he walked over to her.

"Well, are you having any luck finding any books?" she asked as he walked up.

"Sure did. Didn't you say you have an account in a bank here?"

She nodded as she took his arm, "That's where I'm headed right now, do you want to join me?" He nodded, she smiled, "I need to see if my figures compare to theirs. I need to order supplies and I don't want an over drawl on my account."

As they walked into the bank, Ben handed her the bank draft, "Add this to the account."

When she look at the amount she stopped, "Where did you get this?"

"Oh I stopped over at the assay office to cash in that payment I got from Nate last spring. I brought it with us, so when I took the books up to our room, I decided to cash it in. That's why I'm carrying this bag."

Kate laughed as she shook her head, "You know I still got that payment Nate brought last fall back in Garnet. How much more do you have stashed around, my dear husband?"

"Oh, probably twice this much, I really don't know for sure. It's up in my cabin."

Kate just stared up at her new husband.

"I think it's best to keep the business separate from our account." Kate started a new account for her and Ben with the draft.

Later as they headed back for the hotel Ben kept looking at signs over each store as they walked by. "Ben what are you looking for."

"I need something to put those books in until I get them up to Jacob. I was thinking about a used suitcase, you know one of them satchel type?"

"My God Ben, a new one only cost a couple of dollars. If you can't afford it, I'll loan you the money," then she laughed as she squeezed his arm. He grinned as they turned into store.

While Ben was looking through the satchels Kate wondered over to a display case full of pistols. Some of the newest colts were on display along with many other makes. She kept looking at this one short barrel revolver, the bore looked smaller than the rest. Ben walked up and was looking over her shoulder, "You into owning a firearm now?" Then he chuckled.

Kate nodded as she looked up at Ben, she pointed to the revolver she had been looking at. "That one there looks lighter than the one I carry now."

"I didn't know you owned a pistol."

From here shoulder bag she pulled out a short barrel Colt, "I always have this with me whenever I travel anywhere. Dan always insisted I carry one. I've only had to use it once." A clerk had walked up while Kate had been talking to Ben. Kate motioned into the case, "Can I look at that one with the short barrel?"

The clerk reached in the case and handed her the pistol, "This is Colts new 32-20. Not near the recoil as that one in your hand. It, don't have the knock down power as the 44, but it'll stop an animal or man at close range."

Kate felt the weight of the two, she looked at the clerk. "Will you take my old my old one in trade?"

Ben reached around and took her pistol and stood there looking it over. "How about we keep this too? I'm not much of a pistol shot, but it wouldn't hurt to own one." He looked over at the clerk, "Do you have one of them shoulder holsters to fit this?" as he held up Kate's old pistol.

The clerk walked back into back, when he came back he had two different styles, "Both of these will fit that pistol," he handed then to Ben.

Kate opened the new box of shells on the counter and loaded her new purchase. She took five more loose rounds along with the pistol then placed them into the purse. Ben put his purchase along with a couple of boxes of 44's and Kate's extra shells into the satchel.

As they walked back toward the hotel Kate was holding his arm, "It always surprised me that you never carried a pistol. Henry, Clayton and Jesse Garret all carry one."

Ben shrugged, "I always felt my rifle was enough protection, besides with a rifle I can hit what I aim at. With a pistol that's not always the case," then he grinned.

CHAPTER 5

As they sat waiting for the stage to start loading the next morning, a big man in bib overalls walked over to them. "Hello, my name is Tyler Bates. The ticket agent just told me you're Kate Crawford the lady who owns that trading post in Garnet?"

Kate smiled, "Why yes I'm, Mister Bates, but my name is now Kate Jasper." She took Ben's arm, "This is my new husband Ben Jasper. We just got married." Ben stood up and shook hands with Tyler.

"Good to know you both. I own a ranch on the way up to Garnet. I know you folks up there fixed up some of those big wagons that belonged to those people killed in that avalanche. Do you have any of them left?"

Kate smiled, "Mister Bates you lucked out, Ben here is one of the men who fixed those wagons up."

"I wish you folks would just call me Tyler."

Ben laughed, "Okay Tyler. Then you just call us, Kate and Ben. We do have two of those wagons left. There both in good shape."

Before Tyler could answer they called to board the stage. Ben looked over at Tyler, "I guess we need to load up."

Tyler nodded, "I riding up to my place on the stage, so we can talk on the way." I left my wagon here with the wheelwright to rebuild the wheels. That's when I started thinking maybe I need a heavier wagon on my place."

As they rode along they made a deal with Tyler for grain and hay for payment on the wagon. Then next year he could do the same and the wagon would be his. He grinned, "By golly I'm sure glad that agent told me who you were, Kate. Now I got me good strong wagon. Can I come up after that wagon in the next couple of days?"

Ben nodded, "You sure can. In fact you can have your pick of which one you want. We do have the covers for them too."

They felt the stage coming to a halt, "Well I guess this is where I leave you folks. My place is about three miles over that ridge."

Kate looked out at the bare hillside, "You going to walk?"

Tyler grinned, "I didn't figure on it. I should have a daughter with horses not too far away." He looked out, "Yep, there she is, right on time."

"I got a whole house full of girls. Rachel there is my tom boy. She's also my main helper. I'll be up to see you folks no later than day after tomorrow," He stepped out. The stage lurched ahead as it moved on down the road. Kate smiled as she saw the girl in bib overall on one horse leading another as she handed the rein to Tyler. As they rode away Kate saw the long pig tails down the girls back.

Benny and Clayton both hurried out to help unload the supplies from the stage. They just piled them on the porch while they hurried to get the stage back on the road. Ben let the two men handle the heavy boxes as he took the baggage in to store. He got along pretty good just walking but the leg was too weak for heavy lifting, yet.

When April spied the ring on Kate's finger she called the other two girls. They had come over from the saloon to help fix lunch for the travelers. April put her arms around Ben's neck, "If I'd known you could afford a rock that size, I'd fought Kate for you." Ben just grinned.

Life was back to normal by the next day. Ben and Clayton checked over the wagons the next morning. "I'll pay for the wagon he takes, then you fella can divide it up. The hay and grain is mainly for the trading post. I think if the trail stays open up to cabin I might take some grain up in case we need to be up there sometime without feed for the horses."

Clayton nodded, "If I'm here I might ride along, but Henry and I was talking last night about going into Springfield tomorrow on the stage. I need a few things before a big storm hits and closes up the area."

Ben nodded as they walked back into the trading post. Ben was hoping they would be gone. He wanted to take a few supplies up for Jacob without anyone knowing it.

The next morning Kate looked out to see two riders each leading a big draft horse coming up the road. She called to Ben who was in the supply room helping Benny build some shelves. He put on his coat and hurried out to greet Tyler and the rider with him. "Good to see you Tyler. I see you bought along some help."

Tyler swung down to grasp Ben's hand, "Good to see you Ben." He motioned back toward the second rider, "Yeah, I brought my right hand man, this is my daughter Rachel. Rachel this is Mister Jasper." The girl nodded as she walked up next to her dad.

Tyler looked over the big wagons, "Boy these old wagons were built mighty good. When the Mrs. and me come west we couldn't afford anything like this. I wish I had enough money to buy them both."

Ben looked over at Clayton who had just walked up, "Clayton this is Tyler Bates who bought one of these wagons. Tyler this is Clayton Moore, he's one of the men who helped fix these wagons up. If you can use this other wagon, I think probably we could figure out a way for you to pay for it. There's, a few more wagons up there, they need more work but they can be fixed, if you wanted to go that route."

Tyler nodded, "By golly I may think about that. I guess I'd better get hook up and head for home. It's going to be a slow trip going back."

Benny walked up, "Ben, Kate said she had a hot lunch for the Bates to eat before they head home."

Ben looked over at Tyler, "Why don't you and Rachel go grab a bite to eat while Clayton and me hook up for you."

As they were hooking up, Clayton chuckled, "By God it's been long time since I hooked a team like this up. My Dad raised draft horses when I was a kid growing up."

Tyler tied the saddle horses behind, then he and Rachel climbed up into the high seat. "Tell the Mrs. again, that was a mighty fine lunch. I'll get that grain and hay up to you the first chance I get," he waved and the big wagon moved off down the road.

Clayton and Henry caught the stage the next day, so Ben walked in to talk to Kate about riding up with him. Kate looked at him from behind the counter, "Will your leg stand up to that trip?"

He shrugged, "I think so. It's getting better every day. If it's clear in the morning, let's go. We can use one of Henry's pack horses. He hasn't moved them to the river yet. I'll pack up some supplies for Jacob. I also need to take those books I bought in Springfield. Benny walked in as Ben was loading the packs, "You want me to ride along to help unload these supplies for your friend up there?" He smiled, "Don't worry. I won't say anything about him to anyone. I knew he was there even before he saved you."

Ben chuckled, "You know Benny, I'm beginning think Kate's right about you."

Kate had walked into the room and heard all of this, "Ben, being as Benny knows about Jacob already, why, don't you take him instead of me? Then if your leg wears out he can help you more than I could. If worse comes to worse spend the night and come back the next day."

Ben nodded as he looked over at her, "I agree. That's going to be a cold ride." He looked over at Benny, "Have we got a couple of extra sacks of grain I can take up there? Tyler will be restocking us here before long."

"Sure, we got plenty if you want to take more. Do you want to use two of Henry's pack horses?"

A cool breeze was blowing but the sky was clear as the two riders leading two pack horse rode away from Garnet. Both were dressed warm with chaps and slickers to break the wind. They made good time going up. Benny dropped off at the cabin to build a fire then went to help Ben unloaded the packs for Jacob in the barn above the manger. They dumped the grain into the grain bin in the horse barn. They closed up the barn and rode over to the cabin. The fire was now beginning to warm the inside. Soon the aroma of boiling coffee filled the cabin. After they finished the lunch Kate had sent, Benny looked over at Ben, "You feeling like the ride home?"

"Yeah, Benny I believe I can handle the ride home. It's going to be a lot warmer spending the night at home than here in this cabin. I guess we better put this fire out and get going."

Ben looked up at the sheer cliffs, all white with snow. He smiled as he swung up, 'I hope you like those books, my friend.' Ben looked over at Benny, who eyes were watching him, "He will know we've been here and come for his supplies tonight."

Ben unsaddled the horses while Benny took Henry's horses back to the pasture. As Ben started to leave the barn, Kate stepped in. She looked at him, "Well?"

Ben grinned, "I'm dam tired. The leg doesn't feel too bad. About half way back I begin to think maybe I had screwed up, it didn't really get any worse coming on in. Old mother hen Benny was keeping an eye on me all the time. I suppose you gave him all kinds of orders before we left?"

She grabbed his arm, "I'm not saying. Benny never tells tails, so I guess you'll never know for sure what I told him."

Two days later Tyler showed up with two loaded wagons. He had four big draft horses pulling the big wagon and a smaller team pulling the lighter wagon. Rachel was driving the light wagon loaded with hay. They had brought gear to sleep out but Kate put her foot down, "No darn way, are you sleeping in those wagons. Tyler can use Ben's cabin, Rachel can sleep in the spare room here in back."

That night as they were finishing eating April walked in from next door. Kate almost laughed out loud when she saw the look on Rachel's face. April was dresses as usual, like she'd just stepped out of display window in some store. Not a curl out of place. "Tyler, Rachel this is my

61

partner April, she operates the saloon next door. April, this is Tyler Bates and his daughter Rachel."

April stepped over to the table as Tyler stood up and offered her hand, "Pleased to meet you Tyler." Tyler's face was slowly turning red, before he could say anything April turned to Rachel still seated next to Kate, "It's good to meet you too, Rachel."

Rachel looked over at Kate then back at April, "That dress is so beautiful. I've never seen anything that nice before."

"Why thank you, Rachel. I'm glad you like it. Now I need to get back to my place, there's a big cribbage tournament getting ready to start. I just stopped by to borrow an extra crib board."

As April hurried out Rachel's eyes never left her. She turned to Kate, "She sure is a beautiful lady."

Kate smiled, "Rachel how about you and I get started on these dishes while these men chat?" Before dark Ben walked Tyler up to his cabin to show him where everything was.

Back in the trading post Kate showed Rachel where her room was. Rachel looked at Kate, "Mrs. Jasper, what does April do over in the saloon?"

Kate kept a straight face, knowing this girl was asking in earnest. "First off Rachel, how about you call me Kate? To answer your question, April manages the saloon. She has two girls that work for her that entertaining the miners who winter here. They drink and dance with them if that's what the men want. Like tonight they join the men playing cards."

"Momma say's all dance hall girls are bad, is April bad too?"

Kate kept back a smile from appearing, 'This was something she'd never had to do before, answer the questions of a teenage girl.' "Rachel in your mothers eyes these type women like April and the other two girls are in her words, bad. To me, they have just a different way of life than your mother. Now honey don't let what I say get back to your mother about these women."

"Oh I won't even tell mother I even asked you about girls like April. If dad tells her I met April, I probably won't get to come along again." She giggled, "Is there any way I can peek in there without them seeing me? I won't say anything to dad or mom."

Kate shook her head as she smiled at the girl, "How old are you Rachel?"

"I'll be sixteen my next birthday."

Kate turned to walk to the door, she stopped, looked back at the girl in bibs, "My private privy is out that door, it's on the left of the bigger one. Now on your way back in you could crack open the back door of the saloon." She turned and walked back up front where Ben sat talking to Clayton and Benny.

Ben looked over at her, "Did you and Rachel have a good chat?"

Kate laughed, "Well, the main thing she wanted to talk about was April. I never had to try to explain to a girl raised like she's been of what a woman like April does."

It was just dawn as Ben and Benny helped hook up both wagons. Kate had fed the two visitors early. She now was bundling up Rachel for her cold ride home. As Kate draped the quilt over her knees on the high seat, Rachel whispered in her ear. "I peeked in there last night. I think the one woman saw me, I hope she don't tell dad."

Kate kissed her on the cheek, "Don't worry, she won't say a word to anyone. Now you stay warm on the way home. Come back to see us come spring." Then she climbed down and stood by Ben as the wagons moved out onto the road.

The following week it snowed for almost the whole week. When the blue sky finally appeared the snow was over a foot deep right in Garnet. Everyone had moved their stock to the river last week, so all they had to feed in town was Ben's horse and Kate's. The mail stage finally made it through with help of extra riders breaking trail. Kate still had snowshoes that had belonged to Dan so Ben kept working with his leg. Benny went along the first day and almost had to help Ben back to town. The extra weight plus the different motioned really put a strain on that leg. He walked every day, even on stormy days. The first of March brought the first warmer weather, followed by a night of rain. That morning a few rumblings could be heard from the direction of the peaks. By the last of the month bare ground was showing around town and on the ridges close to town.

Just about dark one evening Kate called from the front window of the store, "Ben, there's rider coming this way. He's leading two pack horses. Boy this is early for anyone to be traveling this country."

Ben walked up behind her, "He's sure a skinny guy. Even bundled up, he looks skinny."

"That's woman," came Benny's voice from behind them.

Kate was staring down the road at the rider, "A woman? I don't think so my crazy Indian friend."

Ben looked back at Benny, "You sure?"

The rider pulled to a stop at the hitch rail. The rider unbuttoned his slicker, as he it fell away the butt of a pistol appeared in a cross draw holster. Ben stepped out the door, "Howdy stranger, come on in and get warm. We'll rustle up some hot grub for you."

I low voice came from under the flat brim hat worn by people from down south. "I'm looking for a man by the name of Ben Jasper. Do you know of him?"

Ben nodded, "I'm Ben Jasper."

"I need to be taken to Jacob." She reached into her jacket, "I have a message for you," a small gloved hand held an envelope.

Ben looked up at her, "Your animals look tired. It is another ten miles to travel to get to where I will signal him. We will go come morning."

"I will camp. I'll be back at first light."

As she started to lift her reins Ben thought real quick, "We have a cabin away from everyone you can use. There is no spirits, manmade or otherwise there. We also have grain and hay for your tired animals. Jacob would approve."

From under that hat brim Ben looked for her eyes, but they were hidden. He had noticed that her hand had never moved away from the pistol butt. Kate had moved outside, but the rider's eyes had never left Ben. "Will you let me fix you a warm meal," Kate asked.

"I will prepare my meal later," she looked back at Ben. "I will go to the cabin."

As Ben turned to leave he looked back at Kate, "Fix something I will take it to her later."

She slowly dismounted as Ben opened the door of his cabin. He lit the lamp then added wood to the stove. He had spent the afternoon up here cleaning up some of his gold ore. She stood in the doorway not entering, "It is warm, who lives here?"

"I used to live here. I now live with woman down at the trading post, we are married. I work on my gold ore up here. I was here all afternoon, is why it is warm in here."

"Do you want me to help you with your horses? That little barn out back has hay in the mow, grain in the bin, your welcome to both."

She looked at him now with her hat off, he could see her eyes. They were like Jacob, eyes. They seem to look right through you. "I will attend to my stock."

Ben walked to the door, "I will bring you hot food that Jacob would eat. Jacob fed me for many months while he brought me back to life. I know he would approve of the food I will bring to you. I will be right back with the food."

Kate was standing just outside the door watching as Ben approached, "That rider scares me. I guess she is a woman from her voice, but her hand never left that pistol butt all the time she sat there. Who is she Ben, she don't fit anything you've told me about Jacob and his beliefs."

Ben nodded as he watched Kate dish up a hot meal into a warm Dutch oven. "Kate, I don't know how far that woman or girl has come this winter. The letter I mailed was to St Louis, so if she came that far it had to be tough trip all by herself. She's probably had to use that pistol to survive. Thief trying to steal those well bred horses would be bad, let alone if they found out she was a woman. Kate, I think we need to think well of this woman."

Kate stopped to look at Ben, "Ben, I'm not condemning her. I said she scares me. I suppose if she has traveled that far she would be wary of strangers." Kate finished and put the lid on the pot, "This should stay hot until you get up there."

At the cabin the girl was just coming back from the barn. "I did use some hay, I also grained each horse. I will pay you come morning."

Ben shook his head, no, "You will not pay me for anything. I owe my life to Jacob. Tomorrow I will take you to him. What name can I call you?"

Ben sat the Dutch oven on the table, then, turned to face the girl. She looked at him with those steel blue eyes, "I'm called Ada, after the daughter of, Jeptha."

Ben nodded, knowing that name came from the bible. When he was small his mother would read to her children from the bible, he recalled that name.

Ben motioned to the cupboard, "If you need any dishes, you'll find them in there. Feel free to use anything in this cabin."

"When do we ride in the morning?"

Ben smiled, "Well Ada, there's no sense in a real early start, it is ten mile ride up there. Once we get there I will signal Jacob, but he won't come down for you until it is dark tomorrow night. You come on down to the trading post come morning when you're ready and we'll leave. I hope you like what Kate sent up for you to eat. She's pretty darn good cook."

Benny came walking in from the back door the next morning as Ben was finishing a last cup of coffee. "Your partner is already sitting her horse out front. It looks like she's ready to ride. I already saddled your horse when I saw her riding down."

"Thanks Benny. I guess I'll pour her a cup of coffee and take it out to her to see if she will drink it."

Ben stepped out and walked over to her horse, then offered her the coffee. "This is for you Ada. You can drink it while I go get my horse."

She slowly took the cup, "The Indian already saddled your horse. Is he your slave?"

Ben stopped and turned back to face her, "No, Benny belongs to no man. He is his own man. He does whatever needs to be done around the town. In my world Ada, I do not believe in slaves. Men are born to be free. No man should ever own another human being. That is my belief."

Her eyes never left him as he looked at her, "How about your woman, don't you own her?"

Ben broke out laughing, "No Ada, I sure don't own her. That lady is my wife and she has just as much to say about how we live as I do." He stopped for a moment, "I hope you understand what I just said, Kate, is my partner, not my slave by any means."

That head never moved as she looked down at him, "The coffee is good."

Ben nodded, "I'll go get my horse, while you finish that."

As Ben walked up leading his horse Benny and Kate stepped out onto the porch. Benny was holding a full saddle bags, he walked over to Ben horse. Ben placed them behind his saddle and tied them down. He looked back over at Kate, "I will stay the night up at the cabin. I should be back tomorrow, if I don't show, don't worry. Jacob might have something for me to do."

Kate smiled as Ada handed the cup to Benny. Then the strange rider spoke in a strange language to him. Benny looked up at her, then, answered her in the same sounding language.

Ben swung up, waved as they headed up the street toward the high snow covered peaks ahead. Kate stood with Benny staring after the two riders, "What did she say to you, Benny?"

Benny looked at Kate, "She speaks with the tongue of the spirits of our past. That lady is very wise for her age. Ben rides with a woman who sees everything."

"Damn you Benny, with that kind of talk I wish Ben wasn't riding with her. Now what did she say to you?"

Benny looked over at Kate, "She asked if it was true that I was not the slave of this man called Ben."

66

Kate stared at Benny, "Where would she ever get the idea you are Ben's slave? Benny I don't think anything good will come of this girl being here."

Benny shook his head, "Kate, if Jacob lets her stay, we'll probably never see her again, unless you go into that mountain."

Clayton came walking up, "Who's the man with Ben?"

Kate looked over at him, "He rode in last night wanting to go to the mountain. I think he wants to travel on over when the trails melt out. Ben and I decided he could stay in the cabin until he's ready to move out." Kate mind was racing, 'I hope Clayton don't ask any more questions, at least for now.'

Ben stopped in front of the cabin, as he looked over Ada had removed her hat. She was staring at the high peaks, then back to the buildings. "These building were built by our people. Is this where they died?"

Ben had dismounted, he motioned up the canyon. "They died up that canyon where they built the settlement. This is as far as the wagon could go, they walked from here. I will build a fire then we'll go signal Jacob that you're here. We'll unload your gear in that first barn, then, turn the horses loose in the pasture."

Ada swung down as Ben walked inside, she moved around the railing of the porch railing sliding her hand along the smooth pole. Ben came out he watched as her searched each log on the cabin front. She looked up at him, "I now feel at home."

With two of the torches lite and in place they set about unloading her horses. By evening Ben felt more comfortable around the strange woman. She had watched when he put out the torches like Jacob had instructed, then, they returned to the cabin.

She had hung the gun belt on a peg by the door, but Ben spotted a derringer butt above her waist belt. Ada was younger than Ben had first thought. She might even be in her teens. She had pushed him aside and was cooking supper. As they ate, Ben finally got nerve to ask about her trip. "Did you have any trouble coming here?"

She looked up at him, "Yes, a couple of times they tried to steal my horses. Another time two men caught me in my bed. Usually my horses would warn me when anyone was near, this time they didn't for some reason." She stopped.

"How did you get away from them?"

"I shot them both." She looked across the table at him as he stared at her, a small smile came to her face, "My father was a U S Marshal, my mother was one of the, family, like Jacob. She and my father we're a strange pair. My mother lived by the teaching of her people. Father lived by the speed of his gun. They had three girls, I was the youngest. My older sisters, Ruth and Ester married into the family, Ruth died with the people that came here. My other sister Ester lives with her husband in a settlement in Arizona. Dad made sure all of us girls knew about guns. My mother and sisters didn't like it, but I wanted to know more. So he spent hours teaching me to shoot. It was mainly how to defend myself. I would not be here now if he hadn't taught me all of that. I worry that when Jacob finds out I'm here instead of my sister, if he will let me stay. When he wrote he asked if Ester would come to join him here. She was already married, so mother, ask me to come instead."

Ben shook his head, "So you don't really know Jacob?"

"No, he was small when the people chased his father from the settlement. He later stole Jacob away from his mother and disappeared. How Jacob found an address to send his letter to my mother people is a mystery to them. Mother knew his mother real well, they grew up together. In his letter he wrote about Ruth being killed here. He wrote that when he and his father found the mine, the families were already dead. He knew of Ester being my mother's daughter and asked if she would join him."

Ben nodded, "I do know Jacob found many records when he and his father moved into the mountain. I saw some of them while looking around after my leg healed so I could walk. You see we never knew anyone still lived in those peaks until I was buried in a slide. We had saw Jacob and his father when they passed through Garnet on their way up here. His father was crazier than a loon. He had this small boy with him, we never saw them again so we figured they had died or moved on. His father kept mumbling something about he now owned the gold mine of his people. A year or so ago I found a cache in one of the barns that made me start thinking someone was in that mountain alive. So I brought up a few supplies and added them to the cache. The next time I looked the supplies were gone, but a small bag of gold took its place. It was then I knew someone lived in that mountain." He walked over to the stove to add wood and pour more coffee in his cup.

"When did you first meet Jacob?"

Ben went on to tell of his being trapped by the slide and waking up inside the mountain. He looked across the table at this small beautiful dark haired girl sitting across from him. "When you meet him you'll find a very smart person, about everything. He pulled up his pant leg to show the maze of scares. He rebuilt my shattered leg, without me ever

68

knowing it. He crafts some of the finest gold figures you'll ever see. Lady, I could go on and on about him, but you'll be finding, all of this out for yourself before long. Now when he gets here, I don't know if he will come inside the cabin, he never has when I've been with him."

"When will he be here?"

Ben smiled, "I wouldn't be surprised if he not already here. I will walk to the barn before long to wait for him."

Ben stood up and reached for his coat, then froze in place when he heard a slight noise on the porch. As he reached for the latch, he felt it move and the door slowly opened. A low voice came from the darkness, "Turn down the light, then I will come in."

Ben moved over and turned the light all the way down without putting it out. Ben felt Ada moving along close to him. Jacob stepped inside. "It is good to see you Ben. Your leg seems to be getting better."

Ben stepped forward to take his friends hand, "It is also good to see you Jacob. You look well." He turned to Ada standing next to him, "This lady came to the trading post last evening looking for you. Her horses were very tired from the long trip, so I talked her into staying up in my old cabin last night. I told her that I needed to signal you once we got here and you wouldn't come down until it was dark tonight. Jacob this is Ada."

Jacob eyes went to Ada, "Your name is supposed to be Ester, daughter of Kathleen, my mother's friend."

"Kathleen is my mother. I'm the youngest daughter of Kathleen and Hank Thomas. When mother got your letter, she asked me to come to you. Ester is now married and lives in a settlement down in Arizona territory. I have a letter from mother to you that will explain why she asked me to come." She turned and walked over to her gear and pulled out a letter and handed it to him.

Jacob stared at her then walked over closer to the lamp. He stood there reading the letter. He turned to face Ben and Ada. "Your mother writes very well." His eyes moved to look at Ada, "I must think on this, before I give you my answer. I will return tomorrow night with my answer,"

He turned to Ben, "You will stay here with her until I return?"

Ben nodded, "This I will do, Jacob."

As the tall young man reached the door he looked to the holstered pistol hanging from a peg. The small belt made it apparent that this weapon belonged to Ada. Jacob stopped and turned to face the other two, his eyes shifted to Ada, "How many have you killed with this weapon?" Two, who caught me in bed in my way here to see you. My father taught us girls to shoot when we were small. My mother hated guns, but she knew my father had to use his in his job as Marshal. Ruth and Ester hated having to learn to, shoot, they never touched a weapon again. I wanted to know more and father spent hours teaching me to defend myself. He always stressed that I should never draw a gun in anger or to threaten a person for my personal gain. I shot those two before they could have their way with me. This I would do again if my life or my, families lives were threatened."

Jacob looked at her, then, started to turn to leave, she added, "I dressed as a man for the trip. Mother cut my hair short. I chose to wear a wide brimmed hat to help hide my face. Even with all of this I still had to shoot those men if I wanted make it here to you."

Jacob looked over at Ben, "Do you remember the trail we used to leave the mountain?" Ben nodded he did. "Tomorrow night I will meet you both with all of Ada's gear there. The horses I will need for you to take care of until Ada decides if she will stay."

He turned and reached for Ada's hand, "It is good you have come this far for me. When you come to the mountain tomorrow, bring all of your gear." He nodded toward the gun by the door, "I will make a place for your weapons where we leave the saddles and pack gear." He turned and walked out into the darkness.

Ben felt Ada tremble against him as the door closed. He stepped to the lamp and turned it up. "You spoke well, Ada. I think you convinced him that you are sincere in your action with the guns. Jacob also shoots a rifle whenever he needs fresh meat, this I know from living with him. I never did figure out where he keeps it, but I know he has one."

Ada smiled, "His eyes are so clear. It's like he's looking deep inside you. He speaks so gentle, yet the words seem to just flow from his lips." She turned to look straight into Ben's eyes, "He trusts you. You can see it in his eyes whenever he speaks to you. It's like he's known you forever, yet you say you've only known him a short time. Why is this?"

Ben smiled, "Ada, from the first time I looked up into those eyes, I've known we have a bond between us. As I laid there in the mountain slowly gaining my strength, I felt at home. You will marvel at his home in that mountain. Until I was able to travel around up there I thought this was just a mine his people had opened up. Then I began to see all the different chambers, the forge built into the sheer rock walls along with work benches everywhere. It was then I knew someone else had been here long before those from the settlement. Jacob and I have talked of this. It is known the Spaniards mined for gold south of here long before any settlers ever found this country. They used Indian slaves as labors, then they would murder them when they left a so they couldn't tell of these mines. Jacob has read many books of this but none ever mention the Spaniards being this far north. In the deserts south of here you can find hand built rock walls of structures of long ago. You'll find none of these up here in this area, except for this mountain full of rooms, of well skilled people years ago." He smiled at her, "You can learn a lot more about these people from Jacob. You will marvel at the knowledge of this man."

He laughed, "It's hard to believe this is the same teenager who came through the trading post a few years ago with a crazy man. Now why don't you take that back room? I'll sleep out here on the floor. Now I can sleep out in the barn if you wish?"

Ada shook her head no, "I will be safe with you. Jacob wouldn't have told me to spend the night here if he hadn't totally trusted you. Tonight I can sleep without having to worry about defending myself for the first time since I left home." She smiled, "Good night, Ben."

Ben was up at first light. He put a fresh pot of coffee on to boil before walking out into the fresh morning air. The towering peaks rose up and disappeared into the clouds this morning. Ben just stood there thinking about the first time he ever saw this place and all the times he had ridden by. Since his stay in that huge rock fortress with all its rooms and passage ways, this mountain had a new meaning to him. He wondered if those early miners here had the same slave labor to do their work as they did in the desserts of the southwest. If so there had to be a burial ground somewhere of where they disposed of the workmen when they left. Somewhere he should be able to find at least bones left by the decomposing bodies. In his travels mining, he had met up with many old prospectors who first came to this country as fur trappers. In their stories of the Indians, none had ever mentioned anything about the Indians ever mentioning their people slaves of white men. He nodded, then, mumbled, 'I need to ask Benny of his people ever mentioning slaves to white miners.'

A voice behind him brought Ben out of his trance, "Your thoughts must be miles away this morning, Ben. You looked as if you were look-ing into another world in those peaks. I must say they almost take your breath away, just looking up at them."

Ben turned to face her, "Yes I guess I was off in another land. Af-ter you have spent time up there I would like to sit down and talk of

71

what you're going to see in the next few days and weeks. I often wonder if even Jacob has ever toured all the passages up there.

Ada stared at her new friend, "I too have many questions about
what I'm about to see. In some ways I wish I had never traveled here.
Yet on the other hand, I want to know more and I don't want to leave.
Just talking to you and seeing your relationship with Jacob has calmed
most of my fears of what's to come." She took his arm, "Come, the coffee is ready. I have breakfast cooking."

Ben sat finishing another cup of coffee while Ada cleaned up the
dishes. In the sun light shining through the window Ben couldn't help
but to stare at this young beauty. With dark hair cut shorter than his,
wearing a man or probably a boys size shirt with pants. From behind
the belt buckle the shiny butt of the derringer was visible. On her feet
were small western riding boots. 'I think this small beautiful girl is like
a small scorpion. Beautiful to look at but very deadly if crossed.'

Ada walked to her pistol hanging from the peg and brought it back
the table. From her pack by the door she took bag and then sat across
from Ben. Those small hands ejected the rounds from the cylinder with
ease. Each part she cleaned with a cloth from the bag. Then a light coat
of oil was wiped onto every part as she reassembled the Colt. With five
rounds in the cylinder, the hammer sitting on the empty hole she laid in
front of her on the table. She then took the derringer from her waist and
cleaned it. Ben saw as she unloaded it that it too was a 44 like the Colt.
'This would be one hard weapon to hang onto when fired,' as he looked
at those small hands.

She stood up sliding the derringer back into its place behind her
belt buckle. She pulled her rifle from the scabbard then sat back down
to clean it. When she finished she looked up at Ben, who grinned, "I see
you were taught well on the care of your weapons. I enjoyed watching
you work, it was like you were handling your very dear friends."

"Father was killed when I was in my early teens. Two men broke
out of jail one night and came to our house to kill him for arresting
them. They had a sawed off shotgun they had taken from the jailer. Dad
had heard them ride up, so he slipped out a side door. Out in the dark
yard Dad didn't see they had separated. One had along butcher knife he
had taken from the jail, the other the shotgun. Dad must have seen the
movement as the one man threw the knife. He spun to fire just as the
second man shot him in the back with the scatter gun.

Mother was gone to help with a birth across town that evening and
hadn't got home yet. I was in my room and heard the shotgun. I
grabbed my pistol and went out the back door, as I creep around to look

72

into the front yard. Two men were standing over Dad laughing. One of them said, "Hell, give him the other barrel, just for the hell of it."

"When he started to lift the barrel I shot them both. I heard some-one running up the street so I stepped back into the shadows. It was the Sheriff. The jailer had somehow made it to the saloon where the sheriff was playing cards before he died of his wounds. He looked at the dead men, then, in almost a whisper called my name. I stepped out and told him what happened. He said for my sake he would say he shot both men. To this day you're the only person besides me who knows what happened that night. The Sheriff died a few years ago. Mom doesn't know, mainly because it would kill her to find one of her daughters had taken a life, left alone two. Now on this trip here, she knew of my chances being alone and all. I think maybe she would handle it better, even though those two men had killed her husband."

Ben slowly nodded, "Ada, I would think she would understand them both if she did find out about the first ones. Your Dad must have seen something in you or he wouldn't have spent the time to hone your skills to what they seem to be. Why the cross draw holster?"

Ada smiled, "I noticed that first time I seen you at the trading post you spotted the gun butt. Dad tried many things, at that time I was smaller than I am now. He said the hip holster would draw too much attention, sticking out from my hip. With the cross draw it doesn't show except from a side view. You meet more people face to face than you do from the side. While mounted it doesn't show much either way. Once he decided on the cross draw, I can't even begin to tell you how many rounds I have fired. My hand has been swollen so bad I would soak it every evening to get the swelling down. Then one day my shot was just a second faster than his. He smiled as he took my arm, 'Now Ada, you got to practice to keep that speed, your life will depend on it.'

"Then he brought out the derringer, with a holster to fit inside my belt buckle. It was a left hand draw. Dad looked at me with a small smile, "Ada, people will see the right hand cross draw, so they won't pay any attention to your left hand." We went through the same practice with the short gun. Then one day he sat down on a log by a small fire and motioned for me to join him.

We sat a long while before he spoke again, then he added some-thing I will never forget. "Ada, from now on you won't always have me around to protect you like you've had this far in your young life. All the practice you've been through won't keep you alive unless you do what I'm going to tell you now. Don't ever threaten anyone with your gun. Talking is fine, but when that doesn't work shoot first. No one will take you serious as a gun fighter. They will think the rigging is just for looks. Before you ever draw to fire know your next move, make it all one motion. Then he just sat there looking at me."

I nodded my head toward him, "Dad, I know what you're saying. I will never let you down." A slow rolling tear dropped from her chin, "That was one of my last talks with my Father."

Ben just sat there looking at a little lady that should be teaching school or being courted by all the local boys. As they walked down to the pasture Ben looked over at her, "I notice these animals of yours are well bred horse flesh. You raise them?"

She smiled, "Oh no. Dad's brother is the horse rancher. When he heard about my trip west he showed up with these horses. First off he thought I was crazy for even trying it, then when he found out I was going he gave them to me." She smiled, "I think these horses were part of my problem coming west, they drew too much attention. One lady store keeper saw that I was a woman when I stopped to buy supplies. She scolded me for riding alone, she added, "Honey they will kill you just for those horses. If they find you are just a girl first before shooting you, it'll be a lot worse for you. I see you carry a gun. All I can say is you better really know how to use it.' As I rode away I could see tears in her eyes."

Ben smiled, "Well let's catch them, then go up and load your gear. We'll eat lunch and head up there this afternoon. We can leave your gear up there where Jacob said then come back down to wait for dark. We can ride double up there tonight or you can take your horse and I'll bring it back. I should walk up there to test this leg, but I don't think I could make it back down. It works good, just doing my normal chores, but I still haven't put it to a hard test." He grinned, "I guess the biggest reason is I know how lucky I'm to just have my leg. If it hadn't been for Jacob I'd be dead or at least a one legged man."

As they climbed up the narrow rocky trail turned off the main trail onto another less used trail. He stopped on the same flat where he'd camped that day the slide got him. He swung down, then, motioned for Ada to join him. We'll have to pack the gear from here to the entrance on our backs. He made up a light pack for Ada, "Now up ahead is one place where it gets really narrow for a few feet. Just keep your eyes on the trail, don't look over the side, you'll get along fine."

As they crossed the narrow part Ben heard Ada suck in extra air into her lungs. He never looked back, he just moved on up the trail. Ben dropped off his load and helped Ada slip out of hers. She was gazing about, then she looked at Ben, "I don't see any opening, this trail just goes on up around this cliff."

Ben smiled, "I'll show you when we get all your gear packed up here," he turned and headed back down the trail. When they got the second load to the entrance, the gear was gone. Ben looked back at her. Ada was scanning the area around them. "Come on one more load should do it."

On the last trip as they dropped off their loads a voice came from the rock wall, "It is good, you made the trip alright." Jacob stepped into the trail from what looked to be just a crack in the sheer rock wall. "I have watched all day and no one is in this area, but you two. I will take Ada with me now, Ben. When will you be back up here again?"

Ben looked at Jacob, "Well, Kate and I've been talking. Now that the weathers getting good we're going to start fixing the place up. I'll start moving more of my gear up here next week. I'm not going back mining anymore so I'll be here most of the time. Kate will spend more time up here with me once all the miner have headed back into the mountains for the summer. April and her girls can handle the trading post and the saloon during the slow time."

Jacob reached out to grasp his hand, "I will be down to see you then. I have a list of supplies, we will be, needing. You can bring them when you come back. Ada may find more after she spends time with me." He handed Ben a folded paper.

Ada stepped forward, "Ben, you are so much like my father in your ways. With you around is like having him close to me." She put her arms around him and buried her head in his chest. She then pulled his head down and kissed his cheek, "Thank you for bringing me here." then she stepped back to take Jacobs hand.

Ben turned to leave, then looked back, "Until we meet again," he smiled at the two people then headed down the trail.

When Ben got back to the buildings he looked up at the sun, it was getting into the late afternoon. He, decide, he would ride back to Garnet in the morning. He unsaddled his horse leaving his saddle on the porch then put all the horses back into the pasture. Once in the pasture Ben turned Ada horses loose, then mounted his horse bareback and rode around the fence line just checking it. He found where one top rail had been knocked off, so he put in back in place. From the tracks he figured by the tracks a herd of Elk had knocked it off. When he got back to the gate he turned his horse loose.

Ben spent the rest of the afternoon wondering around the barns looking at things that needed to be repaired. He decided from the looks of things to be done, he'd need to bring the wagon next trip. He sat down at the table while supper was cooking to make a list of supplies he would need. He ate leaving a few biscuits to go along with his morning breakfast. He cleaned up the kitchen then sat down to drink a last cup of coffee. He wrote team down, at the bottom of his list. "I think Kate and me need to be thinking on another team if I start working up here," he mumbled out loud. Benny used the team at the trading post almost every day for one thing or another. Maybe he could make a short trip down to see Tyler Bates if he knew of a team for sale. Out in the barn was all the leather he'd ever need to make up a workable harness. 'I should maybe let Tyler know all the horse gear left by the settlers. He probably put it to good use.'

CHAPTER 6

Benny met Ben as he pulled up to the barn behind the trading post, "Good thing you got here, that Kate has been pacing the floor this morning. I figured by noon if you didn't show up, her and me been heading for the homestead."

Ben grinned as he heard the back door slam, he looked back to see Kate walking toward them. "I see Jacob must have let her stay?"

Ben nodded as Benny led his horse away, "Yes in fact it all happened a little faster than he had told us that first night." He kissed her on the cheek.

She grabbed his head and pulled him to her lips, she stepped back, "None of that cheek stuff, you been gone two nights."

She poured him a cup of coffee while she fixed his lunch. "I told Jacob I was going to start working on the place next week, in case he wanted to see me. I brought back a list of supplies he needs and a list of tools I'll need. You know were going to needing a wagon up there for hauling supplies back and forth. We still got a couple of those big wagons left, but we don't need something that big for this. What do you think about me trading for a light wagon and another team?"

Kate sat down with two plates of food. She nodded, "I think your right about the second wagon and team. You got any ideas of where to look?"

"I was thinking about riding down to see Tyler. He hauls all over, so I'm sure he'll know of something. I also think maybe Tyler would be interested in one of the wagons still up there that needs a little work before it can be used. Maybe tomorrow if you're not real busy we could ride over and see him."

Kate looked up from her plate, "Tyler is supposed to be here Monday with a load of grain, maybe we could talk to him then."

Benny came walking in from the kitchen carrying a plate of food, "I heard you say something about Tyler being here Monday. I can see a big wagon coming up the valley right now, I think he coming in early with that grain. I already got that grain bin all cleaned out, so we're ready."

Ben looked over at Benny, "What we need is a second wagon and another team, I was going to go see Tyler if he knew of one."

"You know Coby down on the river has extra wagons he's picked up from people traveling that river road. He's also got lots of horses too, now if any of them been worked in harness I can't say."

"Okay we'll see what Tyler has to offer then tomorrow we can ride down and see Coby," Ben answered.

Ben and Benny unloaded the big wagon while Kate fed Tyler and Rachel who had come along with her father. Later Ben asked about any light wagons and teams Tyler knew about being for sale. He looked and the ground then over at Rachel, "Rachel, when we were in town the other day who mentioned that team they had for sale?"

"Well Mister Toliver, at the stage stop said he'd taken in a wagon for a grub bill someone had built up during the winter. Remember he said he was going to hold it for a month to see if the man could come up with the money."

Tyler nodded, "That's why I bring her along. Her memory is lot better than mine. I'll keep my ears open if I hear of one for sale." He climbed up to the high seat, "Ben I'll keep thinking about a trade or something for one more of those big wagon still up at the barns. Are you and Kate going to move up there? I always figured we'd see more of that religious bunch if they did find gold in them cliffs. You going to, try your luck up there?"

Ben shook his head no, "No, I just want to build that up into a place for Kate and me to live. I'd like to claim that whole upper end of this valley and start breaking up some of that ground and plant something that would make good hay. I been looking, I think I could irrigate a good part of that ground along the creek and maybe get two crops a year. As far as me mining, up there, no way. That's too rough of a way to make a living climbing around in those cliffs. I always preferred placer mining rather than hard rock. As far as some of them people coming back, I really don't think they will." Tyler, for right now didn't want anyone spreading rumors of people living in that mountain."

Only a few in Garnet, knew about Jacob, so he knew none of them would talk.

"I heard Toliver, told someone that a rider came through the other day looking for Garnet. They said it was a small man, he had three mighty fine horses with him. Did he find you folks?"

Kate nodded, "Yes, he stopped by one evening, then, rode out the next morning. Real quiet person, he just asked directions, got a few supplies and rode off."

As the big wagon moved off down the valley toward the main road, Kate looked over at Ben and grinned. "I'm getting as bad as you are in telling tales."

Ben nodded as she looked over to where Benny stood watching them, "You both do good, at not letting anyone know about Jacob and his mountain home. They're, be more coming who won't be put off as easy as some you've had so far."

Ben nodded, "Kate, do you need this helper of yours today? If not I'm taking him with me down to the river to see Coby."

"Go ahead, about all I got for today is setting out the supplies for Clayton and Henry. They're both getting itchy feet to get back to their diggin's for the summer. Jess and his group aren't leaving until the upper trail is open."

When they got to Coby's, he was working a pasture fence. When he saw them coming he headed for the house. Every time Ben rode down here he couldn't believe the difference in the climate in such a short distance. The green grass was just getting started up at the cabin, and not much higher in Garnet, but here it was green everywhere. When Coby found out Ben needed a wagon and team his eyes lit up, "By golly, Ben I got a couple of deals you just can't turn down. Wagon's is something I'm getting too many of for my own good. It seems every summer more people traveling by who have run out of money. A few supplies and a few dollars and they're on their way. Come on down to the barn. I got just what you're looking for. This team is bred out of some sort of cross, they have draft horse blood from somewhere. There a little heavier than a light team, but yet not huge like a full blood draft. The wagon needs a little care. We could do a quick job of greasing the wheels here before you head for Garnet. Then, you could finish the repairs up there."

Ben walked around the wagons while Coby sent one of his hired hands to get the horse brought up to the corral. Ben spotted the team Coby had mentioned even before they got to the corral. "Okay, Coby. What are these two deals you got all thought up? Let's start with the big team and this wagon?"

Coby grinned, "Now Ben you take all the fun out of dealing when you talk like that. Well first off Benny tells me you still got a couple of those big wagons from the religious nuts from up the valley? I'd kind of thinking about working one of them into the deal. I think with the busy season getting here, I could maybe peddle one of them."

"You know already that I don't own those wagons by myself. It's group ownership. But that's no problem. I just pay my partners for their share. We already have a price on them, so as long as they get their share I can deal anyway I see fit. So what deal have you got in mind?"

Coby took a big chew from a plug he took from his pants, pocket, he offered the plug to Ben. "I'll wait to hear the deal first before I take a crew of that."

Coby looked over at the wagon, then, back to Ben, "Okay, team and rigging along with the wagon for one your big wagon brought down here with the canvas cover and a hundred bucks?"

Ben chuckled, "Now Coby, I thought you said deal? Well now, I got a better idea. I'll have Benny bring down one of the big wagons with the cover loaded in the back. In exchange I want the team, wagon and harness's, then we'll add to that, that pair of blacks over there against the back fence that's looks to be a team. To this I will add a hundred in cash. I don't want anything except the black's. I already got plenty of harness material."

Coby looked at the ground, "Now damn it Ben, I think your deal is a little short on the money end. Add another hundred and you got a deal."

Ben looked over at Benny who was just listening, "Come on Benny, you're the Indian, you're supposed to help me on horse dealings."

Benny never changed expression, "White men talk too much when they deal? Indian trades without all the chatter. Leave this Indian out of this trading."

Ben laughed, "You're a big help, Benny. I think Kate's paying you too much." Ben looked back over at Coby, "I'll split the difference, Hundred and fifty and you get the axles greased so I can take the wagon home."

Coby nodded, "The winter's pasture rent may have to go up if I keep dealing like this. He motioned to his men working in the corral, "Dab some grease on the axles of this wagon."

Two hours later, Ben was driving the wagon, Benny had Bens horse and the black team on led ropes behind him.

Kate walked out as they pulled up to the barn. She looked at the new additions, "You left to get a team and wagon, now you show up with extra horses too. Do you and Benny figure on starting a freighting business?"

Ben grinned, "I just got all involved in horse trading and forgot to quit. To be truthful I think that team of yours is getting a little too old for any hard work. This pair of blacks, look to be good for a few years and the price I thought was right."

Kate looked over at Benny, "I suppose you go along with all of this?"

Benny shrugged, "White men trade like Squaws, too much talk," then he took the blacks into the corral.

Benny helped Ben pull all the wheels and checked over the axles on the new wagon. By evening Ben was ready to load up in the morning and head up to the cabin.

That night Clayton and Henry stopped by to say they would be heading out come morning. Both were going by the lower trail and figured it would be melted out good by now. Kate invited them for supper, later they all went into the saloon for parting drink. Jess and a few of the other miners waiting for the high trail to open came down to see Clayton and Henry off. As Ben and Kate got up to go home Clayton walked over, "Ben I'll stop by and see Nate on my way up to my mine, anything you need for me to take to him?"

Ben shook his head as he stood thinking, "About the only thing I can think of is, tell him that I checked on that paperwork Kate signed for the claim, it's all recorded. He should have received his copy when he got home last winter. If he didn't get them tell him to send word with you when you come in the 4th for supplies."

Kate motioned to Henry sitting with April, "Don't forget I'm feeding you two in the morning at dawn before you take off."

The next morning as they all walked out after breakfast to see the two miners off, Clayton took Kate's hand. "Kate you make sure to keep an eye on this guy so he, don't get lost again this summer."

Kate smiled and looked over at Ben, "Don't worry. His leash is only ten miles long. The cabin will be his limit when he's alone." She squeezed his hand, "You take care, too." She looked over at Henry, "That goes for you too, Henry. We'll see you both for the 4th of July."

Benny helped Ben get loaded while Kate loaded the food supplies for Jacob and for the cabin. When he got loaded Kate buried her head into his chest, Ben could feel her sobbing. He reached down to pull her chin up so he could kiss her, "Don't worry my dear, I will work very careful. Besides I figure I'll have eyes watching my every movement while I'm there. If you get too lonesome once all these miners leave, ride up and spend a few days." Then he kissed her again, "Oh hell who knows I might get so lonesome tonight, that'll I'll be back by morning," then he laughed as she looked at him.

The sun was warm and the fresh team wanted to travel so Ben was up at the cabin in the early afternoon. He spent the rest of the day putting away the supplies. He put Jacob's supplies in the usual place, then, headed back to the cabin. By evening he had the cabin ready for the summer. He walked up to the spring house to make sure the water was clear. When he lifted off the lid, the cool spring water was clear below him. This was the first time he'd ever looked over the rock work the religious group had done when they built building. It was like everything else, well done. He knew that the cistern by the cabin had at one time held water, but it had been dry since he first stayed there. As he looked into the spring house he spotted the end of a pipe in the rock work. As he reached down he felt the wooden plug blocking the pipe, so he worked the plug loose. Water began going down the pipe and the pool in the spring house began to lower and soon the over flow was hardly running. Ben left the lid off and walked down to the cabin and opened the lid of the cistern. Water was already filling the rock tank. A grin appeared on Bens face, 'By golly, I'll be right up town with water just outside my door,' he said aloud.

He closed the lid and walked back to lower the lid on the spring. After supper he checked the cistern, the tank was full but no water was spilling out into the yard. In the growing darkness it was hard to see down into the tank, but it looked like the overflow was disappearing into the rock wall. "Well maybe tomorrow I can figure out how that works," he lowered the lid and went in for the night.

The next morning he walked down to the corral after breakfast to check on his team. He stopped when he noticed a small pond of water in one corner of the corral. He was sure that wasn't there before. A smile came to his face as he got closer, in the corner of the main corral where the water stood was a small low place. The extra water was now running over rocks into the green pasture outside the fence. Ben got down and stirred the bottom of the pool then he felt the rock bottom. This was a manmade pool that over time with horses in the corral was hidden by dirt kicked into it. He decided he would get a shovel later and clean it out, now he knew where the cistern over flow came out.

At the barn he found someone had taken most of the new supplies. He walked to the door to gaze up at those towering white peaks above the valley. A quiet soft voice from, behind him, caused him to jump, "Good morning Ben."

He turned to find Ada standing by the door from the back room. She was dressed like she had been when he brought her up here. She smiled, "Jacob wanted me to talk to you, so I stayed down here last night. He will be back tonight for the rest of the supplies, I will go back with him then."

82

Ben smiled, "How about we go over to the cabin? I got coffee on. There's, a couple of fresh biscuits along with bacon if you're hungry."

Ada walked back by the door and picked up a pack and handed it to Ben. She picked up the second one. "The coffee sounds good, I've had breakfast already."

Ben could tell by the weight of the pack that there was maybe gold he was carrying. Inside the cabin Ada took a pouch from here pack, she handed it to Ben, "This is the gold for the cost of the supplies you brought. Jacob said for you to keep track of the purchases as to what he owed Kate each time." Ben nodded.

Ada then pulled two small objects, wrapped in soft deer hide. She un-wrapped them to revel two gold candle holders. Then she opened the pack Ben had carried from the barn, from it she took an assortment of figurines, all molded from pure gold. She laid them on the table, then handed Ben a letter, "This will explain what Jacob needs for you to do with these."

Ben read the letter. Jacob wrote he needed for Ben to find a way to ship, these east without anyone finding out what they were or where they had come from. He had a list of what was to be sent in three differ-ent packages to three different addresses. Ben looked up at Ada, "Ada I will need time to find a way of sending these without leaving any trace of where they came from. I'm sure between Kate and me we'll figure a way to do this." He looked out the window, then, back at her, "Will there be more, later?"

Ada nodded, "Yes, if you find a way that can't be traced back to our home."

Ben grinned, "When you say our home, I gather that you're stay-ing?"

Ada refilled their cups, "Yes, I'm staying but not as his wife. Jacob has asked me to stay, but only as his partner in the mine. I have letters for you to mail, one is to my mother. Jacob has asked her to find him a woman to give him children, who is of the beliefs of the family. His wishes are that I also remain as his number one, but not the mother of his children." Ada smiled as she saw the look on Ben's face, "Do not be sad for me. I have found here with him a peace that I never had be-fore. I will also be his personal protector from anyone trying to harm him in any way. This is to say that I may have to use some or all of that training that my father taught me."

Ben slowly shook his head as he looked at this small young girl, "Then you're going to be his enforcer or body guard? Does the fact you've had to kill to live have any bearing on this?"

Ada reached across to touch his arm, "Ben, I'm at peace with this. I was hoping you too could understand this."

Ben nodded, "Ada, you have my blessing, if this is what you want."

She smiled, "Thank you, Ben." She stood up, "Now, what do you have planned for the day? You've got help, so let's get to work."

They re-packed the gold into some of Bens packs. Earlier Ben had found a trap door under the bed that led to an opening under the cabin. Then when he crawled in he found a covered opening that opened outside in the back of the cabin. He figured it had been built more for escape route than a hiding place. He dropped the packs into the opening under the floor then closed up the trap door.

Ben checked the cistern, tasted the water, it was cold with a sweet taste like all good mountain water. With a shovel he cleaned the pool in the corral while Ada checked the horses over. When she walked back to him she nodded, "These horses are new to you? I don't remember them when I stayed at your cabin."

Ben laughed as he finished his job, "Little lady you don't miss much do you? Yes I just bought them from a ranch down on the river. Kate and I decided she needed her team for work around town. Besides they are getting old for the work I want to do up here, so I bought this team and a little heavier wagon for my work." He laughed as he looked over at her, "I might as well tell you now, I also have a young black team I bought at the same time. You'll be seeing them up here as the summer wears on." Ada smiled as she followed him back up to the barn.

By evening they had got work done around the buildings where having a helper made the repairs go a lot faster. Ada fixed supper. Later they sat out on the front porch as the sun began to drop below the horizon. Then a cool evening breeze coming off the snow cover peaks cooled the air to almost to a point that a coat was needed. They moved inside to wait for darkness. As the cabin got dark Ben and Ada sat in the darkness. As Ada moved in her chair, Ben heard the sound coming from near the door. The door slowly opened, Jacob was framed in the doorway. "I see you got many jobs done today with the help of my partner? I also watched as you found the workings of the cistern. The pool in the corral was still there when I first came here with my father. The water had been turned off, but it would fill with rain water is the way I first knew of it."

Ben chuckled, "Yes, Jacob this little lady is great help. Besides she cooks better than I do too. Yes, I did find out about the cistern and the spring house. I knew of them but I had no idea they were connected. Then the pool in the corral was a complete surprise."

He walked over closer to Jacob, "My friend, I will start being up here a lot more from now on. Kate is going to be up here part of the time once all the miners are gone back into the mountains for the summer. So feel free to order supplies anytime or just leave me a note in the barn if you like we've been doing."

"It is good to not be alone anymore, with Ada here I feel like spending more time with my work. I have studied the books you brought to me, you did well. I found out many things about the human body I didn't realize before. I also think I could add to some of those articles. I do think too, that many wouldn't go by my ways of using the mind to cure sickness and wounds. You are a true example of this, to me you rose from near death to rejoin us. I could only rebuild your leg. The rest was done by you. I took away your pain so your mind could work on healing you. This is what the books do not teach." He reached for Ben's hand, "These talk's like this is what I missed most when you moved from the mountain. It was then that I found how much I missed having you to talk to. Did Ada ask you about sending my parcels out for me?"

Ben nodded, now with the moon shining outside and filtering through the door, he could see Jacob. "Yes, we talked of sending these packages for you. I will get with Kate and we will find a way to ship these without leaving a way to trace them back to us. One hard thing to hide is the beautiful addressing and your trademark statue on the return. My friend everything you do is a work of art, this people will notice first. I know we can figure out a solution."

Ada got ready to leave, as she stood by Jacob she looked like a small child alongside the tall man. Jacob looked down at her, "My small partner moves about our home in the mountain as a shadow, I never hear her. She also sees all that is around her, this makes my life so much easier. Now I don't have to worry about danger as I work. She has skills so different than anything we have in the family. My father would have been so scared of her to the point of trying to find a way to see her taken from this earth."

Ben frowned, now Jacob was off into something that didn't make sense to him. He knew the man had been crazy, but not to the state of wanting someone killed. Jacob never pushed his beliefs on Ben during their talks, but many things he said puzzled him. This deal, with his father, Ada, that did worry him. Not so much for Ada's safety, but to think maybe more people among this group thought this way. He shook his head, 'Ben, don't let yourself be pulled into this. Keep your relationship with Jacob strictly friendship, not religion.'

Jacob must have known Ben was not comfortable with the topic. Then he again took Ben's hand in a firm grip, "I will keep in touch. If you do, send those packages, leave me a note to know they are gone." Jacob turned and moved out into the darkness.

As Ada walked by Ben to follow Jacob, she stopped, then squeezed his arm and whispered, "That man has a great love in his heart for you. I too cherish your friendship." then she disappeared into the night.

Ben strained to hear any movement in the night, but there was nothing. He dropped down on the bed to get a few hours shut eye before dawn. It never did come as his mind wandered to his friends living in that damn mountain. As dawn, lighten the inside of the cabin, Ben rolled out to start breakfast. Ben worked the morning replacing a gate post in the corral. His leg was getting tired, so after eating a couple of biscuits from supper, chasing them with cold coffee, he headed for the corral. He caught his saddle horse and led him to the barn. He swung up after saddling the horse. He headed up toward where the settlement had once stood. Years before Ben had found one of the trails used by the settlers up through the rocks, was good enough to ride a horse up. It was a slow trip but he ended up among all the wreckage of the buildings. The avalanche pushed all the building down the mountain into a huge pile of rubble. Ben tied the horse and walked around over the lumber and timbers. He sat down to look about, 'With one helper I could get enough timbers here to almost fence the whole place. At least I could get enough to build all the gates and all the main corner posts,' he mumbled. As he worked back down the trail he looked for any place that would stop a pack horse loaded with posts. Back at the barn he unsaddled, then turned his horse back into the pasture. It was the middle of the afternoon, but his leg was telling him to call it a day. He built up a fire in the cabin and put on a fresh pot of coffee to boil. He moved out onto the porch where he could see the surrounding country. He had about dozed off when he heard one of the horses down in the pasture whinny. Ben looked and saw the horse was looking up the road back toward Garnet. Then he saw the reason, a lone rider leading three pack horse was just coming into sight. Ben grinned, he could tell by the hat it was old Jess Garrett. He was the oldest of the miners that wintered in Garnet and usually the last to leave each spring.

Ben walked out as the rider got close, "By God Jess, this is late in the afternoon for you to just be here. You better spend the night and get a fresh start come morning." Then Ben noticed the back animal, "Say Jess I just noticed, that back pack horse looks awful familiar?"

Jess nodded as he swung down, "Hell that's been the plan all along. Kate sent along supper for us and a message for you, it's all back there on your pack horse. Besides I couldn't take another night of them girls making sure I got a good send off," then they both laughed.

Ben turned his pack horse out into the big pasture with the other horses, leaving Jess's in the smaller pasture. Back in the cabin Ben pulled a full bottle from one of the packs and held it up.

Jess laughed, "Kate sent that, she said she heard the snakes were bad up here this year."

As the stew in the Dutch oven was heating up on the stove Ben and Jess sat enjoying the bottle Kate had sent. They watched as the sun was slowly settling lower in the sky. Jess looked over at Ben, "You know I've never seen that Kate any happier than she is this spring. You two just fit each other. Now you've got this place to prove up on. Ben I really envy what you and Kate have. In told her the other night that this might be my last year to mine. We kind of talked a little about maybe I lease the trading post from you folks and try it for a year. You know I got one of the better houses there in town. Later I sort of mentioned it to Meg that I was thinking about maybe settling down. All she said was, 'whenever you're ready Jess, keep me in mind.' Ben could see a small tear in the old miner cheek.

"That Meg would make a man a good partner," Ben answered. "I understand how you feel. I had the same feeling when I head out last year. When I got up to the mine, Kate was on my mind. I had one hell of a good spring cleanup, but gold just wasn't the main thing on my mind. Yes sir, Jess, I fully understand. I wouldn't want to have missed all those years hunting the mother lode, but, now I just don't miss it. You know Jess my only advice to you is, don't wait too long to make the change. I dam near miss my chance in that slide, don't you make the same mistake."

Jess smiled, "Thanks Ben. I knew you would level with me, is one the reason I wanted to stop here."

Ben nodded, "You know that supper Kate sent up should be hot by now."

The next morning before dawn Ben fixed breakfast while Jess loaded up his gear. The top of the peaks were just beginning to shine from the sun coming up when Jess swung up. He looked down at Ben, "I'll see you the fourth of July," he raised his hand in a salute and headed up the trail.

Ben gathered up a saw and a few other tools, then, caught up his horse and one pack horse. He just finished loading the tools on the pack horse when the horse turned its head to look toward the road. Ben glanced that way, a big smile then appeared on his face. He chuckled, 'Sure didn't take her long to get here once the last miner left.' When Kate rode up he walked back to help her down, "Howdy partner, you from around these parts? He kidded as he gave her a big hug.

"Ben Jasper, why are you loading that pack horse? You told me you had plenty to do her on the place so you brought the wagon to use." A slow smile appeared, "I guess I should just say hello before I start grumbling, Right?"

Ben nodded, "You know I really need someone to run the other end of this saw, so why don't you just climb back on that horse. Then I'll show you why I was loading the pack horse."

He held the horse while she remounted. She followed along as he headed up the trail toward the wreckage of the settlement. He loosened the cinches while Kate stood looking over the area. "What are we doing up here?"

Ben walked over to her, "I was up here yesterday just to look for some timbers I can use for post down below. I saw a lot of this that is long enough, but I'll need to cut it to length to get it out of here. That one you standing on will make two good posts if we cut it right."

Kate nodded, "You were going to do this by yourself?

Ben smiled, "Only the ones I could lift without any trouble. I was going to leave the bigger ones for later and bring Benny up here to help me. I kinda wanted to start that fence along the creek before the ground gets too hard to dig. If I could fence part of that I could get a little hay for the barn. Who know we might spend part of the winter up here if old Jess can handle to trading post alright." Then he laughed when he saw the look on Kate's face.

Kate smiled, "Now I know why he was in such a hurry to get packed up yesterday. You do know the stew was his idea."

They load six posts on the pack horse and headed back down the trail. Ben loaded this first trip light just to see how the horse got along with this type of load. Back at the cabin Ben unloaded the posts and put the horses back in the pasture. Kate had taken her gear from her horse before Ben had headed down to the barn to unload. Ben saw her watching him as he walked up toward her. She pointed at the cistern, "I just looked and it's full of water. I looked at it before and it was just an empty tank. Where's the water coming from?"

"I got a little nosy that first night I was here so I looked into the spring box back behind the cabin. I saw how full it was, then, I saw this pipe I'd never seen before. I reached down and pulled a wooden plug and water started flowing. Then I check this box again and the tank was already filling up. Then later I found out where this overflow water goes that's running into the ground there," as he pointed towards the ground. "Look down in that smaller corral, see that pool, it come from here."

Kate looked at him, "This is nice having water right by the door. Has that been there ever since they built this cabin?"

Ben nodded, "Jacob knew it was here. When he came after his supplies, he commented about me finally figuring it out."

That night they sat out on the porch watching the night shadows slowing taking over the valley. Kate was staring up at the peaks as she laid her head on Bens shoulders, "You think they are watching us?"

Ben hugged her, "Who knows about that, but I do know one thing. Jacob already knows you're here. Sometimes I can't believe what he knows about what going on down here. It's like he spends the whole day looking this way. Say I about forgot, you and me have a chore to do for him. I got some packages he wants mailed, but he doesn't want anyone to now where they were mailed from. I told him we would get our heads together and figure it out."

Kate nodded, "I think I already know of a way to do that. I got a very good friend over near the Snake River country. We send things back and forth to each other all the time. I'll just send her a big box with everything in it. She can open it and take out all of Jacobs packages and send them on."

Ben smiled, "I knew you'd have an answer for Jacob's problem. You know I worry about his fancy return address on those packages. Drawing like he does is going to draw attention to anyone who handles or sees them. Maybe we could rewrap them before we send them to your friend."

Kate nodded, "Did he put that same statue on these?" Ben nodded, yes. Kate smiled, "I agree with you, that is beautiful work. Do you think all the packages are filled with his gold figures?"

Ben nodded, "As heavy as they are, I'd say yes. I think if anyone finds out what's in those packages marked with that drawing, then Jacob life would change. Also could changes the life of your friend who mailed them. People would trace them back to your friend, her, life could be in danger. Without that drawing on each package, people's attention wouldn't be aroused by just the weight."

Kate leaned over against him, "Now, you've really been worrying about this little chore haven't you? Ben I'm sure we can do this so everyone will remain safe."

Ben kissed her forehead, "Bed time for me." Kate followed him inside.

For the next week they brought down at least one load of posts a day, one day they brought three. Ben decided he would leave the rest until he got Benny up here to help with the heavier timbers. They had decided over supper that night to ride back Garnet the next day. Kate wanted to see how the girls were getting along and they needed more supplies.

After supper they were sitting out front as they did each night. Ben sat up straight in his rocker. He stood up, "Rider coming," as he motioned off toward town.

As the rider got closer they both recognized Benny. He stopped out front and swung down. Kate walked to the railing, "Something wrong at the trading post, or did the girls chase you off?"

"I just come out to get you both to ride back to the trading post," He looked at Kate, "You got any coffee left over from supper and maybe a couple of biscuits?"

Kate laughed, "Come on in, I'll fix you something to eat. If I don't we'll never find out why you're here."

As he ate he filled them in, "A girl showed up on the stage this morning. I think maybe she's the one Jacob sent for, anyway she wants to only talk to you," as he looked up at Ben.

"Kate and I was going to ride in tomorrow morning anyway, can we wait until then?"

Benny looked up from his plate, "She's not the main problem. There are three men following her. The stage driver took me off to the side. He said those three had been watching when the passengers loaded in Springfield. Then he caught a couple of glimpses of them following the stage. There camped down below the forks in that grove of trees. They've been take turns watching the store, then one of them started following me when I left to ride up here."

Ben looked out into the growing darkness, then back at Benny, who was halfway grinning. "He's probably still trying to find his way back out of the hot springs canyon. I left him a good trail going down to the pools. Then I rode up the cliff trail a few turns. When I rode out from there, I didn't leave him a trail to follow."

Kate looked at Ben, "Maybe Benny's right we should ride back in the dark. You get the horses while I get ready."

90

Ben nodded, "Benny, do you want a fresh horse for the trip back?

Benny stood up finishing the last of his coffee in the cup, "I probably better, who knows what the night will bring. I'll help you get them."

While saddling the horses, Ben walked close to Benny. He spoke in a low tone. "What do they look like?"

"Flat topped hats like you see down south along the border. They ride fine horses and are well armed, so I say they are here on business. I've watched the girl who dresses and acts like those women that used to live up here in the settlement. I can't tell if she knows she's being followed. Riding up here I got to thinking maybe she's with them."

Ben looked over at the half breed. This was a lot more than Benny usually say's at one time. Ben walked over to a feed box along the, manger. He reached inside into the loose grain and came out holding a leather pouch. He took a colt pistol from the bag and a handful of cartridges. He put the pistol in his waist band under his vest and dropped the cartridges into one of the vest pockets. He put the bag back into the bin. When he took the reins of his horse from Benny, "You need one? If you do I got more stashed around here."

Ben shook his head, no. "I got all I need."

As they rode up toward the cabin a grin was on Ben's face, as he thought about this breed. Who was so much a part of his and Kate's life. Well educated but still possessed his Indian blood lines in reading people. He could track about anything and never leave any sign while doing it.

Benny led off into the darkness with Ben bring up the rear. Benny turned off long before being in sight of Garnet. This was a route that was new to Ben. As far as he could tell they weren't following a trail, it looked like they were just moving out through the sage brush. As they topped a ridge Benny stopped, Ben rode up alongside of him. Below you could make out the buildings of Garnet. Benny whispered, "Do you want to stay in your cabin until dawn? If you go to the store you'll scare the hell out of Meg."

They eased down and stopped behind Ben's cabin, Ben dismounted when they did. "I'll take the horses over to the barn. Then I'll be back at first light to get you before going down to the store." Before Ben could answer he walked off leading the horses.

The cabin was warm so they lay down on the bed, fully clothed to grab a little shut eye before dawn. When Ben stepped out just as dawn was breaking, Benny was sitting there. He was leaded back against the wall looking up at him. "The one who followed me into the canyon yesterday is still gone. One of them is over behind that knoll watching the store, the other one is in camp down at the forks in the road."

Ben nodded, "You think Meg is up yet?"

Kate had stepped out as Ben spoke, "I think so. I can see a light in the kitchen window."

Benny stood up, "She lit that lamp about half hour ago."

Kate touched Ben arm, "How about I go down first, maybe I can get her attention without scaring her to death." Ben nodded and Kate moved off down the trail toward the store.

The back door opened as Kate came up behind the woodshed, Meg stepped out looked about then headed for Kate's private privy. Kate moved over to the back porch and stood back in the shadows. As Meg walked back toward the store, Kate spoke her name real soft like, "Meg, it's me Kate."

Meg stopped, then, she saw Kate as she moved out into the light. "Good thing you waited until I was coming back from there," she laughed as she walked up to Kate. "Why are you sneaking around out here?"

Kate took her arm, "Let's move inside then I'll explain."

Before Kate finished tell Meg about everything the back door opened, Ben and Benny stepped in. Kate looked back at Meg, "Where's the girl who came in on the stage?"

"With no one in town right now, I put her in my room over at the saloon. She'd probably have a fit if she knew where she's sleeping." then she smiled. "You know April and I had a little talk last night about her. She looks the part of one of them religious nuts that used to live at the settlement. On the other hand, I'm not so sure she's not putting on an act for us. She might be more at home up in that room than were supposed to think." She shrugged her shoulders, "Who knows, I'm probably all wrong about her."

Ben looked back at Benny who just looked up at Ben, then, he blinked, without changing expression as if to say he agreed.

Kate started breakfast with Meg helping while Ben and Benny sat down with a cup of coffee. The door between the saloon and the store opened, "Well look who's, back. When did you folks ride in?" April asked as she stepped into the room.

Ben looked up at her, "Not long ago. Where's the new girl?"

April nodded behind her, "Charlotte went up to get her."

April poured a cup of coffee, then, sat down next to Ben, "Her name is Alice Chapman. From what I gather from her, she's part of that family or whatever they call themselves. From what I gather, she is supposed to marry that friend of yours who lives in that mountain. What happened to that cute little gal that rode in this spring? I thought she was supposed to take care of him."

Ben chuckled, "Well, I think Ada ended up being more than he bargained for. She is now his partner and I guess you could say his protector."

Before Ben could finish his story Charlotte walked in with a tall blonde girl. Her long plain dress with her hair hanging down her back made her look like all women from the family. Ben stood up as Charlotte introduced her. "Alice, this is Ben Jasper, his wife Kate," as she motioned to Kate standing by the stove. Ben, Kate this is Alice Chapman." She put her hand on Benny shoulder, "Of course you know Benny from yesterday when you came in on the stage."

Ben stepped forward, "Good to meet you Alice. After breakfast we'll see about getting you moved up to our place near the mountain. Right now why don't you sit down I'll bring you a cup of coffee. Or would you like something else?"

"It's good to meet you Mr. Jasper. Coffee will be fine. I'd had never drank coffee until I started my trip here. I found that very few of the stage stops had tea, so I've gotten used to drinking coffee. You mentioned moving up to your place up by the mountain, where is Jacob? I was told you would take me to him."

Kate had walked up with hot food, "Don't worry, Alice, Ben will get in touch with Jacob, he'll come after you. Besides I'll be going back up there with you, so you won't have to eat my husband's cooking while you wait for Jacob," then she laughed when Ben looked up at her.

Alice looked over at Ben, "I thought Jacob lived close by? How far is your place from here?"

Ben smiled, "Not far. We'll take a wagon from here. How much luggage do you have?"

Ben and Benny stepped out onto the front porch as the morning sun covered the town. A chirp of a hawk broke the stillness, Ben saw Benny tense up. He looked up toward the barn. Ben looked over at him, "What's the matter Benny? Is there somebody out there?"

Benny nodded, "You stay here. I need to go up to the barn alone. Don't worry about me. This is not a danger to you or anyone here. I think I have company." He moved off toward the barn and soon disappeared inside.

Ben stood there looking around when Kate walked out to stand by him. "Where did Benny go? I thought he was going to help you hook up a wagon."

Ben put his arm around her shoulders, "When we first stepped out here a hawk call came from that ridge up above the barn. Benny tensed up when he heard it. He told me to stay here and headed for the barn. He said something about he had company."

Benny came walking back from the barn leading a team. "Did you have company in the barn?" Ben asked as Benny walked up.

Benny nodded, "My brother is here. He has brought my son to live with me. You will meet them both later after we get to your place. My brother says the three down by the forks are packing up. So the lost man found his way back from the hot springs."

Kate looked at Benny, "Your brother is here? He brought your son? Benny you never told me you had a family. Where's your wife?"

Benny looked at Ben, "Too many questions. I'll hook up the wagon while you go get your horses. I'll leave my horse here so I can bring the wagon back."

Kate stood staring after Benny as he led the team toward the wagon. Ben glanced over at her as he followed Benny. A grin appeared when he saw the look on her face. Kate turned and walked back inside.

Benny helped Ben load Alice's luggage. Then Kate motioned toward the counter in the trading post, "Those supplies on the counter go too. The pantry up at the cabin is getting a little bare."

As they left Ben was driving the team with Kate and Alice on the seat with him. Benny brought up the rear. He was riding Ben's horse and leading Kate's. Ben motioned to different places as they drove along. When they got to where you could see the upper end of the valley and the roofs of the big barns, Ben stopped the team. "Well Alice those high peaks just above those barn roofs up ahead will be your new home. Jacob lives in that mountain."

Alice sat staring at the snow covered peaks, "He lives in that mountain with all the snow?"

Ben smiled as he looked at him, "His home isn't up that high. When we get closer you'll be able to see opening in the cliffs right above the barns. Those openings are sealed up now, but that is where the miner dumped their ore down into the mill before the avalanche came down cover the settlement. When that happened it ripped the scaffolding from the mountain. Jacob has sealed those opening to keep out the cold winds. You'll find his home in the mountain warm and big. I guess I should explain why I was there. Jacob saved my life along with

94

my leg which was badly mangled when I was caught in a rock slide. I spent almost a whole summer there."

Alice looked at Kate then back at Ben, "How did he save your life, he isn't a doctor?"

Ben smiled, "Maybe not according to the law, but he's probably better than most men that practice medicine in this country." Ben lifted the lines and the team moved on. Benny was riding along side and Ben glanced over at him. Benny's eyes moved over toward the draw on the left of the road, then back at Ben.

Ben stopped the team again, he looked over at Alice, "Why do you have three men shadowing you? I'm not going to send word to Jacob until they are gone." Alice just sat there staring at him. Ben went on, "By gone, I mean plumb out of the country."

"How did you know they were with me? Alice asked as she stared at Ben.

"When they camped down by the forks and kept one man watching the trading post. Then one of them tried to follow Benny when he rode up to get me and Kate." He smiled as he nodded over toward Benny, "If they are going to track people in this country they need some lessons, especially if they try following an Indian."

Alice just sat there for a moment, "I was told when I got ready to leave that the family was sending someone to make sure I made it here. I have never talked to them, but I did notice them watching me every time we stopped during my stagecoach ride here. I rode the train part of the way here. I never noticed them then. It was only after I started riding the stagecoaches."

Ben looked over at Benny, "You got any ideas how we can talk to them?"

Benny nodded, "I will have my brother stop them." He handed Ben the reins to Kate's horse. He lopped off up the valley then disappeared off into draw on the opposite side of the road from where the three men were riding. About ten minutes, he rode back toward them.

"Why don't you have Kate take the wagon on to the, cabin? You and I can go talk to our visitors," he swung down and handed Ben the reins to his horse.

Ben looked over at Kate, then over at Alice, "I hope you've told us the truth about these fellas." He turned to Kate, "We'll be fine. I just want these riders to head for home before I send for Jacob."

Kate nodded, "You and Benny be careful." She took the lines and put the team in motion. As they drove away Ben looked over at Benny, "You sure your brother can stop those three?"

Benny tightened the cinch on Kate's saddle then swung up on her horse. He headed off to the left, with Ben following.

Ben first saw three Indians sitting their horses with rifles across their laps. Then he saw the three men with the flat toped hats sitting on the ground. As they got closer, two more Indians stood behind the men. All five Indians were dressed in white man's pants stuffed into high topped moccasins. All five wore beaded vests with no shirts. Their hats were what looked to have been cavalry issue hats at one time, with a few Indian changes.

Benny swung down. One of the Indians standing behind the three men stepped over to him. Benny looked over at Ben, "This is my brother, Charlie. His Indian name is Two Blood."

Benny motioned toward Ben, "Charlie this is my friend, Ben. He is the husband of Kate who owns the trading post."

Ben swung down, he offered his hand. "It's good to meet you Charlie."

Charlie just nodded then turned to Benny, then spoke on some language Ben didn't understand. Benny looked at Ben, "He asks what you want to do with these three?"

Ben walked over to the three men staring up at him, "Why are you following the girl?"

The older looking of the three, slowly stood up, "What the hell business is it of yours. Besides who says were following anyone?"

Benny had walked up alongside Ben, "Maybe we should just let Charlie and his friends take them when they ride back home. They could drop them over a cliff somewhere along the route."

Ben looked over at Benny, who expression was as always, showing no emotion. His eyes never left Ben. Finally Ben looked back at the man standing before him, "Well I guess that's up to these three. You can tell me now why you're trailing the girl or I guess I'll let Two Blood take you away with him."

The man standing looked at his two friends still sitting on the ground. Then he turned back to Ben, "We were hired to make sure Miss Chapman made it here. We were told this man she's is to wed would pay us in gold for her safe arrival."

Ben smiled, "What makes you think that the man she came to marry has gold? He is just a poor religious nut who lives in a mountain. He has a hard time scrapping together enough gold just to buy what food he needs." Ben said as he watched the expression on the man's face.

The man again glanced at his two partners, then, back to Ben, "He has taken over the mine of the family who mined it before the avalanche wiped them out. We know he has gold, we have seen statues made by him of solid gold."

Ben laughed, "Well friend you seem to know something I don't about that mine. If it was so rich with gold how come none of the survivors never came back to claim it? I now claim and live at the base camp they built. No one from what you call the family has ever even came back to claim anything, let alone the mine you seem to think is so rich with gold. No my friend, you need to come up with a better story or your trip home will be short."

"Just take us to your man living in the mountain. We'll make him tell us of the gold. We have brought his new wife to him and we want our pay," the man yelled at Ben.

Ben looked back at Benny, "Maybe we should bring the girl back to question her about, who, these three really are."

Benny nodded, "Maybe Two Blood and his friends can find a way to make these men talk."

Ben turned back to face the man standing, "I have one other idea, we could take you back to Garnet and lock you up in the cellar they used for a jail when that was a booming town. Then we can send for the sheriff in Springfield to come and get you."

"Hell mister you're all talk. You can't hold us," one of the men on the ground yelled out.

Benny motioned for Ben to follow him away from the men. Once out of range for anyone to hear Benny stopped. With his back to the group he said, "Do you think the girl knows these men?"

Ben shook his head, "Benny, I got a strange feeling she does. You know what Meg said about her and April kinda agreed he wasn't who she was supposed to be. What do you have in mind? I can tell you are thinking about something."

"You know that new gate you built would make a fine place for a hanging. We could ride on up there and string them up or act like were going to and see what the girl says or does."

Ben smiled, then nodded he agreed, "I knew you had an idea in that head of yours."

Benny spoke to his brother again in the same language. He turned and whistled. A rider appeared out of a draw nearby leading four horses, two were saddles, the others, with just packs. The rider was young, maybe in his early teens, dressed like the others.

Benny looked over at Ben, "My son, Thomas. His Indian name is, 'One who walks two trails."

Ben swung down at the cabin, Kate and Alice stepped out. Benny started to lead the other riders to the corral, when Ben called to him. Ben walked out to meet him as he swung is horse toward Ben. "Benny, I've been thinking, Jacob I know is watching all of this. Let's change our hanging to one of the big beams inside the horse barn? I just as soon not let him watch what we're planning."

Benny looked up at the mountain, then, back at Ben, "You are right. I will let you know when we're ready for you to bring the girl," he turned his horse and motioned for the others to follow.

Kate stood there on the porch looking at him, he eyes drifted to the young rider, "Is that Benny's son?"

Ben nodded, "His white man's name is Thomas. His Indian name is something like, 'One who walks two trails,' or something like that."

Ben looked over at Alice who had moved to the far end of the porch where she could see the barns. Benny and the others had disappeared inside. Ben smiled, 'Maybe this will work,' he said under his breath.

Benny motioned from the barn, Ben turned the two women, "Come on with me, I got something you need to see." He took a hold of Kate's arm as she looked up at him, he, winked. He quickly looked away before Kate could say anything. He looked over at Alice, "All of these building were all built by your people before the avalanche whipped out the settlement. Of course you probably already know this from the way they are built." If Alice was really from the family she would be like Ada and recognized the craftsmanship. So far she didn't act like she even understood what he had just said.

At the barn as they walked in he heard both women gasp at the sight of three men with ropes around their necks. The horses that were on were standing under beam with the ropes draped over and tied. Only Ben, and Benny were in the barn, Charlie and the others were nowhere to be seen.

Ben walked over to the older man, "Okay friend, why are you following the girl?"

The man's eyes glared at Ben, "Go to hell. You can't hang us for protecting her on her trip here. I want to talk to the man she came here to marry, I know he will pay us for bringing her safely here."

Ben looked over at Benny who had a quirt in his hand as he walked toward the horses. Kate grabbed Ben's arm, "Ben, you can't just hang these men."

Ben looked over at Alice. Her face was white as she stared at the three men. As she turned toward Ben a voice came from the back of the barn. "This woman isn't Alice Chapman or one of the, family. I know the real Alice Chapman." Ada stepped from the shadows in the back of the barn.

All three men sitting the horses began struggling trying to get their hands loose. You could see the fear in their eye when they saw Ada. She walked over to look up at the older man struggling to free himself from the ropes on his wrists. The man stopped struggling as he looked down at the little lady dressed in black. Ada walked over next to Ben, "That one is Horace Spalding and the other two are his cousins. They were kicked out of the family many years ago. Horace was whipped by the elders for beating his wife before they chased him off." She turned to girl who was claiming to be Alice Chapman, "Where is Alice?"

She slowly walked up to stare right into the eyes of the girl, who started to tremble as she stepped back. Ada moved to stay close to her, then the girl back bumped the wall of the barn, she threw up her arms to cover her face. The older man still struggling with his bonds yelled, "Keep your mouth, shut, or I'll kill you." His voice suddenly went to a whisper, when Ben looked over at him the rope around his neck was tight. Benny was standing next to the post under the beam where the three ropes were anchored. He had one rope in his hand. He had pulled all the slack from that rope, the man Ada called Horace was standing in his stirrups to keep from choking.

Ben looked back to where Ada stood before the girl, who now was crying. "I don't know what happened to the real Alice Chapman. Horace offered me five- hundred dollars to come here in her place."

Horace was trying to yell but Benny was keeping to much tension on the rope around his neck. Ada stepped back next to Ben, "This is a family problem. They should be the ones to deal with Horace and his cousins."

Kate had walked over to grasp Ben's arm, he squeezed her hand, then, looked back at Ada, "How close is the nearest settlement?"

Ada smiled, "We don't need to get them to a settlement. The family has many members who live among you. You have two who are a less than a day's ride from here." She looked over at Benny, who just nodded.

Ada motioned back to the girl, "She isn't a family problem, so I will leave it up to you about what happens to her. I will talk to Jacob, if he wishes to seek another wife."

Benny walked up next to Ben, "I will leave with these three to-night. Charlie has taken the others to camp in the canyons of the hot water for a few days. When, I return I will bring Thomas to live with me."

"How did Ada know that you knew members of the family?" Ada has taken the girl off to one side and was talking to her in a low voice. Kate was still standing by Ben.

Benny shrugged, "Who knows, maybe I'm one of them."

Kate looked up at Ben, then over at Benny, "If Ada hadn't shown up, would you have hung those three?"

Ben smiled, "I guess we'll never know."

Kate punched him in the side, "Well don't ever do that again without letting me know, Okay?"

As late afternoon was setting in Kate started supper for the four people left at the cabin. Ada was waiting for darkness before heading back to the mountain. Ada had gotten the girl to tell her real name, it was Hattie Gatfield. She had been working in a boarding house Colorado when she met Horace Spalding. He had been living off and on at the boarding house in the small mining town south of Denver. Ada told Ben she believed her when she said she had no idea what happened to the real Alice Chapman.

Kate called them all to supper. Hattie sat real quiet as she picked at her food. Finally she looked up at Ben, "What are you going to do with me?"

Ben looked over at Kate, "Oh I will take you back to Garnet as soon as Benny gets back from his little trip. From there we'll buy you a stage ticket to someplace you pick. I don't like the way you tried to work your way into Jacob's life. He doesn't deserve being taken by someone like you." He stopped then grinned, "Really I don't think if you had fooled us you'd ever got past that little lady sitting next to you. For your sake, it's lucky we stopped you here. If you'd got past us I don't think any of you would have ever made it alive to see Jacob."

Hattie eyes searched Ben face, she, looked at Kate who slowly nodded her head she agreed. Hattie looked at Ada sitting next to her. You could see Hattie's shoulders tremble as she looked down at the food still on her plate.

Ben walked out with Ada as she headed for the barn. "What are you going to tell Jacob about all of this?"

Ada stopped to look up at Ben who almost towered over her. "I will just tell him what happened. He will then decide if he still wants a wife from the family to mother his children. Our life will go on no matter what he decides."

Inside the barn Ada started making up a backpack of supplies from the cache in the store room. As the pack got bigger Ben looked over at the little lady dressed in black, "Ada you can't carry a pack that big."

As Ada turned toward Ben a familiar voice came from the back of the barn, "I will carry that pack for her."

As Ben turned Jacob walked up offering his hand, "You have been busy today my friend."

Ben grasped his friend's hand, "Yes, we had a few who tried to cheat their way into your home. Even before Ada here confirmed my suspicions about the girl, I had decided not to signal you to come down. When she didn't recognize any of the work done here by the family, then I knew she was with the three who were shadowing her. We faked the hanging to get her to tell us the truth about the men. Ada doesn't think this girl ever knew what happened to the real Alice Spalding and I agree. I will take her back to Garnet buy her a stage ticket out of this country."

Jacob looked at his partner, "The three men, the family will make sure they never talk. The girl might not have had, a main part in the scheme to get into the mountain, but she still knows of me and the gold. I think we should take her with us tonight."

Ada nodded, "I think as you do, Jacob. We shouldn't rely on her never speaking of this in her travels."

Ben looked from one friend to the other one, but he didn't say anything. "I will go get her ready to travel," Ada turned and walked out.

Jacob sat down on the bench looking at Ben. "I since you don't agree with our discussion to take the girl into the mountain, my friend?"

Ben shook his head no, "Jacob I don't disagree with you. I think as you do about her telling of this and it getting to the wrong people. When I first thought of putting her on a stagecoach and sending her away, these same thoughts were going through my mind."

Jacob eyes searched out Ben there standing in the dark. "I have Ada to protect me as I work in my shop. Outside the mountain, I have you also protecting me. Coming back to this mountain and meeting you has changed my life. Then with Ada coming into my life, I have the peace I never thought to be possible. If too many show up looking to find me or what is inside the mountain, Ada and I will move on to keep what we have together."

Jacob stood up as Ada and Hattie walked into the barn. Ada motioned to Jacob, "This is Jacob." Ada looked at Jacob, "This is Hattie Gatfield."

Jacob stepped forward and reached for her hand, "You will come with us to my home. You'll be safe with us."

Ben watched as Jacob shouldered the big pack, the three disappeared into the back of the barn. Kate stood on the porch in the darkness watching Ben as he walked up from the barn. "What will they do with her?"

Ben gave her a big hug, then, walked with her into the cabin. "I don't know for sure, but knowing Jacob she will live. Maybe he can't change her way a life and she can learn to live in his world. Who knows?" He sighed, "These, last couple of days are like, we been living in a dream."

The next morning Ben hitched up the team, tied both saddle horses behind the wagon. He pulled the wagon up to the cabin. Kate walked out of the cabin carrying a small pack. She put it under the seat. Ben looked over at her and grinned, "How about we load up our freight we got stashed under the cabin? We need to get these packages moving for Jacob. We can put them in my cabin until we ship them." Half hour later Ben pulled a tarp over the load.

It was a cool clear morning as they drove a long, Kate looked back at the towering peaks behind them, then put her head on Ben's shoulder. "Do you think there will be more people showing up, looking for Jacob?"

Ben nodded, "I hope not, but I think too many people have heard about the mine in those peaks. Even with the family not trying to move back here, there's bound to be stories told by the survivors. It's like those three Benny took away, at one time they had been connected to the family. Then greed took over, they forgot their religion for gold. You know just like I do stories grow each time they are told especially when money or gold is involved." He shook his head, "I think Jacob days in that mountain are numbered. I just hope Ada is good enough to keep them alive."

Kate nodded as they moved along, "Ada is so small, she moves like a cat stalking, its prey. Her eyes never miss anything. When she came to get Hattie, her voice was so gentle. Hattie seemed to trust her. She went along without saying a word. Ben, why would a father, teach his daughter to be gun fighter?"

102

Ben looked over at his wife staring at him, he shrugged, "Kate I can't really answer that. The way it worked out, she needed that training to survive getting here. Another thought is, maybe that was the only thing he had to offer her. With his wife and other daughter were so against what he stood for, he just wanted this daughter to be able to take care of herself in life." He put his free hand on hers, "For whatever reason, he did a good job."

They stopped behind his cabin and unloaded, Jacobs packages before going down to the trading post store. Kate headed for the store while Ben put the horses in the back pasture. As he looked over town he saw two riders approaching town from the east. As he watched he grinned, one of the riders was Benny. Coming from that direction Benny had been to canyon of the hot springs. Ben waited until they rode up. Benny motioned to Thomas, "I'm going to take Thomas up to my place so he can get moved in. Then we'll come down to the trading post so Thomas can get acquainted.

The girls all came over from the saloon to meet Thomas. He was very quiet as the girls made over him. Kate notice that his eyes followed ever movement they made while helping her get lunch on the table. Kate was almost sure this was the first time he'd ever been around woman like April and her two helpers. She could also see Benny was also watching his son. From the look in his eyes, she was sure he was amused by his son actions.

Later outside Benny sent Thomas off to do some work in the barn. As soon as he was gone Benny turned to Ben, "I need to find him a job to keep him busy. His mother has done a good job of seeing to his formal education, now I need to teach him how to live in the white man's world. Maybe you could take him up with you to cabin. You said you needed help and he's good and strong. You will have to teach him that type of work."

Ben smiled, "You need to spend time with him too, you know. I'll be glad to have him along and I know Kate will be all in favor. She doesn't like me being up there alone," he chuckled. "I guess she still thinks I'll get myself buried in another rock slide."

The rest of the afternoon Ben spent loading supplies he needed to work with up on the place. Thomas was helping him. The boy was quiet, but easy for Ben to be around. He spoke good, English, you could tell he'd had a lot of schooling. Ben had a list Kate she had made up of things he'd mentioned he needed while they were up at the cabin. Thomas had no problem reading it. When he added a few items Ben mentioned his writing was very good.

The sun was just clearing the peaks as Thomas led the team down from the barn. Benny helped him hook them up to the wagon. Kate opened the door to let them know breakfast was on. Inside Ben was working at the counter on a tool belt for Thomas to use. "Try this on, Partner," Ben said as he handed it to Thomas. He marked where he needed to punch a hole for the buckle to hook.

On the way up the road Ben handed the reins to Thomas, "Here, you need to practice driving a team."

Thomas grinned as he took the reins, Ben smiled. "I know you can handle a team real well, I'm just being lazy. Besides you're a lot younger."

It was late afternoon by the time they got all the supplies put away. Thomas walked around the big barn looking all around, "I've never seen a barn this big. How did they lift all those big timbers up there?" As he, pointed to the big beams above them.

Ben just shook his head, "Those people were and are true crafts-men. All the work they do is almost perfect. I've always wondered why they didn't come back here and claim all of this after the avalanche. Kate and I are lucky to have this."

As Ben lite the fire for cooking supper Thomas started getting out tools to cook with. He looked over at Ben, "I too can cook white man's food. Benny said before we left that you were a bachelor type cook, whatever than means."

Ben looked over at him and laughed. Ben noticed Thomas always call Benny by name never dad or father. Maybe as they worked together Ben would find out more about Thomas life before coming here.

Thomas turned out to be great helper. He and Ben made a good team. They finished one fence Ben wanted. Then, started fencing what Ben called his hay field. As they drove the wagon back toward the cabin one night they saw strange horses in the corral as they neared the buildings. Then Jess Garrett stepped out of the cabin to wave at them. As they pulled up Ben laughed, "By God, it must be getting close to July 4th for you to be here." He swung down to shake his old friend's hand, "Good to see you Jess." He motioned toward Thomas, "Jess I'd like you to meet Thomas, he's Benny son who has moved here to live with his father. Thomas, this is Jess Garrett. He lives in Garnet every winter, during the summer, he mines for gold."

Jesse reached out to shake with Thomas, "Hell I didn't know Benny had any kids. Good to know you, Thomas."

"I figured you were working close by so I started supper. I need to add one more plate I didn't know you had a helper. By the time you fellas get those horses put away I'll have her on the table."

Ben thought he smelled fish frying when he walked up to the cabin. As he sat down at the table Jess placed a plate of fried trout before them. Jess grinned, "I stopped up there at Loon Lake and dropped my line in the water on my way down. Damn they were biting, good. So I decided to bring down a mess for supper."

Jess and Ben both laughed as Thomas cleaned up every bowl on the table onto his plate. He grinned when he looked up and saw the two men looking at him, "Mister Garrett you are a great cook. These trout are good. I will do the dishes as soon as I finish eating."

Jess nodded, "By God boy, you got a deal."

Both men walked out on the porch to smoke while Thomas worked in the cabin. Ben looked over at Jess, "Well how was spring cleanup?"

Jess nodded as he looked at Ben, "Damn good. In fact it was one of my better spring clean ups." He looked down at the floor then back up at Ben, "You know what we talked about this spring when I left? Well I sold my claim and loaded my gear. I'm no longer a miner. As soon as I get to Garnet I'm going to see if Meg will go down to Springfield with me so we can get married. If that happens then I'm going to take Kate up on the deal at the trading post."

Ben laughed then offered his hand, "Jess, I wish you the best on this. I'm sure Meg will be all in favor of being Mrs. Garrett. You two will make a fine couple. If you like Jess, we can load your gear on the wagon and you can leave your spare horses up here, I got lots of extra pasture."

Jess the next morning with Thomas help unpacked his gear and loaded it onto the wagon. They put all the pack gear in the barn and hung it up. Later Thomas took the extra horses down to the big pasture and turned them loose. It was noon when they hooked up the team and headed for town. Ben drove the wagon with Jess sitting beside him, Thomas followed along behind with Jess's horse.

As they moved along Jess motioned to a peak off to the south. "You know, Ben, I think you got somebody watching this area. I noticed as I came over the pass a faint smoke coming from the tree line of that peak. Then while I was fishing in Loon Lake I caught another glimpse of smoke up there. I've prospected up there and that's rough country. I didn't find any mineral worth mining on that whole peak. So unless I really missed finding something, whoever up there, is not mining for gold. I also noticed a couple of places along the pass coming over where someone has camped. They weren't in the usual camping areas along that trail. You know you usually camp where you got water and feed for the stock. These camps were dry camps, no feed or water but with a view of the valley here."

Ben shrugged, "I guess maybe we need to keep our eyes open for nosy people." He thought for a spell, "Jess, you must know about Jacob living in that mountain? Well after you left this spring a girl showed up, she was supposed to be a girl from the family Jacob had sent for. Well Benny spotted three men following her and keeping an eye on the trading post. When he came up to get me at the cabin he spotted one of the men following him, you know Benny's Indian blood kicked in. He led the guy off into those hot spring canyons then lost him before coming on to the cabin. To make the story shorter we found out the girl was a fake and then rounded up the three following her. It ended up they were going to use her to get the gold they thought Jacob had. They had found out about a girl coming to live with Jacob. Somehow they done away with her and paid this other girl to pose as her. It didn't take us long to find out she hadn't been raised by the family, so we knew something was up."

Jess smiled, "Hell, I missed all the fun, what did you do with her and the three men who was with her?"

Benny took the men to some people connected to the family who live around here. All three at one time were members of the family, so it was decided they should handle it. The girl, Jacob took her into the mountain with him. What he does with her is up to him. I know for sure he won't kill her."

Jess just shook his head, "So you think more of these people will be showing up thinking this Jacob has gold in the mountain, does he?"

Ben looked over at the man next to him, "Yes, those miner, who were working there when the settlement was wiped out were doing well. I have never figured out why they never came back to the mine. I was going to ask Jacob one time about it, then, I decided it was none of my business. You know I often wondered if maybe it has something to do with them thinking the mountain has a curse on it. I don't know whether that religion believes in such things."

"You know you could be right about someone snooping around. If those other men knew about the gold, it could be there'll be a lot more showing up. Can people find their way into that mountain without that Jacob fellow knowing their there?"

"It's possible, but Jacob has blocked the entrances the miners used. So it is unlikely people can find the other passages. I know of few of them from spending that time in there while my leg healed. I really only know one way for sure."

Jess looked over at Ben, "What happened to that girl that showed up last winter, you took her up to the cabin to meet him?"

Ben smiled, "Ada, she's still there. She's his body guard."

Ben chuckled when he saw the look on Jess's face, "It's, long story Jess, I'll tell you more about it sometime when we got a lot of time. I will say I think anyone trying to sneak in there will meet a very deadly little hell cat in a fight."

They were just coming into town about then, "Jess, how about we go to the store first, then later you and Thomas can go up to your cabin to unload your gear?"

"That sounds good to me, Ben. I kinda like Meg to know I'm back in town for good."

As they stopped out front Kate stepped out onto the porch, "I see you found a wondering miner, Ben." She stepped to the wagon as Jess stepped down and gave him a big hug. "There's a gal over there that's been watching the road every day for you to appear."

About then the door of the saloon opened. Meg came hurrying toward them. She grabbed Jess and pulled him close then kissed him. It's about time you showed up. The 4th is only three days away."

Jess held on to her, "Meg, I sold the mine. How about I stow my gear up at the house, then you and me can catch the afternoon stage for Springfield and get married?"

Kate started laughing, "Jess, you been the brush too long. I'll bet you could wait until morning to catch the stage and still get married."

Meg looked over at Kate, then back up at Jess who was still holding her, "You go get your gear stowed, when you get back, I'll be ready. The stage is due in about an hour, so hurry." She kissed his cheek and hurried off toward the saloon.

Ben smiled as he looked over at Kate, "I better go along to make sure our bride groom doesn't miss the stage. Come on Thomas, you can help me get him unloaded." He climbed back up on the wagon seat as Jess climbed up on the other side.

Benny looked over at Kate, "Maybe I should go along to hurry them up. Or at least I can take care of the horses and put the wagon back in the yard." He hurried off toward where Jess's house was behind the blacksmith shop a block away.

Kate was left standing on the porch as April and Charlotte walked up. April grinned as she looked at Kate, "If we got all this right, Meg and Jess are heading for Springfield to get married? I didn't even know Jess was in from the mine."

Kate nodded. "That's a whirlwind engagement." Jess spent the night with Ben and Thomas up at the cabin and rode in with them. He just swung down from the wagon and asked Meg if she wanted to catch the stage for Springfield to get married. Now you know as much as I do."

April and Charlotte both laughed, "She came though the saloon and up the stairs at almost a run shouting something about Jess and marriage. It looks like Charlotte and me going to have to find a new partner for the saloon."

Meg, in her best dress, Jess, in his best dress up clothes stepped aboard the stage. Jess looked from the stage window, "We'll see you for the big 4th celebration."

Kate called out, "What no honeymoon?" The stage jerked into motion and was gone before Jess or Meg could answer.

That evening Clayton and Henry rode in from their mines. That evening the saloon was in full swing. Ben, Kate, Thomas sat with Benny as they joined into the gay time. A couple of other miners that neighbored Henry's claim had, rode in with him to celebrate the holiday. Many stories were swapped as the evening wore on. Benny and Thomas left first, leaving Ben and Kate to party with the miners.

The day before the big celebration Jess and Meg stepped down from the morning stage. Jess then helped another lady with her luggage as she stepped from the stage. Kate walked out to greet the newlyweds, "Well look at you two, new duds and everything."

Meg swung around so Kate could see all of her new dress. "This new husband of mine is already spoiling me, with new clothes, new furniture, for the, house. You know, I think I'll keep him."

She turned to the lady Jess had helped down from the stage, "Kate I'd like you to meet Elsie Roberts. Elsie, been working down at the Wild Horse saloon, in Springfield for the last couple of years. When she found out I was got married she asked if she could work up here for April. So I brought her along to talk to April about taking my place."

Kate stepped forward to offer her hand, "Welcome to Garnet, Elsie. I'm sure April will be glad to see you." She laughed, "You may have to wait for a while or at least until after noon to talk to her. I think

108

her and Charlotte had a busy night with all the miners in for the 4th. Henry brought a couple of his neighbors in with him. I also saw a few strangers in the crowd last night."

Elsie laughed, "I needed a change from the rat race at the Wild Horse. Pay was terrible, the condition were even worse. A new owner from back east just bought the place. His idea of a saloon is a lot different from what this country is used to. I don't think he's going to last long, before someone catches him in a dark alley. He skims cream off the top of the gaming tables, bar and girls, before handing out your share. Even if I don't get, a job here, I'm not going back down there."

"Well, Elsie why don't we put your luggage in the store, you and me can get acquainted while you wait to see April," Kate said as she picked up one of the suitcases.

Jess picked up all the packages he could carry just as Benny came around the corner with a team and buggy. Benny jumped down to help Jess load everything in the back of the buggy. Benny looked over at Kate, "This was all her idea, she said I should make sure the new bride and groom didn't have to walk to their new home. Jess you drive, I will walk across the back lot to help you unload. Then I'll bring the buggy back." Meg hugged him as he reached to help her up into the seat.

Ben and Thomas were over in the blacksmith shop sharping their tools from the cabin. Kate had Benny busy getting everything ready for the big day tomorrow. She told him at breakfast to hook up the buggy incase Jess and Meg were on the stage. So when he heard the stage coming up the road he watched to see if they were aboard. So when he appeared Kate was all smiles.

Ben had the back door of the blacksmith shop open and saw Benny walking across the back yard. "Where you headed, Benny? I thought Kate wanted you to hook up the buggy in case Jess and Meg got back."

Benny nodded his head toward the street where the buggy was just coming into view. "They got so many packages there wasn't room for me in the buggy, so I have to walk."

Ben laughed as he looked back at Thomas, "Come on partner we'll go help the newlyweds unload."

With everything in the house, Benny headed back for the barn while Ben and Thomas went back to work in the blacksmith shop. At noon they walked over to trading post for lunch. Kate introduced them to Elsie. "As soon as April gets up I'll take her over to meet April."

Ben looked up at her as he sat down at the table, "I think she might be awake now. I heard movement in the saloon as we walked by.

It sounded like chairs being moved, like someone is cleaning up in there."

Kate sat two plates down in front of Ben and Thomas, "When Benny comes in tell him to serve himself, while I take Elsie over to meet April."

Ben was pouring a fresh cup of coffee as Kate walked back in grinning. "Boy was that easy. I thought April and Charlotte was going to kiss us both when I introduced Elsie. When I walked out Elsie had already jumped right in to help clean the place up from last night."

Kate filled a plate and sat down across from Ben. "I told the girls lunch was on so they should be showing up. By the way Ben, that friend of Henry's, Rocky Bingman was in a while ago. He said he needed to talk to you about maybe running the blacksmith shop. He's been having leg trouble up at his mine. He said he broke it a couple of years ago, now when it's cold or gets wet it bothers him. He was wondering if he could make enough here in the shop to put grub on the table."

Ben looked up, "Hell Kate, that shop don't really belong to anyone. When everyone left, that fella who ran it just moved on leaving everything behind. As far as I'm concerned he could just move in anytime. I suppose he should go down to Springfield and check on the taxes. If he paid the back taxes then he could claim the place. You and Dan knew the original owner, what do you think?"

She nodded, "His name was Culver, if I remember right. He said when he left he was heading back to Missouri to see his family. He just never came back. Is there enough work to keep a man busy?"

Ben looked over at her, "I think so. You know all of us been using the shop to fix anything we need. I know the miner would pay to have drill steel sharpened and tools fixed. The stagecoach is always in need of a horseshoed or something fixed on the stage itself. It might be slow at first but I think a man could make a living and not starve. If Rocky comes over I'll tell him what I think about it."

That evening a big wagon was coming up the road to the trading post, Tyler Bates could be seen on the high seat. As it got closer more heads began to appear in the back. "Howdy, folks, me and the family decided to join you folks for the 4th. Where would be a good place for us to camp close by? We brought everything to camp out."

Ben stepped out to the wagon, "Good to see you Tyler. Sure we got room for you folks, just follow me. I'll take you up to a lot next to my cabin. I got a good well so you can get water real easy."

110

As the wagon moved off, Rachel appeared waving out the back at Kate. "Hi, Kate, I'll be down to see you as soon as we get camp set up."

Kate laughed and waved, "Good to see you Rachel." Kate was thinking back to the night Rachel and her dad spent with them. Rachel was fascinated by April dress and the girls from the saloon bright clothing. She sneaked a peek into saloon that night. Later she asked Kate questions about what the girls did in the, saloon. Kate had trouble answering her on this.

Garnet was a roaring place the day of the fourth. Even a few people came up from Springfield to join in. Coby Kline and his crew from the ranch on the river showed up. The morning, of the 5th things was, real quiet. The first movement was Tyler big wagon stopping out front of the trading post. Ben walked out, "You ready to load those supplies you bought, Tyler?"

The big man laughed, "I was hoping you were open this early. I sent Rachel down to make sure before I drove down. Boy things are sure quiet compared to yesterday. You folks really know how to celebrate. The Mrs., here already said she wants to come back next year. I think Rachel got her eye on one of those cowboys from down on the river," then he laughed when Rachel called out from behind him.

Kate walked out to say goodbye to the Bates family, she carried a package under her arm. Rachel had climbed down from the wagon while the supplies were being loaded. She walked over to Kate, who handed her the package, "Don't open this until you get home. It's from all of us," she leaned closer and whispered, "That includes April and her girls. I saw you sneaking a look in the back door last night, don't worry that's our little secret."

Rachel giggled as she leaned over to kiss Kate on the cheek, "Thank you." She hurried back to climb back up into the wagon. With a wave the Bates family was headed for home.

Most of the miners spent the day, loading up on the supplies they need to last them until the snow chased them from their claims. Jess spent the day with Kate watching how she handled the many orders. Meg came in later to help with the orders. Ben and Thomas loaded their wagon, then right after lunch headed back for the cabin. Kate and Benny had decided she would stay to help Jess until he felt he could handle the business. He and Meg had leased the trading post for six months, to see if they like the life. Kate said as soon as they felt comfortable with the store she would move her personal gear up to Bens cabin. Then she would ride up to join Ben and Thomas.

111

Benny had told Jess he would stay around to help like he did for Kate as long as they needed him. In the meantime Thomas would keep working for Ben. Ben and Thomas topped the small ridge to look down on the cabin and the big barn, Ben stopped the team. On the creek below the main corrals stood two, teepees. Ben could see extra horses in the pasture. He looked over at Thomas, who nodded toward the teepees, "Uncle Charlie is here."

Ben flipped the reins and the team moved on down the road. As they neared the cabin saw Charlie sitting on the porch. When Ben stopped Charlie stood up, "I rode to town two days ago to see you. Everyone was partying so I rode back here. I figured you'd be back before long."

Ben dropped down from the seat, "Good to see you Charlie. Did you come all this way alone?"

Charlie shook his head no, "I brought my wife and my two kids. They fear you will make us leave, so they hide. She has never seen mountains so high, she thinks that spirits are living in those peaks."

"What brings you back to this country, Charlie? I figured once you got Thomas here delivered to his dad you'd long for that warmer climate."

Charlie motioned to the mountains all the way around them, "When we got back, all I could think about was getting back to this. In my heart the desert was no longer my home. I could see why Benny never came back to his people."

Ben laughed, "Well Charlie you're sure welcome to stay. If you'd like a better place to live than down in the pasture, I know of such a place you might like. When we get the wagon unloaded, I'll saddle a horse and take you on a tour of places you might like to build your home."

When they stopped by the teepee Charlie brought out his wife to meet him. Ben almost stared as a very small attractive girl looked up at him. He could tell she wasn't Indian, but instead Spanish. Her eyes never left him, as Charlie led her closer, "This is my wife, Rosa." Two small kids had followed them out of the teepee. The boy was maybe, ten or twelve and a younger girl. The boy showed his Indian blood, but the girl looked like her mother. Charlie spoke to them in Spanish, then, turned to Ben," This is my son Pedro and my daughter Maria."

Rosa stepped forward, "It is good to meet you Senior Jasper," she said in broken English.

Ben smiled, "It's good to meet you Rosa, please call me Ben. I know my wife Kate will be glad to have neighbors when she gets moved up here." He looked over at Maria, then back at Rosa, "I know one thing she'll probably try to steal that daughter of your or at least spoil her." Rosa smiled as she moved back close to Charlie, Ben could tell she understood English, but that she was also was very shy.

Later they sat their horses looking down at the widening valley below where the settlement had been. The grass was green with a creek lazily winding its way down the valley. Many small beaver ponds were visible throughout the valley floor. Ben looked over at Charlie who was just staring at the view below them. "I can live here without being run off by white men?"

When Kate and I files on the building we also files on this valley. I need to get something built over here to keep the claim valid. If you build a cabin, I will say you are building it for me as a line cabin once we bring in some stock. Then you and your family can live here without being run off by someone else wanting this valley."

They rode a little higher up the ridge before Ben stopped again, he pointed to the wreckage of the settlement. "We can get much of the material you need to start building from up there. That is what's left of the religious settlement after the avalanche can down to cover it up. I think with work we can get a wagon up from the valley to the settlement. It would be easier to haul the timbers rather than packing them on horses."

When they rode back toward the cabin Ben looked over at Thomas, "If Charlie needs help moving his family to the valley you can help them. I got plenty of things to do I can handle alone." As he started to ride on he stopped again, "If a wagon would help to move them, go ahead and use one."

Ben glanced down toward the pasture later as he worked below the cabin. The teepee was down and a wagon was slowly moving over the small ridge. Ben grinned as he turned back to his work, 'Having company close by would be nice. With Charlie and his family up in the valley Ada and Jacob could still come down without being seen.'

Ben was cooking supper for himself. Thomas had said he would spend the night up with his uncle. Darkness was making the barns hard to see as Ben sat smoking his pipe on the front porch. He was thinking about Kate being up here with him full time. This would be their first time all alone with only each other to worry about. With Jess running the trading post and April the saloon, Kate's big worry's, would be over. They had talked of adding on to the cabin, but it was plenty big enough as it was really for the two of them. They had quit talking about that lately.

Ben stopped breathing, a small crunching noise came from behind him, "You are very alert," came Ada's voice from behind him.

Ben chuckled, "You stepped on that rock on purpose, my cunning friend. Ada, you scare me the way you travel in the dark. Most people can't move that quiet in the light let alone in the dark."

She touched his shoulder, "Is the coffee still hot?" as she moved off into the cabin. She stepped back out to sit on the railing next to him. "You make good coffee."

"What brings you out of the mountain?" Ben asked.

"Jacob wanted me to talk to you. Did you know many people are watching the mountain and your place here? We've been watching them for a couple of weeks, there seems to be five all together."

Ben nodded in the darkness, "Yes, some of our mining friends that came to town for the 4th of July told me of finding cold camp sites as they came in over the pass. I didn't know they are still here."

"Do you know why they watch us? Does it have anything to do with the gold Jacob works with?"

Ben looked at the shadow sitting close to him on the rail of the porch, "Yes Ada, I think it's all about the gold. I think these people are no different than the men that brought the girl posing as Alice up here. Somehow it's leaked from the family members that Jacob lives in the mountain. Gold has ways of turning the most religious man in the world to a thief that will do anything to get his hands on the yellow gold. In fact I think these types are far worse than any of the most hardened criminals. I know the three who brought Alice never passed the word along to anyone after the Indians took them away. Who they had talked to before coming here or how they found out is something we know nothing about. I worry more about them getting inside that mountain before you know they are there."

114

"Jacob has sealed up all the entrances but two. The one you know about, the one in the valley of the bones. I've been there once. I know no one will find that opening from the outside. Jacob worries that they will try to force you or Kate to show them the way."

"Kate knows nothing of passage into the mountain. If I took any-one up there, they would be dragging me. That last few feet on that ledge would be a problem dragging a body," then he chuckled. He then became serious, "Ada, you mentioned the valley of the bones. Have you seen that valley?"

"I've only been to the opening, looking into the small valley. Once it looks like there had been what looks to be a good trail into the valley. Now the brush and trees hide the trail. Maybe a person on foot could find his way up or down the trail. It would be very slow going. Why do you ask?"

"I've read and heard stories of the first Spaniards who mined this country. They probably were the miners that built what you and Jacob, now live. Most tales are of them mining far south of here, but I think those tunnels in that mountain had to be them. It is said they used slave Indian labor to do all the work then killed them when they left the area. That way the location of each mine was known only by the Spaniards. Most everyplace they have mined bones have been found in great num-bers, like they were all killed together. I think what you call the valley of the bones is where they killed their slaves here."

Ada reached over to touch Ben, "You have really studied the his-tory of the early Spaniards. You and Jacob should spend time or maybe you already have talking of this. I know he thinks like you do on the bones in that valley."

"Does the Indian boy know of us? I see you now also have a fam-ily living in a teepee. They moved today to the valley below the settle-ment."

Ben laughed, "Do you two miss anything we do down here? Yes the family in the teepee is Charlie, Benny's brother and his family. We will build them a cabin up there. His wife is Spanish and they have two kids. Now back to our other visitors, does Jacob have any ideas about getting rid of them?"

It was silent for a long spell before Ada spoke again, "You know Jacob, he hates violence, but when crowded he will fight back. It is my job to protect him and now Hattie since she now lives with us. I guess we can only wait for them to make the first move, so far we don't know for sure what they are after. I will tell Jacob you are aware of our visi-tors." She walked into kitchen and put her cup on the table. "I will be heading back home now. Ben did your new friend, Charlie, tell you that when he came back into the valley he wasn't alone? The others who were here with him last time are camped again in the canyons of the hot springs."

Ben stood up, "No, he didn't say anything about others being with him. Are they the same ones that were here with him when he brought Thomas to live with his father?"

"At least two of them are the same, the third one I don't know for sure. When I watched them in their camp in the canyon the third one was hunting for meat so I didn't see him that close."

"Ada I worry of you traveling alone now that we have people watching the mountain and this valley. Maybe for a while you shouldn't travel so freely about."

"I will be careful. Jacob and I have talked of this many times, he agrees with me. We must know what these people are up to. Now I must go before dawn catches me on the open hillside going up to the mountain entrance." With that she walked off into the darkness.

Ben lay in his bed thinking of this wisp of a woman who had just visited him. He sat up in bed when a distant noise came from the direction of the mountain. It had sounded like a lone shot from a hand gun. Then all was still again. He swung his feet off the bed and started to pull on his boots, then, he stopped. What could he do in the darkness? It would be light by the time he made it up to the mountain, so anyone watching would know he had heard the shot and where it came from. For Ada and Jacob's sake he should stay here and go on like he hadn't even heard that shot. He laid, back down, 'I hope you are alright my small friend,' he mumbled in the darkness.

As he sat waiting for the skillet to get hot and the coffee to boil his thoughts went to that noise during the night. The more he thought about it he decided it could have been Ada's derringer that made the noise. It wasn't the sharp crack like a rifle or normal pistol would make.

Thomas came driving the wagon into the yard just as Ben stepped out to go about his work day. "Well, did you get Charlie all moved in?"

Thomas nodded, "He likes the place you chose for him. He said he would ride over today to help us."

Ben grinned, "You got the wagon all hook up so let's haul a load of posts up along where were building that new fence. That way whenever we got time we can work on that project."

It was about noon as they drove the empty wagon back into the yard. Thomas pointed down in the meadow as Charlie came into site. "Now he comes when we got the posts already hauled."

Thomas was un-hooking the team when Charlie rode up. Charlie stopped and sat looking down at Ben, "There is a saddled horse standing on the ridge behind the house. I've been watching him coming down from the trail, no rider is anywhere about."

Thomas looked at Ben, "Do you want me to go get him?"

Ben nodded and the young boy was off at a run toward the hill. Ben turned to Charlie, "You did not come to this place alone?"

"No, three of my blood brothers, that were here with me before wanted to come back too. I was going to tell you today when I got here. Will they have to leave?"

Ben looked at the Indian, who like his brother Benny showed no emotion. "Charlie. That will up to them. If they live in peace and cause no problems I see no reason they should leave. Charlie, can you get word to them to show up after dark tonight?"

Charlie looked at him, then, slowly nodded his head. "Charlie I think when Thomas gets here with that horse, I will know for sure if I need your brothers. We've had some men watching us from all the high ground around here. If that horse belongs to one of them, then I need to get rid of them before the others, come, nosing around."

Charlie looked at Ben for a moment before speaking again, "Walking Bear has told me of the men who watch you. One was close to the barn last night. He followed the girl when she left."

Ben looked up real quick when he heard Charlie speak of the girl. "You know about her? How long have you known of her being here?"

"Walking Bear said she has been watching their camp in the canyon. Walking Bear says she moves like the mountain lion. He also says she knew the man was behind her last night as she left."

Ben shuttered, as he muttered, 'If the man had followed her onto the narrow ledge near the opening, his body would never be found.' As he looked up Charlie was staring at him. Ben smiled, "I was talking to myself."

"She is now at home in the mountain. You were right, the man never made it across the ledge."

Ben grinned. Talking to Charlie was just like talking to Benny at times. Maybe Kate is right about Benny being a spirit or something, if she is right, then it must be a family thing with Charlie. He motioned toward Thomas coming down toward them, "Let's go put that horse in the barn until it gets dark."

They spent the afternoon building fence. Ben's leg was getting tired and began to ache a little. He motioned to his two helpers, "Let's call it a day, this leg is telling me I've been on it too much today."

As they got to the house Ben opened the lid of the water tank and filled a pail. He sat it and dipper on the railing. The water was cool and sweet to the taste. He handed the dipper to Charlie, then sat down and leaned back against the cabin wall. "You two are great helpers. With you both here this place will really be shaped up by fall."

Thomas stood up, "I hear our supper down there along the creek," he trotted away. Ben looked over at Charlie.

Charlie motioned down to the meadow along the creek, "Grouse." Then he looked back toward Ben, "Do you want Walking Bear to chase the men watching you out of the valley? He could make them totally disappear if you like."

Ben studied the emotionless face looking at him. "Charlie, that's a hard decision to make. Yes I would like them to be gone, but I worry about killing them. I also wonder about what Jacob will say and I worry too about Kate finding out. I know she would not be happy with me if I, okayed Walking Bear doing away with them. Also if it leaked out the law would be after Walking Bear and I don't want that."

A small smile appeared on Charlie's lips, "The Spirits could chase them away. I think if that happened they probably would never return to this land."

Ben laughed, "Now Charlie you sound like your brother. Kate has always wondered about things Benny has said about the spirits, now you worry me with your talk." He studied the Indian looking at him, "You know Charlie I would go along with that way of moving them." He hesitated then went on, "Charlie one thing I'd like to find out before the spirit gets involved. Why are they here? Also, how many more know about Jacob mining in this country? I keep thinking it has to be someone involved with the family or used to belong to them. Deep back in my mind I keep thinking our troubles are just beginning if we don't get this stopped now."

Charlie nodded, "This I will talk about that with Walking Bear when he gets here tonight. Now I will ride to tell Rosa, I will be gone for a while tonight. I will be back before Walking Bear gets here."

Supper was over, so Ben and Thomas moved out on the porch. Charlie rode up and joined them as they waited for darkness. It was totally dark when Charlie leaned over next to Ben, "You have company at the barn, they, have come from the mountain. Walking Bear is also, here, while you talk to them I will tell him your wishes."

Ben walked into the big barn, he stopped just inside next to the bench where he usually left Jacobs supplies. "Your Indian friends are like Benny, they too are very good." Jacob's voice came from the back

118

of the building. "I usually can move about without people knowing I'm even in the area. Ada said as she headed back to the mountain last night she knew she was being followed by one of the men who watch the valley. Before she got to the ledge she knew a second person was close by, but she knew he was friendly. After the man fell over the ledge, the second man turned away leaving the mountain."

Ben walked over toward the voice, then, he saw Jacob and Ada in the shadows, "I was worried about Ada after I heard the shot last night. Later, I decided it was her short gun that had made the noise, so then I figured she had made it home alright. I'm glad you're here. I was going to signal you later to come down. Jacob, Charlie say's Walking Bear can move these men away from here without killing them. He also says they could make sure they never talk of this place again. I have a problem believing in this spirit world talk, so I'll just say Walking Bear will use his powers to take them away."

A soft almost a chuckled broke the stillness, "Ben, one reason I think of you as a brother is you say what is in your heart. This is good. Walking Bear no doubt has ways of making things happen that to you aren't possible. When you slept through all the pain as I repaired your leg had nothing to do with me using the spirits. I used the juice and other parts of plants to make your mind feel free of all pain. Walking Bear too will also use what mother earth has to offer to make these men see all types of strange things. They will view things beyond this world like you have never seen. So my good, friend, in your wisdom you are right in not believing about the power of spirits are doing things to these men bodies. It is only their minds that will see the spirits."

"Okay Jacob, I maybe understand what you're trying to tell me. I guess from what you said you have no problem with having Walking Bear move these men. I ask Charlie to ask him if he could find out how they first heard of you living in this mountain. We must find out who's spreading this about and get it stopped. If we don't our troubles are just beginning."

Ben felt a hand on his shoulder, "Yes I agree. I have a letter for you to mail. I too look for answers of who is after the gold in this mountain. I also have a list of supplies whenever you go back to Garnet. Now Ada and I will return to our home. I will leave this chore of ridding us of unwanted strangers, to you and your Indian friends. Ada has told me all along you would only resort to killing these men when you were left with no other choice. My brother you do what you deem best, I know you will do it right." He squeezed Ben's shoulder before stepping away.

Ada moved up next to Ben, "You have eased his fears, Thank You," then she moved off after the tall man, soon to be swallowed up by the darkness.

As Ben walked back toward the cabin, his thoughts were on what Jacob had said about the spirits. Ben smiled into the darkness. He still had many questions that were still left unanswered. They may use drugs to work on people's minds, but that still didn't explain how they knew what was going to happen. How did Charlie know about Jacob and Ada, coming down from their mountain home? His knowing of Walking Bear also being close could have been some of the many night sounds in the air. Ben had noticed even Thomas seem to know every sound of danger while Ben just thought they were small animals and birds making these sounds. He chuckled as he stepped up onto the porch, 'This is way too deep for me. I'll leave this up to Kate and her spirit world.'

"You talk to yourself as you walk. Is this good?" asked Thomas from the dark porch.

Ben laughed, "Thomas, I can't answer that. I call it thinking out loud instead of talking to myself. It's just so many strange things are happening that I just don't understand. I always until now thought I was well aware of everything around me. I've mined alone for years, I always knew when people were getting close or wild animals were near. When I'm around Benny, Charlie and even you it's like I'm a stranger to this land. Does that make sense to you?"

"Yes, I have noticed you only read a part of what is being said in the night air. Like Benny said of you and uncle Charlie agrees, you read the night well for a white man. Your friend from the mountain almost never misses what is being said. The girl, she is cunning like a wolf, she moves without being noticed by most. Uncle Charlie says Walking Bear is about half scared of her. She has moves among them in the canyons of the hot springs and only leaves a sound when she wants to. He says it's like she is testing them, this makes Walking Bear very nervous."

All went quiet on the porch when footsteps of two people were heard. Charlie and Walking Bear appeared. "Walking Bear says the men you seek are now in the canyons of the hot springs. If you wish you can ask them why they come to this place searching for gold. Walking Bear said he has asked, but they tell him nothing. They only say they are here to take what belongs to them."

Ben sat there for a spell not, answering, then, he looked up at the two shadows sitting on the porch rail. "You said if Walking Bear took them away they would never return to this land to bother us again? He can do this without killing them?"

In broken English Walking Bear spoke, "This I can do, without killing them. I will follow them out of this valley to make sure they leave without harming anyone in your other home. Then I will return to my new home in the canyons of the hot water." He started to move away then stopped, "You are a friend of the little one, why does she watch us?"

Ben chuckled, "She is only protecting the man who lives in the mountain. She means you no harm as long as you don't try to enter their home. Her name is Ada. Someday I will bring her to talk to you. You will find you and her, have many things in common, you just are of different beliefs and ways of life."

Walking Bear walked away without answering, Charlie followed him. Ben was about ready to turn in when he heard a horse coming toward the cabin. Charlie's voice broke the silence. "I go home now. "I'll be back come morning to help you build fence," then he rode away leaving Ben and Thomas alone on the porch.

"I don't know about you Thomas but I'm going to bed, this has been a day like I'd never had before. I just hope I can go to sleep," with that he walked into the cabin.

Sleep finally came. The next thing he heard was Thomas building a fire to cook breakfast. 'Maybe today this place can get back to normal. He swung his feet out onto the cool floor, pushing himself up to get dressed.

Thomas and Ben finished hooking up the team as Charlie rode up. He stopped by the small pasture to turn his horse loose, then, walked up to join the two in the wagon. Ben looked over at him as he settled down to sit on a pile of posts in the back, "Well how is Rosa getting along in her new home?"

Charlie nodded, "She is busy making it more comfortable. They are building a sweat house by the creek. She has already picked a place where she wants her cabin built."

Ben nodded, "Good, we'll finish the fence I need along the hay field today, so tomorrow we'll start getting you the material to build your house. First we need to see if we can get a wagon up to the settlement, or if not maybe we can fix it so we can get a cart up there. I've looked at that before, I think we can get that lighter wagon up there. We'll need to load light loads but that will still be better than having to pack the timbers down there on a horse."

121

That evening as they topped the small ridge overlooking the building smoke was coming from the chimney of the cabin. Ben pointed, "I'll bet we have a cook tonight, Thomas." Then they saw Kate step out onto the porch and wave.

They stopped at the cabin, Ben stepped down and Thomas and Charlie took the team to the barn. Ben put his arms around Kate, "Good to see you finally missed me. How's Jess doing as a store manager?"

Kate kissed him, "Good to see you too. You seem to have another helper, isn't that Benny's brother with Thomas?"

Ben laughed, "My dear it will take me all night to tell you what all happened here since we got back from the fourth celebration. You now have a family of four living close by for neighbors. Charlie has brought his family here to live, his wife Rosa, a son Pedro and one very cute daughter, Maria. Knowing you you'll try to steal Maria first off."

Kate smiled, "Where are they living?"

"When I got back from town they had their teepee down in the pasture. I moved them up in that valley below the old settlement. We're going to start building them a cabin tomorrow. Charlie's been helping on the fence work and we got that hay field fence done. We're going to try to get a wagon road cleared up to the settlement so we can haul a few timbers for the cabin from there. If we can't we can just use green timber from across the valley to build it."

Kate hugged him, "You have been busy. This Rosa is she Indian or white?"

Ben smiled, "She's of Spanish decent I would say. Charlie talks to her in Spanish, but she knows English too. I think those kids speak both or maybe even three languages. She seems very nice. Tomorrow you can go up there with us if you like. We can take your horse along and you can ride back after you meet the family."

After supper Thomas helped with the dishes then said he was moving his sleeping gear down to the barn. Kate started to speak as Thomas went on, "I fixed up a good place to sleep in the tack room in the horse barn. It is a good room for me."

After Thomas left carrying his bed roll, Ben looked over at Kate, "I told him we could build a small bunkhouse, but he said the tack room was just fine with him. I think from the looks of the inside of that room it was built for the workers to sleep in. Most tack rooms don't have windows. Its better he's staying in the horse barn than the other one, this way Ada and Jacob can come and go without maybe him knowing it. I doubt it, but it is a thought. You know he's just like Benny and Charlie when it comes to knowing what is going on. We had a talk one evening about the sounds in the night." He chuckled at the look on his wife's face, "I know dear, I was thinking about you as I listened to him talk. You and witch doctor partner as you call him with all your spirit world talk. Thomas doesn't believe in spirits, he believes only in what he can hear and see."

Kate smiled, "I'm glad I'm free now to live with you full time, now I protect you from all of this you don't understand," then she broke out laughing.

Ben drove the light wagon with Kate sitting beside him and Thomas followed riding Kate's horse. Ben looked about as they stopped at the teepees. A fire pit was ringed with, rock's. The new small sweat lodge was near the creek in the meadow. Rosa and the kids had been busy. Charlie came walking from the bigger of the two teepees. He turned and spoke back into the teepee. Rosa appeared alongside of him.

Ben helped Kate down from the wagon, "Kate you know Charlie," he turned to Rosa as she clung to Charlie's arm. "Kate this is Rosa, Rosa this is my wife Kate."

Kate stepped forward holding out her arms, "It's good to meet you Rosa. With you living here now, I have another woman to talk to. I'm so glad you have moved here."

Rosa took her hand, "Charlie has spoken of you. I'm too glad to have a woman close by to talk with." She turned to look toward the other teepee, "Pedro, Maria come out to meet out new neighbor."

Both kids came out and hurried over to their mother side, Rosa put her arm around Pedro shoulder, "This is our son Pedro," then she reached for the girl clinging to her dress, "This one is our daughter Maria."

Kate stepped over and took the boy's, hand." It's good to meet you Pedro. "She turned and kneeled down in front of the bashful girl peeking out from behind her mother, "Maria, you are a very pretty young lady, no wonder Ben thought I might try to steal you. You and I will have many good times together."

The men took the wagon and started up the valley, while Kate stayed to talk to Rosa. Ben and the two worked clearing a right away for the wagon. Charlie motioned back toward the valley, "We have company coming."

Kate and Rosa had brought lunch up to the crew. Ben smiled as he saw Kate had a passenger behind her. Maria was peeking around Kate to look at the men. Kate looked over at Ben and smiled, "I've got me a helper."

By evening they had the wagon up to the edge of the settlement. They left the wagon there for the night and took the team back down to Charlie's camp. Thomas had brought his bed roll, so he stayed with Charlie and his family, Ben and Kate rode home alone.

While Kate fixed supper, they talked about their new neighbors. Kate laughed, "Maria informed me as we rode back from taking your lunches up to you that she had her own horse. She was riding with me so I wouldn't get lost."

Ben smiled, "I saw you were already spoiling that cute kid. Charlie really seems to be a good worker, I'm glad he decided to come back to this country. I sure would like to know more about how and where he and Benny were raised. They both seem to live well in two different worlds."

Kate nodded as she sat down across the table from Ben, "Yes I agree. You know Rosa is very well educated too, you can tell by the way she talks. I think you are right about her being Spanish."

A week later they had the cabin going up. That had built the base from the big timber and used lumber on the floor from the settlement. Then they decided to build the walls from logs. So while Charlie and Thomas cut trees, Ben made up a list of things would need from town. Kate got Rosa to give her a list of supplies she needed. The morning they were going to leave Ben walked out to go get the team hitched up while Kate cooked breakfast. As he opened the door he noticed a rolled up paper dropping onto the porch. He smiled when he saw the small statue figure drawn on it. Inside he found written, 'Check the cache.' Ada.

Ben stepped back into the cabin, "Mail lady was here during the night," then held up the paper.

"What was the message," Kate asked as she looked over at Ben.

"After breakfast I need to check and see, right now I'm just going to check on the horses."

After breakfast Ben walked to the barn. He scooted the ladder over so he could climb up into the loft where he used to hide the food for Jacob. As he topped the ladder he could see small boot tracks along with larger moccasins prints. Inside the big trunk he found it full of smaller wooden boxes. Well made, but unmarked except for a small leather pouch attached to each one. He opened one pouch and took out a small white paper, written on it was only an address in Jacob's beautiful printing. He put the note back in the pouch. As he stood up he noticed tracks leading to the second trunk, when he opened it he found more of the boxes like the ones in the first trunk. On top of one boxes in the second trunk the name Kate was carved into the wood. Ben took this box, climbed down. As he moved the ladder back to its normal place he heard Kate call, his name. He stepped out into the sunshine as she walked up. What did you find?"

He handed her the box with her name on it. In the light Ben could see this box was made different than the other ones. This box had a hinged lid. The others looked to be nailed shut. Kate opened the box on top was a letter address to Ben, under that was another smaller box. Ben was opening the letter when he heard a small cry come from Kate. He started to ask her what was wrong when he saw what she was holding. A beautiful small wooden box of shiny wood, decorated with what looked to be gold designs drawings all over it. Kate handed the small box to Ben, "Ben I've never seen anything so beautiful as this. Are all of these designs really made with real gold?"

Ben was just shaking his head as he looked at the box in his hand, somehow Jacob had figured out how to use gold in his drawings. About then Ben remembered one of those books he bought when he and Kate got married in Springfield for Jacob had stories about this type of work. He looked up at Kate, "Our friend is something else when it comes to craftsmanship. Did you look inside of it, yet?" He handed it back to her.

Kate unhooked a small gold colored latch and opened the lid, "Oh my God, look!" Then she looked up, Ben as he stared into the box. Inside was a miniature set of silverware, only made of, gold. The fork knife and spoon, on green velvet lined box. They were so small, maybe three inches long at the most. Every detail was perfect, with a design engraved into each handle. Kate reached down and took the knife from the box, when she turned it over a smile appeared. On the other side of the handle was an engraved statue like the ones Jacobs used for his signature.

Ben read his letter then handed it to Kate. He waited until she finished it, "Well, you got any ideas on doing what he asks?" The letter asked if Ben could find a way to ship this entire shipment to England.

Kate nodded her head yes, real slow. "Ben, if we could go to Springfield and buy one of them steamer trunks, it would hold all of this real easy. People ship their belonging all the time back to the old country, when they go home. We could pack the top with old clothes people have left in the houses when they left. I gathered up all that stuff and washed it and packed it away. I've handed out a lot of it to people down on their luck who traveling through Garnet the last few years."

Ben backed the wagon into the barn and loaded all the small boxes from the trunks in the loft. Coby Kline, from down on the river had bought another of the big wagons over the 4th while he was in Garnet. He told Ben he wanted the tarp cover whenever he had a chance to bring it down. So Ben back the wagon over under the rope hoist hanging from the rafters With Kate's help they rolled a tarp from the back room and loaded it. It completely covered the bottom of the bed so the boxes were well hidden in case they met someone on their way to town.

Ben pulled the team to a stop in front of the trading post. Benny came rushing around the side of the store to help Kate down. "Good to see you two. I was going to ride up tomorrow to spend a few days with you. I kinda wanted to see Rosa and the kids."

Ben got down and grasped Benny's hand, "That brother of yours has a great family. That's why were in town, we need a few things for their new home. I may have to go down to Springfield to get them. I brought that cover Coby wanted for that wagon he bought," as he nodded toward the wagon. "Can we unload it here somewhere until he comes after it? I got some things under it I need to unload up at the cabin before we head for Springfield."

Jess and Meg had come out of the store to greet Kate and Ben. It was decided they would come down and have supper with everyone when they got the wagon unloaded. As Benny helped Ben pack all the boxes into the house he never asked a question about what was in them. When they finished he grinned at the two watching him, "What has Jacob got for you to send this time?"

Kate told him about her idea of a steamer trunk. Benny looked over at Ben, "Come with me, I think we already have one of those. You know the more I think about it we may have two of them. Kate remember that old Scotsman who had that mine up on Nasty Creek. His name was something like Duggan or something like that. Well when Coby and his crew found him dead that spring up near the mine, the sheriff notified a nephew in California. When he showed up he sold the mine to that Bishop bunch. He brought all of the old man's personal stuff to his house here in Garnet, then, he went back to California. Clayton bought that house for back taxes a year or so later. I remember helping him pack all the old man's gear into two of them trunks. We put them up in that company warehouse you bought when the company moved out. Hell Kate I guess you own them trunks now."

Kate grinned, "Yes I remember when Duggan died. I guess I never went up there when Clayton bought the place. Well let's go see what we got in that warehouse?"

Both trunks were in good shape. Both were still full of the old Scotsman's personal gear. Kate looked through the one with just clothes in it. "Let's take this one. I'll see if Jess and Meg kept all of the stuff I used to keep for people traveling through who were down on their luck. If not I'll find a place for it, these clothes are too good to just throw away."

Back in the cabin Kate was shorting through the clothes when a knife fell out and hit the floor. Benny picked it up, then stood there staring at it. "This is one nice knife. It looks to be of the finest steel you can make. This edge is like a razor. Kate what are you going to do with it?"

Kate looked over at Ben, who shrugged, "I got a good knife I don't need it. Why don't you just keep it Benny, you're the one that remembered the trunks even being here."

Kate nodded, "I guess you own the knife, Benny. You already have a knife on your belt, why do you want two?"

Benny looked over at her as he pulled his knife from the sheath. "Kate this is a good knife, but nothing compared to this one the Scotsman owned. I will make a sheath for my new knife so I can wear it. I thank you both for this gift."

After Benny left Ben and Kate spent the rest of the day packing the boxes into the big trunk. Jacob has sent in the letter an address in London where he wanted the boxes sent if they could all be shipped together. Otherwise he'd sent address's for each box if they were sent separately. After supper Kate spent evening painting the address on the big trunk, while Ben went down to see how many of the supplies Jess had on hand. When Kate finished her job she walked down to the saloon to see April and the girls. She found Ben and Jess playing crib as they sipped on a drink. "Sure you leave me up there slaving away while you're down here drinking," Kate said as she walked up behind her husband.

Ben grinned up at her, "I would buy you a drink. Jess and me, here have been figuring out all the supplies we need for Charlie's cabin."

Jess nodded, "We sure have Kate. I did like you, said, I stocked up when I was down in Springfield a couple weeks ago. Some of it came in, Monday. The rest will be here tomorrow when the wagons come through. I told Ben what I don't have I can get here next week so you folks won't have to make a trip to Springfield."

Kate looked over at Ben who nodded, knowing what Kate was thinking. "Jess, we got a steamer trunk we need to ship. Will the wagons coming tomorrow take it?"

"Don't know why they wouldn't. They should be here a before lunch tomorrow."

127

Ben motioned to April to bring a round of, drinks, she nodded and moved off to the bar. "Okay then Jess, I'll take the wagon up to the cabin before I come down to load it with the supplies. I'll bring the trunk down, then, Benny can help me load it."

Charlotte and Elsie came in from the back room to join them. Ben had saw three men walk out the door just after Kate had come in. He had glanced over at Jess when he saw them, Jess had just shrugged. Ben looked over at Charlotte, "Newcomers?"

Charlotte nodded, "That one fella was in a week ago, but he was with a different guy then. They've been asking all kinds of questions about all the different gold mines around here. I told them all the ones I knew that were still being worked. When those two were here last week they asked about those religious people who used to live up where you and Kate live. I just told them you and Kate had filed on the land and you're turning that into a ranch."

Ben nodded, "I was just curious, I never saw them around before." he turned back to his crib game.

"When those two came in last week to buy supplies, they asked how long I'd owned this place. I told them I had just leased it to see if I like running a trading post. I never mentioned anything about you and Kate and they never asked."

Benny brought up the team and wagon the next morning, Kate invited him in for breakfast with her and Ben. While they were eating Ben looked over hat his good friend and grinned, "Benny, how much do you know about those men asking about all the mining around the area?"

"They've been riding everywhere looking over all the old deserted mines. To me they don't look or act like miners. I think maybe they are snooping around trying to find Jacob."

Ben nodded as he ate, "God I hope not. I really worry about Jacob's safety. Ada will be watching but I'm afraid they will find a way to sneak too many in there for her to handle at one time. Benny, there's got to be someone close by who keeping this all stirred up. If Walking Bear did what he said he was going to do with that last bunch, they shouldn't have told anyone."

Benny looked over across the table at Ben and Kate, "The ones Walking Bear took away are very far from here now. They remember nothing about where they have been, this I know for sure."

Ben pushed back from the table, "Mighty good breakfast, Kate. Now Benny and me, will see if we can load that trunk."

128

Kate followed them out, "I will help you. You just think you're as strong as you used to be. I know the leg is getting better, but you still favor it," she said as she goosed him in the ribs.

Kate went back into the house as Ben and Benny headed down to the trading post. As they rode along Ben looked over at Benny, "If you hear anything about what going on with those newcomers let me know." Benny nodded.

It was a little after lunch when Ben and Kate climbed up onto the wagon seat for their trip back to the place. Jess and Meg stood waving as they moved out, April waved from the front of the saloon. As they passed in front of the saloon they looked up when they heard their names called, Charlotte and Elsie were waving from the upstairs balcony.

About half way to the ranch the road swung over to pass through an opening in an out cropping of rocks. It was an odd formation out in the open prairie. As they moved through the biggest of the boulders Ben caught a movement in the corner of his eye. As he turned to look, Walking Bear rode out from behind a large boulder. Ben stopped the wagon, "It's good to see you made it back Walking Bear."

"You have men again looking for the man in the mountain. The ghost woman knows of them, but they do not know of her watching them. Do you wish for me to take them away?"

Ben looked over at Kate, then back to the Indian, "Walking Bear, do you know how many they have this time?"

Walking Bear held up one hand with the finger spread, "Five are close by. There are three more over the pass to the east, one days ride from here. They don't look for man in mountain they just watch the trail."

"Walking Bear, I think right now we will just watch these men, if trouble starts you let me know. If the woman Ada gets in trouble you fight with her. She knows of you she will know you're fighting on her side. If trouble starts, get rid of them, I don't care what you have to do."

Walking Bear turned his horse and disappeared back behind the big rocks bordering the trail. Ben looked over at Kate who was just smiling at him, "You seem to have many friends watching over Jacob and you. I heard what you and Benny said about someone around here is working with these people. Ever since I heard that I've been trying to think of someone we know that even knows of Jacob. Sure Benny, Jess, Meg, April and Charlotte know about him. A few of our winter miners know of him, but they are back in the mountains now working their claims. Besides that you, me and Benny are about the only ones who know about the gold we've shipped for him. Ben, I don't like this idea of one of the people we know is causing all of this."

Ben nodded, "I agree, Kate. I just don't want anything to happen to Jacob or Ada. I'm hoping whoever it is will slip up and leave some clue for us to find. With Benny, Walking Bear and Ada on his or their trail, this will happen. I know I would hate to have those three on my tail."

For the next week everything was quiet. Benny had showed up with the rest of the order of supplies from the trading post. He spent the night out in Thomas room in the barn. Kate had tried to get him to spend the night in the cabin with them but he said no. He told her he wanted to sleep where he could hear the night talk. Kate looked over at Ben, who just grinned at her. Later after they were in bed, Kate rolled over close to him. "What did Benny mean when he said he wanted to listen to the night talk?"

Ben chuckled, "One night Thomas and I talked about how Charlie, Benny and Walking Bear and Thomas himself always seem to know what was going on. He said it was the night talk, he said most white men miss hearing it. Now you know as much as I do about your buddy Benny and his family."

Benny came in for breakfast with them. "How is Charlie's cabin coming along?"

"If you got time before you head back we could ride up so you can see it. We got the roof on yesterday."

Benny nodded, "I told Jess I'd be back before sundown, so I got lots of time to waste."

Kate looked over at Ben, "How about saddling my horse too, I'll ride up with you. I haven't spoiled Maria for a couple of days."

When they topped the small ridge Benny could see the new cabin, he stopped. "You and Charlie did good, picking a place for the cabin as you call it. To me it looks more like a house."

When they rode up Charlie and Thomas were on the roof. Charlie looked down at the three, "I see you brought big brother to help today."

Benny waves his hand, "I only came to see you and my son work, and to give advice." About then Rosa and Maria stepped out of the teepee. Benny walked over to Rosa, "Before long you will have a new home Rosa. Who is that girl hiding behind you?"

Before Rosa could say anything Maria went running to Kate as she stepped down from her horse. Rosa smiled, "I guess your niece thinks Kate will protect her from you. Don't feel bad, when Kate is close by she has a shadow."

Kate with Maria sitting behind her rode back with Benny. Benny caught up the team and brought them up to the wagon. Kate and Maria sat on the porch steps watching as Benny climbed up into the seat. "What are you and your helper going to do today, Kate?"

"I promised her we would make sugar cookies. Ben accuses me of spoiling your niece, but you know I wouldn't do that," then she grinned. Benny nodded and put the team into motion.

That afternoon Kate saddled up to take her visitor back up the valley. As they rode along with Maria was holding a bag of fresh cookies. Maria squeezed Kate's side just as they topped the ridge, overlooking the new place. When Kate looked back her partner she was pointing across the valley. As Kate looked the way she was pointing she saw three riders sitting their horses under a tree on the far ridge. As Kate rode along she kept looking, then she saw them moving off, 'I think those are Indians,' she said to herself. She kept watching as she rode on up to Charlie's place, but never saw the riders again.

Later as she rode back with Ben she told him about seeing the riders. "I couldn't believe it when Maria spotted those riders. Most kids her age aren't that observing."

Ben nodded, "You got to remember in many places Indians are fair game. Even though Charlie is only half Indian to most people who hate Indians he's just a renegade half breed. Rosa may be Spanish but to most when she's with Charlie she's just another Indian squaw. Those kids are just stuck with the parent they have. With the life they have lived so far those kids have already learned to watch for trouble. Rider watching them usually means trouble. I think it was probably some of Walking Bears men watching you today."

Kate nodded, "I know I've had a few people at the trading post who wouldn't buy anything Benny touched. In fact one time I sent a whole group of wagons away because they wouldn't buy anything as long as Benny was in the store. They were real sort on supplies too, but this one lady just kept scream at me about the filthy Indian. Then she called me his squaw, that done it. I told her she wasn't welcome any longer and to move on. Later one man from the same train showed up with a pack horse to buy supplies they really needed. He tried to apologize for what the woman had said. I told him the only reason I was selling him supplies now was I saw all those kids in those wagons and I felt sorry for them."

Ben grinned at her, "I'm sure glad you're getting mellow, as you get older."

As they rode into the yard Ben spotted three horses with blanket saddles drinking from the small pond in the lower corral. About then Walking Bear stepped from behind the cabin. "I saw you coming back from Two Bloods new house, so I waited to see you. The five riders who watched this place have, gone. I think maybe they ride to Springfield for supplies. The three camped on the high trail are still there. Each morning one of them rides to cliffs where the miners have worked. They look all around then ride back to their camp. One time the rider crawled up through the rocks above the trail and picked up something and then rode back to camp. Later he rode the back trail up to where the other five were camped. It was the next morning that the five moved out."

Ben frowned, "Could you tell what he picked up?"

Walking Bear shook his head, no, "It was too far away to see what it was. It looked like he dropped part of it, then he put something into his pocket before he went back to his horse."

Walking Bear started to move away, then, he stopped, "The little ghost knows of this." Then he headed down toward the lower corral. Ben grinned when he looked down at the pond. Two Indians were now standing by the horses.

From behind him, Ben heard Kate, "Where did they come from? They weren't there a minute ago."

"My dear wife, I stopped worry about such things along time ago when you're dealing with Benny and his friends. I'll go put our horses in the barn."

At supper Kate looked over at Ben, "What do you think Walking Bear was talking about when he mentioned that rider up under the cliffs each morning?"

Ben gave a slight nod of his head, "You know I've been thinking about that ever since Walking Bear told us. The only thing I can think of is maybe our spy were trying to find is already in the mountain. Maybe someway their dropping messages from above. When Jacob sealed those opening the miners had opened up I think he probably left an opening just big enough to look out."

"My God, Ben, there's only three people up there. We know it's not Jacob, If Ada's is watching the rider each morning we know it's not her," she hesitated, "Unless she's making sure they found her message. Ben, if it isn't Ada. That only leaves Hattie."

"I know, that's what bothering me. I just know it isn't, Ada, she's dedicated her life to Jacob and protecting him. If it is Hattie, then she has fooled us all, especially Jacob. I need to talk to Jacob in private

132

without the two women knowing it. Fooling Hattie is easy, but Ada is a different story, she's always with him.

A week later the work was just about competed on Charlie's cabin. One evening Ben and Kate sat out on the porch watching the sun slowly disappearing in the west. The nights were beginning to tell everyone fall wasn't far away. "Kate, in the morning, why don't you walk down to the barn with me. I'll climb up in the mow of the barn where the trunks are and get some of that furniture out where you can see it. If you see anything Rosa could use in her new home, we'll get it down and clean it up. I know they'll need some repairs and I can do that."

Kate nodded, "Okay I can do that." She stopped rocking for a second, "Better yet, why don't I ride over and get her first thing bring Rosa back with me. That way she can tell us what she needs as you dig it out."

While Kate was gone to get Rosa, Ben climbed up into the loft. When he first started climbing up here he had fumbled around in the dark until his eyes got adjusted. Then one day he found a window opening with a wooden door instead of a window glass. When he propped this open he had all kinds of light to see even into the darkest corners. He looked through the furniture and picked out what was in the best condition and carried it over next to the ladder. Before long he heard horses outside the barn and Kate appeared in the doorway. She laughed, "The whole darn family came along, even this one as she reached around behind her to grasp Maria."

Ben motioned to Thomas, "Why don't you grab that rope hanging on the peg by the door, then bring it up here. Bring that pulley hanging next to it, too. That way we can let it any of this stuff Rosa wants down with the rope, instead of trying to pack it down the ladder."

With Thomas help they held up a table so those standing below could see. Rosa looked up at Ben, "Can I come up there? I want to see it better."

Rosa rushed up the ladder to the mow. She looked at the table, felt all the smooth craftsmanship in building it. "This I want, can I have these chairs too?" She took a rocking chair that needed work and bedstead along with the table and chairs. She looked about, "I need a bigger house. Then, I could take all of this." As she started to climb down she spotted a big wooden tub hanging on the back wall. She looked at Ben, "Will that old tub still hold water?"

Ben shrugged, "We have a smaller one up at the cabin I got from up here, I soaked it in the horse trough overnight, once, it got wet it holds water real good. I think this one will be the same way."

133

With dust all over them they had everything down from above. "If you like I'll work on this making a few repair, then I'll bring it up to you," Ben told Rosa.

Thomas walked up next to Ben, "Can I help? I like working with wood."

"I'll do better than that, I turn this job over to you," Ben told Thomas as he put his arm around his shoulders. There's all kind of wood working tools over in that tack room where you was sleeping. There in those big cupboards along that back wall."

In a week all the furniture was moved over to the new house. All had been quiet, then, one morning as Ben stepped out to take care of the stock he found Walking Bear waiting for him. Ben walked over to where Walking Bear was sitting his horse, "Do you ever sleep, Walking Bear?"

The Indian never changed expressions, "The five riders are back. They camp now just south of here. Last night they were up on the trail above here. They didn't go close to the trail that the little ghost uses. They waited there a long while before they rode away. It was like they were waiting for someone. I think they will die if they go up that trail."

"Did you see Ada last night while you were watching these men?"

"No, I did not see her, but I know she was close by. When she is close, I feel her presents without seeing her. I will watch tonight to see if they come back."

As Walking Bear turned his horse Ben asked, "Would you like some coffee before you go?"

Walking Bear stopped and turned back to face Ben, "Not this morning, we need to get back to camp. I will have coffee with you soon."

As he started away three riders came from behind the lower barn to join him. Ben was grinning as he headed down to check on the horses in the corral. When he walked back into the cabin Kate looked up from the stove, "I see we had company already. What did Walking Bear want?"

Ben told her what Walking Bear had told him as they ate breakfast. "I wish Ada would stop by and let me know what she thinks is going on. I could lite a signal fire, but if were being watched they would see it too and figure out what it means. I guess we should always figure it like the old saying, 'no news is good news.'

Charlie and Thomas rode into the yard just after Ben stepped out from breakfast. "What brings you two out this fine morning?"

Charlie dropped from his horse, "We got everything pretty well done, we thought maybe we should go back to work for you."

Ben nodded, "Well I guess we got a lot of things to do before winter. Kate and I will probably spend most of the winter in town, but you'll need a good supply of wood up at your place. We also need to bring down more of the materials from up at the settlement. Another year and some of that won't be worth the work to get it. We can store those better timbers in the barn to keep them from going through another winter. While you working up there bring down anything you think will be good wood for winter. I can handle most of the work around here. If I decide to try cutting a little hay off the meadow along the creek, I'll let you two know so you can help.

One morning Ben walked into the big barn and noticed a pouch hanging from the wall where Jacob left messages. Inside was a list of supplies. A short letter was written at the bottom of the list. Jacob said he would have another shipment before the big snows. Then Ben stopped reading as he looked back at the sentence he had just read. "I will be down to see you once these men trying to get into my mountain are gone. I worry that they will, cause, you harm if they find I visit you at times, so I will stay away. Trust me my friend that I will make sure no harm comes to you and Kate. Your Brother," signed with the statue figure.

Ben and Kate made an overnight trip to town for supplies. Kate had ridden up the day before to see if Rosa needed any supplies. With the three separate lists to fill they had full wagon for the trip home. Jess had told Kate the business had been kinda slow lately, but he like the new job. Come winter he and Meg wanted to talk to her about a new deal on the place. When Kate visited the saloon, she found a happy group. Elsie had fit right in with the other two. April had just got back from a buying trip to Springfield. She had bought a lot of new clothes for herself and the girls. She was going to remodel a part of the saloon and had bought a lot of the new fixtures while in town. Benny had found a couple of men to do the work for her.

As they loaded up to leave Benny was helping them. He said he was going to come up the following week and stay for a couple of weeks. Jess was talking to Kate when Benny motioned for Ben to follow him. They walked to the barn, inside Benny tuned to face Ben, "Walking Bear was here the other night, he was telling me about your visitors. What do you have in mind for them? I know we can't just kill them unless they start something, but I also think you and Kate are in danger with them around."

Ben looked back out by the wagon where Kate was still talking to Jess, then, he turned back to Benny. "Benny, I worry more about Jacob and Ada. If what happening is what I think, our spy is in that mountain now. Walking Bear tells of a rider watching from below every morning like he waiting for a message from above. I really want to talk to Jacob, but I don't want to signal him with those fellas watching. I got a load of supplies for him in the wagon, so maybe I can catch him when he comes down for them."

Benny looked at him, then, slowly nodded, "You and Charlie be real careful as long as those men are around. I don't think they will bother my brother or his family, but they know you have some connection with Jacob. While I'm up there, maybe we can look around more."

"Okay Benny, I guess we better get back or Kate will think something is going on."

Later as they bounced along heading back for their valley Kate looked over at him, "What did Benny want to tell you without me being around?"

Ben grinned, "Oh he has been talking to Walking Bear and knows about riders. He thinks we might be in danger if they get desperate. I told him we were aware of them and would be on our toes if they start getting too close." Kate looked over at him and smiled.

The clouds had been building up all afternoon as they drove home. They had just started unloading the wagon when the first rain drops started to fall. "When we get what you need right now off, I'll take the wagon down to the barn and park it inside. We can deliver Rosa supplies when the storm quits. While I'm down there I'll put Jacob's supplies in the normal hiding place in case he shows up during the night."

Ben unloaded Jacob's supplies into the room where the last few tarps from the big wagon were stored. When he opened the cupboards to put the supplies away he grinned. The empty packs Jacob used to carry his supplies were laying there. As he moved one of them to make room for the supplies he saw the wooden boxes hidden back in a corner of the shelf. Jacob hadn't come down with empty packs. There were six of them. Ben took them back to a small cupboard partly hidden by the big canvas rolls. With this done he moved one of the rolls enough to hide the cupboard door. After packing the supplies into the cupboard where the packs were he took the team over to the horse barn. When he walked back to the cabin the rain was coming down hard.

Inside the heat from the stove felt good as Ben took off his hat and coat, "That coffee sure smells good." Kate poured two cup and sat down across from him at the table, "You were gone a long time."

136

"Oh I had to make room for Jacob's supplies. It seems our message carrier also brought down a few items. I had to move them to have room for the supplies. I left Rosa's supplies on the wagon.

The next morning the clouds still hung low over the valley, but the rain had stopped. After breakfast Ben walked down to the barn to check on the wagon and to see if Jacob or Ada had been down during the rainy night. Inside everything was just as he'd left it the night before. Seeing that, Ben walked over to take the horses out to the upper corral so they could drink and get a little exercise. Later if the rain stayed away he would hook up the wagon and he and Kate would take the supplies up to Charlie's place.

The sun was breaking through a little before noon, so when Kate called him for lunch he asked if she wanted to ride up to deliver the supplies to Rosa. It was a nice ride with the air so fresh from the rain. When they got up to the cabin Rosa and Maria were the only ones there. Charlie and Thomas had taken the wagon up to the settlement for more timbers. They had taken Pedro with them. They unloaded the supplies on the covered front porch so Rosa could sort through them as she put them away. They were just finishing when Maria came around the house to say the wagon was coming down from the settlement.

Kate nudged Ben as the wagon stopped out front. Pedro was riding behind the wagon on his pony with a blanket type Indian saddle. As he dropped from his horse Maria was standing next to him. Pedro scooped up his little sister and boosted her up on the horse. She went lopping off across the meadow with her pig tails flying in the wind. Kate looked over at Rosa, who was just smiling, "She is becoming a very good, rider. Thomas has spent much time teaching her to be a good rider. That pony will be hers as soon as Pedro's new horse is safe for him to ride alone. He rides him now but only when Charlie or Thomas is riding with him."

Maria come riding back to the group she dropped from her horse like she was used to doing it. Pedro took the reins and led the horse over to the hitch rail alongside the cabin. Maria raced over to Kate who kneeled down to grasp her, "Say young lady you seem to be a good rider. I will come up one of these days and you and me, will go for a ride. Is that okay with you?" Maria nodded as she gave Kate a big hug.

Ben walked over to the wagon to look at the timbers they had brought. "These still look good, you must be getting deep into the ruble to find these that show no sign of being out in the weather. We need to get them under cover before the winter snows. We have all kinds of room in back of the horse barn to stack these in the dry. Why don't we

137

stack these somewhere around here and later we'll bring a bigger wagon up to take them down to the barn. You know I've been thinking of taking a couple of those carts that were made from parts from a big wagon and making a new wagon without the box. With those wide wheels it would haul a good sized load of these timbers. Later on if we need green logs for something it would work good for hauling them."

Charlie nodded, "Yes we are getting into the deep part of that ruble. We found a skeleton this morning as we dug out a timber. These were the second set bones we've found, the other one the bones were scatters about, this one was all together. It was a skeleton of a woman. We have opened up a grave up where the others are buried, before winter I will fill it in. Then I will mark how many we have buried in each grave."

Ben nodded, "I always figured after I started digging out these timber that I might find more victims. It's good you are burying the remains."

As they walked back toward the cabin Charlie stopped, "Ben, as we dig through that ruble we are being watched. Then this morning as we moved the bones up to the burial spot, I saw footprints in the fresh dirt where someone has been there since I buried the first one. Thomas and me, both are carrying a pistols now. I really don't want trouble, but I will protect my family if I'm pushed."

"It's good you have armed yourselves. Kate and I both carry a pistol with us at all times. According to Walking Bear we are all being watched too. They're mainly watching the mountain, but he says the others are watching our cabin. He fears for our safety, I told him you and I would talk about this and plan out what we need to do. I think we should just go on like we've been doing, but keep a gun handy. How about the first sign of any trouble you bring your family down to our place and we'll move them into Garnet. Then we'll come back to do what we have to, to get rid of these people."

Thomas had been listening, "Kate carries a gun?"

Ben laughed, "I guess she always has. When we went to get married she saw a newer, lighter pistol, in the hardware store, she bought it. She pulled this other colt from her purse to trade in. I bought it for myself and she got the new one. She said her first husband had bought her the pistol when they first opened the trading post. She said she made it a point from then on to always carry it."

Ben decided to cut some of the hay down along the creek, the grass was high and thick so it wouldn't take long to cut enough for back up this winter. Ben took two of the scythes down from the wall in the barn and spent the afternoon sharpening them. Kate wanted him to go up and get Thomas to help, but Ben told her he would just work until his leg got tired then quit for the day.

Ben took the team and wagon and loaded the two scythes. He headed down to the hay meadow along the creek. It was near noon when he saw two riders coming his way. He knew Kate was going to bring his lunch. One of the riders was her. Then he grinned when he recognized the second rider, it was Benny.

Kate looked at the hay already cut, "You been busy this morning. How's your leg feeling?"

Ben grinned at her as she walked up, "Good, so far. I see you brought me some help. I can go easier now that he's, here, he's probably real soft from just clerking at the store."

Benny walked over to Ben, "You didn't tell me I was supposed to bring my own scythe. I guess I will just watch you work."

Ben nodded toward the wagon, "I brought an extra one this morning, it's in the wagon."

Kate rode back home after they had ate, she took Benny's horse with her. Both men were tired early in the afternoon so headed back for the cabin. Benny decided to ride up and see Charlie and his family for the evening. Ben spent a little time putting a good edge back on both scythe before Kate called him to supper.

The next morning heard Kate laugh as she looked out the kitchen window, "You must have worked Benny too hard yesterday, he, brought two helpers with him. Wait a minute he brought two, and a half helpers, Maria is riding behind her father."

Maria came, racing up to Kate soon as Charlie helped her down. "I get to stay with you."

Charlie walked up, "Rosa and Pedro will be down to get her later on. Pedro wants a berry pie for his birthday. Rosa told him only if he helped her pick them. When they take this one along to pick berries she eats more than she picks." When Kate looked down at Maria she was shaking her head that she agreed.

Kate went about her day, but his time she had a shadow. A lunch time they took it down to the men in the meadow. As they got closer Kate couldn't believe how much hay they had cut. She noticed a few shocks of hay piled up where Ben had cut yesterday. When Kate rode back home Rosa and Pedro were coming down the valley toward them. Kate fixed them lunch, then with Maria perched behind her brother they headed back for home.

Two days later Charlie and Thomas went back to bringing timbers down from the ruble at the settlement. Benny and Ben brought the hay in from the meadow and put it up in the mow of the barn. The next day Benny headed up to help Charlie while Kate helped Ben haul the last load from the hay field.

CHAPTER 8

Ben woke up when he felt Kate shaking him real lightly. "Ben listen, I can hear horse racing by from up on the trail."

Ben pulled on his pants and walked out on the porch, he could hear the fading sound of running horses on the road toward Garnet. Then from above came the sound of another horse racing down to where the trail met the road. As the sound of the running horse faded away the night was silent. Then slowly the normal night sounds came back. Kate had moved out to stand by him, she clung to his arm.

They both jumped when from the darkness came, "One white man and the woman fall from the cliff trail. The others, race away, I think the ghost woman must have scared them." Walking Bear rode up where Ben and Kate could see him.

"Damn it Walking Bear, you're going to cause me to die of heart attack if you don't quit sneaking up on us. What do you mean the white man and woman fell from the cliff. Was it Jacob and Ada?"

"Other white woman from the mountain and one of the men from those who watched you fell. I only heard them scream as they slipped from the ledge. I was on the ledge across from the trail, but I couldn't see good enough to see why the man slipped, but I did see that he pulled the woman over with him. I think the ghost woman was close by. I didn't see her, but I feel it in my body that she was close by. Right now, I think she is near."

"Walking Bear, ghost woman as you call her is no different than Kate here. She is like you, she can move about with no sound, but she doesn't have any magic powers."

"If anyone has magic powers, it's you Walking Bear," Ada said as she stepped up on the porch. Walking Bear started to back his horse away from the porch.

"Walking Bear, you stay here." Ben turned to Ada, "What happened up there tonight? Who fell from the trail?"

"Hattie, she tried to sneak out tonight. She fell over the cliff with the man who came to get her. Jacob and I found out she has been dropping messages to someone below off the cliff where the miners worked.

141

Jacob when he sealed up those mine openings, left a small hole for us to look out over that area below. She must have explained to them in a note of where the lower opening was. The man who came to get her found the cliff trail, but he couldn't find the opening. He was standing there when she came out. He took her hand to help her around the narrow place. He slipped and when he fell he took her with him. The others were waiting where Jacob said you had camped the night the slide covered you. One of them had walked up to where the trail got narrow and was waiting for them. When they fell he turned to run back to where the others were. I was in the rocks above them so I loosened a few rocks and let them roll down the cliff. This started a small rock slide, the man running tripped over the loose rock in the trail. The other riders heard the noise above, them. They mounted their horses and raced away leaving the other man stumbling to get through the rocks on the trail. As soon as he got to his horse he went racing after them."

Ben looked over at Walking Bear and chuckled, "You were right Walking Bear she was close by." He turned back to Ada, "How much do you think she told them about the gold?"

Ada stood there for a minute before answering, "Jacob and I wonder the same thing. He thinks maybe we should leave the mountain for good. He has already figured out how to seal up the mountain if we do go."

Kate had gone back into the cabin earlier to put on more clothes and to build up the fire. She walked back out, "I got hot coffee boiling on the stove."

Ben turned to Walking Bear, "You want some coffee?"

"I will ride to see where the men went after they left here. If I find them still in the valley, do I kill them or just make them think the ghost lady is still after them?"

Ben grinned in the darkness, "Maybe we should try to make them think there is really spirits in the mountain first. If that don't work we may have to use stronger measures later."

Ben could see Walking Bear turn to look behind him, "Do you want to ride with me, Two Blood?"

Charlie stepped from the darkness, "You go ahead Walking Bear, I will stay here in case they, double back on you."

Then Walking Bear was gone, Charlie, followed by Benny and Thomas stepped up onto the porch, from the darkness. Ada had moved inside with Kate before Walking Bear had left, she now stood drinking a cup of hot coffee when Ben and the others walked in. Kate had lit a candle earlier and had placed it back out of the way. It caused ghostly shadows as people moved around.

Ben sat next to Ada, "We figured out messages were coming from in the mine after Walking Bear spotted the rider from the camp on the pass. Every morning he would show up under the cliff. Then one morning they saw him climb up above the trail to pick up something. How did you and Jacob find out she was sending notes?"

"Jacob saw her first. She was sneaking along the passage coming from the mine tunnel one night after she thought everyone was asleep. Unknown even to me he sprinkled dust below each one of the sealed up openings. A few days later he found her footprints below one window. That's when he told me that he thought she was sending messages to someone below." She grinned, "I too saw the rider pick up the message the same time Walking Bear did. I don't understand her way of thinking, Jacob had told her she could live with him as his wife. She has, fooled, a lot of people since she first came into our lives. I thought she was planning to leave a couple of days ago. I found a small pack hidden close to the opening from the mountain. She was trying to leave with enough gold to last her a long while. When she fell you will only find rocks in her pack at the bottom of that canyon. She died the way she came to us, broke."

She turned to Benny who had been listening to her story, "Would you take me up to the cliff now so I can back into the mountain before the sun rises?" She turned to Ben, "If you come up to the opening, be careful I will leave the trail very unsafe after I get across the place where they fell." Ben nodded as she walked out behind Benny.

An hour later, Benny rode back in from taking her up to the mountain. Kate had breakfast waiting for him. The others had eaten while he was gone. Ben was sitting at the table when Benny sat down, "Ada said to tell you her and Jacob will be down soon to talk to you."

For the next few days things were quiet, Benny came back down from Charlie's to help Ben around the place. One night as Ben and Kate were getting ready for bed Kate heard a scratching on the door, "Ben something's outside the door."

Ben moved over to the door with his pistol in his hand, as he slowly opened the door Ada spoke, "Ben, it's me Ada." He opened the door and she stepped in, "Jacob is out in the barn packing the supplies in the pack sacks. He wants to talk to you."

Ben pulled his boots back on, grabbed a jacket as he followed her out the door. He stopped just before he closed the door to look back at Kate, "You want to come along?"

Kate smiled, "I'll wait here. You go ahead."

As Ada led them toward the barn she pointed to the horse barn, "Benny is staying in the tack room in there? Maybe he should join us for this talk."

Ben smiled, "I think he already knows you're here." He looked toward the barn just as Benny stepped out from the door. "Come, join us Benny."

Jacob sat on the bench waiting for them as they walked in, the two full packs lay on the bench by him. He stood up to grasp Ben's hand, "I'm truly sorry about cause you all this trouble. This greed for the gold is getting out of hand. Now that we have found part of the cause of this trouble, I think this is an off shoot of the original family doings. A few things Hattie said unknown to her, leads me to think she too belonged to the family at one time or at least grew up with parents that belong to it. If this is true, then I think maybe if these men leave now they will spread the word, then more trouble will come."

Ben looked at his old friend, "Jacob, are you saying you don't want these men to leave? Do you know if they are still here close by?"

Jacob looked over at Ada, she nodded, "Yes, they are in their camp south of here. Walking Bear is watching them. I think tomorrow morning they will find they are afoot."

Ben smiled in the darkness thinking, 'This little lady covers a lot of ground.' Then he looked back over a Jacob, "Do you think they're other besides these riders in the area?"

"Ada has known for a long spell that they have a message point between their camp and Springfield. One of Walking Bears men is watching it now to see if they can find out where the messenger lives. He spends days after leaving the message or picking up one just riding around before he heads back to town. He back tracks and lays watching his back trail for hours before moving on. It's like he checking for any sign of someone following him."

Ada spoke up, "This man doesn't look like man who is so good at hiding his trail or reading trails left by others. He looks more like a man who should be working in a bank or store somewhere. He dresses like a farmer, bib overalls and homemade shirt. He carries what looks to be a shotgun, but it also has a rifle barrel. As I watched one day he shot an antelope for camp meat. The shotgun is a double barrel and I think that the rifle barrel is underneath. Anyway he always carries it whenever he is off his horse."

Ben slowly shook his head, "Maybe we should have Walking Bear bring those men into the canyons of the hot water. Then he could bring the messenger too. If we had them all together maybe we could figure this out. The problem with that is, what do we do with them once we get this information? If we turn them loose we're back to the problems we have now."

Jacob stood up, "Ada and I will return to the mountain. We will watch for one more week to see what our intruders have in mind. We will meet here seven days from now to discuss their fate. In a month we will be again into our winter season, or close to it. Once the snow starts falling we will be left alone until spring. Ada and I can always get out of the mountain through the valley of the bones even in the worst winter snows. So I will seal up this side of the mountain until spring once the snows start falling. We will meet here on the seventh night." He reached for Ben's hand, "If you can make it to trading post between now and then, maybe you could get our winter supplies. I left you a list and gold in our regular place." He helped Ada into her pack, put his on. With a small wave they walked out into the darkness.

Kate had breakfast started as Benny and Ben walked into the cabin. As they ate Kate looked over at the two men, "Well, you two, what happened tonight?"

Ben smiled as he looked over at Benny, then back to Kate, "We need to make a trip to town in the next couple of days. Jacob left his list of supplies he needs for the winter. He and Ada will be back in seven days to make final arrangements for our friends. Jacob wants us to watch them until then to see if they will slip and let us know what their plans are for us."

Kate looked at Ben, "What do you mean arrangements for those men. I can't believe Jacob would want them killed for what they have done. Chase them off, yes, but kill them. I just can't believe he would go along with that."

Benny looked at Ben, shrugged, then he looked at Kate, "Letting them go back for more people will only make it worse next year after the snow leaves. Kate, Jacob, is saying if this keeps up he will seal up that mountain and him and Ada will leave for good. This I don't want to happen, I like having him and her around, I really enjoy our talks."

Kate stared at the man who had been her right hand man for years, "What do you mean, you're long talks with them. When have you ever spent time talking to either of them?"

Benny looked over at her. A slight grin appeared on the usually sober face, "Kate, I've had many long talks with Jacob in his mountain. Ada, since she found out that I'm not really Bens slave, we have become good friends. We have met many times in our travels."

Kate looked over at Ben, "Did you know about this?"

Ben held up his hands, "No Kate, I'm like you, this is all news to me."

Kate looked at Benny, then, she picked up a hand full of dishes off the table and took them to into the kitchen counter. Mumbling as she left, "I don't know why this surprises me."

Benny decided to ride up to see if Rosa wanted anything from the trading post before Ben and Kate headed for Jacobs supplies. Ben walked down to retrieve Jacob list from the trunk. Inside he found three more small boxes to be mailed, along with a small heavy pouch to pay for supplies.

Ben then thought of the boxes still hidden in the room of the rolled up tarp's that Jacob had brought down earlier. 'I need to get those to town when we go. Jacob probably thinks I've already mailed them.'

As Ben read the list he shook his head, thing to himself, 'This is one big list for one wagon load. Benny may have to drive the second wagon."

That afternoon Benny rode back in, he had Thomas with him. They got two wagons ready for the trip to town. Since Ben had built the wagon for hauling the timber from parts of wagon scattered around the place, they hadn't used the second wagon around the place. It was decided to head out first thing the next morning for Garnet. The next morning Thomas was the only one in for breakfast with Kate and Ben. "Where's Benny this morning?" Kate asked as they sat down to eat.

Thomas shrugged, "He took off last night with Walking Bear when he rode in. He just said for me to drive the extra wagon and he would meet us later in town."

"Did Walking Bear say anything about our guest living south of here?" Ben asked.

"I didn't talk to him. Benny woke me he was going out to talk to Walking Bear. Then later he walked back to grab his coat and told me to go with you this morning. I heard them leave not long after that."

Jess greeted them as they pulled up in front of the trading post, "Howdy farmers. I thought maybe you folks had moved on. Since you stole Benny, I haven't got anyone to keep me up on the gossip."

Kate kissed him on the cheek, "You can have him back whenever you want him. Where's that wife of yours?"

Jess grinned as he motioned toward the door, "I think she's got a surprise for you inside."

Kate stepped inside to look around her old store just as Meg came from the living quarters in the back. Kate let out a laugh, "Meg, what did you let that old fool do to you? Or was this planned?" she asked as she noticed her old friend was carrying a child."

"Oh Kate, I think it's great, so does Jess. I just couldn't believe it when I started seeing the signs that I might be this way. Kate, I just can hardly wait to hold a baby in my arms."

Kate held her close, "Well that's great. I know you and Jess will be good parents. Wait till Ben see you, he'll give Jess all kinds of trouble."

Meg laughed, "Oh Jess is ready for all the kidding, he said it's going to be a long winter as soon as the miners start coming in. He said the worst will be Clayton and Henry when they get here."

Ben gave Jess the list for Jacob, Rosa, then gave him Kate's list, "I need to keep these bills separate, Jess." He and Thomas took the wagons up to cabin. Kate came walking up as they finished putting the teams away.

Kate looked in the cupboards, "We got coffee, that's about all we'll need if we're only going to be here over night. We can give Jess and Meg more of our business by eating down there." She smiled over at Thomas who was looking at her, "The way you eat, I will do my best to pay your grub bill too," then she winked at him. "Ben. Wait until you see Meg! You're going to get a surprise."

Ben and Jess were sitting out on the porch having drink after supper. In rode Benny leading a long string of pack mules and horses all with empty packs. He waved as he rode around the corner and up toward the bigger correl. Thomas has been sitting with them listening to the stories, he got up and followed Benny with the horses. Jess nodded that way, "What's that all about?"

Kate had stepped out about then, "What's with the pack string Benny's leading? Is he going into business for himself?"

Ben glanced over at her, "He's your Indian. We were going to ask you the same thing?"

Kate frowned at him then grinned, "Well get up and go around there and find out."

"Kate he'll be here as soon as he gets those horses and mule taken care of. In his own sweet time we'll find out what he's up to now." Kate shook her head, turned walked down the front door of the saloon and went in.

Benny stuck his head out of the trading post, "Meg fixing me some supper, you fellas want anything?" He had come in the back door from the corrals.

Ben and Jess walked inside, they each got a cup of coffee then sat down to join Benny. "Okay friend," Ben started off, "What's with the big pack string?"

Benny looked up from eating, "I saw that list of supplies you had for Jacob. I decided I could pack his supplies through the valley of the bones and save him a lot of trips up from the barn. Besides we got a good storm coming and that narrow ledge could start getting slick. I went down and borrowed these pack animals from Coby down on the river. He owed me a favor." he went on eating then he stopped again, "This way our nosey friends won't know about the supplies."

Ben looked at Jess, "How you going to explain about the supplies you load up. People are bound to be curious, what Jess here supposed to tell people who ask?"

"Just tell them they're for Walking Bear, most people around here know he lives down in the canyons of the hot water. I'm going to go in that way anyway."

"Does Jacob know about you bringing in his supplies from that way?"

Benny nodded as he ate, "I told him last night when I rode with Walking Bear. Ada had told Walking Bear Jacob wanted to talk to him. She told Walking Bear to bring me with him, I would know the way. So that's why he came after me at the barn. Ada and Jacob met us in the canyon not far from Walking Bears camp. While Walking Bear and Jacob were talking Ada and I decided the pack string would be a good way to get the supplies in there. You are to take one good load for two pack boards with you in case someone is watching the mountain when they come to see us next week. This way it will look as if they only had come after supplies."

"They're only seven of them left now, from both crews. The man who leaves messages at the post office on the trail left note say to keep watching until the mountain snows get deep. If they get a chance they are still supposed to try to get in there to see how much gold Jacob has stored in his vault."

"How did Walking Bear find out what was in the message?"

Benny looked up as he started on big piece of wild berry pie, "Walking Bears nephew Spotted Antelope, who rides with him, can read and write. The man who came after the mail got bucked off when a hornet's nest fell into the trail. He was knocked out for a spell from the fall. Spotted Antelope read the message then."

148

Ben chuckled as he looked over at Jess, who was just, shaking his head. "That's one big worry in this country this time of the year is, hornet's nest falling." Ben nodded.

Kate and Jess packed each packsack as Ben and Thomas brought them in the back door of the trading post. Weighing each pack, then Ben and Thomas took them out to help Benny load them on the animals. With the supplies loaded Benny swung up on his horse, then, he motioned for Thomas to do the same. "We will meet you back at cabin sometime tomorrow." with a wave the loaded string moved off down the alley and soon disappeared over the hill behind the old school house.

Charlotte who had come over earlier to help in the kitchen while Meg feed this crew breakfast stepped out to watch. "Why Benny going that way, your place is down that road?"

Kate walked over to put her arm around her shoulder, "Charlotte with that Indian we never ask questions. He just does his Indian thing." Charlotte looked at Kate with a weird look on her face, Kate laughed as they went inside.

Later with Kate driving the light wagon with Rosa's supplies, led out, Ben with the bigger load following as they headed for home. About half way home Charlie and Pedro, came riding in from a side trail. Kate stopped when they rode up, "Here Charlie you can drive this wagon all these supplies belong to you. You can just take it home with you."

When they got to where you could see the hay field Charlie turned off to go that way. He could save about a mile by missing the building and going this way. He waved and called, "I will bring the wagon back tomorrow."

Ben waved, "Just keep it up at your place until it snows, you might need it or the team."

Pedro was off riding his new horse around the hill. Charlie had tied his horse on the back of the wagon.

The next afternoon Benny and Thomas came, riding in on the road from town. Ben who saw then coming from the bigger barn walked over to wait for them outside the horse barn. "Well how was your trip any problems?"

As Benny swung down he nodded, "Went good. Now Thomas knows the lower route into the mountain. Some of the horses didn't like being in the mountain, but the mules didn't seem to mind a bit."

Ben glanced over at Benny, "Inside the mountain, how far?"

"Those earlier miners made a small barn in the rock to keep a few horses. We could only take four at a time in to unload them."

Three nights later Ben, Kate and Benny sat in the dark cabin waiting for Ada to show up. It was a little before midnight when they heard the light, knock. Ben opened the door, Jacob was standing there. Ben took his coat from by the door and stepped out onto the porch, "You want to come in or go down to the barn to talk?"

"I need to load up and head back, our visitors are back tonight. Ada stayed up near the entrance to make sure they don't get inside. Walking Bear is also up there with two of his men.

As they walked toward the barn Ben could feel the wind that had started to blow sense it got dark. "That wind feels like snow is on its way before morning." As they got to the barn Benny had caught up with them.

Inside Jacob started checking over his pack, "I will leave Ada's pack for another time." He looked at Ben, "Is there anything in her pack I need to take now? If it snows too much I won't be using this entrance until spring so these supplies may not be used."

Benny picked up Ada's pack, "I will carry it up to the cliff trail for her. That way you'll have everything up there with you."

Jacob turned face to Ben, "I don't know what will happen tonight up along the cliff, but I know for sure those men will not make it inside my mountain. Benny will let you know what happens when he and I get up there. Ben once were snowed in, let's just wait until spring, then if those men show up again I will seal up the mountain, and leave."

Ben took his hand, "Okay Jacob, we'll do just that. You and Ada have a good winter. Charlie and his family are going to spend the winter up in their new home. He says he and Thomas are going to do some trapping to keep busy. Kate and me are going back to our house in town once the snow starts getting deep."

Ben was alone to walk back to the cabin, inside the heat from the stove felt, good. He looked at Kate as she walked up to him, "I think come morning the ground is going to be turning white, that wind is getting cold."

"Where's Benny?"

"He took Ada's pack up to the cliff trail for Jacob. She stayed up there to watch our visitors who are back looking for a way into the mountain. He says she's not alone watching them, Walking Bear and a couple of his men are there too."

Kate put her head on his shoulder, "Why can't they just leave Jacob alone? I'm tired of always having to worry about those men sneaking around. Ben, when will all of this end so we can enjoy our new home up here?"

Kate was cooking breakfast the next morning when the door opened and Benny walked in. "It's beginning to snow. Kate, you better put on more breakfast, I could see Clayton dropping down this way from the high trail as I walked from the barn. He must have ridden all night to be here this early. The smell of snow in the wind must have made him nervous."

Ben nodded as he set a cup of coffee on the table for Benny, "I'll bet Henry's not far behind if he figured on coming out the high trail. From his mine it's a tossup which route is shorter."

As soon as they heard the horses outside Ben and Benny put on their coats and walked out to meet Clayton. "You want us to help you unload those packs, before or after breakfast, stranger?"

"Boy was I glad to see that smoke coming from your chimney. I've been riding all night to get off the trail before it snowed too much. I was going to ride on in but these pack animals are tired. Let's unload them now, then, I can enjoy that warm fire."

Ben motioned, "Follow me, we'll unload in the big barn, then put the horses in the other barn and give them a little grain."

Inside Clayton gave Kate a hug, "How's my favorite gal?"

"It's good to have you back, Clayton. How come you're coming in so late?"

"We had a good water year in the high country, so mining's been good. I guess I kinda forgot what time of the year it was. Henry coming in on the low trail, he might have got into Garnet last night or for sure today. Say Ben what was going on the high trail up above here last night? With that skiff of snow this morning I could still see these, strange track up where the trail passes by the last flat before you hit the cliff trail. It looked like six or eight riders had a wild party up there."

Ben looked over at Benny, a faint smile appeared. "Our visitors had a little cougar trouble last night."

Ben looked over at Kate as she stared at Benny, then back at Benny, "Manmade?"

"Spotted Antelope killed a cougar down by their camp yesterday, somehow the hide got into the rocks near the cliff trail."

Clayton looked over at Ben then at Kate, "Who in the hell is the visitors and who is Spotted Antelope?"

All three turned to look at Clayton, then, Ben laughed, "Clayton that one of those stories for the trading post this winter. We'll fill you in on part of it as we eat."

Kate was clearing away the dishes as the men were finishing the last of the coffee. Clayton was shaking his head, "So that little gal who tried to fool you people is now dead? You also have more people trying to break into that damn mountain to get any gold Jacob has stashed away. Now you folks have had a busy summer or at least since I was here over the fourth."

Clayton went out to the tack room where Benny and Thomas were sleeping for a few hours. Later he came back over to the cabin, "That wind has kinda let up a little, I guess I could pack up and go on into town before dark. That old, Mountain, sure is beginning to look white up on those highest peaks this afternoon. I'm sure glad I rode on through last night, I doubt anyone else will try that trail until spring."

Ben and Benny had been out closing up the buildings for winter had walked in right behind Clayton. "Why don't you wait until morning, we'll just load your gear in the wagon and go in then. We can just bring your pack animals in when we bring ours. We still got grass down along the creek they can get too. Then when we bring them down, we'll just take them all down to Coby's for the winter."

They woke the next morning to a clear beautiful winter day. The sun was just beginning to hit the higher peaks. Ben opened the door and stepped out to sweep off the small porch deck. As he looked toward the barn Benny and Clayton were just walking out. As they walked toward the cabin the snow looked to be about ankle deep. Ben stepped back inside, "You got company coming up from the barn."

Kate nodded, "I think I'll go in with Clayton and start warming up the house if you don't mind?"

Ben looked over at her, "Good idea. I think I'll stay up here for a few more days getting this place ready for winter. I'll bring the horses down when I come. I need to see if Charlie's got enough wood to last until spring. I'll bring his extra horse down too."

Benny and Clayton walked in. Benny nodded his head toward the door. "Charlie and Thomas are coming across the meadow. It looks like their bringing the wagon back. They got two saddle horses tied behind."

It was a little afternoon when Kate and Clayton headed for town. Clayton had loaded all his gear, packs and all for the trip in. Thomas and Charlie had gone back up to Charlie's to work on sawing up all the wood they had hauled in. Thomas was going to stay to help Charlie until they got it done. Then he was going to stay on with Charlie to help with the trap line for the winter.

Ben and Benny finished getting the place closed up, so they decided to ride up and see how many horses Charlie wanted to send out with them. As they got near the place Ben motioned to Benny, "What's that building, up there on the hill, it looks like it's built right into the hill? I can see smoke coming from it."

Benny looked over at Ben, "Thomas said something about his new sleeping cabin. That must be it. I was wondering where he figured on staying this winter. Charlie's cabin isn't that big for him to stay there with all the family."

They stopped at the hitch rail, then, walked over to where Thomas and Charlie were working. Ben looked at the pile of logs and at the timber wagon piled high with logs. "Charlie you must figure on a damn hard winter with all this wood."

Benny had walked over next to Thomas. He motioned up toward the building built into the hillside. "Is that your new home? I see smoke. Did you build a rock fireplace?"

"Charlie helped Pedro and me, build it. I found a good small stove up in the ruins while getting out the timbers. In fact we found a good stove for Rosa, too. So I have a very warm place for me to winter while helping Uncle Charlie trap."

Later Ben and Benny walked up to see the new place. It was bigger inside than they thought just looking from the outside. Ben motioned to the two bunks, "You figuring on company?"

Thomas smiled, "That is Pedro's bunk. He said if his mother gets mad at him he will sleep up here."

After looking over all the new addition to the place, Ben and Benny took all but two of Charlie's and Thomas horse, they headed for the main place. The next morning they closed up the place and headed for town with the horse herd. A cold wind was blowing as they rode along. Both men were bundled up to keep warm. Benny had said earlier he wanted to spend the night down at Coby's, so they stopped at the edge of town. Ben rode in to see if anyone else had horses to be taken down to the winter range. Kate saw him riding in and she stepped to the porch of the trading post to call to him. As he rode up she motioned toward Benny sitting with the other horses on the ridge above town. "High stranger, how come you're partners not coming in?"

Ben nodded, "He's headed down to Coby's the horses. We were wondering if anyone else had horses ready to go down to the river?"

Clayton had walked out to stand by Kate, "Henry took his down the other day, along with a few from other miners who have come in."

Ben waved and Benny disappeared over the ridge with the horses.

The next day Benny came riding back in. He swung down in front of Ben and Kate's house. Ben opened the door as Benny walked up onto the porch. "How come you didn't leave your horse down at the barn, you just riding through?" Then he laughed.

Benny just looked at him with his same blank look, "I got some news you might like to hear. Walking Bear went to check on our friends in their camp. He found all seven of them dead. They had been shot in their blankets. From the ridge where Walking Bear stopped, it looked like whoever killed them used a shotgun at close range. He couldn't ride any closer to check them without leaving fresh tracks. With the new skiff of snow, he didn't have any tracks for him to follow to see where the shooter went."

Ben looked up at Kate who had walked up to stand beside him, then, he looked back at Benny. "Ada and Walking Bear both have spoken of the man, who delivered the messages to the post office. He carries a double barreled shotgun with a rifle barrel underneath. Maybe that fellas figured he didn't need those boys anymore and didn't want them talking to anyone."

Benny nodded as he sipped the hot coffee Kate had set before him. "Spotted Antelope is waiting on the ridge for me. I told him to wait to see if you had anything you want Walking Bear to do? Do you want for them to go up through the valley of the bones to let Jacob to know about this?"

Ben thought for a moment, "Yes, that would ease Jacobs mind about them still trying to get in the mountain. Of course tell him the messenger with the shotgun is still out there somewhere."

Benny nodded finished his coffee and pulled his coat back on. After he left Ben sat there looking at the ceiling, then he looked over at Kate. "To shoot them in their beds is pure cold blooded murder. Kate whoever this man is or who he works for are very crude men. I think come spring we need to think over how we want to spend the summer up there at the cabin. I think maybe we need for the law to get involved in this. I left them out of this so far to protect Jacob and Ada, but now it getting a little out of hand."

A week later Ben was cleaning out the barn when he heard Jess calling his name from back of the trading post. He stepped out to wave at Jess, "What up?" He hollered back.

"You need to come down here." Ben waved, then, he stepped back inside to grab his coat. When he stepped back out Kate was standing on the porch of the house.

"What's all the hollering about?"

Ben shrugged, "Jess said for me to come down there. It kinda sounded serious. You want to come along?" Kate grabbed her coat and hurried after Ben.

When they walked to the front of the building from the back door, two men with badges on their vest were talking to Jess. Jess motioned to Ben, "Ben, Kate, this Marshal Moore and Sheriff Collins from Springfield." Both men stepped forward to shake Ben's hand. Kate stepped forward to offer her hand, then, Jess went on. "A hunter found a camp with seven dead men in it on that ridge south of your place. The Marshal here says they were shot in their beds by someone using a shot-gun."

Ben glanced at Kate. Then, back to face the two lawmen, "We've known most of the summer men were camped up there. For a while they had two camps, three of them were camped up on the high trail through the pass. They have spent the summer watching the mountain where the family was mining before the avalanche whipped out their settlement. They never have come by the place to talk to us, but they sure did a lot of night riding." Ben was hoping these two would just believe his story and not push the issue. He really didn't want to get Jacob involved.

Jess spoke up, "We've had a few strangers stop by the saloon that asked the girls all about the mining in this area. Mostly, if anyone, was still mining in those cliffs. A couple of the same men did buy a few supplies from us during the summer. I never did know where they were camped."

The sheriff nodded, "When we got the report from the hunter, I sent a couple of deputies out to investigate. There was a new skiff of snow covering the area since the shooting. The only track they found was on the ridge behind the camp. They were unshod ponies and they never rode anywhere close to the camp of the dead men. We've been hearing of a few Indians being in this area most of the summer. So far, there's, been no complaints about them bothering anyone. A shotgun killing, don't sound like Indians, anyway. I think they rode up, saw the dead men. Turned, rode away. Leaving the men just where they were shot."

The Marshal looked over as he ate, "Are you the Kate Crawford that used to own this place?"

Kate grinned, "I am. My name is Jasper now. Ben and I got mar-ried last year down in Springfield. Jess here is leasing the trading post from me to see if he likes this better than mining."

155

He grinned, "I've always heard of this old town of Garnet and the lady who wouldn't let it die."

Kate laughed, "Well maybe part of that might be true. My first husband and I had faith in this place, so we stuck it out after most of the miner raced away for another strike. The he died after the big avalanche killed all those people in the settlement. I stayed on here along with my friend April, I run the store while she took over the saloon. Then many of the miner from the high country started taking over these vacant houses for their winter homes and Garnet lives on. Then I got this one to quit roaming the Mountain," as she grasped Ben's arm, "Then we took over the buildings up near the mountain for our home."

"Well it was nice to meet all you folks, I guess the sheriff and I better head back to Springfield. If, you hear anything, that would help us to learn more of these dead men. Sent, us a message on the stage-coach."

As the riders rode out of sight, the door of the saloon opened. Clayton, Henry along with a few more of the men from town walked over to the trading post, "What's with the law being here?"

Jess filled them all in on the story, while Ben and Kate sat back listening to him. When he finished Clayton looked over at Ben, "Those, the same fellas that's been nosing around your place?" Ben nodded, yes.

Later Kate and Ben walked back up to the house to find Benny nursing a cup of coffee. "How come you didn't come down to listen to the law talking," Kate asked.

"I was in the kitchen I heard most of what they said." He looked over at Ben, "You did a good job. I think they believed your story. Now we need to find out what happened to the mail man. Maybe he left the country?"

For the next two weeks the weather changed, it rained for three days then the wind changed to the north. When the sky finally cleared a foot of snow covered the area around Garnet. The stage finally made a run after the weather cleared. Ben and Kate walked down as they saw the stage leaving down the road. When they got to the trading post Benny and Jess were packing in all the freight from the front porch, Ben jumped in to help.

Meg and Kate sat out coffee for everyone at the big table back by the heating stove. Benny looked over at Ben, "The stage driver was just telling us that daughter of Tyler Bates found a horse in bad shape not far from their place. The horse still had a saddle on when she found it. She took it home with her and I guess it's going to live. No gear was on

156

the saddle except a double barrel shotgun in the scabbard. I guess Tyler tried to back track the horse, but he lost the tracks in the new snow. He found where the horse had been during the storm, but that's all he found so far. I guess the Marshal is combing the area for the rider."

Ben looked over at Kate, then back at Benny, who just gave a slight nod. Clayton looked over Ben, "You figure this fits in with those dead men the Marshal told you about?"

Ben glanced at Kate, he knew Clayton and the miners who had come in for the winter didn't know anything about the mail man as they called him. He didn't want these men involved. The less they knew about those dead men and the mail man was best right now. Clayton and Henry knew that Jacob lived in the mountain, they also knew about Ada, but the others Ben wanted to keep in the dark right now. At least until they found out who was in back of all this trouble.

Everyone eyes were on Ben, ever since Clayton has asked him about the dead man. Finally Ben nodded, "Yeah, I do think maybe it all does fit together. If they found that horse south east of Tyler's place, then that must be close to where they found those other men. My only question is who in the hell are these people? You know I can see some crooks trying to find some easy gold to steal, but why are they so sure there's any gold in that mountain. I don't recall anyone from around here ever seeing any gold from that mountain before that slide wiped out the settlement, do you?"

Everyone was looking at each other shaking their heads no, then, Clayton looked back at Ben, "No, I guess we've always figured they were mining gold or they wouldn't have spent that much time building what they did."

Ben eyes were on Clayton to see if he mentioned Jacob being in the mountain to these other miners. When he didn't, then he figured his little spiel had let Clayton know, he didn't want Jacob being in the mountain brought up. He glanced over at Kate she was looking at Jess, then, he noticed Jess was really looking her way. Then Ben picked up a small nod from Jess to Kate, Jess turned to look back at Ben.

Later the miners who had been in the trading post headed for the saloon, except Clayton. Ben smiled over at him, "I'm glad you and Jess didn't bring up Jacob being in that mountain. Until we find out who's behind all of this, I'd just as soon we keep it among just the ones sitting here now. I hope if the Marshal finds the rider of that horse he lets us know. I'm really curious who he is, I suppose that depending how or when they find him. I would think if his shotgun was in the scabbard maybe he was shot or at least knocked off his horse. With this new snow they may never find him, if he's dead or badly wounded."

Later Ben and Kate went back to their place, Benny showed up later. "I think come morning I will ride up to see how Charlie and his family are making out. I think they should know about the mailman, so he and Thomas can watch as they move around trapping. If he's dead, the birds and wild animals will soon be eating on him. Both Charlie and Thomas read sign real good they might spot him from watching the birds." He shrugged, "Who knows I may see Walking Bear on my travels. He might know something we don't." The next morning was a bright cold winter morning, with not a cloud in the sky. Benny bundled up and swung up on his horse for the ride up the valley. As he rode along watching the hills for tracks, two riders rode out of the rocks near the small summit above the buildings. They dropped in alongside Benny as he rode on down into the valley. "What brings you two out so early on the fine clear morning?"

Spotted Antelope who was riding in the middle looked over, "Walking Bear figured you'd be out and about today. So we've been watching for you. We been watching you since you rode over the first little hill from town. Walking Bear wanted to make sure no one was following you."

Walking Bear looked over at Benny, "We found where the mailman, as you call him lay's. The man with the badge was just over the ridge from the body yesterday so we rode away before he saw us. We were in a place with no cover, so we rode away before he got to the body. Two other riders with badges were not far away as they looked for him. Later we heard one lone pistol shot. We figured he was signaling he had found the body."

Benny glanced over at his two friends, "We heard from the stage driver that Tyler Bates daughter found a saddled horse wondering around close to their ranch. A shotgun was still in the scabbard."

As they rode near the barns and the cabin, Benny watched for any tracks in the snow close to them. The only tracks were elk along the creek bottom in the lower pasture. Ben had dropped all the gates to see if the elk would use them instead of breaking down the fences. So far Benny could only see one place where the top rail had been knocked off.

Charlie leaned his axe against the chopping block as he saw the riders coming up the meadow. He motioned to Thomas who was stacking the chopped wood under a lean-to on the side of the house. "We got company," as he pointed to the meadow.

Benny swung down along with Walking Bear and Spotted Antelope. "I thought I better check on you brother, to see if you still had my son living with you." He looked over at Thomas, "You getting the hang of trapping yet? You know you've got a good teacher here working on you."

Benny rolled a block of wood over next to the fire. Charlie was burning some of the big knots, a coffee pot set off to one side. Charlie motioned toward the house, "We can go inside if you like."

Benny shook his head no, "I'm dresses for riding. It would be way too warm inside." Walking Bear grunted he agreed and moved a block over closer.

Rosa came walking out carrying a big pot of coffee, Pedro and Maria was tagging along behind each carrying extra cups. Benny grabbed Maria, "How come you and your brother aren't in school?"

Rosa laughed, "I called recess when I saw you three riding up. I knew they wouldn't get any school work done until they got to see you. It is good to have company."

Rosa and the kids went back inside in a short time later. Benny told Charlie about the dead men and about Tyler daughter finding the mailman's horse. Charlie looked over at Thomas, then back at the three visitors, "We spotted a body yesterday, or at least something dead in the snow. I didn't want any lawmen seeing our tracks so we didn't ride any closer. Thomas and I were going to ride over to Walking Bears camp this afternoon to let him know about it. I figured if we were being watched they would just thinking we were checking out the hot springs for game. Thomas was checking traps when he saw the lawmen taking the bodies away from that camp. We didn't know how they died. He did see tracks of Walking Bear and Spotted Antelope on a ridge overlooking the spot, so we knew they knew of the camp." He stopped and looked over at Benny, "You think the dead man is the one called the mailman?"

Benny shrugged, "The stage coach driver is the one who told everyone at the trading post about the girl finding the horse. With a shotgun in the scabbard, I just think it must be him, not that many people carry just a shotgun in this country."

Thomas looked over at his dad, "Before the tracking snow, Uncle Charlie and me were scouting that area for game. We found many tracks, then, when we back tracked that one time we found we were being followed by a lone horseman. So we headed for home."

Charlie nodded, "One thing we did find was tracks of a two wheel cart. It had real wide wheels, you know like the ones on the timber wagon Ben built sitting over there," as he motioned to the wagon. "Whoever had the cart was staying away from the main horse trails and sticking to the open ridges. He was traveling just off the ridge top so he wouldn't skyline himself. Now since it snowed his tracks are nowhere to be found."

Benny looked over at Walking Bear, "Did you see any cart tracks before or after it snowed?"

Spotted Antelope spoke up before Walking Bear could answer Benny, "I saw something one day when the storm was still just rain. Now I know it must have been that cart you are asking about. It was sitting on a point west of where that camp was. From across valley where I was, I couldn't figure out what it was. When I first saw it I thought it was a tent tucked under that tree on the point, now I think it was what you called a cart with a tarp over it. It was open on the back side under the hill top. I think the horses were under it too. A person looking out over the other side could see all the country around Springfield. Maybe on a good clear day, even a few buildings of the town."

Benny looked over at Charlie, "Maybe you and Thomas should forget trapping in that area."

Charlie nodded he agreed, "That's no, problem, we didn't leave any traps out over there. That's too dry a country for what were after."

Benny motioned up to the peaks above them, clouds were beginning to appear and you could see the drifting snow swirling around those rocky crags. "I think we have a snow coming, I also think I will head back for town. All three riders swung up. Benny looked back down at brother and son, "I'd ride together until we figure this cart out."

Charlie and Thomas both nodded as the riders headed down the valley back toward the main buildings of Ben and Kate place. At the rocks Benny stopped, "Walking Bear, you and Spotted Antelope ride with care. Maybe you could kinda keep Charlie's place on your schedule of places to watch?"

Walking Bear almost grinned, "We do check it often. Also the little ghost watches them from her perch in the mountain. She will let me know if I need to go up there."

Benny looked over at the two staring back at him, then he laughed, "You two have many strange ways of dealing with the one who you were scared of not long ago. I do not want to know more for now, maybe later I will need to know. Now I must go before the wind gets any colder."

As Benny was rubbing down his horse Ben walked into the barn, "Was everything alright up in the valley?"

Benny looked over at him, "Tonight after supper and after I get warmed up, we need to talk. Many things my brothers know of what's going on south of here, besides the dead men."

Ben nodded, "Just you and me or do we include Kate, Jess and Clayton?"

"For right now, I'd rather it just you and Kate. Later we'll decide who else needs to know. I think we are getting close to who's causing all of this. I do not like what happening."

Ben nodded, "You coming up for supper or are you going to eat with Jess and Meg?"

"I will eat with Jess and Meg like I usually do. That way I can listen if they have anything to add to what Charlie and Walking Bear have found out. You know those stage drivers are always telling tail of some sort."

Later Kate and Ben where finishing supper, Kate looked over at Ben, "What do you think Benny found out? If he doesn't want anyone but you and me to hear it, it must involve someone from here in Garnet. Ben I hate it when our own neighbors might be the ones causing all of this trouble. It was so much easier before those religious nuts ever showed up in the first place."

Benny finished tell them all he had learned from Charlie and Walking Bear. When he finished both Ben and Kate just sat there looking at each other. Then Ben looked over at Benny, "So it sounds like our mailman's luck run out too? We, kind of figured he must be the one who bush wacked our night riders, because of the shotgun being used to kill them. Now were back to finding someone else is behind all this. I wish we could find a place where we could get a good look at those wheel tracks. If those tracks, were made by wheels from a freight wagon, or like the ones, we sold from up at our place. We can trace the ones we sold, Tyler's got two of them, Coby's bought two. He sold that first one to a wagon train moving through last spring. Does he still have the second one he got?" He glanced over at Benny who just shrugged he didn't know. "We know Tyler is using the good one we'd fixed up to haul freight. The second one he said he would work on it over at his place during the slow time to save a little money. If I remember right the running gear on it was good, it just needed work on the box and bows for the cover. I guess we need to ride down to see Tyler to see if it got all its wheels under it. Then check with Coby to see what happened to his second wagon."

Kate had been listening to the men talk. She held up her hand to slow up the talk between them. "You know Ben when we were in

Springfield last spring we stopped by the freight office to see if they'd bring up all the furniture we bought for us and the saloon. I remember all the parts of wagons of all kinds scattered about in that back field behind the horse barn. I think I mentioned the one sitting by the black-smith shop was just like the ones you and Clayton rebuilt."

Ben grinned, "Your right, I remember that now. So I guess our theory about tracing down the wagon we restored isn't so important now. Hell those wheels could have come from anyplace along that main road where some wagon was left after it broke down. I still want to see those tracks, but I want to see fresh tracks. Not one left after the snow melts."

Benny scooted his chair back, "Well, I guess I'll head for bed. Now you two know what I found out today, so come morning we can figure out what we're going to do."

"Tomorrow is stage day, maybe the marshal sent along a message if he found the body. If not maybe the driver heard a rumor or two about them finding another body," Ben said as Benny walked toward the door.

Ben and Kate walked down to the trading post the next morning to see if anything came in on the stage. They had just sat down with a cup of coffee when Jess called form behind the counter, "Here comes the stage." He walked over toward the table, "Ben how about you help Benny and me unload our freight and get it inside?"

The stage, come to stop as Jess and the other two stepped out. Clayton and Henry came walking up as the driver dropped down from the high seat. With the five men and the driver working the freight was soon unloaded. The two passengers were inside eating as the men fin-ished. The driver sat down with Clayton, Henry and Ben at a separate table. Meg brought the driver lunch as Benny walked over with the big coffee pot. "We'll what's new in Springfield?" Ben asked as the driver started eating.

"By God Ben, them lawmen been busy. They found another body not far from where Rachel, Tyler Bates daughter found that horse I told you folks about. When I was loading up this morning I saw two depu-ties riding in with another body loaded on a pack horse. I don't know anything about this one, but I did notice they were coming in from the other side of town. Like maybe, this one was from down on the main road west of town. I think the Marshal sent you a letter in that mail sack, Ben. Anyway he said he was going to when I ate supper with him last night."

162

Ben got up and walked over to where Jess was sorting the mail, as he walked up Jess handed him a letter. Ben opened and read the short note. It was just about what the driver had said, except he mentioned again seeing unshod horse tracks on the surrounding hills. He was asking if Ben had any ideas who these riders were. The Marshal knew Ben had at least one Indian working up on his place. Ben grinned as he handed the letter to Kate, then he walked back over to the table. Clayton looked up at him, Ben shrugged, "The letter just says what Harry here just told us about finding the body. He didn't mention anything about the one you saw them bringing in this morning. I imagine we'll be seeing that Marshal before long. He's real curious about the unshod horse tracks up where these bodies have been found. I need to send him a note to let him know that Charlie, Benny's brother and Thomas are trapping this winter. I just figure he's seeing their tracks." He glanced over at Benny who was just looking at him, with that same blank look as usual. "Harry when you come back through tomorrow I'll have you a letter to the Marshal about them trapping up there in that area. He did say none of the tracks are close to where the bodies have been."

Later as Ben and Kate headed back up to their place Benny walked with them. As soon as they were away from everyone, Benny looked over at Ben, "You do real good at telling only what you want people to know. I sometimes wonder about how you keep these stories straight when you leave so much out?" A small grin appeared.

Ben smiled, "Hell Benny, I better keep it straight. The way things are going I could be talking to main guy himself. This bugs the hell out of me, not knowing who's behind all of this. I just about ready to think maybe it's not the gold as much as it is getting rid of Jacob. I really think when all of this is settled it will have something to do with Jacob and the family. Like maybe Jacob's father did something before they chased him off and now someone or the family in generals trying to get even?"

Benny looked over at Kate, "Now, he's, having, to just guess to try to figure this out. Too much thinking, Ben, we just need to be ready when this all breaks loose. Before spring we'll know who's behind this. Jacob and Ada are safe in that mountain now, unless these people know of the valley of the bones. With Walking Bear out there I doubt if anyone will find the back door to the mountain without him knowing it. Knowing the Ghost Lady as Walking Bear calls her, Ada is probably well aware of what's going on. Between her and Jacob that lower entrance could be hard on anyone trying to sneak in there. A couple of places that trail is, very narrow."

Ben nodded, "I suppose your right. I'll get that message done and take it down to the store so it can go out tomorrow. I think the Marshal will be showing up if the weather stays clear."

Benny headed down to the store to help Jess. Ben wrote his note to the marshal. Later he and Kate walked down to the trading post to mail the letter. Meg sat back at the table alone when they walked in, you could tell she was getting close to being a mother. Kate walked up behind her and started rubbing her neck and shoulders, "You doing alright, Meg?"

"Kate I hurt all over. My legs are all swollen up. I can hardly move around. I wish this kid would show up," Kate could feel her sobbing.

"Easy girl, I think it could happen any time. Do you want Benny to ride into town and get a mid-wife to come stay with you?"

Meg shook her head no, "Elsie says she can handle everything. I guess she was the oldest of eight girls, she says she helped her mother with all of them with no midwife. I'm leaving this up to her."

About then Elsie walked in, "Good you're here Kate. I think by evening were going to have a new addition to our town. How about you stay here with her while I get her bed fixed up for this?"

Ben had gone over to the saloon leaving just the three women in the store. When Elsie walked out from the back of the store Benny was with her. He looked close at Meg's eyes, then, looked up at Kate. "You take her arm on that side. We'll move her back to the bedroom." He whispered to Elsie as he walked by, "Maybe you should go get Jess," she nodded.

It was close to evening when Jess heard a scream. He started toward the back of the room just as Kate stepped into the room. She smiled, "Easy Dad, she's fine. With Elsie and that witch doctor in there with her she in good hands."

Jess looked at Kate, "What's Benny doing in there?"

Kate smiled, "Jess I think we're lucky he's in there with her. Like Elsie just said before I left, this isn't the first time he's help with a birth of a child. That Indian knows a lot about pain and natural type medicine to ease it." She smiled, "Jess, I still think he was a witch doctor, medicine man or whatever before he decided to come into white man's world to live," then she laughed.

Ben had gone back up to the house earlier to build up the fire. He came walking in from the back door, "How's the father to be holding up?"

About the same time a sound of a new born crying broke the still-ness. Kate jumped up from her chair, "I think we have our newest addi-tion to Garnet." She hurried off toward the back room.

A while later Elsie came carrying the new born into the room, "Jess, meet your new son."

Jess peeked into the blanket, "I forgot how small new born babies are. How's Meg, Elsie?"

Nobody noticed Benny had walked into the room, "She's fine Jess. That lady is a real trooper."

Ben nudged his friend, "I'll bet you were a lot of help in there."

Elsie spoke up before anyone, "Ben, this man knew just what to do. This wasn't his first time helping with a birth. In fact he taught me a few things I'd never seen before." She walked up next to Benny, "You do good work my friend."

Benny took baby and Jess into see the new mother. Elsie looked at Kate, "I'll stay with her for a while, you, want to stay the night?"

Kate nodded, "Sure, I'd be glad to sit with her."

"No need for you to stay, Kate. I just told Jess and Meg I'd spend the night," Benny said as he walked into the room. Why don't you two go tell everyone in the saloon about our newest, citizen? Elsie and I can handle things here."

Kate tended bar while April and Charlotte hurried over to see Meg and the new baby. Later after they were back Kate and Ben headed up the hill for home. "I wonder what name they will give, him?" Ben asked as they walked along.

Kate smiled, "Well unless they changed their minds, Meg said his name would William Garrett. If it would have been a girl they had picked out Wilma."

CHAPTER 9

Marshal Moore rode up to the trading post one clear day in early April. As he swung down Jess stepped out into the sunshine, "Good morning for a ride Marshal. I think maybe we've survived another winter."

"I don't suppose you'd have any breakfast still sitting on the back of the stove? I got a real early start this morning from Springfield."

"Come on in Marshal, I know Meg is still cooking for a few of those sleepy head miners who partied most of the night." He held the door open as the Marshal walked inside. Clayton and Henry were both sitting at the table nursing a cup of coffee.

Clayton held out his hand, "Good to see you survived the winter marshal. What brings you out so early?"

The marshal pulled out a chair and sat down, "Oh, I just need to see Ben Jasper. He's still around isn't he?"

Clayton nodded, "Yes and no. Ben, Benny and Kate rode out yesterday for their home in the valley. They took supplies for, Charlie, Benny's, bother who spent the winter up there with his family. I think Ben wanting to get back to work up there, so he wanted to see if the snow was gone yet. They'll probably be back tomorrow."

The marshal nodded, "I guess that's another fifteen or so miles, right? My horse is kinda tired I might have to wait until later to ride on up there."

Jess had heard him as he worked over behind the counter, "Marshal we can solve that problem for you, we've got a pasture full of horses that need to be rode. Benny brought up part of our herd from down at Coby's on the river. Benny and Ben spent a day trimming and shoeing them before they left. You're welcome to anyone out there." He chuckled, "A few of them might have a few kinks to be smoothed out."

The marshal nodded, "By God Jess I'll take you up on the offer. It's been awhile since I been on a horse with a hump in his back."

Clayton went out to help the marshal change horses. "I'd ride along with you, but my head is a little on the sore side this morning. We kinda had a wild party last night, it was April's birthday. Of course by this time of the winter we usually don't need a reason to party," then he laughed.

As the marshal swung up he grinned, "I was wondering why the hung over looks. Thanks for the help."

Kate was busy cleaning up the cabin while Ben was busy outside opening up the barns. He had turned on the water last night so this morning she had water in the tank by the porch. Benny had spent the night up with Thomas in his dugout. Rosa was thrilled with all the supplies he had brought. Benny loaded up the furs that they had trapped during the winter. He told them he would take them down to Coby when he got back to town. Coby bought furs for a buyer who traveled the main road on the river.

Benny pulled up at the corral as Ben came walking down from the horse barn. Benny motioned to the road above the cabin, "Companies coming. I see a shiny badge on his vest. It looks like that Marshal Moore."

As he pulled to a stop he looked over at the packs they were unloading, "Boy it's been a long while since I've see furs like those you fellas got there. They must be the winters work of those Indians you said work for you up here."

Ben nodded, "Charlie is the man you speak of. He's Benny's here's brother and his helper is Benny's son Thomas. Their place is up that draw over there," as he pointed. "As you get up toward the old settlement that draw turns into a good size valley. We staked that too when we took over this p0lace."

The marshal swung down, "If this horse looks familiar, it's because I got it from Jess at the trading post. He loaned me this horse, mine was kinda tired from the ride from Springfield. We need to talk about our problems up here." He looked over at Benny.

Ben laughed, "Come on up to the house, we'll talk over a cup of coffee. You can talk about whatever you want around Benny and Kate."

"Well, the day before yesterday I got a report that another body was found between Springfield and Tyler Bates place. When I got up there the body was Tyler himself. Now comes the part that's got me buffaloed, he was driving a wide wheel cart. Whoever shot him took the team, or turned them loose. Tyler was slumped over in the seat with a lone bullet in his head. On the seat beside him was a double barreled shotgun. When I got to the Tyler place, it was deserted. In the bunk-house we found who my deputies said was a hired hand, dead. He'd been shot in his bed. As we looked around everything was in its place. They had turned the small calves in with the two milk cows. The corral gates were open the livestock was in the pasture. Inside the house nothing was missing, except the people."

Ben looked over at Benny, who was studying the marshal, "Marshal, did you find any tracks so you know how many people were involved?"

"Why don't you folks just call me Drew? That would sound, more friendly if we're going to be working together. As far as, tracks. Not really. It almost looks like they turned the extra horses loose in the yard when they left. Didn't Tyler have one of those big wagons you fellas sold him?"

Ben nodded, "In fact he had two of them. We sold him the first one that we had fixed up. Later I sold him one from up here that needed some work done on it. Why are you asking?"

"There's not a wagon of any type on the place that I can find. One of my deputies has been trying to court Rachel, Tyler's oldest daughter. He says at least two of the big teams are missing. If they took the wagons, why leave all the household goods? I can't find anything missing in the house."

Ben looked over at Benny, "You think Walking Bear could know anything about this?"

Benny stood up, "I will go see? I don't think he does or he's been over to see some of us. Charlie said they had been by a few times this winter."

Drew was looking from one to the other, "Who in the hell is Walking Bear?"

Benny walked out as Ben turned to the Marshal, "Drew, when I told you about Charlie living here I didn't tell you we have a few more Indians came with him. They live down in the canyons of the hot water and they live very peaceable. I didn't mention them to you because they want to stay here and not go back where they came from. You'll have to ask Benny where that was because I really don't know. Some of those unshod tracks you were asking about last fall were made by Walking Bear and his, half-brother, Spotted Antelope. The reason they never rode down closer was because they didn't want any trouble."

Drew sat there looking at Ben then his eyes went to Kate, "How much more don't I know about? Is there someone living in that mountain?"

168

Kate grinned, "Marshal, I think you'll have to have Ben fill you in on most of this. I know most of it, but all this started before Ben and I got married."

An hour later as Kate sat supper on the table, Drew sat staring at Ben. "Holly Christ man, do you realize what all you just dropped on me? Hell I'll be the laughing stock of the country if any of this ever gets out. I'm supposed to be the marshal of this area, now I find I don't know anything about it, except my little corner, here around, Springfield."

Ben nodded, "Don't feel bad most of the miners wintering in Garnet no nothing about any of this either. When Jacob saved my life, is when I really came involved with him and later Ada." He smiled, "Drew when you first meet Ada, don't misjudge her from her looks. She very small, but she is a deadly fighter and a very good tracker. Even Walking Bear is a little scared of, her. He calls her the Ghost Woman. Lately they have worked together and he's beginning to find she is human," then he laughed. "You know her Dad was a lawman like you, with three daughters and a wife who belonged to that religious group who tried to mine that mountain. They are known as the family by all who has dealt with them. Anyway two of the girls when with the beliefs of their mother, Ada took after her dad. So he taught her the art of gun fighting and he taught her well. When two men broke jail one night they bush wacked him, Ada heard the shooting and killed them both before they could get away. The local sheriff covered for her on the shootings so her mother and sister wouldn't find out. One of her sisters died up above here when the avalanche covered up the settlement."

"How do you communicate with them, if they're in that mountain?"

Ben smiled, "I've got signals I can use, but I won't use them unless it's a life or death thing. I'm sure they already know you're here. I don't know how they do it but very little happens down here without them knowing it. Drew I want most of all to keep Jacob and Ada out of this as much as we can. They have harmed no one, but these people just keep coming looking for the gold."

"What happens if they do break into the mountain?"

"Drew I know Jacob well enough to know he will seal up that mountain and disappear. If that does happen, whoever breaks in there will never leave."

The marshal just sat there looking down at the floor. Then he glanced up at Ben, "You got a place I can bunk for the night around here? I need to think this thing out before you drop something else on me."

In the tack room the marshal looked around, "This looks good enough to live in full time, who belongs to these bunks?"

"Benny stays here all the time and when Thomas is here, he sleeps here to. Since he built him a dugout up at Charlie's he's been staying up there. Once I get moved back up here full time Thomas will probably stay here while he helps me. Now don't get gun happy tonight if Benny comes back, don't shoot him," then he grinned.

Drew rolled out his bedroll, "I doubt if I sleep much. I still can't believe all of this I've learned today about the happening in my own territory."

"I'm going to check the other building before I bed down, so you might hear me moving around outside." He walked out leave the marshal staring at his back.

Ben and Kate were drinking their first cup of coffee when Benny walked in followed by the marshal. Kate poured a cup of coffee for both of them, "Benny, when did you get back last night," she asked as she poured.

Drew spoke up before Benny could answer, "You folks should have warned me about this guy. I woke up this morning to find I had company that moved in during the night. Hell I'm a light sleeper anyway I've always thought I was. I never hear anything when he came in."

Benny looked over at Drew, "You snore too loud to hear anyone coming or going."

Ben laughed, "Hell Drew, he does that to us all the time. Now Benny, did Walking Bear know anything about these dead man?"

"Only Crow was at the camp. He said Walking Bear and Spotted Antelope have been gone for two days. They were watching someone who rides from town to the river each day. They were going to see who he meets with on the river road."

Ben looked at Benny, "Is Crow the other man's name who rides with Walking Bear? He always stays off to the side away from them."

Benny nodded, "Crow speaks very little English, so he stays away whenever English is being spoken. He speaks very good Spanish along with our tongue. He is good at hand talk, if you ever need to speak to him."

Kate was cooking breakfast as she listened, she turned away from the stove, "Benny tell him I can speak Spanish if he ever needs to talk to someone around here."

Benny and Ben both looked over at her, "Since when?" Ben asked.

Kate turned back to the stove, "Since I was a very young girl. In fact I almost spoke that before I did English. My nanny was Mexican."

Ben looked over at Drew, "I think there maybe a few things I don't know about my wife?" Drew grinned as he nodded.

Benny went on, "I told Crow to have one of them come over as soon as they get back."

"Benny, I think they got your message, look outside the door," Kate said as she motioned toward the door.

Walking Bear and Spotted Antelope were sitting their horse facing the door as Benny stepped out. Both riders suddenly sat up as they looked past Benny, Benny looked back and saw Drew standing in the doorway.

Benny then spoke to them in a language that Ben recognized as their own. He had heard Thomas talking to Charlie using this same language. Both Indians turned their attention to Benny as they all three talked back and forth. Benny turned to face the Marshal, Ben and Kate who was standing behind Ben. "Well I guess maybe the new blacksmith, Rocky Bingman, is the man we've been looking for." He slowly shook his head, "The part I don't like is maybe Coby's involved in this too. Walking Bear said each time Bingman went to the river Coby was the one who rode out to meet him."

Ben looked back at Kate, "Of all the people in Garnet, Rocky would be the last one I ever figured would be a member of the family. I never remember him being very nosy about anything going on around the country. He mostly just sat around listening to the guy swap stories about their summer mining jobs."

He looked again over at Kate who just shrugged. Then she looked back at Benny, "Come to think of it Benny, remember last fall when Tyler Bates came to town, he spent time over at the blacksmith shop. He said Rocky was doing some repairs for him. Now as I think back he was, horseback, he couldn't have brought anything for Rocky to work on. Then a week later he showed up again, this time he had Rachel with him and was driving a wagon. He dropped Rachel off at the store while he went and loaded the wagon over at the shop. Rachel had Jess fill a good sized order of supplies for the ranch. Tyler stopped by the store, they loaded the supplies and left. That was the last time I saw Tyler or Rachel."

Spotted Antelope had been listening to all of this talk held up his hand to get their attention. "I talked to one of Coby's wranglers, the one they call Lazy, he said the girl Rachel was with that last wagon train that went by. I asked him how he knew, her, he said she had delivered many messages to the ranch for Coby."

Drew stepped close to Ben, "Ben, I'm going to cut across country from here to Springfield and get a few of my deputies. I think I better start rounding up some people for questioning. I'll keep you posted on what I find." He headed for the barn to get his horse, he stopped. "Hell my horse is in Garnet, I guess I'll have to go that way to get him, before Jess gets me for stealing this horse I'm riding."

Ben stepped down from the porch, "Just keep riding the horse you rode here, you can trade back whenever you go through Garnet."

Drew waved, "Thanks, I'll do that."

Benny turned to Walking Bear and Spotted Antelope, "Ride with him to make sure he makes it to Springfield, or at least until you can see the town. Keep your eyes open. Don't get ambushed by someone with a scatter gun."

When Drew rode up Ben stepped out to stop him, "Benny is sending these two along to make sure someone, don't try to gun you down on the way. Do you want them to ride with you or just shadow you? I think it would be better if they rode with you."

Drew looked down at the three people standing looking at him, "You think it's that bad?"

Ben nodded, "Hell killing people don't seem to bother these people. I just don't want to hear about someone finding your body all blown to hell."

Drew looked over at the two Indians looking at him and nodded, "Thanks, I'll see you soon, I hope."

As the three dropped from sight Benny looked over Ben, "I think I'll head for town. I think someone needs to watch for trouble there."

Ben motioned, "Come on, I'll help you saddle up. As they neared the barn Ben looked over at Benny, "You going tell Jess about what's going on?"

Benny just shook his head, no, as he walked into the barn. Ben walked along behind him, then, a smile appeared on his lips. 'I agree my sly friend. Right now I'm beginning to think I don't know any of these people I've been living with.'

Ben kept busy taking care of the stock, then about noon headed back for the cabin. As he walked in Kate was sitting at the table staring off into space. Ben chuckled, "As the old saying goes, a penny for your thoughts right now?"

Kate looked over at him, "Ben I'm scared. One of the people we considered a friend is now dead, another we've dealt with for, year's maybe involved in all of these killings. My God Ben who can we trust?" A tear began to slowly roll down her cheek.

Ben walked over and put his arm around her neck and kissed her on the forehead, "Well lady, we know we have a few Indians and two people in that mountain we can count on. Anyway that's my feelings right now. I feel better about April being in there alone now with Benny being in town. I think Charlotte is straight, Elsie we can only hope isn't involved." Ben could feel Kate shutter as he said the last part.

"I think tonight I will light my signal to Jacob that I need to see him. The snow is melted far enough now they can get out the lower entrance if he hasn't sealed it off. I'm almost surprised Ada hasn't already been here. In some ways that worries me."

Long after dark and nearing midnight Ben sat on the knoll waiting to light the signal. Later he put out the torches and head back for the cabin. "Tomorrow night I hope I have company,' Ben said under his breath as he put the torches back in there hiding place in the barn. As he walked up to the cabin he saw a shadow of Kate sitting in the rocker on the porch. She stood up as he walked up onto the porch, "Do you think they saw the signal?"

He put his arm around her, "Yes, if their still in the mountain, they saw it. Tomorrow night will know for sure."

Later as Kate snuggled up to him in bed, "Ben why did you say, if they are still in the mountain? Why wouldn't they still be in there?"

He pulled her close, "Kate. That was just a figure of speech. Maybe I should have said it differently. I'm sure they are there, or they would have sent us a message of their leaving. Now go to sleep my dear wife, dawns going to be here before long."

Unknown to Ben and Kate miles away Drew sat by a small fire looking at a dead man at his feet. "How in the hell did you two know he was hidden here in these rocks? Hell he'd blown me to kingdom come if I'd been riding alone."

Spotted Antelope nodded, "In the moon light I saw a coyote sitting there on that rock over across the draw looking this way. Another one was over, there, he also was watching this rock. They were not hunting for prey, they were watching an enemy. So I watched real close, then I saw a flash of something reflecting from this small cave. I think this one got careless and lite a cigarette. He does not know the ways of the hunter or the hunted."

173

Drew grinned just as dawn began to break in the eastern sky, "I think I need to hire you two to teach me the ways of the hunter as you called it. When you stopped last night and said we needed to rest for a spell, I thought you both were nuts. Hell Springfield's only a couple hours ride from here."

Walking Bear reached for the coffee pot on the fire, "Before, you leave for town. We will ride on ahead to where the main trail goes into town. This one might not ride alone."

Drew nodded, then, he reached down to pick up the double barreled shotgun laying by the dead man. "Every one of these fellas carries one of these dam things. It's like maybe they don't know or handle ordinary firearms very good." He looked over at Spotted Antelope, "I sure hope the undertaker don't ask me why this fella was killed with a knife. Hell I don't own anything but a pocket knife," then he laughed.

Drew stopped where the little used trail he was on met the main road to, Springfield. He looked about but saw no Indians. He started to turn down the main road when he jumped, "A second rider is just ahead of you," came Walking Bears voice from a clump of willows along the edge of the road. "He was camped near the creek back there where he could see the road and the trail. I do not think these men are after just you, they are watching for anyone traveling in this area."

From across the road from where Drew talked to Walking Bear, Spotted Antelope appeared out of a draw, "Two riders come this way. They both have shiny badges on the clothes. We will go now, before they see us."

Drew waved, "Thanks for the help." Both Indians disappeared as Drew headed on down the road leading the horse with a body draped over it.

When the two lawmen saw Drew they kicked their horses into a lope. As they pulled up Drew smiled, "Good to see you fellas out working. Did you happen to see another rider between here and town?"

The older of the two grinned, "Where in the hell have you been, Drew? The sheriff has been pacing the floor of your office all night. He kicked us out to look for you at dawn. To answer your question, we haven't seen a soul since we left town, why? By the way who's the dead guy?"

Drew shrugged, "I'll tell you the whole story when we get back to the office."

Both riders felling in alongside as they moved on toward town, Drew's eyes scanned the area around them without moving his head, a grin appeared. Just above them sat two riders who about then melted

174

into the surrounding. Drew just shook his head slowly, as he thought, 'If Benny hadn't sent those two along I'd now be back there along that trail filled with buckshot.'

Ben walked down to the barn in the dark, Kate stayed at the cabin. He sat on the bench waiting for either Ada or Jacob to appear. As the night drew on Ben became more worried, it knew it was now well after midnight. As dawn broke the sky outside the window, Ben headed back for the cabin. When he opened the door, Kate was standing there, "Who came down?"

Ben shook his head, "Nobody showed up. I afraid something has happened up there."

Kate had walked to the stove to pour Ben a cup of coffee. She stopped as she looked out the window. "Ben, we have two visitors outside. It's Walking Bear and Spotted Antelope."

Ben opened the door. Both were sitting their horse at the hitch rail. "Come on in, Kate has hot coffee on the stove."

Walking Bear looked over at Spotted Antelope, he nodded his head. Both riders dropped down from their horses. Inside booth sat on the floor with their backs to the door as Kate brought them a cup of coffee. "Well how was the trip to Springfield with the Marshal?" Ben asked.

Spotted Antelope, who spoke better English of the two, spoke up. "Not good. A man laid in ambush along the trail for the lawman. He is now dead. We stayed with him until he was on the road to town. Two other men with badges came, riding from town looking for him. We left before they got to him, so they wouldn't know we were with him."

Ben looked over at them with a frown on his face, "How in the Hell would they know Drew was going to use that trail?"

Spotted Antelope went on, "People are watching all of the trails. That is why we didn't get here last night. We spotted a couple of riders after we started back, so we split up to find out how many there was watching the trails. It is like they are looking for someone on all of the trails from this part of the country. These men are not wise to the ways of the land. It is easy to move among them without being seen."

"Who can they be looking for?" Ben asked as he looked over at Kate.

Then he looked back at the two Indians, "I signaled the night before last for Ada or Jacob to meet me last night. They didn't show up. Could it be they have left the mountain and these men have found out and they are searching for them. Why else would they be covering all the trails? Spotted Antelope can you and Walking Bear get up through the valley of the bones to see if find out where Jacob and Ada are?"

Both men stood up, "We go by way of our camp to see if Crow has seen anything, before we go to the valley of the bones."

Kate stepped forward, "Can I fix you two some breakfast before you leave?"

Walking Bear looked over at her, then, in Spanish said, "We ate on our way here. The coffee was good." Kate smiled and nodded.

Ben pushed back his plate, "Damn it Kate, this is getting all out of hand. If anything happens to Jacob or Ada. Someone's going to pay for it." He stood up, "I'm going down to feed the horses. I think later on I'm going to ride up and let Charlie and Thomas know about all of this."

Ben finished in the horse barn and stepped outside. 'I think I'll check the other barn again, maybe they left me a message I haven't found,' He mumbled to himself.

He stopped just below where the trunks were located in the mow when he saw the small boot prints in the dust. Then he could see where the ladder had been. As he moved over for the ladder he heard Kate holler, "Ben, come quick. Ben where are you?" she almost screamed.

Ben run outside, he saw Kate looking his way from the cabin porch waving her arms. A rider less horse stood at the hitch rail. Ben ran toward the house then he saw the body of a man lying at Kate's feet. "Ben, its Crow he's been shot."

Ben with Kate's help moved Crow inside. Kate cut away his shirt and looked at the ugly wound low in his side. "Ben, he's lost a lot of blood. I think the bullet went plumb through."

About then they both heard horses loping into the yard. Ben looked out just as Rosa and Maria dropped to the ground from their horses. "Who's hurt? Isn't that Crows horse?" Rosa asked as she rushed past Ben to kneel alongside Kate. She rushed over by the stove and grabbed a pan. She turned and handed to Maria. "Run to the creek and fill this with moss, hurry."

Maria raced out the door as fast as her short legs would go. Rosa looked up at Ben, "Can you go to the pool in the corral and get me some sticky mud."

Ben grabbed a wash pan from outside the door and headed for the pool. He saw Maria already coming up from the creek with the moss. Kate had moved to the side to give Rosa more room to work. She could tell this wasn't the first bullet wound this little Spanish girl had ever worked on. Maria sat the pan next to her mother. "Kate, would you boost Maria up on her horse? Maria, go get your father and Thomas, hurry but don't go so fast that you'll fall off."

Kate watched as the little girl loped her horse up the valley, then she was out of sight. She looked back at Rosa working on Crows wounds. She shook her head. This was just ordinary way of life for these people, just to survive. A girl as little as Maria, just went about doing what needed to be done. Ben walked in with the pan of mud, he sat it by Rosa.

Rosa looked up at Ben, "He was shot from behind at close range. Maybe you should check his horse, it might be wounded too." Ben nodded and walked out.

The horse shied away as Ben felt along its front shoulder. Then Ben saw blood on his hand. As he eased his hand by the wound he felt something just under the skin. He kept stroking the little horse's neck as he worked the lump toward the opening of the wound. Then he picked a small ball from the wound, "Shotgun shot? How in the world did you only get one lone shot in your shoulder, my tough little mustang?" Ben said out loud.

He lead the horse to the water tough for a drink then on to the barn, he thought for moment the little horse was going to balk on going inside the building. Ben poured as small amount of grain into the small tough mounted on the manger. The horse sniffed the grain then started eating. Ben pulled the Indian saddle and rubbed salve on the wound to keep the flies from keeping it open. Then he forked hay into the manger knowing this little horse had probably never eaten hay before. He opened the gates and closed others so the horse could go out into the corral. He stood in the doorway looking all around, "I wonder how many people are watching me right now?"

When he got back to the cabin Crow was lying on a blanket by the door. His eyes were following every move Ben made. "Ben, he says men went into the valley of the bones after they shot him. They thought they had killed him. He lay still, until the rode away. Then he crawled back to his horse and got on, then, as he rode away a loud noise came from the cliffs. He looked back. Rocks were falling over the opening into the mountain. He's been riding all night to get here."

Rosa looked over at Ben, she motioned out the window. "Charlie is here."

Ben opened the door just as Charlie pulled up. His horse was blowing hard from the ride. "Maria said to come quick. Is Rosa alright?"

Ben motioned to the cabin, "Rosa, fine, it's Crow, he's been shot. Kate found him on the ground out front of the cabin. Rosa has him patched up. Come on in you can talk to him."

Charlie kneeled down, "Crow what happened. Is Walking Bear and Spotted Antelope alright?" They were speaking in Spanish so Ben only understood when he mentioned Walking Bear and Spotted Antelope. The door was still open as Ben looked out he saw two horse with three riders riding up. Thomas dropped from his horse and lifted Maria down from behind her brother on his horse.

"Maria says Crow is wounded?"

Ben nodded and motioned into the cabin, "Charlie is talking to him now. Rosa and Kate patched him up. I think he will be alright in time. He's lost a lot of blood since he was shot in the valley of the bones."

Thomas nodded, "When Maria rode up she just said that Rosa wanted us to come quick. Charlie horse was already saddled so he headed here. I had Pedro go catch his horse and mine while I rubbed down Maria pony. She rode him pretty hard. So I had her ride with Pedro and left her horse to rest up. While we were saddling up she said it Crow who was hurt, Charlie thought something had happened to Rosa when he rode out."

Charlie walked out on the porch, "Whoever shot him was using a big bore rifle. Luckily it never hit any vital organs. He had to be pretty close to the one who fired the shot."

Ben nodded, "Charlie the strange part is when I checked his horse over I found a wound in the left shoulder, but it wasn't a bullet. When I worked it out of the wound, it was a round shot from a shotgun. How does a man get shot in the back off his horse with a large bore of some sort and his horse has one small ball from a shotgun?" At that range a shotgun should have blown the whole side out of that horse."

Charlie shook his head, "That I don't understand. I also wonder where Walking Bear and Spotted Antelope could be. Crow says he hasn't seen them since they rode over here to see Benny."

Ben filled him in on where the two Indians had been. "They were here early and had coffee. They said they were going over to camp to check on Crow when they left. Then they were going to ride up through the valley of the bones to see if they could locate Jacob and Ada. They're probably up there by now or at least on their way, to the valley of the bones."

178

Unknown to Ben he was right. Two riders sat their horses looking at the huge rocks blocking the opening into the mountain. Spotted Antelope dropped down from his horse and pointed down below them. The trail from here to the closed entrance was carved from a pure rock wall. Where they had stopped was just before the narrow ledge. Walking Bear walked over to where Spotted Antelope was looking over the edge if the cliff. Down below was a dead horse that had tumbled or had been knocked off the ledge by the slide. Spotted Antelope looked back at his partner, "I don't see the rider down there." He moved back down the trail they had just ridden up, he dropped to one knee. "I think we have a wounded or hurt man somewhere close by.

He pointed to the rocky trail. Two spots of blood covered a smooth rock. Walking Bear led the horses as Spotted Antelope moved along the trail. Across the canyon from the plugged entrance a brushy draw came in from the side. Spotted Antelope stopped, he looked about someone was shot here." He pointed to a blood on the bushes and on the ground. Walking Bear walked over to look, then, he pointed to where a shotgun blast had pitted a big rock on the edge of the trail. He moved on up the draw following, a single horses tracks. He found where a horse had stood behind a few small trees. "One lone horse stood here. I can find a couple spots of blood here too."

Spotted Antelope was walking up toward him, he pointed to blood a bush. "Whoever was shot back there crawled out of the bushes right here. I think whoever it was got on the horse right here."

Both Indians moved back down on the main trail out of the valley of the bones. A couple of times Spotted Antelope dropped from his horse to kneel down and study the trail floor. "The rider is badly wounded the way he bleeds. I don't think he will make it very far," Walking Bear nodded.

Both Indians almost as one stopped as they sniffed the air, both dropped to the trail. They moved off along the edge both searching in the rocks below. Walking Bear held up his hand, he pointed down through the brush along the trail. Below them he could see the legs of a human in the rocks below. Walking Bear eased down closer. He stopped, looking back up at Spotted Antelope on the trail above, he held his nose. "A bear has been eating on this man. He left a pile before he left. That is what we smell. It is like this bear has been eating on dead flesh for a long time."

Spotted Antelope has moved down close to where Walking Bear stood, "That is not a bear you smell, that pile was left by a Wolverine. That smell is the way they mark their territory. Haven't you ever found a Wolverines den, they smell terrible." Walking Bear looked over at his partner and shook his head, no.

"Bears don't usually eat on a man who has just died." He moved over to where the man lay, "See those claw marks? That is a wolverine for sure." He, raise his rifle and pulled back the hammer, "We better keep a sharp lookout for him, they, will attack without warning."

Walking Bear leaned down to look at the body, "I think this is the man, who's, horse, we seen up at the slide. This isn't the man, who left the blood trail we've been following.

Spotted Antelope nodded, "He wears the same clothes as the mail man did."

Just as they got back up on the main trail the horses started moving around, both Indians grabbed their reins to hold them. Both horses were looking back up the trail just as a few rocks began to roll into the trail from above. A snarling black animal came out of the brush just above the trail, he was hissing as he ran directly at the two men trying to hold their frighten horses. Spotted Antelope grabbed the reins of Walking Bears horse. Walking Bear dropped to one knee and fired at the on rushing ball of fur. The shot dropped the animal for just a second then it was again rushing for them. Walking Bear fired twice more before the animal lay still on the narrow trail not far from where the Indian kneeled. Walking Bear hurried back to help Spotted Antelope who was being drug down the trail by the terrified horses as they tried to break away. They both finally got their horses calmed down. They walked on down the trail until they were out of sight of the dead wolverine. They tied their horses and headed back up the trail.

"That was one tough warrior," Walking Bear said as he gazed at the still form.

Spotted Antelope nodded, "They say even a bear gives these animals a wild birth, rather than tangle with them. From now on you will remember the smell of one so fierce." Walking Bear nodded as they turned and headed back for their horses. Just before they got to the horses Spotted Antelope dropped to his knee, "We still follow the wounded man from the draw."

Both Indians dismounted and searched along the trail, then, Walking Bear walked off down a little used trail heading toward the valley below. "He rides toward the valley below. Maybe he is heading for Ben's place for help. If he is, it must be someone who knows this country."

Ben saw both riders as they topped the hill just above the place. He motioned to Charlie, "Here, come's our two lost Indians."

Later after all the stories were told everyone sat around the porch. Ben looked over at the two Indians, "So you say that entrance to the mountain is closed. How long would it take to clear the rocks to get inside?"

Both Indians looked at each other, then, back at Ben, "The rocks covering the opening are bigger than this cabin," Walking Bear told the ones on the porch. "The other riders are buried in there along with their horses. Like we said only the horse in the rocks below and the man the wolverine was eating didn't get covered up. Now we know the man shot was Crow, that leaves four men buried in that mountain if we read the tracks right. When we rode up there we were trying to figure out all the tracks on that rocky trail. I think there, was five shod horses and one with no shoes."

"We know now the one unshod horse was Crow. Now do you think Jacob and Ada are in the mountain?" Both Indians just shrugged. "I think I need to go up and see if Jacob did seal up this lower entrance like he said he was going to. If he did how in the hell are we supposed to know if they are alright?"

Walking Bear glanced over at Ben, "Ghost woman will let us know if they are still in the mountain."

"How Walking Bear? If she can't get out how's she going to let us know?" Ben asked as he spun around to look at Walking Bear.

Everyone's eyes went to the big Indian, who never changed expression, "They have other ways from the mountain. They still have the trails of the ancient ones used. If they use them they will not come out in this country."

Ben looked at him, "Trails of the ancient ones? Jacob never said anything about other entrances when I lived in there with him. Walking Bear are you sure about this?"

Walking Bear nodded. "More, I do not know."

Ben kept looking at Walking Bear, he turned to Charlie. "We need to let Benny know about all of this. No one would even notice if Thomas rode into town, they would think he just rode in to see his father. I think he should go."

Charlie nodded, "You ride careful my young nephew. You know the ways of the hunted, so use that knowledge to cover your tracks."

Ben motioned to Thomas, "Come on, I'll help you get a fresh horse from the pasture."

Ben watched as Thomas went out of sight over the small rise above the cabin as he walked back to the others. It was decided they would move Crow up to Thomas dugout, so Rosa could treat him. They hook up the lighter wagon, filled the bed with hay to lay Crow on. Ben started to climb up to drive when Charlie touched his arm. "You should stay in case we are being watched. Walking Bear is going to go up with us to help unload him. Spotted Antelope is going to head for the canyon of the hot water, then he will double back to see if we are being watched."

Kate and Ben stood watching as Charlie and Rosa headed up the small valley in the wagon, moving along real slow. Pedro and Maria were riding behind leading the extra horses. Kate put her head on his shoulder, "What are you going to do now?"

Ben smiled, "I'm going to finish what I started to do when you hollered when you found Crow. I need to check all the places in the barn where Ada and Jacob have left messages before. I still can't believe they would leave without leaving us some sort message."

Ben checked the cupboards in the room of the tarp's, then the bench where he left supplies for them to pick up. He moved the ladder over and climbed up onto the loft. He opened the shutter on the window so he could see, better. As he walked over to the two trunks, he could see the tiny boot tracks in the dust. Then he saw the imprint of moccasins, too. They both had been here sometime this spring. When he opened the first trunk he found more of the small boxes. In the second trunk was an envelope on top of more boxes. Ben walked to the window as he took out the message. It was done like all of Jacobs work, it was printed in beautiful script. 'You be well my brother. I will see you again one day.' It was signed with the familiar statue.

Ben stood there for a long while, then, he closed the shutter over the window opening. He climbed back down, put the ladder away. When he walked into the cabin, Kate could tell he had found something. Before she could ask, he handed her the note. Kate looked up after she read the brief note. Finally she smiled, "Ben, now we do know they are alright."

He nodded, "At least they were when they were here. They could have left that any time after we left last fall. I think from the tracks in the dust it wasn't long ago, but we really don't know for sure." He poured a cup of coffee, then, sat down, "We got more boxes to take care of, too."

That evening Ben and Kate sat on the porch watching the sun slowly dropping behind the horizon. Ben pointed as two riders appeared riding down the small valley. Kate walked inside then came out carrying two cups and a pot of coffee just as the two riders stopped at the hitch rail.

Spotted Antelope dropped from his horse to sit on the edge of the porch, "No one is watching you. I found old camps above here where they have been watching both places, but not for many days. I think they are all gone now. Maybe they all died in the valley of the bones."

Walking Bear joined Spotted Antelope as they drank their coffee. "We will go home now. Crow is going to stay with Charlie until he is well. Rosa is a good healer of wounds, so he will heal quicker being close to her." Later both Indians were headed for their home in the canyons of the hot water, leaving Kate and Ben still sitting on the porch. Darkness covered the area when they finally stood then walked into the cabin hand in hand.

Benny and Thomas rode in about noon the next day. Ben had finished his morning chores and was sitting on the porch thinking about what needed to be done. Both riders swung down, Thomas took their horses to the barn. Benny sat on the top step as he looked at Ben. "Coby and the blacksmith are both gone. Coby sold his outfit to a couple of his riders real cheap. What Coby didn't know was Clayton furnished most of the money. I also think maybe Henry may have had a little of the deal too, anyway those two are gone. You know, I just can't figure Coby. I thought I really knew him. Bingman, hell we hardly knew him."

Ben nodded. Kate had walked out and had heard what Benny had said, "I agree Benny. We all have dealt with Coby for years. I just can't believe he would go along with all this killing that's been going on."

Benny shrugged, a small smile appeared, "Jess and Meg said to tell you folks, that the two day trip you two said, you were going on when you left the trading post," he stopped.

Kate laughed, "I suppose we did kind of miss judged this trip."

Benny nodded, "I check your house, everything, is good. Clayton had been checking it every day too. He and Henry were getting ready to head out. Henry's taking the low trail. Clayton said he was coming this way. I wouldn't be surprised if he shows up this evening or by tomorrow for sure."

"Have you seen the Marshal?" Ben asked.

Benny gave a slight nod, "He brought back the borrowed horse He, rode down to Coby's to check things out. He sent word on up the road to other lawmen to watch for that group. He figures they will probably skip off by themselves and by pass most of the towns. Anyway he got posters out on them. His deputy that was trying to court Tyler's daughter Rachel thinks he will see her again. Like Drew says he don't have any charges against her, but he would like to ask her some question."

"I wonder what will happen to that place now Tyler had some fine buildings and a productive place there. You don't suppose they will do with it like they did this place, just move off and never come back?" He looked over at Kate, "Maybe we should watch to see what happens, if it starts going up for taxes we'll see if we can buy it."

"Ben, what in the world would we do with it? We got more here than we can handle?" Kate asked as she stared over at her husband.

"Hell Kate, I know that. I was just thinking maybe we could let Charlie or even Thomas run it and later on they could own it. I just hate to see something like that place just go to ruins. Most people that travel that road don't even know that place is there. You know thinking back about that now, maybe Tyler built that place out of sight for a reason. He could have had all kinds of visitors and no one would be the wiser. Like a base for the family to use."

Kate smiled, "Your always thinking aren't, you?" Then she laughed at his expression.

Benny went on, "I think the Marshal will be up to see you folks. I left him a note with Jess after Thomas showed up to tell me about what happened in the valley of the bones. I figured you'd rather he found out from you that find out later from someone else."

After lunch Benny decided to ride up and see how Crow was getting along. Thomas was going to help Ben clean out the horse barn. Benny also wanted to see Rosa about his foot, Kate had noticed he was limping more today than usual. He was so touchy about talking about it so Kate never brought it up when he first rode up and she saw him limping to the porch.

184

Ben and Thomas were just leaving the barn that afternoon when on the upper trail two riders were heading down toward them. One rider was leading two pack horses. "That's Clayton, the second rider looks like Drew. Thomas why don't you go tell Kate we got company, in case she starting supper. I'll help those two take care of their horses."

Clayton grinned as he rode up, "You and Kate forget where town is? You said you'd be back in two days when you rode out."

Ben laughed, "I know Benny already gave us hell for not letting you folks, know, what was going on. We didn't find out all of it until it was over, then I did send Thomas in to let Benny know." He took Drew's hand as he walked up, "Good to see you, Drew. Benny said he left you a note before he headed back here."

As they unpacked the horses Thomas came back from the house, "Kate said supper will be ready in about an hour. She wants me to help her, so I'm going back to the cabin."

Later while they waited for supper they sat sharing a drink. Ben told them both of the fight in the valley of the bones.

When he finished Drew looked over at Ben, "You think there's four men buried in the mountain and the one the Indians found along the trail? That makes five. Do you think that is all of them?"

Ben nodded, "Spotted Antelope is sure there were only five rider went up the trail, ahead of Crow. They ambushed Crow before he ever saw them to know how many were in the party. When Spotted Antelope and Walking Bear stopped by last night they said all the camps around the valley are empty. Now if that's all of them, I have no idea."

"Ben. What about that guy and gal living in the mountain, are they still in there?" Drew asked with his eyes glued to Ben.

Finally Ben shook his head, no. "Jacob left me a message sometime in the last month in our hiding place. Drew, I want him left out of all of this if you can do that. You know he never had anything to do with any of this. He was just the man they thought had the gold they were after. Ada is just his companion and his body guard. Now back to the message, it was short, mainly saying we would meet again one day." Kate had walked out, she had heard the part about Jacob, Ben looked up at her, "Right?"

Drew and Clayton looked at her as she shook her head, yes. "Ben's telling you all of it, I read the note too."

Drew shrugged, "You said before there are only two entrances to that mountain? Now with the slide covering the one, can they still get out?"

Ben shrugged, "Drew, all I know last fall just before it snowed Jacob said if he ever left, he would seal up this lower entrance. Now it must have been open sometime since the snow started melting up there, they were here to leave me a message."

Drew nodded, "Ben, I'd like to see that entrance where those fellas are buried?"

"Okay, I'll have Thomas take you up there tomorrow. After your back from there, I will take you up to this lower entrance. I think we'll find part of that trail missing. I don't think you'll want to try to work yourself around it once you see it. If you toss a rock off that one place, you don't hear it hit below for a long time, if you ever hear it at all."

At supper Kate looked over at Clayton, "I suppose you're headed for your mine come morning? Are you coming back in for the 4th again this year?"

Clayton looked up from his plate, "Well Kate, I may be back before that, if I sell my mine. You see me and Henry been doing some thinking the last couple of days. Drew here is going to help us see if we can take over that place of Tyler's. We both have put away a good nest egg the last few years. We talked it over and we're both not looking forward to spending another summer working our asses off up there all alone. In fact Drew's older brother Fred is real interested in buying Henry's claim. Henry's in Springfield right now talking with him. He's also trying to get answer on us tying up paperwork on that place. So if Fred does buy the claim Henry will take him up there next week. We're hoping he can know for sure about us buying or claiming or the place by then. My claim is only a half a day's ride from his, so he'll let me know when he comes up."

Kate laughed, "Now it must be catching. First Ben decided he like my company better than his lonely summers at his claim. Then Jess decided he wanted a partner and settled down in town, now you two are settling down. Henry's older than you and Jess, so this doesn't surprise me. You, I figured we'd bury in those mountains. You were always the first out and the last one in every year, kinda like this fellas was," as she leaned against Ben.

Clayton grinned, "Maybe I see a glimmer in Ben and Jess's eyes that wasn't there before and it's made me curious."

"Do I hear a talk of maybe there's a female somewhere in this story? Clayton, are you telling the whole story?"

"Now, Kate, one thing, at a time. You know I can't speak for Henry, but right now I'm just working on buying a different way of life."

Drew had been listening to Kate questioning Clayton, "Clayton I believe you got yourself in tight corner. I don't believe this gal is going to give up until she maybe hears the whole story," then he laughed.

"That is the whole story. I knew I shouldn't tell Kate about any of this when I rode in."

The next morning Ben was helping Clayton get packed up after breakfast. Drew and Thomas had already left for the valley of the bones. Kate came walking down from the cabin as Clayton was getting ready to head out. "Clayton usually you'd be gone for a couple of hours by now. You don't seem to be in any hurry this year."

Clayton grinned, "Well Kate, usually I try to get up to Twin Peaks the first night. Then the second day gets me into my place in the early afternoon. This year I'm going to stop by and see a couple of miners on Pid Creek and stay with them tonight. One of them offered to buy my claim a few years ago, so I thought I'd see if he's still interested, if not he might know of someone looking for a proved up claim. I can still make it on up to my place tomorrow. It'll just be a little later than usual."

He shook hands with both of his old friends, then, swung up. "I'll see you two sometime before or if all of this other deal falls through, I'll be back for the 4th." He turned his horse and with the two pack animals headed back up for the main trail through the pass.

Kate took Ben's arm, "Well my always thinking husband. What's next?"

Ben looked down at her, "While I was talking to Drew about the entrances, another thought came to me. Now the more I think about it, I think maybe Jacob and Ada were on their way out when they left the message. Come on I want to check something in the barn."

Ada's gear and one other saddle were gone from the tack room. Ben grinned, "Let's walk down and count the horses in the lower pasture." Kate looked up at him. A small smile appeared as she squeezed his arm.

Ben looked out over the big pasture. A big grin appeared on his weathered face. Both of Ada's horses were gone. "I guess now we know they're not in the, mountain now." He looked back toward the mountain with its snowcapped peaks, then over at Kate who was just staring at him. He shook his head, "I will really miss having him close by. Even though I didn't see him that much, it was just the fact I knew he was near if I needed to talk to him." He took Kate's arm and headed back toward the buildings.

"We'll see them again, Ben," Kate answered as she saw the sad look on her husband's face.

It was evening when Drew and Thomas, came riding in. Ben noticed they were coming down from above where the lower trail went to the lower entrance. Ben walked to the barn to help put up the horses.

Drew looked over at Ben, "On our way down I had Thomas here show me the lower entrance. You were right the trail is missing along that shelf. Hell man, a Billy goat couldn't get across that gap."

As they walked toward the cabin, Ben looked over at the marshal, "What did you find up above in the valley of the bones?"

Drew glanced at Ben, "Well, your two Indian friends joined us on our trip up the valley. Spotted Antelope told me the whole story as we rode along. I have no reason to doubt his story. In fact as we stood there looking at the big boulders blocking that entrance a faint smell of something dead was drifting out. Like you told me before opening that back up would be one tough job. Those early miners carved out all of that from a solid rock mountain, so with time it could be reopened. Thomas told me the story about the, bones that gives the valley its name. It's really hard for me to believe those early Spaniards were this far north. Using Indian slave labor is the same story you hear about down south in the deserts where they mined. Dumping them over a cliff after they were through mining to keep the mine location a secret," Ben looked over when Drew had stopped talking, to see he was just shaking his head.

"I'm like you, Drew. It's all hard to believe. With the mountain all sealed back up you missed seeing the unbelievable work they did in that mountain. They must have been here working for a long time or they had a lot more slaves than we realize possible." Ben never mentioned what Walking Bear had said about other ways out of the mountain. If that became known, more people would be trying to get into the mountain, this way maybe things would quiet down.

Drew rode out the next morning, heading back for Springfield. Thomas had ridden back up to his dugout home last night after supper. After Drew rode away the next morning Ben walked back to the cabin. It was warm out on the porch so Kate and him sat there nursing a cup of coffee. Kate was facing the direction of the small valley going up to Charlie's place. She motioned with her hand, "Here comes Benny. Maybe he'll have Rosa supply list. I told Thomas to tell her we were going to be going in if she needed anything."

Benny swung down at the hitch rail, "You got more of that coffee, Kate? I think Rosa must be getting short on coffee beans, her coffee this morning was just, hot colored water." Kate laughed as she got up and went into the cabin.

Benny took a sip and gave slight nod, "I think you got me spoiled Kate. Now this is good."

"You think I got you spoiled, Benny, I've known that since the first week after you started working for me!"

Benny looked over at Ben who grinned, "Don't look at me I know she's got me spoiled. She does make a mean pot of coffee."

Kate looked over at her longtime friend, "I noticed you lost your limp, Rosa must have fixed your problem."

Benny looked over at her, then, gave her a slight nod, "It's good now. Thomas said you are going to town, when?"

"I think sometime today, right Ben?" Kate said as she looked at Ben.

Ben nodded, "Might as well, you want to ride along Benny? We'll come back tomorrow."

Benny shook his head no, "I think I'll ride up and spend a few days with Walking Bear and Spotted Antelope. I think a few days in the hot springs will do me good."

As Kate and Ben topped the hill Kate looked back at their summer time home. "Do you have a strange feeling that, Benny is going up to see those two for a different reason?"

Ben looked over at his wife and grinned, "I was wondering if you picked up on that too. I got that same feeling when he said he was going up there. I think if we'd follow him, he'll go to the hot springs but later he'll be in the valley of the bones. Of course following him would be the big problem. First off he would know were following him before we went a mile, then he would ditch us."

Kate laughed and nodded she agreed. Kate dropped off at the trading post while Ben drove up to the house to put the team away. As Kate walked in Meg came around the counter, "It's about time you showed up," she hugged Kate. "I kept hounding Jess to send someone up to check on you two. He'd just laugh and say, they'll be back one of these days. Kate took lots of supplies when they left. She said she wanted to start getting the pantry filled up there for the summer. Then Thomas showed up to let Benny know you were alright. Sounds like all kinds of things happened up there."

Kate nodded, "We've been kind of in the middle of all that's happened but yet we never considered ourselves in danger. That's enough about us. Where's that kid of yours?"

Meg motioned to a basket behind the counter, "He's sound asleep."

About then Jess and Ben came walking in the back door. Jess grinned at Kate, "Ben here brought me up to date on your living up there in the wilds. He also tells me you got a big order for me to fill."

Kate handed him two separate lists, "This one's Rosa's, this other one is ours."

Meg picked up the basket and motioned to Kate, "Let's you and me go back to the living quarters, we can keep up on each, others gossip," then she laughed.

April and the girls all showed up to see Kate, while her and Meg were in the living quarters. April reached over to hold onto Kate's arm, "Kate, did Clayton tell you about him and Henry taking over that farm of Tyler Bates?"

Kate nodded, "He just said he and Henry were trying to figure a way to take it over. I guess Drew was going to help them with the legal part of it. Clayton said Henry was in Springfield working on it when he rode out for his mine."

"Well the deal went through on Drew's brother buying Henry's mine. Henry filed on the Bates place, so now they have to see what the courts going to do. In fact Henry is back over in Springfield this week to see what the court is going to do. He's supposed to get word to Clayton whenever he takes Drew's brother up to take over his mine."

Kate laughed, "It seems when Ben and then Jess quit chasing the mother lode. It has started a trend with these older miners. You better look out April, you'll be losing more of your gals," then she laughed.

April grinned, "Hey, partner I'm not too old to catch onto a man yet."

A smile slowly appeared on Kate's face, when she saw the expression on her friends face. She smiled, at her longtime friend and partner, then, she nodded. 'As her mind was busy thinking about what April was hinting, Clayton or Henry.'

Ben stuck his head through the door, "Kate, Jess, has a few questions about your order that I can't answer. Kate walked out into the store and over to the counter piled high with boxes.

Jess looked over at her, "Kate, I must be reading this list wrong. The amount of coffee you got down here would be enough for a cavalry unit for a month. Same with the salt, you got table salt here when I think you really mean you want stock salt. It's kind of early in the year to be starting to salt down meat for winter."

Kate looked at him, "Now Jess, why would you question my list, you remember I used to be on your side of the counter. You're supposed just to fill the order the way it's written down. Now if you can't read the list, then you can ask questions," then she laughed. "Jess, the coffee is mostly for our Indian friends over at the hot springs. I guess they don't want to waste water, so they make what I call syrup instead of coffee the way we know it. I'm hoping Benny can get them to cut down on the coffee beans per pot. Same with the salt, only I don't have any idea why they wanted so much. I've never had the chance to eat what they cook."

That evening Ben and Kate walked down to the saloon to visit. Most of the miners were gone back to the mountains, so things were quiet. Most of the talk was about Tyler and Coby. Everyone agreed, about those two being involved in all of this just didn't make sense.

Everyone kept looking over at Ben as the conversation went on, finally Ben spoke up. "One thing I have trouble with is how much of this did Jacob know about. I never got a chance to talk to him after we found out about those two being involved. He was raised by a member of this group until his father was kicked out of the family. His dad was crazy as far as I concerned, Kate dealt with him more than I did. How Jacob ever survived with him is a wonder. When I lived with him in that mountain, he never really said how or when his dad died. Maybe if his father would have been alive when Tyler moved into this country he might have known him. As for Coby, maybe they just didn't ever see each other. I guess we will never get an answer to any of this now they're all dead. I often wonder if Tyler's daughter Rachel knew about any of this. One of the marshal's deputies was trying to court Rachel when all this blew up. He keeps telling Drew that she will be back one of these days. Who knows maybe she can clear up some of this if she does show up."

Kate stood up, "It's been a long day, I, think I'll head for bed." She looked over at Ben. He stood up and grabbed his hat from the top of the piano. Kate looked over at Jess, "We'll load up after breakfast in the morning."

Ben and Kate were packing the supplies into the pantry when Thomas rode up. "I think Rosa is in a hurry for her supplies. She kept telling me all morning I should ride over here to help you unload."

Kate laughed, "I think from her order she must be getting low on lots of items. When we get through why don't you just take the wagon up and unload it? You can bring it back tomorrow or whenever you're come back."

That evening as they sat on the porch watching the sun dropping in the west, Kate looked back up at the mountain towering behind her. "This will be the first summer we won't have someone watching us from above. It is sad to think we won't be seeing any more of that beautiful gold figurine he made. You know we never have shipped those last ones he left."

Ben nodded, "I guess we should bring them up here and get them ready to mail the first time we're over to Springfield. In some ways, I hate to send them out. It might start a new bunch looking for Jacob." Kate looked over at him, then, turned away.

"You know what we should do is get them ready, then find someone going to Cheyenne or Denver. If they were mailed from a place like that they would be hard to trace, especially if we wrapped them without his statue mark showing on each package," Kate said without looking over at Ben.

Ben nodded, "Tomorrow I'll bring a couple of them up from the barn. When we get them ready then we can put them under the floor until we find someone to mail them. Then I'll bring a couple more."

With Charlie and Thomas help Ben started on a ditch to take water from the creek out onto the ground had fenced to raise hay. By using a one of the plows left by the family, the ditch job went along good. Before long Ben had water on most of his hay ground. With the warmer weather and the water Ben could see a big difference in the area being watered. Ben looked up the valley one day and saw three horses coming toward them. Charlie looked up and nodded that way, "That is Crow out for his first long ride. I see Rosa sent Pedro and Maria with him."

As they rode up Maria turned off and headed for the cabin. "I will go see Kate, when you're ready to ride on come by the house." Pedro waved to his sister as she rode off.

"How are you feeling, Crow?" Ben asked.

Crow looked at Thomas who nodded at him, "Go ahead, he will understand you alright." He looked over at Ben, "He worries his English is not good enough to talk to you. Rosa makes him speak English to her and the kids."

"I feel better. Rosa is a good healer. I think I will be tired before we get back home. Rosa told Pedro to take me from here to the settlement, then down the valley to Charlie's place."

Ben nodded, "I think you speak very good English, Crow. When you get up to the house tell Kate you need a cup of coffee."

A few days later Walking Bear and Spotted Antelope rode up to where the three were working. They looked at the ditch, then at each other. Spotted Antelope dropped from his horse, "Benny said to tell you he went back to town."

Ben smiled, "Did he feel better after he soaked in the hot springs?"

Both Indians looked at each other, then Spotted Antelope answered, "His foot was better when he left." Ben nodded.

"We came to get Crow. Rosa said he was doing real good when we stopped by a week ago," with that they rode off up the valley.

Ben decided to cut his first cutting of hay before the big celebration for 4th of July. Kate joined the three as they worked in the hay field. The second evening as they got home, they found Clayton sitting on the porch. "I wondered where you two were. Then I saw the two riders split off and head up the valley when I spotted you riding this way. I knew you were somewhere around close when I saw the dough rising in the kitchen."

Ben stopped the wagon so Kate could climb down, "Kate can fill you in on what's happening while I put the team away." When he got back to the house Kate and Clayton were having a drink on the porch.

Kate motioned to a glass on the table by the door. Ben picked it up and sat down to join them. "Well, are you still a miner or a farmer?" He asked, as he looked over at, Clayton.

"I do know, one thing for, sure, I'm a miner without a claim to work if the land deal didn't go through. Henry brought me word a few weeks ago that we were well on the way to being a land owner. His deal with the marshal's brother went through, so he's without a claim too. He said he was going to be back in town by the 4th, he's coming back on the low trail. Hell, he might even be in town by now."

After supper Clayton stood up from the chair on the porch, "Kate that was a great supper. It's been a long day getting here, so I think I'll turn in." He looked over at Ben, "How about I spend a few days helping you folks with the hay crop. If I'm going to be a farmer or rancher, I'll need the experience."

Ben nodded, "Hell, I'm not about to turn down help."

"Okay then, I'll see you for breakfast," he turned and headed for the tack room in the barn.

They put the last of the hay in the barn two days before the 4th. Ben had asked Charlie if he and his family wanted to join them in town. He said no, Spotted Antelope had been by and told Rosa the snow and ice was gone at Spirit Lake. It was decided they were going to camp up there over the holiday along with the Indians from the hot springs.

Thomas was going to spend at least one day in town with Benny, then come back out here. Kate was trying to get him to spend more time in town, but so far she wasn't winning.

They loaded Clayton's gear he had brought from the mine in the wagon and left his pack spring at the place. He said if the deal went through he would come out to get them once he was settled in his new home. "I saw three riders leading pack horses on the high trail a while ago when I took my horses down to the lower pasture. I'm sure that one rider was Sherm Grover. I figure it's our winter group coming in for the celebration and supplies. I bet we'll have a full town for the 4th,"Clayton said as he walked up to where Ben was hooking up the team for the trip to town.

Clayton tied his saddle horse behind the wagon, then joined Ben and Kate on the wagon. Thomas had gone off to check the water on the hay field. He had asked Ben when they got the ditches all built if he could do all the irrigating, he liked working with the new ditches. Kate had decided that was the reason he was coming back the day after the 4th.

Town was booming as they pulled in. A crew was unloading a freight wagon parked in front of the trading post. Kate waved at Deb who was checking in all of the supplies. Ben stopped at their house. He helped Kate down from the high seat. "I'll take the wagon over and help Clayton unload at his place. Then I'll come back to unload our gear."

As Ben packed the gear from the wagon into the house he sat two bigger boxes by the door. Kate looked over at them. When Ben walked in carrying more stuff she nodded that way. "Ben that freight wagon unloading down at the store is, Fred Jamerson. Why don't we load up that box address to my sister in St Louis and take it down and have Fred ship it off for us. When she gets it she will open it and ship all the smaller packages off to wherever Jacob had them addressed."

Ben smiled, "Good thinking." He walked over and picked up one of the boxes and headed for the door. Kate said she would walk down while Ben drove the wagon to the store. Fred was just finishing unloading the supplies, when Ben drove up. Kate was already talking to him. They loaded the box into the big wagon then Ben headed back up to the barn. By the time Ben put the team away Kate was back at the house.

That evening Kate and Ben headed down to the saloon to visit with old friends in for the big celebration. Clayton spotted them as they walked in. He motioned for them to join him at a table in the back. "Henry rode in a while, ago, he went into Springfield on his way in

194

from the mine. He's got our paperwork. So now were owners of Tyler's old place. This calls for a drink."

Kate laughed, "Clayton, sense when did you need a reason to take a drink? Why don't we toast our friendship now, then when Henry gets here, we can toast the new partnership."

Kate could tell Clayton had already had a few drinks before they got here. "Good idea. No wonder that big lug you're married too beat us all in getting you to marry him. Your always think ahead, Kate. I need to find me a thinking woman."

Charlotte had walked up behind Clayton, she looked at Kate grinning, "What's this about a thinking woman?"

Kate laughed as Clayton turned his head to look up at Charlotte, "Oh, he thinks he needs a thinking woman now he's a land owner. Do you know any available thinking women, Charlotte?"

Charlotte leaned down, "Clayton honey, I'm a thinking woman. Will I do?"

Clayton nodded, "By God you'll do, Charlotte. You want to get married now or in the morning?"

Charlotte looked over at Kate and winked. She leaned down and put her cheek against his. "Honey with the hangover you're going to have in the morning, let's wait until about noon."

"Bye God, noon it is." He looked over at Ben, "You and Kate make sure you're here, I want all my friends to be at my wedding."

April, who had walked up, had heard most of the last part, "Who's getting married, Clayton?"

Clayton grinned, "April, I want you and Elsie there too." He looked up at Charlotte, "Right Charlotte?"

April reached down and turned Clayton's face toward her, "Clayton honey, I know you've had a lot to drink since you came in, but what I want to know is, who's getting married?"

"April, my old friend, me and Charlotte are getting married tomorrow at noon."

April looked over across the table at Kate, then at Charlotte, "Did I miss something, before I walked up. I didn't know this was going on."

Kate started laughing, "April, I don't think Charlotte knew it either," then she looked at the expression on Charlotte's face, she laughed all the harder. By then everyone in the place was laughing.

With a few more drinks Clayton was done for the evening. Ben and a couple of the other miners took him up to his house. Ben covered him with a blanket and they headed back for the party.

195

With the big celebration planned for the next day people started clearing out before it was real late. Kate and Ben stood up to leave, April walked over smiling. "Do you think Clayton will remember any of this tomorrow?"

Kate nodded, "You might warn Charlotte, I think she got a wedding tomorrow unless she finds an easy way to let that man down. I think he was serious about getting married."

April stood there looking at Kate, "You really think so?"

Kate nodded she did. Ben smiled, "April, I agree with Kate. I been on many a party with Clayton, he always seem to remember everything that happened during the party no matter how drunk he gets." As they walked out April was watching them.

Henry came walking up behind her, "Shall we break our news to them tomorrow?"

April reached for his hand, then she smiled, "Let's see how this all comes out," then she squeezed his hand. "If Ben's right and Clayton does remember all of this. Charlotte would be foolish not to take him up on the offer. I know there's no love involved yet, but with a little time they would make a nice couple. In our profession if we wait too long, there won't be any white knight to steal us away from this. I think I'm almost to that point, now you've come along to change all of that." She put her arms around him and pulled him close, she looked up into his eyes, "Henry, I will make you a good wife."

He kissed her forehead, "April, I've never thought any different."

April turned out all the lights but one over by the bar. She brought out two wine glasses and a bottle of wine. She poured then sat down next to Henry. "April have you had a chance to talk to Kate yet about all of this?"

"No, but I've been talking to Jess and Meg. Jess is going to buy out Kate on the trading post, but he doesn't want the saloon. Kate already said if Jess doesn't want it, then I have first chance to buy out her share in this place. Before she heads back to their place I'll get the paper work started on buying it. Are you sure it's okay with you if we buy this place? I've already talked to Charlotte and Elsie, neither one of them wants to buy in on it, so it's just you and me."

Henry nodded, "Like I said before, I have no problem with us owning it as long as you got one of them to manage it. What are you going to do if Charlotte does take Clayton up on his offer, wasn't she going to manage it for you?"

April shook her head, no. "I guess I didn't tell you, Elsie going to run the place. Both girls know I've got a couple more girls coming to take my place. Anyway I thought I did, they were supposed to be here before this. I told Connie to be here by the first of July."

At first light the morning of the big celebration Garnet was coming alive. Kate and Ben walked down to have their morning coffee with Jess. Benny was eating when they walked in. They sat down with him as Jess placed two cup of hot coffee on the table. "If you need more serve yourselves, I need to get a mail sack ready for the stage."

Kate looked up, "The stage is running today? How come, this is a, holiday?"

George said the day before yesterday when he was here that the stage would be here this morning, something about a special." Jess called back from behind the counter.

Thomas came walking in the front door, "There's a stage coach coming up the road." About then he could hear the sound of a teams out front. "Hey, there is two women getting out of the stage," Thomas said as he stood staring out the window.

A short time later a tall blond woman stepped into the store. Kate stood up and walked over to the woman, "Are you looking for April?" She asked the woman standing before her.

The woman smiled, "Why yes I'm. My name is Connie Korell. April is expecting me."

Kate smiled, "Come with me, we'll get her up."

The front door was never locked in the saloon so Kate just walked in and headed for the back to April's quarters. She knocked on the door, "April, you got company."

She heard rustling inside, "Kate is that you? Come on in, what do you mean I got company?"

"April, it's me Connie." April rushed to the door as she pulled on a long silk rap. She threw her arm around the newcomer.

"Hey girl, I thought you were going to be a no show. Where's Candy?"

"I'm right here," the second girl said as she walked into the room. She too got a big hug from April.

April turned to Kate, "Girls meet my partner Kate. Without her I wouldn't have all of this. Kate I was going to tell you all about this last night when you got in here from your place in the hills. Well you know how last night was? Connie and Candy are here to take my place so I can get married. Kate I still want to own the saloon, Elsie going to run it for me. I know I should have asked you before I sent for these two, but you've been hard to catch up with this spring."

197

Kate started laughing as she hugged her old friend, "April, slow down. First off, I wish you and Henry a happy life. Next thing is whatever you do with this place is up to you. Connie, Candy, I'm glad to meet the both of you."

April was looking at Kate, "How did you know it was Henry, I'm marrying? I suppose he told you last night. It was supposed to be a surprise when we announced it together."

"April, anyone who was watching you two last night could have figured this out, besides I notice you two all huddled up all winter. Now before you get all over him, he didn't say a word, I just figured it out. I'll have Thomas and Ben bring you girls luggage over from the store." as she walked to the door, she stopped, "I hope you girls slept on the stage, if not you've got along day ahead of you," she was laughing as she walked out.

Back in the store, after Ben and Thomas moved the trunks to the saloon, Kate motioned to Ben, "Lets head back up to the house. These people have a celebration to get ready for. Thomas why don't you come along, I'll feed you too?"

As they walked up the hill, Ben motioned toward the house, "We got company."

Kate laughed, "He looks worried. You think he's remembering last night?"

Ben looked at his old friend as they walked up, "Clayton, you don't look well? You need some hot coffee with a little something added to it."

Kate stopped to look down at him, "Do you want some breakfast? I'm going to cook some for us?"

"Kate did I make a fool of myself last night? All I can remember is. I think Charlotte and me are getting married today. I won't be able to look her in the eye again if I embarrassed her in front of all of those people."

Kate leaned down to look into his eyes, "You do know she did agree to marry you. Are you telling me your backing out on the deal?"

"No, no, Kate, I wouldn't back out. I like Charlotte. Are you sure she agreed willingly to marry me?"

Kate turned to walk into the house, she called back over her shoulder, "Maybe, you should walk down and ask her after breakfast."

Ben smiled as he sat down by his friend, "New ranch or farm or whatever you call it, a new wife all in a couple of days. I thought my life changed quick, hell you beat us all with adventures in one night."

He reached over to grasp his arm, "Hell Clayton, you'll survive. Charlotte will make you a good partner."

After breakfast, Thomas sent everyone out on the porch while he did the dishes, "Someday that boy will make some girl a good husband," Kate said as she sat down.

Clayton looked over at his two friends, "We really can't get married today, right? Don't we need a license or something before it is legal?"

Kate smiled, "Well Clayton, many folks have been married and never had a license. Ben and I got one because we went to Springfield to get married. With you and Charlotte, I wouldn't worry about it. If you want later you can go into Springfield and get a license and get it recorded. Today, with all of us witnessing the ceremony you will be married even in the eyes of the law. Now who are you going to get to do the ceremony?"

"Benny, if he'll do it."

Kate and Ben's eyes both looked at Clayton, "Benny? How in the world did you ever think of him to do it?" Kate asked as she stared at Clayton.

Clayton shrugged, "Maybe I better go check with Charlotte before I make too many plans," he stood up. If we go through with this, how about you two stand up with us?"

Under the awning of the trading post with a large crowd standing in the street, came these words, "With the entire town of Garnet in attendance, I now pronounce you man and wife. You may now kiss the bride." Benny stepped back still holding the Bible.

Kate eyes had never left Benny during the ceremony, when he finished she smiled. 'Benny, you still amaze me.' As he, preformed, the ceremony Kate couldn't find a word he missed. She turned to hug the bride and then she kissed the groom. As the crowd moved forward to greet the newlyweds, Kate moved over next to Benny, "My little man, how come you know all the words in that ceremony? I think I was right after all, you were a damn bible thumper before you came here," then she laughed as she hugged him.

Ben had moved up alongside and had heard the last part, Benny looked up at him with no expression on his face, "Crazy woman." then he walked off.

Kate rolled over and put her head on Ben's shoulder, "Can we go home today? I don't believe my old body will stand another day like yesterday."

Ben chuckled, "I agree. I don't believe I ever spend a day and night like yesterday. Garnet will never be the same old place again. You know there can't be a drop of booze left anywhere in town."

Kate kissed her partner, then swung her legs out of bed, Ben heard a muffled laugh, then. "Oh god my head hurts. One wedding was bad enough, but that second one at midnight is what about killed me."

The aroma of fresh coffee filled the kitchen, when a knock came to the door, then it opened a head appeared. "You both dressed? I smell coffee. I think you two are the only people moving about this morning. There not a soul in the trading post, the stove is even cold."

Kate smiled, "Here preacher man, drink this," Kate said as she placed a cup before him.

A little before noon Kate saw smoke coming from the chimney of the store, "Why don't you hook up Ben while I go down to see if Jess can find the supplies we ordered. If not we may have to wait until to-morrow to go home."

"How about I just sit here until you signal me there's someone alive down there. Then I'll go hook up the team."

Benny and Ben loaded most of the supplies while Jess sat nursing a cup of coffee. Meg walked out with Kate. She looked over at her husband, slowly shaking her head. "I thought for a while this morning he was going to just die on me. Kate how come, Ben, not in the same shape as, Jess?"

Benny came walking by just as Meg was talking to Kate, "White man drinks too much. You don't see an Indian all hung over."

"Oh Bull, my bible thumping, friend, if you ever took a drink you'd probably go on the war path or something worse." Meg laughed, as Benny looked back at Kate.

With the wagon loaded Benny came walking from the barn leading his horse. Kate had gone over to the saloon to leave a message for April. She knew her and Henry had gone up to his house after the second wedding. Elsie met her at the door with an empty cup in her hand, "Meg's just got to have some hot coffee in the store. I'll be back in a minute, Kate."

Kate climbed up into the seat of the wagon she laughed as she looked over to the bench in front of the store. Elsie still in her robe and Jess sitting by her was a sad sight. Meg looked up at Ben, Kate and Benny on the wagon seat, "If they don't make it, I'll send word about the funeral," as she nodded to the two on the bench.

200

A few miners moved along the high trail for the next few days as they headed back to work. Clayton and Charlotte rode in one afternoon to get his stock. They spent the night, so Kate and Ben caught up on the gossip around Garnet since the forth. They were living in the big house where Tyler had lived. Henry and April were building a new house in Springfield and spending time in Henry's house in Garnet. Henry had decided he just wanted to be a silent partner in the place until sometime Clayton wanted to buy him out.

"I told him I had a better idea. I'd trade him my share of Coby's place for his share in the ranch. So now I own the ranch free and clear. Henry and those two riders own Coby's store and business. Then I heard from Jess a while ago that Henry is buying out the two riders."

Clayton told Ben while they were away from the women that few lone riders and one family in a wagon had stopped by the ranch. He figured they were looking for Tyler or someone connected with the family, otherwise everything had been calm.

When they got ready to head for home the next morning Kate mentioned about Charlotte riding horseback. She was wearing man's pants and shirt, "Looks strange to see you on a horse, but you look right at home."

Charlotte laughed, "Kate I was raised on horse ranch in the breaks of north Texas. Hell Dad didn't even own a wagon, so if you went anywhere it was straddle a horse. I rode into town one time with my dad and saw my first saloon girl dressed in one of those frilly dresses. A year later I ran away from home and got me one of those dresses. In fact I haven't been back since."

With two cuttings of hay, along with one small patch of oats to harvest it was a very quiet summer. On one trip to town Kate got to see April one evening. Henry was off buying more supplies for the business along the main road. Jess told Ben over a drink on the same trip into Garnet that Henry was almost doubling the size of the business Cody once owned. "In fact Ben, Henry said now he owns that lay out and sees how much business Cody missed, he thinks that was just a front to cover up his main business of supplying the family."

Ben shook his head, "He sure fooled the most of us that dealt with him each winter. Is Henry going to hurt your business when he makes his operation bigger?"

Jess thought a moment, "No Ben, I don't think so. Garnet is far enough off the main road that I didn't get much business from those wagon trains going through. Kate and I talked about that when I first took over the store. The bigger trains already have plenty of supplies they picked up before they leave the main Oregon Trail to head north. I get enough business from the miners who live here in the winter and the ones mining in these close mountains for me and Meg to survive. We did make a deal we'll start sharing loads of freight coming in. That's going to help him more than me, but he made the offer, I agreed to do it."

The first snows hit the mountain peaks, so Ben and Kate started getting ready to move back to town for the winter. On the last cutting of hay they hauled it up to Charlie's place. The two of them built a cover over it. With the extra hay Charlie and Thomas were going to keep three horses at the upper place. Walking Bear and Crow had gone on a trip south, Spotted Antelope was the only one staying at the hot springs camp this winter. He had made Ben and Charlie a deal he would winter the extra horses in the canyon for enough grub to last him though winter.

Kate and Ben moved back to the house in town in early November. Clayton and Charlotte along with Henry and April spent Christmas with their friends in Garnet. Business was slow after the snow got deep just after Christmas. Jess didn't have full time work for Benny, so Benny packed up to go spend some time in the canyon with Spotted Antelope. In late February Thomas and Spotted Antelope showed up using two extra horses to break a trail over from the hot springs camp. On their trap line Charlie and Thomas had kept the trail open from the ranch to the hot springs. Rosa had a list of supplies she needed so they decided to ride in before it stormed again. They spent the night in Benny cabin and headed back the next day.

Kate had asked Spotted Antelope how Benny was getting along this winter. She found out he'd only spent a week at the hot springs camp before he headed out. When Kate asked where he went Spotted Antelope just shrugged, "He just said he wanted to go visit a friend. He said he would be back as the snow melted."

Grass was beginning to show on the south slopes when Ben decided to see if he could get up to the place under the mountain. The night before he figured on leaving Kate started getting ready to join him, "Kate this might be a rough trip, you sure you want to ride along?"

Kate glanced back at him, "Ben Jasper, if you think I'm going to let you go alone, forget, that. I still remember your one trip to that mountain alone, so you're stuck with me."

Later they walked down to the store to pick up a few item to take long on the trip. Inside they found a couple of the miners playing crib to pass the time a day. When the conversation got to Ben going up to the ranch the two card players looked up. "Hey, Ben how about I ride along to join you? I need some air and those horses of mine need some work," Clay said. I brought them up from Henry's place on the river last week and their feeling pretty foxy. Homer the other card player nodded, "Count me in too, I need the exercise too."

Ben looked over at Kate, she grinned, "Okay, go ahead without me. I know when I'm not wanted." Both men were looking at each other, Kate laughed, "Don't worry fellas this is a family thing. I just told Ben he wasn't going alone, so if you two want to ride along, it's fine with me."

Ben was building a fire in the house when he heard Clay say from outside on the porch, "We got company coming this way, Ben."

Ben stepped to the door, then, he waved, "That's Thomas and Pedro, Charlie's boy coming down from the upper place. Thomas said he and Charlie had a good trapping season, with lots of pelts to take out. Ben told Thomas to see if Rosa had a list of supplies she needed then they would bring them when they moved up in a couple of weeks. Later in the day Pedro along with his sister Maria, came riding down with Rosa list. Maria was a little bashful when Ben told Clay and Homer she was the queen of ranch.

This was the first time either of these miners had seen the ranch, they always used the low trail to their mines. "Dam, you got a pretty place here, Ben. These old mountain peaks looks big from the lower trail, here they really look huge. I've heard you fellas talking before about when those religious nuts tried to mine those cliffs. Hell man I'd hate to even ride along under that one bluff up there."

Homer has been listening to Clay talk about the mountain spoke up, "Ben didn't you get trapped under a slide a somewhere up there?"

Ben nodded, "I sure did. That's when I first met Jacob the man who lived in that mountain for a spell after the big avalanche killed all those people who built this place. He's long gone now, but I truly owe him my life." Ben didn't say more hoping they didn't ask more about Jacob.

They rode back the next day in the warm sun, the tracks through the snow where they'd broke trail yesterday was already melting out. Ben figured one more week he could bring the wagon without any problems. He was anxious to get back to their mountain home and he knew Kate was the same way.

With a heavy loaded wagon they topped the ridge above the house. Kate smiled, "Someone knows were coming, smokes coming from the chimney. There's also horses in both pastures," as she pointed to them. As they got closer Benny came walking up from the barn, Kate waved.

"Hi stranger, we heard you've been traveling around the country this winter? You look well so the travel must have been good for you."

Benny looked over at Ben and shook his head, "She is no better than when I left. Maybe you should have left her in town."

"Okay you damn bible thumper, that's enough out of you." As he helped her down from the high seat she took his arm, "It's good to see you, Benny. You got any fresh coffee on?"

After coffee they started unloading the wagon, leaving Rosa supplies loaded. Benny decided he would change teams and take the supplies up to Rosa. As they were changing teams three riders appeared coming down the valley. Kate stood on the porch, then she waved when he figured out the small one was Maria. About then the smaller rider came racing toward the house, waving as she came. The pony came sliding to a stop at the hitch rail, Maria was already off running to grab Kate. "Hey young lady, you're growing up way too fast. I'll be losing my cookie maker one of these days if you keep growing." She hugged her partner to her. "You were riding kinda fast coming in. I don't want you getting hurt."

"I race Pedro all the time. I won't fall off, Kate." Kate nodded as she held her close.

Charlie took the wagon up to unload it, so Benny spent the night with Ben and Kate. After supper they sat talking about Benny's travel that winter. "Kate, you and Ben need to ride with me this spring before you get busy with the hay. I want to show you something I think you'll really like."

Kate looked over at Ben then back to Benny, "Well what is it, you want us to see?"

Benny just looked at Kate, "We leave in two weeks. Spotted Antelope is going with us. Walking Bear and Crow are back in the canyon camp. They both brought back squaws, wives as you call them. They are going to build their camp on down the canyon from where they have been living. Spotted Antelope will still stay in the upper camp, when he's there."

Ben looked over at Benny, "How many days will we be on the trail to this place?"

"Four if we ride slow, three if we hurry."

"Then I better figure on two pack horses?" Ben asked as he looked over at Benny.

"Maybe three would be better," he answered.

Thomas had spent the night to help Ben get the horses ready for their trip. As dawn was breaking Kate swung up on her horse, "I still wish I knew where that crazy Dad of yours is taking us." said as she looked down at Thomas.

A slow smile appeared, "Kate I can't help you with that, he didn't tell me anymore than he's told you. I'm sure he wouldn't let anything bad happen to either of you." He waved as Ben led off up the trail toward the hot spring canyon trail. As they reached the forks, there sat Benny and Spotted Antelope. Ben grinned as he looked at the five loaded pack horses, "You moving, Benny."

He led off up the trail that would lead them into the valley of the bones. Kate was riding right behind Benny, just ahead of Ben and his packhorses. Spotted Antelope was bringing up the rear with the other pack horses. Kate looked back a few times, Ben just grinned and shrugged. Benny stopped and pointed a across the canyon, "Kate, you see where that trail stops along that cliff, that was the opening into the mountain. In that small valley below where that opening was is what we call the valley of the bones. Those real white rocks below that ledge are really petrified bones, not rocks." Kate looked back at Ben who nodded yes.

"Oh. My God, I've heard you men talk of this but I had no idea it would be like this. Those poor people, worked to death then shoved over that cliff to keep them from talking about the gold."

"Greed, only worse than it was when Jacob still lived in the mountain. You wonder how much gold those Spaniards really got by working that many slaves," Ben answered from behind her.

That night they rode up a small draw away from the trail they had been following. There they found old fire rings of many people who had used this same draw. After the pack animals were unloaded Spotted Antelope took them away from camp to stake them out to feed on the thick grass. No one had used this camp spot for a long spell, you could tell by the green plants growing up in the ashes.

The third day the country began to change as they dropped down in elevation. Wild fruit trees were in bloom along with all the other plants. Benny pulled up near a stone cabin with the roof caved in. He turned to Kate and Ben, "If we keep going it will be well after dark before we get to where were going. I say we, camp, here, then we'll be there before noon tomorrow."

As they all finished the last cups of coffee before turning in Kate looked over at Benny, "Benny this house is old. Who lived here? There's no farm ground, but I noticed a few apple and other fruit trees just above the house. There all in a rows so you know they were planted."

"From what I know from local Indians, this was built by what I would say from the description, it was Monks. The stories tell of the men in robes and their heads covered, who never talked. Above this house you find a, couple more smaller ones, like maybe sleeping quarters. There's stone cellar built into the mountain over there," as he pointed into the darkness. "Tomorrow as we ride out you'll see more small stone structures and more fruit trees along with places that have been leveled out for gardens. You know many priests and monks from Canada came in with the early fur trappers. They tried to convert the Indian with very little luck. I think this group just came deeper into the mountains than most of them did to set up their settlements. What happened to them I have no idea."

A slight laugh came from Kate, "If you don't know my weird Indian witch doctor, I don't think I'll ever find out. Now it's my bed time."

They dropped into a long narrow valley. A few cattle were grazing along the timber line. Then Ben spotted a smoke coming from the trees and could see the roof line of a cabin in the trees. As he watched he saw more buildings and what looked to be a set of corrals. Benny just kept riding along one side of the meadow, then, the meadows suddenly stopped. A small timbered ridge ended the valley. Benny kept following a trail up through the trees, then before them another valley appeared. This valley was round with a fairly large creek cutting through the middle of it. It was completely surrounded by timber, mostly large yellow pine. Smoke was coming from the chimney of a large low logs house. Many out building surrounded the big house. In the back ground a big barn was starting to take shape, it too was built of logs. Kate looked back at Ben, "This place is beautiful," he nodded he agreed.

As they got closer two people stepped out onto the porch. One was a tall man dressed in overalls, a homemade shirt. On his head was a western style hat, on his feet, high topped moccasins. The woman was small. She was holding a small child in a blanket. Another child just learning to walk was clinging to her skirt. As the couple stepped down from the porch, Ben heard Kate suck in her breath, "Oh my God, Ada is that you?"

A smile appeared her face as Kate swung down to rush to hug her. The tall man walked over to Ben as he swung down, "Welcome to my home, Ben. I've always known we would meet again. My life is been lonely without having my talks with you." He grasped Ben's hand then smiled.

Ben just shook his head, "Jacob, I'd never recognized you dressed like that. I too have missed having you to talk to. This is a beautiful place."

Kate was holding the baby as Ada walked over carrying the other child, she smiled. "It is so good to see you, Ben. We owe you so much. I suppose you can see I no longer have to guard the man who is now my husband and the father of my children. When Benny showed up last winter I was so happy when he said you both were well. I too have been waiting for you to get here."

Kate walked over next to Benny still carrying the baby, "Benny, sometimes you really test me don't you? You know damn well you could have told us where we were going and why. Oh no, you have to make it a big secret." Then she smiled and touched his sleeve, "But I still love you and thanks you for bring us here."

"Too much talk." he winked at Ben when he turned to Jacob, "We got most of the supplies you wanted.

Jacob nodded, "Let's take those pack animals around back to the supply cabin." He turned to Ben and pointed to a small cabin, "You can put your gear in that cabin, Ben. As soon as we get these packs off I'll show you where to put your horses."

As Ben walked to the corral he saw Benny and Spotted Antelope putting their gear in a dugout that was built away from the other buildings.

Later the four men sat talking on the porch. Ben looked over at the man he's always seen in a long robe with hair to his waste. Now he was dressed alike any other rancher except for the moccasin's. "Why the big change Jacob? You look to be doing right well here, but this life for you is so much different than when you lived in the mountain."

Jacob grinned, "Ben, I decided if I was to have a decent life to bring my children into, I needed to change my life. I almost missed having Ada for my wife. I looked at her as my protector, not a woman who could have my children. Then I saw the need to leave that mountain and my life in there. So with Ada at my side we left without any of you knowing. I knew I needed to shed the robe and hair, then, fit my thinking to a normal man with a family. I still do work with my gold, but only as a way to relax. With that the few gold items I sell, along with the cattle and horses we raise, we do well. I have also legally changed my name to Jake Marsh." He looked at Ben, "Benny say's since I left the mountain the strangers trying to get to me, are also gone. He also says a couple of the local people turned out to be tied up with the family. I knew the family had contacts around Springfield, but I had no idea those two were involved. Tyler I didn't know. Coby I knew of because of his business on the river road, but I didn't know he was a family member."

"When those five were killed at the opening into the valley of the bones, all of the mystery riders came to a stop. We've had a couple of calm summers since then. Kate and I both enjoy our ranch under that mountain. I now have water on some hay ground, last year I had two good cuttings. I also tied a few acres of oats. I'm just a farmer at heart."

Jacob nodded, "That is a beautiful place you have."

"Jacob," Ben stopped. "I guess I better get used to calling you Jake instead of Jacob, I might slip sometime when strangers are around. Anyway if it's any of my business, where do you mine gold here to have material for your hobby?"

Jake looked back at Benny, then back to Ben. "Well first off Ben, I understand you might know that, there is another entrance to my old home. Before Ada and I left I moved most of my gold to a hidden vault near the other entrance. Only three people know of the location of that entrance as far as I know. That's Ada, me and Benny here. Last winter while Benny was here we brought a good load from the mountain. I will tell you no more about its location my good friend, for your own protection. Benny I know will never reveal it to anyone."

About then Kate stepped out with the bundle in her arms, she sat down next to Ben, he could see a tear slowly rolling down her cheek. "Why, the tears? It's looks to me like your spoiling these two kids."

Kate reached over to grasp Ben's arm, "Ben, this bundle in my arms name is Katy. They named her after me. That one hanging onto your knee happens to be named, Benjamin, so that's what caused me to have a few tears."

Ada stood behind Jake with her hands on his shoulders, both of them were smiling. "You both were involved in getting us together. Now with our children bearing your names, you'll always be with us."

Ben, Kate and Benny spent ten days with Jake and Ada. As they saddled up to leave Kate again had tears in her eyes as she hugged everyone and the kids a couple of times. "We will be back," she said as she, hugged, Ada for the last time before she swung up on her horse.

That first night as they camped Kate was real quiet as she cooked supper. While they ate she looked over at Benny, "Where did Spotted Antelope go? He was just gone one day soon after we got to the ranch."

Benny looked up from his plate, "He likes to look at new country." He shrugged, "He might too be looking for a squaw. I think since his partners came back with wives he been thinking maybe he should have one too."

Finally Kate smiled, "Are you next?" then she laughed as he looked up at her.

Benny spent one day at the ranch with them after they got back. Then he rode over to see the other two in the canyons of the hot springs to let them know about Spotted Antelope. From there he rode back to town for a few days. He told Ben he would be back to help with the first cutting of hay.

When Ben rode down the next day to look over the hay crop he found Thomas already there. Ben could believe the hay crop, the field was green and taller than he's ever saw before. Thomas was grinning as Ben went on about the crop. They decided they would turn off the water that day and start cutting in two days.

That afternoon Kate called from the house to Ben working in the barn sharping the scythes. When he looked out she was point up the road toward town. Over the hill came two wagons, when they got closer Ben could see Benny was driving the lead wagon. Benny pulled to a stop. Ben looked up at him, "You moving out here for good or something?"

On the seat of the second wagon was Henry with April perched alongside him. "Howdy folks, we thought we'd come spend the night with you. I think April misses her talks with Kate," then he laughed as she punched him in the ribs.

As the girls hurried into the house, Ben turned to the two old friends, "Okay what's in the wagons?"

"Well by golly Ben, I think I found something you'll like," Henry said as he climbed up on the wheel of the wagon and pointed to the inside the bed. "It's one of them new style mowing machines they've

209

been using back east. One of those, farmer coming by the trading post was short on money to buy supplies for his big family sold me this thing. In Benny wagon is a dump rake, anyway that's what he called it. There both horse drawn."

By evening they had both new things unloaded, with Kate reading from the book on how to make it work they put in together. With the rake they only need to put the wheels back on.

"Now Ben, that man told me you need a calm team to pull this mower. He said when the cycle start cutting it makes a noise. Then when you turn a corner it makes a loud clicking sound in the wheels. He said a high strung team will run away when they hear all that noise behind them. You got a calm team?"

Benny looked over at Ben, "Kate's old team from the trading post is the calmest we got. I think if we go real, slow with them in the morning they'll be alright. We can get Thomas and Charlie to snub up next to them to keep them from running if you think they'll spook."

They hooked up the older team the next morning and drove them around the yard. Their ears flew up on the first turn they made, but soon they didn't even pay any attention to it. There was some tall grass just outside the low corral so Ben shifted the mowing into gear to see how the mower worked. He made one pass then everyone walked back looking at the smooth cut it had made. "I can hardly wait until the day after tomorrow to start cutting that hay field," Ben said as they walked back to the mower.

Henry and April stayed over another day just to watch the mower work. With a crowd watching Ben shifted the mower into gear and started around the field. Charlie and his whole family were there to watch. By noon Ben had more hay cut then the four of them could have cut in three good days the old way. Henry and hooked up his team, April climbed up alongside and they headed back for Garnet. Henry told Ben he'd keep everyone entertained in the saloon that night telling about Ben's new hay machines.

The farmer who sold the rake to Henry told him how to use it and how long to wait for the hay to cure before raking it into windrows. It was decided Benny would use the other team to rake the hay, so that first morning Charlie and Thomas rode alongside the team as Benny tripped the rake a few times. After a couple of rounds they totally ignored the noise of the rake dumping so the two riders quit riding along side. Ben checked the hay in the windrows they first cut. He decided Thomas and Charlie could start hauling hay that afternoon. In a week they were through cutting and raking. Using two wagons they soon had the first cutting all done. Thomas was back to irrigating the same day they hauled the last load of hay. Charlie asked if Ben and Benny would ride up to his place the next morning.

They were off just after breakfast for the ride up the valley. Once up in the upper meadow they saw Thomas and Charlie riding toward them. As they got close Charlie motioned to follow him and Thomas. They stopped just after they crossed the creek. Charlie motioned to the high grass all along this side of the creek. "With your new mower we could cut all of this good grass hay and still have plenty of feed for the stock until the snow comes."

A week later they were back to haying. They filled Charlie's hay shed and had some left over to stack. Kate, Ben and Benny made a trip to town when the grass haying was done. They spent three days in town catching up on all the gossip. Clayton and Charlotte showed up the last day they were in town, so April sent word to Henry at the store on the river to come home that night for a big party. The big story that night was Charlotte said she was with child, due in early part of the year. Kate looked over at Henry and April, they both held up their hands saying together, "No Way, we are too old for that now!"

Questions about Jacob came up during the night. Clayton just couldn't understand why he never had contacted Ben if he was alive. Ben just shrugged, "I just have a feeling he's alive. Someday he just might ride in, who know?" As Ben looked over at Kate he could see a slight nod.

When they got back to the ranch Thomas had more news for them, Spotted Antelope was back and he did have a new bride. She was Shoshone, from a village on the upper Snake River country. Spotted Antelope said he would build their home in the upper camp where he now lived.

When they finished the second cutting Ben, Kate and Benny were headed back down through the valley of the bones. Ben and Benny helped Jake and his crew, finish the barn. On the back of the barn the ground was higher than in the front. They had dug, the in to the hill and the back wall was a rock wall. The log walls didn't start on the back until they were near the second level of the barn. Then Jake had built wide doors into the loft on that end. Four long peeled poles ran from the ground into the big opening. They were notched into the top opening so the door would close over them. A small rack built from small poles was mounted on sled like runner. Two cables were attached to this sled through pulleys into the barn along the big poles and then through more pulley back outside. They would fill the rack with hay from a wagon outside. Then with a single horse hooked to the cables outside the sled would travel up to the end of the poles inside to a stop. Then the rack was dumped into the loft, the horse backed up and the sled was back outside for another load. Jake had saw something like this before and built this from memory.

Benny and Ben looked at each other while watching Jake's crew taking hay into the barn. Ben, was, nodding his head as they watched, "Benny we could do something like this on the big barn and get a lot more hay in it."

The last night before they headed back home, Jake brought a rolled up paper and spread it on the table. On it was a drawing of the biggest barn back at the ranch. Then more drawing of cables and pulleys were laid out. Jake, explained these to Ben, Benny and Kate, then handed them instructions how to build all of this. He looked at Kate and a slow smile appeared, "Kate you'll have to be the one to supervise this, while Ben and Benny build it. It's altogether different than the one I use, but this will work on your barn."

Benny looked over at Ben, then at Kate, who was holding both kids on her lap, "Maybe I'll stay here until you finish this."

Kate smiled, "Oh, no you don't. You know darn well you couldn't live without me keeping you straight." This brought a laugh from everyone in the room.

As they hugged and got ready to leave the next morning Kate mentioned the ruins they rode through each trip. "I still would like to know more about the people who once lived there. It is so peaceful in that canyon."

Jake walked up to stand next to Kate, "Next summer when you come back, we will camp up there together, then I will tell you of those people."

Kate put her arms around the tall man, "You will always be Jacob to me, my dear friend. I can hardly wait now for spring and our stay in the canyon of the ruins. I will also look for word to your stories," as she swung up onto her horse she looked back down at him, "I may even talk Ben into building us a place in that canyon for us to spend out our old age."

Charlie and Ben decided with all the hay, they needed a few cows on the place. So Ben and Kate took Thomas and headed for Springfield. They bought twenty young cows and two bulls. Ben and Kate also bought a new buggy for them to use. Kate drove the buggy back up the road to Garnet, while Thomas and Ben took the cows cross country.

The second day brought a grin to Ben's face as Charlie and three Indians showed up to help move the cows. Ben headed for Garnet that afternoon, leaving them to take the cows on to the ranch.

As Ben rode by the store than evening it was just getting dark, "Is that you Ben?" came, a call from the porch of the store.

Ben pulled, "High Jess, I didn't see you sitting there."

"Your wife is in the back with Meg. Put your horse away and come on back. We'll find you some grub and a drink or two."

The next morning Ben tied his horse behind the buggy and climbed in the seat with Kate. She handed him the reins, he shook his head no. "It's your buggy."

When they got home to the ranch you could see the cattle grazing in the upper meadow. It had already snowed a few times on the peaks above when Ben and Kate got ready to move into town. Benny sat eating breakfast when he announced he was spending the winter with the Marsh family. Kate looked up from the stove, "When did you decide this?"

Benny glanced over at her, "When we were there, I ask if I could stay in that upper cabin all winter."

Kate just shook her head as she sat down to eat, "Benny, I swear you do this just to keep me guessing. It would be so easy just to tell folks when you're going to do something like this, especially the people you live with."

"Then if I changed my mind, then I'd have to tell you about that. This way I only need to tell you once," he answered back.

"Well come spring, Ben and me will be back down to see you. We've been talking to Charlie and Thomas about taking over this place so we can travel around to see things. I still want to spend time in the canyon with all the ruins." Her eyes stared right at him, "I also think you know a lot more about those people. I think your just baiting me so I'll have to beg you're to tell me more. You could find a good place there for my cabin if you really wanted to please me," then she laughed at the blank look he gave her.

"I will meet you there on the full moon in April. Bring lots of supplies so you can stay awhile. Jacob said he could get free then too. He, Ada and the kids will come at the same time."

Kate looked over at Ben, who smiled, "I don't know any reason we can't be there."

CHAPTER 12

It was a very open winter in Garnet with the road to Springfield being closed only twice all winter. Clayton moved Charlotte into Springfield to be close to a doctor when the time got close. Then one day in early February as the stage driver tossed down the mail sack to Jess. "I'm supposed to tell Kate Jasper, "It's a boy," Can someone pass that on to her?"

Jess nodded, "I can do better than that," he walked to the door. "Kate, you want to step out here, this man has a message for you."

Kate looked up at the stage driver, "Hi, Al. You wanted to see me?"

"Sure do Kate. I got a message for you, "It's a boy." Clayton ran a block this morning to give me that message before I left town."

Ben had walked out onto the porch, Kate spun around, "It's a boy. Ben, were headed for Springfield."

A week later Kate, had helped Charlotte move back to the ranch. Ben helped Clayton around the ranch for a couple of days while Kate made sure the new mother was doing alright. Then they headed back to Garnet. In mid-March the road was open to the ranch so Kate and Ben moved back. The cattle had all survived the winter and Charlie and Thomas had hay left over. Charlie and Rosa and the kids rode over the second day they were back. Kate asked how come Thomas hadn't been around. "Rosa laughed, "Two of Crows new wife's sisters showed up to stay with her while she has their first child. It's due any day. Well Thomas is really been spending a lot of time over there all winter."

Kate asked Maria if she would like to stay with them for a few days to help her. Rosa said it was okay with her so when they left Maria said she would be back before dark. She wanted to get some different clothes.

Ben started putting his coat on when Kate looked up, "Where you going, supper about done?"

"Our new boarder is coming up from the creek. I was going to go put her horse away for her." Kate grinned then motioned for him to go.

214

Ben started getting their pack gear ready and making a list of what he needed to take. A week before they were to take off Ben, Kate and Maria headed for Garnet with both wagons. Kate had a big list of supplies she wanted to take with them, plus she had a large order for Rosa. This was Maria's first trip to town since they first came here. She was all wide eyed as she looked at all the shelves full of supplies lining the walls and isle the trading post. Meg just couldn't get over the beautiful young lady Kate had introduced to them. "Kate this young lady we'll raise some eye brows." Maria ducked in behind Kate who laughed. " She's a little shy."

With the horses all loaded, Kate gave Rosa and Maria a big hug before she swung up on her horse. "We'll see you folks when we get back. Don't worry about us if we're not back for the forth." With a wave she fell in behind Ben and the pack string. Thomas had decided to stay at the house while they were gone, so Kate didn't have to worry about her home while they were gone.

The only sound was the horse's hooves on the hard trail, along with the birds singing in the trees. They were just coming into the canyon of the ruins. Ben turned to look back at her and motioned to his nose like he was sniffing the air. Then Kate began to smell the fresh wood smoke coming from close by. She looked about then she saw a roof of a cabin on a flat above the trail. When she glanced up at Ben he nodded he saw it too. Kate jumped as Benny stepped from the brush above the trail, "I figured you'd be here today."

Benny motioned to Ben to head up the hill toward the cabin. At the cabin Kate smiled as she swung down, "Benny, did you build this?" He nodded.

About then Ada stepped from the cabin and rushed to hug Kate. "I've been counting the days until you got here. Jake and a couple of the men from the ranch are up finishing up your cabin."

"My cabin, you mean you built one just for me and Ben?" Ada nodded, then, pointed into the blooming apple trees off to the south of where they stood.

Later with the horses all unpacked they sat around a fire ring enjoying a cup of coffee. Kate sat there holding both kids on her lap. "Oh, this is so beautiful and so peaceful."

Jake's crew went back to the ranch leaving just Ben, Kate, Benny, Jake, Ada and the kids to stay in the canyon. A couple of days after they were settled in Jake took them on a walking tour of the ruins. High on the canyon walls they found large flat areas with rocks piled along the edges into almost fences. The rock piles were where they had cleared these flat places to raise crops. Jake said this was where they grew all the vegetables and fruit to feed the slave labor in the mines back in the mountain. The story of the monks Benny had told them was true, only they came long after the Spaniards had left. They used the same buildings and gardens to survive. Their biggest problem was the Indians still living in this area remembered stories of their ancestors being killed here. So they hated anyone living in this canyon. That's why the monks didn't last long here.

"The day after tomorrow I will take you into the mountain. Benny will stay here with Ada and the kids and the three of us will go. It will take us three days to do what I need to do and show you the place. Kate, Ben has already seen the part where I lived, but not any of the other parts."

They rode a narrow trail through the brush to a small basin. A rock cabin sat off to one side, a curl of smoke could be seen coming from the chimney. In a small corral were a dozen small burros. As they stopped, an old man came to the door. Jake motioned to him in sign language. The man motioned back, then, went back inside.

Later with all their gear on the burro's they started up a narrow draw filled with brush. Kate had never ridden a burro, or ridden Indian type sidesaddle. As they rode through a thicket all of a sudden it was dark and every step of the small animal she was riding made a hollow sound. 'We're inside the mountain,' she gasped.

She could hear Ben chuckling behind her as the burro stopped, then, ahead a torch brightened the darkness. On up the dark tunnel they went. It seemed like forever, then Kate could see light ahead of them again, soon they were riding in the sunshine along a very narrow cliff. In a short while they were back in the dark tunnel following Jake with the torch. Twice more they rode out into the open before they stopped in a large room. Light was shining in from an opening not far from them. Kate could tell by the smell they were in a barn like room, with feed troughs along one wall. Water could be heard running in a small stone tank off to one side.

Jake motioned to take the packs off the burros. "We will walk from here to my old home before we stop, for the night. Ben recognized his old room and where Jacob had cooked all their meals. As Jacob built a fire in the stone fireplace he glanced over at Ben, "Show Kate the view."

Ben took her arm, "Come, I'll show you something you won't believe."

"Oh My God, this is almost unreal. There's our house and the barns. Ben, you can see some of the roofs of Garnet from here." She looked back at Ben, "This is where Jacob had you when you were hurt so bad?"

Ben nodded, then he pointed off left of where she had been looking, "Down there is Charlie's place, see it?" Kate nodded as she stared at the beauty below her.

The next morning when they finished eating, Jake stood up, "Ben, how about you give Kate the tour while I get to work. I will meet you both back here tonight." Then he left down one tunnel Ben had never walked, while he lived here.

Kate just shook her head as Ben led her through the maze of rooms inside the mountain. In the small room down where the entrance to the lower trail had been, Ben stopped. He eased out through the opening to see how Jacob or Jake had sealed it. He froze as he stepped around the last narrow place before going outside. Before him was the cliff, but now the trail was missing it was straight off into the void below. Ben eased back bumping into Kate who had followed him. "I figured he had closed the entrance with stones, instead he just took the trail away. You step out there now. It's straight down for a long ways."

The next morning while Ben and Jake packed up the burro's, Kate walked over where she could look through the small opening to look at her home below. She shivered, then turned to walk back to join the men. She noticed now all of the burros were loaded. Coming in four of them had empty pack saddles, now they were loaded.

Back at the rock cabin they, packed up the horses, leaving the pack saddles on the burro. Ben started to pull the pack saddles from the tough little animals, when Jake took his arm, "Leave that for the old man. I want him to always think he is needed here."

As they rode away the old man had never shown himself. Kate wanted so bad to ask who he was, but something told her to just let it go. If Jacob wanted them to know he would already told them.

The next morning Ada got the kids ready for the trip home while Ben and Benny helped Jake load up. After much hugging and tears Kate stepped back as Ada handed the little Ben up to Jake. When she got settled on her horse, Benny handed Katy to her. "How about we meet here again to harvest the apples this fall?" Jake asked.

"We will be here during the harvest moon," Benny answered. He looked back at Kate and Ben who both nodded.

That night as they sat before a small fire in open fire pit, Ben and Kate with a drink, while Benny nursed a cup of coffee. Kate looked over at her helper for many years, "Benny, are you riding back with us?"

Benny looked over at them. Finally he shook his head, no. "I think I'll stay here. Jess doesn't need me anymore at the store and I really feel good here. I got a lot of work to do on this place. Spotted Antelope and his new wife Morning Star are living over in the next canyon right now, so I have someone close by if I need help. They figure on making their home here, instead of in the canyon of the hot springs. Spotted Antelope had told me Morning Stars family hunted this area each fall while the women gathered fruit to dry. So I suppose we'll be seeing them once in a while too."

A few small tear came to Kate's eyes as she turned her head away from the two men. Unknown to her she hadn't, fool anyone by turning away. Both men looked at each other, to Ben's surprise, Benny showed a slight smile. Then he looked back at Kate who by now had wiped the tears away. "Kate, times are changing. The life as we've always known it is slowly slipping away. As I look back now, I'm so glad I met you. You made me feel wanted and needed around the trading post and at that time I needed that. Now I'm plumb comfortable with life, I have everything I ever wanted. Friends, family and now with Thomas being close by. Soon he will be married and have his own family to care for. This is all good, thanks to you and Ben."

Kate nodded, "You too have added to my life, Benny. After Dan died, I was lost for a while. With your help around the trading post I could finally see I was better off than most women that lose their husbands early in life. Then Ben came into my life, even though he wondering off each summer looking for the mother lode. The ranch under those peaks has been a blessing for both of us, including you, Benny. With Charlie and Thomas to run the ranch we are free to be sitting here together in, God's country. She leaned over to put her head against Ben's. Tears were again flowing down her cheeks. The fire was slowly dying down as the three people sat there looking at the stars and listening to the sounds of the night.

The End